BREAK THE BODIES,
HAUNT THE BONES

"I can't stop thinking about this book. It's a haunting story that burrows under your skin like an insect laying eggs that hatch within you in the middle of the night. Hicks's mesmerizing imagery kept me turning the pages and asking myself: How is this book happening? What sort of literary witchcraft am I witnessing?'"

— Maurice Broaddus, author of *Buffalo Soldier*
and *The Usual Suspects*

"A tour de force of the imagination. Hicks has created a world that is beautifully and brutally surreal and yet, at the same time, *Break the Bodies, Haunt the Bones* stands as a hyperrealistic psychological portrait of the death of the American factory town. My own identity as an American was disturbed and changed by this novel; some dormant understanding was shaken awake. This is a stunning and profound debut."

— Julianna Baggott, best-selling author of
New York Times Notable Book *Pure*

"Hicks's debut novel is a thoughtful tour of the rotted and haunted heart of America. Highly recommended."

— Jeremiah Tolbert, Shirley Jackson Award nominee

"*Break the Bodies, Haunt the Bones* is a breathless wonder of a debut novel. Amid robots and a city of pigs and residents haunted by their own personal ghosts, Micah Dean Hicks explores economic uncertainty, the violence of bigotry and hate, and the tremendous weight of the past. In Swine Hill, no one escapes the horrors of grief. And yet this is a novel infused with hope, and with the most gorgeous sentences evoking the sublime wonder of this world. Hicks is a magician with words and has written a spellbinding, haunting, and necessary book."

— Anne Valente, author of
Our Hearts Will Burn Us Down

"In *Break the Bodies, Haunt the Bones,* Micah Dean Hicks has crafted a haunting story with multi-generational appeal, where the very real horror of poverty meets supernatural horror, and social issues like xenophobia, racism, and economic anxiety are addressed organically through allegory and gripping storytelling. I finished this book three nights ago and still feel the chill of Swine Hill in my bones."

— Chris L. Terry, author of *Black Card* and *Zero Fade*

"The novel's concept, and Hicks's prose, are strong enough to fold in dozens of big ideas, from racism and poverty to police brutality and manufactured nostalgia. Readers of Jeff VanderMeer, Kelly Link, or Carmen Maria Machado will feel at home in Hicks's prose . . . A book that will haunt you long after you've finished it."

— *Criminal Element*

"Daring readers with a hunger for the arcane and the New Weird style of writers like China Miéville will enjoy this singularly strange novel."

— *Booklist*

BREAK THE BODIES, HAUNT THE BONES

MICAH DEAN HICKS

A John Joseph Adams Book
Mariner Books | Houghton Mifflin Harcourt
BOSTON NEW YORK

First Mariner Books edition 2020
Copyright © 2019 by Micah Dean Hicks

For information about permission to reproduce selections from this book,
write to trade.permissions@hmhco.com or to Permissions, Houghton Mifflin Harcourt
Publishing Company, 3 Park Avenue, 19th Floor, New York, New York 10016.

hmhbooks.com

Library of Congress Cataloging-in-Publication Data
Names: Hicks, Micah Dean, author.
Title: Break the bodies, haunt the bones / Micah Dean Hicks.
Description: Boston : John Joseph Adams/Houghton Mifflin Harcourt, 2019. |
Identifiers: LCCN 2018032618 (print) | LCCN 2018032768 (ebook) |
ISBN 9781328566775 (ebook) | ISBN 9781328566454 (hardback) |
ISBN 9780358133636 (paperback)
Subjects: | BISAC: FICTION / Fantasy / Contemporary. | FICTION / Fantasy /
General. | FICTION / Science Fiction / General. | GSAFD: Fantasy fiction.
Classification: LCC PS3608.I2825 (ebook) | LCC PS3608.I2825 B74 2019 (print)|
DDC 813/.6—DC23
LC record available at https://lccn.loc.gov/2018032618

Book design by Carly Miller
Title lettering © Chris Thornley

Printed in the United States of America
DOC 10 9 8 7 6 5 4 3 2 1

For Brenda

PART I

SWINE HILL WAS full of the dead. Their ghosts were thickest near the abandoned downtown, where so many of the town's hopes had died generation by generation. They lingered in the places that mattered to them, and people avoided those streets, locked those doors, stopped going in those rooms. But you might encounter a ghost unexpectedly — in the high school where Jane had graduated two years ago, curled into the hollow of a tree, hands out and pleading on the side of the road. They could hurt you. Worse, they could change you.

The haunted downtown of Swine Hill had been slowly expanding for years, stretching its long fingers into empty neighborhoods where grass fissured the roads and roofs collapsed into rooms of broken furniture and shattered glass. For the people who'd lived and died on those streets, it was anguish to see the vine-choked houses, to know their descendants had run away from all they'd worked for. Their spirits, most present in the stillness of night, raged in the empty places. Even if she was late for work, Jane knew to drive around those neighborhoods.

It was easy to feel alone. There were more dead than living in Swine Hill. Jane's aunts and uncles had gone out of state after the collapse of the tire factory and the lumber mill. The town jealously cleaved to the pork-processing plant that had chewed up its sons for generations, hoping that in the end, it would be enough. Most people Jane's age had already gone, scraping up enough money to start over somewhere else. The only ones left were those so poor that they couldn't make it out, or so haunted they couldn't see a world outside their ghosts, or just clinging to a past they couldn't bear to leave behind. But Jane wasn't alone. Her ghost flashed bright and quick through her mind.

Her car's engine coughed as she turned the key, something sputtering under the hood like a laugh, and finally groaned to life. It accelerated slowly, heavy with the weight of spirits. The speedometer and gas gauge waved their orange arms erratically. Her windshield wipers often turned on without warning, and sometimes her horn would scream out of nowhere. She was happy the CD player still worked at all, though sometimes a ghost would settle into the discs, craving the bright sound of music, and then the stereo would play only noise.

Jane flipped open a case of burned CDs and put in one after another until she found one that played, throwing the dead ones onto a pile in her back seat. Music crashed out of the tinny speakers: sticky electronic pop, the lyrics full of secrets, gossip, and drama. The cold weight of her ghost swelled inside her, thrilling in the sound.

Though Jane didn't know the ghost girl's name, it had been a part of her ever since she was a child. It was nosy, listening in on other people's thoughts and telling Jane what they were thinking and feeling. If the ghost didn't have anyone else to listen to, it would burrow deep into Jane's mind, unearthing her regrets and fears and making her fixate on them for hours. If it felt unappreciated, it might lie to her, withhold what it knew, or tell her the most vicious things people thought about her. But Jane had learned to manage it over the years, using music to placate it. The ghost had been her first friend, and now that she was still in Swine Hill after her classmates and family had gone away, Jane wondered if the ghost would be her last friend, too.

Something like fog rose as the sun slipped behind the trees. A chain of spirits so wispy and immaterial as to be little more than air, a mass of faces and trudging feet bleeding in and out of one another, drifted up the road to the Pig City meatpacking plant. These ghosts weren't dangerous. They had somewhere to go, a purpose still. The plant that had employed them all their lives was older than the town, the only reason that Swine Hill hadn't crumbled back into the earth. The ghosts were the unofficial night shift, still swirling through its rusted doors, crowding its blood-splattered hallways to do their phantom work.

Jane plowed through them like snow, their distorted faces stretching over the windshield. She turned into the grocery store's cratered parking lot, the sodium lights casting deep shadows at the building's edges, the storefront murky yellow and cluttered with signs.

Near the front of the store, the specter of a man slowly spun up from the asphalt and took on substance. He lay on the ground, holding his stomach and bleeding, a phantom box of strawberries broken open on the ground beside him. Decades ago, a police officer shot him while he was leaving the store. The cop had been called about another customer, someone yelling at the cashiers. It was a mix-up. A mistake, but one that had happened and would happen again. The ghost looked at every person who entered or left the store, his face a mask of pain and surprise, and mouthed, *Why?*

Jane, her shoulders tense, tried not to look at him, and jogged through the doors.

There weren't any cashiers at the front. A flood of customers milled around, waiting for someone to check them out. Jane went straight to her register — just stuffed her bag under the counter instead of taking it to the back — already apologizing as she scanned the first customer's items.

She felt her ghost move away from her, felt it filter in and out of the minds of the customers, bringing her the avalanche of their thoughts. Everyone who looked up and saw her immediately thought, *Black.* Whatever else they thought about her, this always came first. Her ghost spoke their minds into Jane's ear: *Probably late. They always are. Lazy.*

People like her. Must have overslept. Kept us waiting. Why doesn't some-one fire her? I'm going to speak to the manager. Too dark. Such a shame. Might have been pretty otherwise.

The ghost knew that Jane didn't want to hear all this, but it couldn't help itself, because its whole tie to the living world was bound up in its hunger for secrets and pain.

"Sorry about your wait," Jane said. "Have a nice day."

Her register's phone rang. Jane held it with her neck while punching in produce codes, looking up to see her balding, squint-eyed manager staring at her from his glass-encased office. He was terrified of ghosts and wouldn't go near Jane or anyone who was possessed. Even when the store was busy, he stayed in his booth, interacting with customers as little as possible. Jane's ghost had told her that he worried he might already be haunted. He spent hours looking in his mirror, searching his pupils for a flicker of ghost-light. Jane had told him that he was clean, but he didn't believe her.

"One cashier never showed up, and the other called in sick," he said. "Kathryn left early. I was alone for a while. Don't put me in that position again."

Jane wanted to protest that it wasn't her fault, but the man's voice was so weak. Her ghost told her how afraid he was, how fixated on the thinness of the glass in the booth. "Yes, sir," she said. "I'm sorry."

Many shoppers wore stained Pig City coveralls, plant workers picking up hamburger meat and pasta on their way home. Most were old, with silver hair like spun metal under the harsh lights, limbs bruised, eyes half closed in exhaustion. Those few still in their twenties or thirties looked much older, weathered by long days at the plant and too little sleep at home. Jane's ghost told her what they were feeling: lonely, tired, a slow-burning frustration like a long fuse leading to an explosion still a few decades away. Defeated down to their bones, they would have gone somewhere else, anywhere else, if only they had the money, if only they weren't eaten up with ghosts and their ghostly needs, if only they didn't fear that the rest of the world was just like Swine Hill.

Her ghost passed along splinters of worry: crumbling houses, dying marriages, resentful children. Jane asked about their problems, and they answered, grateful to have someone listen. No one questioned how she knew. They had grown used to strangeness, were grateful for the kind that didn't bite.

The last customer put down four cartons of eggs, a canister of protein powder, and an armload of vitamins. Her ghost told Jane that the young woman was thinking about running down a basketball court, her body thrown forward like a spear, the faces of people in the stands ripping by like confetti. Jane knew it was Bethany before she looked up.

Jane had played basketball all through school. Their team wasn't the best in the region, but they had a good time playing. That was until Bethany Ortiz came. She was two years younger than Jane, and she'd spent her entire life training, doing drills, lifting weights, and playing every sport from tennis to swimming. She'd begged to play football with the boys, but the principal wouldn't allow it. As Bethany burned through the trophy cases at the school, she picked up the ghost of every failed athlete who'd wanted to be the best. Now she boiled with them. Even Jane's ghost couldn't tell her how many spirits moved under Bethany's skin.

If there was a game, Bethany played it, and no one could beat her. It was exciting, at first, to win game after game. But soon Jane and the rest of the team realized no one needed them, that they weren't the ones winning games at all: Bethany was. They, like the rest of the world, were just there to watch.

Bethany looked hard, like a Greek goddess cut from marble or an android that had been built to humiliate humankind, some woman-shaped machine whose skin stretched over steel. Jane's brother, Henry, was the closest thing Bethany had to a friend. The two of them didn't have a lot in common, but they were both prodigies in their own ways. Whereas Jane was stuck in Swine Hill with little real hope of leaving, everyone thought that it was only a matter of time before Bethany would burn off across the horizon like a rocket and leave the town far behind.

"Hey," Jane said. "Good luck with the game tomorrow."

"Thanks. Is your brother okay? I haven't seen him at school all semester."

The ghost pushed past Bethany's concern and dug deeper, looking for some secret desire or hidden cruelty. Jane flinched, not liking it when the ghost pulled the worst out of people, but she didn't think the ghost would find much. Every night, Bethany went to bed knowing that she was the best at whatever she'd done that day. Her sleep must be easy.

But there *was* something. Deep below Bethany's obsession with times and weights and records, she was angry. She didn't like that entire sports were off-limits to her and always would be. She didn't like how people frowned at her when she shouted after sinking a basket or crossing a finish line. Even her parents, loving as they were, wanted her to be more humble and meek, less brash. And if Bethany went on to play professional sports, women didn't get the kind of money and fame men did. No matter how dominant she was, people would always assume that somewhere there was a man who was better, and she'd never even get the chance to prove them wrong. Bethany resented the entire world. But deeper still, at the core of her, Bethany was afraid that the army of ghosts inside of her would never let her leave Swine Hill.

Jane's ghost was pleased, fattening itself on Bethany's secret fear.

"Henry's working on some big project," Jane said. "He's been going to the plant every day for months."

Bethany nodded, used to Henry disappearing. "You should come to the game," she said. "Almost no one does. You remember."

"I have to work during the day tomorrow," Jane said. When her ghost told her how disappointed Bethany felt, she added, "But maybe I can head over after and catch the end of it."

"Yeah, sure."

As soon as Bethany left and the front was empty, Jane's manager called again.

"A gallon of milk burst in Dairy," he said. "Grab a mop, clean it up." He paced inside the small office. Her ghost told her that he had to pee, that he'd been holding it for an hour. He would stand, legs shaking, until he risked darting out to the bathroom or until he pissed himself. Her ghost loved it when that happened, stretched out his self-loathing like a hammock and lay in it.

Jane was halfway through mopping up the milk when the manager called for a cashier over the intercom. She finished, pushed the mop bucket against an endcap, and sprinted back to the front. Her shift went this way for hours, the manager sending her all over the store, calling her back, demanding that she be in three places at once.

As soon as the store seemed empty, Jane buzzed her manager on the phone. "I need a break."

"Make it quick."

She laid her apron over the register and went to the break room. She kept a loaf of bread and jars of peanut butter and jelly in the fridge. With things always going out on her car, she had to save money. She made and ate a sandwich, then made another, wrapped it in a paper towel, and carried it to the back of the store.

She pushed through double doors into a dim storage area, the floor wet from a problem with the air conditioning unit, then out through the back door by the loading dock. Here, under the blinking snap of a streetlight, were a pair of dumpsters, a metal folding chair, and a stray tire rim overflowing with cigarette butts. Bottle glass shimmered over the tar and asphalt, and strips of trash in washed-out blues and reds blew over the lot.

"Dad?" Jane called.

Her ghost couldn't tell if her father was near. It couldn't read his mind, didn't know if he had much of a mind left. He had left their house when Jane was ten. She saw him around town about once a week, hunched under an old sweatshirt, quick and furtive. He didn't speak, didn't meet her eyes, ran if she tried to touch him. She tried to make sure that he had clothes and stayed fed. He was the only person she knew who could walk the abandoned city center without being devoured by ghosts. He had disappeared so deep inside himself that the spirits didn't even know he was there.

Jane had reasons for staying in Swine Hill. One was money. Saving enough to move to a new city and find a place to live, to be stable while she hunted for a job, was almost impossible when she needed new tires or when tooth pain drove her to the dentist or when something broke in the house and her mother needed help paying for it.

Another reason she stayed was that she was afraid she would lose her ghost. The ghosts were tied to what reminded them of their lives. If she left Swine Hill, her ghost might not be able to follow. Most people didn't like their ghosts and were glad to have them gone, but not Jane. She'd had hers for so long, she couldn't imagine who she would be without it.

But the biggest reason she stayed, more than all the others, was that she was afraid something would happen to Henry and her father if she wasn't there.

Jane waited for ten minutes. Finally, she laid the sandwich on the chair and went back inside, hoping that her father was okay.

While it was slow, Jane thought about texting old friends who'd moved away, just to see how they were doing. But having to answer the same question, to say that she was still here, still working the same register, made her slip the phone back into her pocket.

Her ghost swam in Jane's chest and said, *He hurts, he's sorry, he's alone.*

The sliding glass doors whitened with frost so suddenly that Jane could hear them sheet with ice. A wave of cold moved into the store. It was the kind of dry, deep cold that hurt all on its own, without need for wind.

The ice on the doors broke apart as they gasped open, and someone walked into the store — a stocky guy in a white hazmat suit, a breathing mask hanging around his neck. He was young, with an innocent, sad face. He kept his eyes down and swept past her, going to the deli. The column of cold moved with him. When he was out of sight, blood and warmth came back into her hands.

Jane knew him. Or she used to. Riley Mason. He'd left school in the tenth grade, and Jane hadn't seen him in years. She asked her ghost what was wrong.

The ghost of his little brother is in him. It's so angry. It says that it barely got to live at all.

Jane grabbed an old sweater from beneath her register and pulled it on, the sleeves falling to swallow her hands. Soon, the cold moved over her again. There was a faint sound, too, a high-pitched ringing. A smell like gunpowder.

Riley walked to the front, holding an armload of deli sandwiches and sodas. He met Jane's eyes, recognized her, and looked around to see if there was a different cashier. He remembered sitting in math class with her, his embarrassment when she had to explain a problem to him and he still didn't understand. He was ashamed that he hadn't finished school, that she might think less of him. It was such a strange feeling, so unusual for someone to think that Jane was better than them, that she wanted to reach out and touch him, to tell him that everything was okay.

He put everything down, and sores of ice opened on the rubber conveyor belt where his fingers touched.

He's worried you'll ask about the cold.

Jane rang him up, rubbing her sleeve hard on the glass scanner to brush away the ice. "I haven't seen you in forever. Did you move away or something?"

He gave a weak smile. He thought she was pretty, was afraid to look at her, glanced toward the door instead. "No, I've always been here." His voice broke, like he wasn't used to talking to people. "Except for work, I just don't go out much."

"You left school at a good time. It was all downhill after Algebra Two."

"I'm surprised you're still here."

"Yeah," Jane said. "For now. What about you? What's with the suit?"

"My dad got me a job at Pig City a few years ago. Night shift. We clean the place once everyone goes home. Spray everything down to sterilize it. That's why I left school."

No, no it's not. He left because something happened.

Jane started to ask about his family, but her ghost said, *No.*

She tried to think of something else to say, not wanting the conversation to end. "Working nights, you probably see more ghosts than people."

"It's nice. I like the quiet."

Gratitude that she would talk to him at all, a warm, sweet feeling, bloomed in the boy.

A truck honked in the parking lot. Riley fumbled with his wallet, then handed her his debit card, sharp and cold.

Jane held on to it, not swiping the card right away. She wanted to ask, What the hell happened to you? But that would only scare him off. "You going to the game tomorrow?"

He looked at her like he didn't understand.

"High school girls' basketball game. Bethany Ortiz is playing, so no surprise about who's going to win. You should come, though. Before work."

Her ghost relayed a stream of feelings: surprise, confusion, caution, gratitude. "Okay," he said. "Maybe."

The truck honked again from the parking lot, three angry blasts.

"I should go before I'm late," he said.

"Sorry." Jane swiped his card and handed it back. She hugged her sides. It was so cold being close to him. Her breath poured out in a ribbon of white. She wondered what his skin felt like.

Riley angled his body toward the door, sacked groceries in hand, but he didn't leave. "You were really smart in school. I was sure you would have gone off to college somewhere."

Jane started to answer, but her ghost said, *Wait.* She stared at him, silent, letting a quiet pressure build between them. She wanted to defend herself, to tell him that leaving cost money, that people needed her here, that nothing was wrong with staying. She wanted to turn the question back on him, ask what the town possibly had to offer him.

"I'm glad, I mean. That you're still here."

Oh. She silently thanked her ghost.

The door opened, and an older man in the same white hazmat suit and mask walked in. His eyes flickered across Jane and she felt a blast of contempt. He held his arms out to Riley. "We're late, kid. What's going on?"

"It's my fault," Jane said. "I run my mouth sometimes."

The man had a salt-and-pepper beard, long hair, stony eyes. He looked at Jane and dismissed her in an instant. It was unimaginable to him that his son might want to talk to her.

The man put an arm on Riley's shoulder, and his son tensed. "Say bye to your friend, Trigger."

Trigger?

Her ghost filled her ear: *Don't ask about that. If you do, he might not talk to you anymore.*

Jane tore the receipt off, but before she handed it back, she wrote her phone number on the back of it, shielded behind the register where his father couldn't see. She pressed it into Riley's hand, getting a shock of cold when her fingers met his, like touching frozen glass.

The two men went out the door in their bulky suits, looking more like astronauts than Pig City workers, like they were headed up to rake the dead white surface of the moon. Trigger held the receipt deep in his palm, thinking of her hand.

He and his father don't like each other.

"Even I could tell that," Jane said.

Riley had left a pile of dead leaves on the floor behind him. Jane reached down and picked one up, the point beaded with blood, its veined body crucified by lines of frost.

He's not bleeding, her ghost said. *The leaves are just part of his ghost. They'll fade away soon.*

Jane held the leaf in her hands, watching as it turned glassy and light, until it was gone and the cold with it.

You gave him your number.

"He seems like he needs a friend." Jane often spoke out loud when she talked to her ghost. It was the only way to keep the ghost girl from talking over her, breaking up her train of thought, running her in circles.

Maybe you're *the one who needs a friend.*

Jane felt a flush of embarrassment, unable to hide anything from the ghost, and it howled around her body in an exulting, invisible wind.

A FEW MINUTES UNTIL closing time, the manager turned off half the lights, leaving the store dim. Jane leaned back against her counter, palms behind her, staring at the clock.

The door sighed open again. With no warning from her ghost, a giant ducked its head and squeezed through the doors. He wore denim coveralls, oversized black boots, and a blue Pig City cap. But he wasn't a person. His swollen arms, thicker than Jane's waist, strained the fabric of his sleeves. Thick gray hair shot from under his cuffs and up from his collar. His hands, resting on the small bar of a grocery cart, had four thick fingers, their nails flinty black. He glanced at her with an inhuman face.

The creature had the head of a pig. Tusks protruded slightly from the sides of his mouth. His eyes were small and sunken, snout wet. Tall triangular ears stood up on either side of his head. His face was a puzzle of scars, like he'd been pieced together rather than born, the seams still showing.

Jane squeezed the lip of her counter, waiting for the spirit to do what it would do. It was so solid, seemed so real. There would be no getting away from it. She hoped it hadn't come to haunt her.

Her ghost rose in her, sensing her terror. *What's wrong, Jane? It's only a man.*

The hulking pig man pushed his cart toward the meat department.

"It can't just be a man," Jane said softly. "What does he want?"

Him? Her ghost swirled thoughtfully. *Nothing. He's thinking about work. Thinking about pigs.*

"He *is* a pig," Jane whispered, afraid the man would hear.

Being as close as they were to the haunted downtown, Jane had seen plenty of strange things walk through the door. People so weighed down with ghosts that they could barely speak, bent double over their carts, flinching from sound or light. But a pig — a walking, grocery-shopping, plant-working pig — *this* was new.

Jane walked down the aisle toward the meat section, letting her ghost get close enough to listen in on the pig man's thoughts. "Is he angry? Is he here for a reason?"

He's just thinking about meat. Prices. Nothing at all.

Jane could feel the spirit's irritation. There was nothing worse to her ghost than someone calm, in the moment, without a gnawing secret or worry. The pig might as well be a newborn, his flighty thoughts catching on the noise of his cart or the flicker of the lights above. The pig man's cart creaked closer, and Jane went back to her register.

Her manager waited, a key in his hand. He dropped it onto her counter and backed away, thinking of the pig, but thinking too of Jane's ghost, of any ghosts that might already be invisibly closing in.

"I need to get home," he said. "You can lock up tonight."

He fled the store, leaving Jane alone with whatever the pig man was. *He thinks it's a ghost. He's afraid it came into the store just for him.*

Jane picked up her phone and pressed the intercom button, announcing that the store would close soon. She was pretty sure the pig man was the only one left.

Here he comes. Thinking about sausage, of all things.

The pig man was easily twice the size of the biggest man Jane had ever seen. His shopping cart groaned with weight. In it, he'd stacked hams, tubes of hamburger meat, big cylinders of tenderloin, and plastic bins of pork chops. There was nothing in his cart *but* meat, most of it pork. He dumped it clumsily on the conveyor belt, and Jane started checking him out. The cheerful Pig City logo, a cartoon pig giving a thumbs-up, passed again and again under her hands.

Jane tried not to look at his snout or ears. He pressed against her counter, smelling strongly of metal and blood. She felt surrounded by him, his towering height, his shadow, his bellows breath.

She rang up six hundred dollars worth of meat, then bagged groceries while he fumbled a wallet out of his pocket and carefully tweezed it open with brutish fingers. He handed her a Pig City company charge card. The name on it read "Walter Hogboss." She rang him up and handed the card back to him.

"Thank you," he said, his voice a snarl, a collection of grunts and wheezing squeals pinned with meat hooks and stretched into words. With that, the pig man pushed his cart to the door and went out into the night.

Jane locked the doors after him, thankful that he was gone. "He may not have been a ghost, but he wasn't a man, either."

He seemed like a man to me.

She wondered if the pig man had come out of the haunted downtown somehow. There had been odd visitants before. Last year, right at dusk, a crowd of ghosts had flooded into the store and rushed the bakery, their semi-translucent bodies bleeding in and out of one another. They stayed there all night, the manager putting up CAUTION: WET FLOOR signs so the living would know to keep their distance. Afterward, Jane learned that it had been some holiday that no one in town celebrated anymore. The ghosts were looking for a special kind of bread that the store had carried eighty years ago. The living might forget everything, but the dead still sang their old songs.

As close as they were to downtown, lots of strange things slipped into the store, most of them small and invisible. Sometimes Jane went down the aisles touching everything, feeling for the special electricity of the dead. Any boxed dinners or pasta sauces or flour sacks that were possessed were thrown out with the expired goods. The stray dogs that ate from their dumpsters snapped at things no one could see.

Jane locked up and walked across the parking lot, keeping an eye out for ghosts. She heard the creaking groan of a shopping cart somewhere in the dark. She fumbled her keys out of her pocket, ready to quickly unlock her car or to defend herself.

The pig man pushed his cart out from behind a Pig City work truck, blocking her path.

His basket-like hands rested on the thin rail of the cart handle. His gray fur looked white in the wash of the parking lot lights. He let go of the cart and took a step toward her. Jane felt her mind stop, her body freeze. Even her ghost retreated deep within, both wondering if they would be dragged into a black place, snuffed out between his big hands.

"Excuse me," the pig man said. "Something is wrong with my truck."

Her ghost leaned against her chest, listening. *He's worried his meat will spoil.*

Jane took a breath. "Okay. I can take a look at it for you." She wished Henry were here. Machines were his thing, not hers.

Jane walked toward the pig man's truck. He pushed his cart behind her, fretting about the meat. She didn't have to pop the hood to know what was wrong. The whole truck trembled with ghosts. They filled its engine, pinging about inside the cylinders. They floated through the gas lines and the tank. They curled in the tires, and entwined their bodies with the electrical. She couldn't see them, but her ghost told her they were there, told her what they were feeling. *A pig working at our plant. A pig wearing our uniform. A stranger taking what's ours. Send the pig back where it came from. Don't let it take what little we have left.*

"Did you drive through downtown?"

The pig man pointed across the dark smear of the city center. "I live on the other side."

"You have to go around. Otherwise, the ghosts mob you. You're lucky it's not worse than this." She was surprised the pig man hadn't ended up haunted himself. The ghosts must not have seen anything in him that reminded them of themselves.

He grunted. "Can it be fixed?"

"Let it sit here for the night. By morning, most of the ghosts should have moved on. Maybe your truck will start then." She doubted it, but there wasn't much else to do.

The pig man thanked her and stood there with his cart. He sniffed the air. Her ghost read his thoughts, how he weighed pushing his cart straight through downtown against taking a longer way and risking the meat going bad.

Jane sighed, already regretting what she was about to say. "I can give you a ride home, if you want." She hoped this wouldn't be a mistake, that the pig man hadn't been planning to get her alone in the close space of a car.

"That would be very kind of you," he said.

She opened her trunk, finding stacked circuit boards and coils of wire, junk Henry had left there. The pig man layered his meat on top of it.

He pushed the passenger seat back and lowered himself in, one arm holding the roof to steady himself. The car sank low on its shocks, and his bulk pressed against Jane in the driver's seat.

He was mostly quiet on their trip across town, letting his arm and shoulder hang out the window. The car swept through foggy ghosts on their way to or from the plant. When they burst through one, the pig man sniffed deeply. "They don't smell like anything," he said.

He's thinking about pigs, meat, the plant workers, ghosts. It's a little hard to follow. He's tired. It's all mixed up.

"Do you work at Pig City?" Jane asked.

"I'm the plant manager," the pig man said. "But I was only recently promoted."

Promoted from pen and straw. Promoted from four legs to two.

His house was in an abandoned neighborhood close to downtown. Only one block separated him from the worst of the haunting. A light was on inside, a yellow glow through the white curtains of his kitchen.

He got out, the car heaving up with him, and unloaded his groceries from the back.

Jane was about to leave when he knocked heavily on her window. She rolled it down, and the pig man reached a hand inside. She didn't move, hands tight on the steering wheel.

"Take this," he said, "as a thank-you."

He dropped two sticky packages of steaks on her lap.

"And please tell Henry that I'll be calling him soon," he said.

The pig man stood, grocery bags looped like shower hooks over his huge arm, and went inside.

Jane rolled up her window and backed out of the driveway, then drove fast out of the neighborhood toward home. "How does he know my brother? What does he want with him?"

I don't know, the ghost said. *He wasn't thinking about much. But when he mentioned Henry, he remembered pain.*

3

HEN HENRY'S GHOST finally released him, he found himself in bed. The wall clock read 7:01, and the light outside was dim. Was it morning or evening? He had the kind of brutal, nail-spike-to-the-back-of-the-skull headache that told him he hadn't slept in a long time. The blankets stuck to his arms and chest. He pulled them away, finding that he was covered in dried blood.

He showered with the bathroom light off. After scrubbing away the blood, he ran his hands over his arms, legs, chest. He wasn't hurt. No cuts or scrapes that he could find. He stood with the water crashing against the top of his head. He felt an electric, full-body awareness, realizing that the blood must belong to someone else. What had his ghost made him do?

Henry's ghost cared only about the technical: engines, angles, formulae. When Henry came across an interesting problem, it woke up the ghost in him. Sometimes Henry would only be out for minutes, with no memory of where he had been or what he had done. Sometimes, the ghost rode him for much longer. Usually, whatever he made was harmless, beautiful, a miracle of science and invention. But every once in a while, he made something dangerous. It was all the same to the ghost. If it could be done, it was worth doing.

Henry dressed and moved through stacks of broken electronics mounded on his floor and into the hallway crisscrossed with extension cords and dotted with drifts of laundry. Music played from Jane's room, so he pushed open her door. Her back wall was stacked with speakers, CD players, and disc towers, headphones and aux cables falling down over it like vines. The rug was scattered with CDs, detailed notes written in Sharpie on their white faces. Jane slept to the noise of her stereo.

Henry shook the edge of her bed, and Jane sat up.

"Is that you?" Jane asked. "Or just your ghost?"

"It's me."

"You were out for two months. Bethany was worried about you."

"Months?" What had he been doing before his ghost took him? He couldn't remember. "Did I make anything? Have you seen it?"

"You went to the pig plant with Mom every day. You'll have to ask her what you were doing up there."

Downstairs, he heard his mother talking on the phone and the click of silverware against a plate. He stumbled into the kitchen, holding his head and shading his eyes from the light.

The robot towered over the stove, making breakfast. Henry had made it out of what he could find — a busted hot water heater tank for its torso, a tin pail shielding a pair of outdated camcorders and auto lights for its head, the key levers of an old typewriter for its delicate fingers. Inside its body, a dense ball of junked computers and VCRs were soldered to car batteries and the power supply from a vacuum cleaner. The frayed end of an electrical cord swung behind it like a tail.

The robot dressed itself in his father's old clothes — something Henry was certain he hadn't programmed it to do. Its work boots and jeans were stiff with mud. Bright stars of rust and bleeding tracks of

white battery corrosion dotted its limbs and chassis. It moved erratically, slamming down plates and dropping silverware, movements
jerky from spirits that had taken up residence in its servomotors. His
ghost had driven Henry to build it after his father left, when Henry
worried that someone needed to take care of his mother.

The spirit haunting his mother was a lonely, hot-burning ghost desperate to be loved. Her skin was scorching to the touch, the ghost
translating its desire into heat. People were drawn to her, felt thrilled
to be so wanted. Those who stayed by her side ended up burned to ash.
After suffering burns all over his body and the mental trauma of being drawn like a moth to what was killing him, their father vanished.
His body was still there, but everything inside him had been snatched
away. Henry and Jane still saw him occasionally, but he wasn't the same.

His mother was dressed in her blue Pig City jumpsuit. She'd gotten
a coveted Pig City job before Henry had been born, but she'd never
been promoted or gotten a raise. There weren't many black workers at
the plant, and no one management considered a problem would work
there for long. She did her work invisibly, without objection or com-
plaint, like another ghost.

But his mom liked her work. She was in the pig houses, keeping the
animals healthy. She could touch the pigs without searing their skin.
When she fed them from her hands, she didn't have to ask whether or
not they really loved her. More than the men who floated in and out of
her life and bed, the pigs were a comfort. A shame, Henry had always
thought, that it was her job to bring them to the slaughterhouse.

His mom was on the phone with her brother who lived out of state,
but the two of them didn't have much to say to each other. Their extended family had gotten out of Swine Hill and left their ghosts behind. It hadn't been easy, and they didn't want to hear anything about
the place, didn't want to remember the hungry touch of spirits. They
had new problems now. And Henry's mom didn't want to hear about
her brother's new wife or how well his kids were doing. Sometimes the
two of them would spend an hour on the phone and barely say anything, listening to the background noise of each other's houses. The

plastic of the phone receiver deformed in his mother's burning hand, hot from all the things she held in.

Henry sat down, and the robot dropped a plate in front of him. It was a huge steak, falling over the edge of the dish and oozing blood.

"Is this breakfast or dinner?" Henry asked.

"One of Jane's customers gave it to her. She cares more about them than she does about me."

Henry put aside the weirdness of Jane's customers giving her steak. "What day is it?"

She ignored him and kept talking to his uncle. "My own daughter doesn't hug me anymore."

Henry sighed. They *couldn't* hug her. They'd get burned.

His uncle must have said as much.

"But they don't even *want* to hug me," his mother said. "That's what matters."

It was like sitting in front of a furnace grate. Henry leaned back in his chair in spite of himself.

His mother glared at him and stood, picking up her keys, her cell phone still against her ear.

"Are you going to work?" he asked. "Does that mean I have school today?"

"Have your sister take you."

It was easy for him not to take his mother personally. Her ghost made her this way. And unlike Jane, he didn't have a window into their mother's mind, couldn't see just how deep ran her river of selfishness and need.

Henry finished breakfast and gave his dirty plate to the robot. His backpack lay against the foot of the stairs, but it didn't hold any clues to what he had been doing for the last two months. He felt impatient, wanting to see what he had made. It might be dangerous, and then he'd have to take it apart. Still, it had to be amazing if he'd spent months working on it.

His head felt tight with pain from lack of sleep. Everything seemed a little softer, farther away, less real. He yelled up the stairs for Jane to take him to school.

Her car wouldn't start. Henry had offered to fix it for her before, but his inventions had a habit of turning out to be dangerous: a dishwasher that turned dirty plates into pottery shards and powder, rewired sockets that cooked electronics, a cell phone that picked up only strange, inhuman frequencies. He knew Jane was afraid that his ghost would snatch him away again if he came across an interesting problem, but there was no other option. She laid her head against the steering wheel and gestured for him to see what he could do.

He spent twenty minutes looking for his father's jumper cables in the mess of the garage, but the car wouldn't start until he opened the battery case and filled it with water. Finally, the engine moaned to life. It was only a temporary fix. Jane needed to buy a new battery, but money was always tight.

They rumbled over the pitted road and past the neighborhood's sagging porches, which were like hands slowly closing to fists around their doors. The whole town was like this, with few people left on any street. Everything weather-damaged and gray, the lawns overgrown and cratered with junk. When a washing machine's electric hum seduced a lonely ghost and then the motor seized up and refused to turn, people could do little but throw the possessed hulk out on the lawn. Henry wondered what it must be like for a ghost, finding in the spin of a motor or the minuscule architecture of a circuit board some shadow of what its life had been.

"I haven't seen Dad in a while," Jane said. "I leave food out in places where we've seen him. I think he's finding it, but who knows."

"I'm sure he's fine," Henry said. He thought of his father's ropey scars and twisted face. The way he could appear suddenly at a car window or staring out from an abandoned building. How he spent his nights walking among the most brutal and angry ghosts. The only reason he wasn't haunted was that he had somehow become more ghost than man.

"You don't have to be afraid of him," Jane said. "He wouldn't hurt anyone."

Henry tightened a fist on his bag and looked out the window, ashamed. His sister could always see the worst parts of him. He tried to refocus, to think of something else before her ghost pushed deeper and found something uglier.

"Two months. I've never been out that long before. Did Mom tell you what I was working on?"

Jane was quiet for a moment, focusing on the road like she hadn't heard him. "I met someone at work last night. His name was Walter Hogboss."

Henry felt his ghost stir slightly, a small flare of recognition. "Was he from the plant? Did they need help with something?"

Jane pulled into the student parking lot behind the school, the gray brick and glass building rising before them.

"He wasn't human."

"It was a ghost? You talked to it?"

"Not a ghost. It was a walking, talking pig. It was stitched together, like a butcher built it out of spare parts. I think he's here because of you."

Henry stared at his hands. Crusted blood collected dark along his nails. "You don't think that *I* made it."

"Where else would it have come from?"

"Why would I make a talking pig? Bacon doesn't taste any better if it can talk. What would be the point?"

"He said he's going to call you." Jane squeezed his shoulder. "I think you did something really bad this time. Worse than the robot."

"Mom needs the robot. A lot of the things I make are good. They help. If I made this pig, there must have been a reason." He fought to close off his mind, to think of anything else to keep her ghost from laying him bare.

"That's what you want to believe," Jane said. "That's what you're telling yourself."

"I have to go." Henry snapped off his seatbelt and shouldered open the door.

Henry passed through the sagging chain-link fence that divided the high school from the haunted arms of downtown Swine Hill. The school was filled with its own strange species of ghost. Most weren't dangerous. Unlike the downtown ghosts who'd lost everything they'd lived for, the dead students still had the school. And in the eighty-odd years the school had stood on this spot, nothing had been torn down. The school buildings crumbled across a stand of hills, their sad ghosts still moving through the hallways and waiting for their lives to begin.

No two structures were alike, all in various stages of decay. Shingles shed from rooftops and piled under the eaves. Bricks tumbled from the sides of stairwells, masonry cracked, and painted boards flaked their layers to show decades of neglect. Old pieces of pipe jutted out of the ground randomly, gas lines that went nowhere and had hopefully been disconnected. There were picnic tables between the buildings for lunch hour, but half of them were broken in some way, little more than wooden hulks for students to perch on. The school buildings sat at odd angles from each other, had protruding stairwells and doors chained shut. Whole floors were closed down due to water damage and low enrollment. With all the secret corners and resident ghosts, it was hard for the teachers to keep track of their students. They'd mostly given up trying.

Henry went into a gray annex off the main classroom building for first period. It was supposed to be a Gifted and Talented class, but Henry wasn't there because he was smart. The principal liked to keep any student with an especially strong ghost out of the way.

They called it the laughing room. Years ago, an entire classroom of eighth-graders had started laughing, afflicted by some chorus of gleeful spirits. The students laughed until they cried, pounding their fists and clawing at their desks. The teacher yelled, threatened to write them up, but they couldn't stop. With a roar, the entire class simply disintegrated into laughter, their mocking voices rising to foam around the ceiling.

When Henry opened the door, ghostly voices came shrieking out. It was an ugly sound, as if the ghosts were laughing at you. It was important not to listen to what they were saying, or else you could be swept away too. He pulled out a bulky CD player and headphones. Before he sat, he picked up a binder of work from the teacher, who was playing solitaire on her computer.

The CD player whirred to life, the disc making a quiet scrape, and Henry was flooded with music. Jane had put together the mix for him. The songs were soaring anthems about saints, inventors, and mythic heroes. The vocalists wailed about destiny, and the words felt true, oracular. It was embarrassing that his sister knew him so well. Henry did want to remake the world, to build some new age. And why else would his inventive, powerful ghost have been drawn to him, if not because he was meant to do something big?

His Gifted and Talented binder was full of Byzantine problems the faculty had created to test the limits of what Henry and his ghost could do. He may have been the brightest student to ever come through the doors of the school, but half the problems were unsolvable, ridiculous, impossible. Sometimes Henry looked at them and saw only a closed door. But his ghost bent what was possible, wouldn't accept that something couldn't be done. The problems in the binder were written to wake it up.

He needed to keep control of himself, to find out what he had done before the ghost carried him away again. He didn't want to be a passenger in his own body. Henry took a deep breath and opened the binder.

The first problems in the binder were merely mathematical or dealt with chemistry. None of them was strange enough to interest his ghost. Henry breezed through them, balancing out equals signs and dispensing with unknown variables like he was tying his shoes. While he worked, the door softly opened and closed. A girl, always late and careful not to look at or touch anyone, hurried to the back of the room. Her footsteps were soft, like crushing paper. Henry wondered what kind of ghost she must have to be so afraid.

The next problem dealt with a complex waste disposal mechanism at the plant. There was a diagram of an intake chute, a furnace, gas lines. A list of work orders detailing problems with the chute getting clogged or the intake belt jamming. Everything was drawn out to scale, neatly annotated with measurements and angles. Henry tensed, waiting for his ghost to rise in him. It loved anything that dealt with the meatpacking plant.

Thankfully, it didn't come. Henry looked over the schematics, found the point of failure, and sketched out a better design. In the back of the binder, Henry found a plastic bag full of trash: a flattened soda can, some bottle caps, random screws and bits of wire. The instructions told him to make a battery. He stared at it blankly for a second, took a breath, and then . . . he found himself staring at a soda can wrapped in black electrical tape. It was heavy when he picked it up, sloshing with some improvised electrolyte. His hands were scraped and his thumbnail cracked. The gutted remains of a stereo speaker and a VCR rested on the floor beside him. Looking at the clock, he saw that he'd been out for thirty minutes.

The final problem in the binder was from his English teacher. On a clean sheet of paper, she'd written, *In three hundred words, describe how it feels to not remember what you did, but to know it's your fault.* The ghost was silent inside him, utterly uninterested in matters of feeling or ethics. Henry palmed the battery he'd made.

He'd decided a long time ago that it wasn't worth being afraid of his ghost. It was a part of him. His inventions almost never hurt anyone. Even when they did, he was trying to do something good. In a place like Swine Hill, where so much was wrong, that's what counted, wasn't it?

Second period was Mr. Nichti's math class, but the material was so basic that Henry had already worked ahead and finished out the semester. He went to the counselor's office instead. It had been a supply closet at one time, just enough room for a desk, two chairs, a bookshelf vomiting files, and small, pale Mr. Bradford.

The counselor repainted his office and the walls of his home every month, his clothes spotted with white. He drove to the next town to purchase food or appliances so that there would be no ghosts in his home. He drank bottled water so that nothing could come through the tap. He never went outside. He wasn't from Swine Hill and didn't plan to be here long, spending his careful life avoiding ghosts. But as excited as Bradford seemed by the things Henry's ghost could do, Henry wondered if the man wasn't a little jealous that he didn't have a ghost of his own.

Henry gave him the Gifted binder and battery, taking a seat.

"Good to see you," the man said. "Is your internship with Pig City done?"

"I was doing an internship?"

"Apparently HR had a problem they needed help with. Something to do with worker satisfaction."

That wasn't the kind of problem that usually excited his ghost. It was too social, the variables too numerous, the contours of the problem too hard to express mathematically.

"Have you thought any more about me graduating early?" Henry asked. "We were going to talk about robotics programs maybe."

Henry had a vague idea that somewhere out there were colleges where he could build machines, wear a lab coat, work on tech that would help people. And he'd heard about people getting scholarships and grants, that you could get far even if you didn't have any money. Nobody in his family had ever done it, though. He'd always thought Jane would.

The counselor gave him a serious look, full of pity and sympathy, like he was bracing himself to deliver hard news. "I don't really think that's doable, Henry. You don't have any AP classes or extracurriculars."

"There aren't any of those here."

"And your grades are fine, but not great."

This was true. He missed a lot of school because of his ghost. His teachers didn't really seem to care, but they weren't giving him A's, either.

The counselor gestured to a shattered remote control car on the bookshelf behind him. "I just don't think Caltech and MIT are going to be impressed by the video of you repairing a roach."

Henry winced. He was usually thrilled by what he made, but the roach was different. A few months ago, the Gifted binder had a bag with the dead insect, glistening brown, and a box full of tiny tools and electronic parts. The problem was simply stated: *Repair the roach.* His ghost had surged up in him, and when Henry awoke, he found himself in the school's science lab after dark, days later. He'd connected the roach via electrodes to a remote control car. But stranger, he had done something to the roach itself, coating its bruised exoskeleton with glue, its dead body swollen with chemicals and issuing tiny wires feeding electricity into it at the smallest voltages. When he turned it on, the roach car sprinted off through the halls of the school. It took them days to find it, dead again after submerging itself in the flooded basement. When Mr. Nichti had brought him the wreckage, congratulating him on something so amazing, Henry had only felt sick.

"Aren't you afraid that if you leave Swine Hill, your ghost will fade?" the counselor asked. "You don't want to throw yourself into an environment you're not ready for."

He was willing to take the risk. No way was he going to stay in Swine Hill for the rest of his life. People didn't understand. The ghost didn't make him smart. It had been drawn to him because he was already brilliant. It was the same with Bethany. People thought she won because she was a human haunted house, all those ghosts pushing her to victory. But the reason she was full of ghosts was because they craved victory and they could only get it from her.

"Other people have left and been fine. What about Meghan? Didn't she get a scholarship to some big school in Texas? I think she wanted to be an engineer."

The counselor shrugged. "You're not Meghan, are you?"

Henry looked down at the desk, feeling embarrassed for coming, as if he'd done something wrong by even asking about schools. No, he wasn't Meghan. He didn't need Jane's telepathy to understand why.

"Of course, you're only in tenth grade," Bradford said. "There's still plenty of time. You might think about community college once you're ready for it, but honestly, I think your best bet would be to do maintenance work for Pig City. After this internship, I'm sure they'd hire you."

Henry glanced at a university brochure on the desk, photos of machines wrought in silicone, aluminum, and industrial plastics. The glasses-covered eyes of kids like him, slender-armed and heavy-headed, bending together over a computer terminal. This was where he wanted to be, away from his claustrophobic house, the family he couldn't fix with electricity or metal.

"Thanks." Henry left the brochure where it lay and stood up. "I'll think about that."

ALL FOUR GRADES of the high school were sent to lunch at the same time. When all the students were in one place, the school didn't seem so small. But everyone knew that enrollment was down each year, that they were laying off teachers, moving some students ahead and holding others back just to have full classrooms. The principal had said there would be no need for a school in twenty years, because only the old would be left in the town, and only because they had nowhere else to go.

The cafeteria tile was blotted with inky stains on the grout. Many seats at the long tables were broken, so students shared or ate standing by the windows. Henry was swept up in the spiraling line, his classmates' voices mixing into a roar that sounded more like wind or water than speech.

Bethany came out of the lunch line balancing a tray on each hand. In a tank-top, the curved swell of her shoulders and biceps fit together like articulated plates of medieval armor. Her long braid swung like a flail. She was all quiet power, something like a bolt of lightning slowed down in midstrike.

Henry had been in love with her at first, pathetically so, a problem his ghost couldn't help him with. But he'd soon learned that Bethany had no interest in him or any other boy. Her focus was singular. Where Henry wanted to make amazing machines, Bethany's sole work was herself. But in a school filled with the strange, they were the strangest two of all. Apart from his sister, Bethany was the only friend he had.

"You were gone a long time," she said. "Were you working on that thing we talked about?"

Bethany hadn't been able to leave town in the last three years. Her hundreds of ghosts wrapped her wrist and ankle, twining their dead fingers around her limbs, keeping her from leaving Swine Hill. They needed her to win. Unless she found a way to break loose from them, she'd spend the rest of her life in the ruins of the town, running and shooting baskets for the spirits living through her.

It wasn't a hard problem to solve. Henry had told her what she needed to do. She had to start throwing games. Lose on purpose. It might take years, but with every defeat, more of the ghosts would bleed away. That was the only way she could make it out. Bethany had told him to come up with something else.

"Nothing new on that," he said. "Sorry. I was working on a project for Pig City."

The students near Henry turned to stare when he mentioned the pig plant. Those who weren't leaving were hoping for a job there. No matter how brutal it was, it paid better than anything around. They'd pinned their every hope on it. Henry hunched his shoulders, sank into his baggy shirt, and lowered his voice. Being noticed too much was dangerous. It was one of the hard things about being friends with Bethany. She couldn't help but draw attention to herself, wasn't afraid to claim things that other people thought were rightfully theirs.

"I'm going to the weight room," Bethany said. "See you at the game later?"

Henry nodded.

After making it through the line, he found an empty seat near a group of towering senior boys. They all had after-school or weekend jobs at the plant. They were talking about the pig man.

One of the boys had been hoping his father would be promoted to plant manager. They needed the extra money so he and his sisters could move out of state. Now he might be stuck here.

Another said that the pig man asked strange questions. One day he'd walked onto the butchering floor, waved his scarred hand at the pig carcasses and the men carving them up, and asked, "Why are we doing all this?" He didn't seem upset, just confused.

If pigs could work, would the plant lay people off? they wondered. It hadn't happened in a long time, but now anything seemed possible.

"How does a pig turn into a person?" one of them asked.

Henry kept his eyes on his food, but he could feel them staring at him. Finally, he got up and dumped his tray, keeping his sandwich and walking out of the cafeteria with it.

Clumps of students lounged on picnic tables and derelict staircases. It was loud here too, people making petty drama and arguing about love, doing anything but thinking of work or family, the ghosts and problems that began at the border of three o'clock.

The counselor had said that Henry was fixing a worker satisfaction problem. Surely he had only been trying to make people happy. The whole town was small-minded, quick to worry. The pig man couldn't be that bad.

Henry walked toward the weight room to find Bethany. He passed behind the cafeteria, alongside the fence that divided the school from the surrounding abandoned streets. There was a line of dumpsters here, overflowing with trash.

A man perched on the edge of a dumpster. He wore a tattered jacket, the ends of it shredded from catching on fence wire. His face was an overlapping pattern of scars. Imprinted on the man's skin, as if he were made of clay, were handprints, the impression of lips and teeth, caresses mapped onto him in bright burn scars. It was his father.

Henry resisted the urge to run. He felt an unexpected grief. He wanted to help, to do something selfless, to prove that he wasn't so different from his sister. He extended his hand, holding out the half-eaten sandwich, and forced himself to take a step forward.

The burned man dropped onto the pavement and vaulted the fence, loping off into the quiet streets. He was gone at once, like a deer slipping between trees.

Henry pulled out his phone and texted Jane. *I just saw Dad.*

How was he?

He sat down and ate his sandwich, typing and deleting the message several times, not sure what to say. *Better than usual.*

The bell rang, but Henry didn't feel like facing his classmates. Word would have spread that he'd been at the pig plant all spring, that he was connected somehow to the pig man. They would want to know why he had done it. He wanted to know himself.

He found a set of double doors chained shut and, pulling them wide, was able to slip between. They opened into a stairwell, which Henry climbed to the third floor.

The sunlight coming in from the sooty windows had a gray cast. The floor was spongy with rotten carpet, fallen insulation, and shredded paper. Panels of drywall had been ripped away from the walls, exposing wires and pipes.

He passed a closed classroom door and looked inside. The room was full of students, as pale and insubstantial as smoke. A knot of them surrounded a girl in the middle of the room, holding her down. The ghost girl yelled with an airless, soundless voice. Something horrible had happened here, was still happening. One of the students turned and met eyes with Henry through the glass. She gestured for him to open the door, to come in. She opened her lips and mouthed, *Help.*

Henry hurried away, his steps the only sound on the floor. Down the hall, he leaned against the window to catch his breath. The glass was broken here, giving him a clear view of the Pig City meatpacking plant sitting turret-like on its plateau.

He found an old drama room and went inside, hoping to find somewhere to sit. He froze in midstride. There was a girl on stage.

She was tall and long-limbed, with an explosion of curly hair hanging over her face. The girl moved through a dance routine, watching her feet and silently counting out the steps. Her bare feet hit the old stage with a quiet slap. The bright trickling of a piano played, from where Henry wasn't sure.

He didn't know her, but he didn't pay much attention to people. She might be an upperclassman.

"Sorry," he said. "I didn't think anyone was up here."

She focused on her dance, brows knit in irritation. "Why are you here?"

Henry sat down in a stray chair, coating his back in dust. "Cutting class. Trying to remember what my ghost made me do."

She kept going through the patterns of her steps, drawing lines in the air with her hands and feet. "Do you always blame your ghost when you do something?"

"It's not like that. I give my ghost a problem, and it takes control of me to solve it. We're a team. Usually, it's great. But I think it might have made a mistake this time."

"If you're a team, why did you say that *it* made a mistake?"

"I guess that's fair," he said.

Why did she seem upset that he'd called the ghost an it? They were always called it, never he or she. He'd been told that ever since he was a boy, ever since he'd become old enough to tell the difference between the living and the unquiet dead. Every child in Swine Hill was taught that. Ghosts were not people; they were things. Selfish and unchanging. Refusing to leave when their time had run out. To think of them as people was to owe them love and loyalty, to doom yourself to staying in Swine Hill forever, living out someone else's past.

The room was uncomfortably warm, stuffy and close. She extended a hand toward him. "Come here. I need a partner for this next bit. I can show you the steps."

Henry had never danced before. Jane had tried to teach him once. He'd seen people do it on TV, and it always seemed like a foreign language, something that neither he nor his ghost could decode. But there was no one here to see him but the girl. And her hand was out, waiting. He went to her.

Climbing onto the stage, Henry noticed a wooden cabinet lying against the wall. It was black with mold and rotten through. Yellowed chips spilled out of it, piling on the old carpet. Piano keys. The bones of a piano. The music came from it.

The girl spun toward him over the stage. The heavy dust lying on the wood was smooth and undisturbed under her feet. Henry was inches away from taking her hand, his fingers almost in hers, when he dropped from the stage and backed away.

"You're dead."

She stared fire at him, her hands balled into fists. "Am I an *it*, too? Come here. You said you and your ghost were a team. Be on my team for a while. I can't finish my dance alone."

He could feel it now, an aura of violence and frustration coming off the stage like wind. Whatever this girl wanted, she wanted badly. It would probably hurt. He might not survive it.

"I'm sorry. I can't." He went to the door, feeling like an idiot. It was his headache, his exhaustion. He wouldn't have been so stupid if he'd been more awake.

"You're useless," she said. "No wonder your ghost picked you. He never helped anyone either."

Henry stopped at the edge of the room. He knew next to nothing about the spirit that haunted him, but he'd always been curious. "You knew my ghost?"

She was back to dancing now, the piano playing fast and loud. She beckoned to him as she twirled. "Come up here and take my hand. I'll tell you all about him."

Henry left the room and shut the door on the ghost girl. Why should he care what kind of person his ghost had been when it was alive? It helped him. That was all that mattered now.

He sighed. If Jane was here, she would say, *That's what you want to believe.*

He got some headache medicine from the office and slept through his last few classes. The school didn't have a dedicated computer lab, but the yearbook room had several computers. At the end of the day, he picked the lock on the door and let himself in.

Once, the yearbook teacher had found him here, Henry in the midst of cleaning up and repairing the old desktops just to have something to do. She told him that he wasn't supposed to be there, but she hadn't turned him in or asked him to leave.

The yearbook teacher, Ms. Miller, had the unpopular idea that the pig plant was the source of all the town's problems. Instead of producing a yearbook, she sent her students to photograph polluted streams and pig bones dredged from the river, did interviews with workers who'd lost limbs working there, made updated maps of the growing downtown and its army of furious ghosts. She told her students that one day she would have proof that something was wrong.

Henry didn't know why she bothered. It was clear that things weren't okay here. Just telling people wouldn't fix anything. Something big would have to change, not just in Swine Hill, but in the world. Henry wanted to be that change.

Jane texted that she had to work all afternoon, so Henry would have to stay at school until the basketball game later. Unless he wanted to walk home, and he didn't. There were too many angry people around the town, resentful and bored. Cars loaded full with older kids. Bitter men and women sitting out on their porches. Cops roving in their aging cruisers. And there were always the ghosts, so desperate to find someone they could see themselves in. Henry stuck out too much. It was best not to be caught alone.

He defragged and ran virus scanners on the desktops. One wouldn't boot until he reformatted the hard drive and reinstalled the OS. Some ghost had probably found its way onto the drive, wandering through old .jpegs and .mp3s, looking for the life it had lost.

He laid his head on his arms, listening to the whine of the computers getting hot with use. His phone buzzed, clattering over the desk and dropping into his lap. The screen read WALTER HOGBOSS. The number was already in his contacts. He hadn't thought to check. He answered the phone and raised it to his ear, afraid of whatever was coming next.

"Hello?"

"Henry." The voice was cavern deep. "Your modified pig project is right on schedule. If things go well, Corporate would like to send you to some of their plants in Kentucky and Iowa."

"I don't remember you. Can you tell me what happened?"

There was a moment of silence on the line, then breath searing into the receiver. "You sound sad, Henry. How can I help?"

"People are nervous about you. Did anyone see us together?"

"Workers at the plant saw you come and go for months, working alone in one of the labs. One day, you stopped coming, and I put on my uniform and walked out. I haven't said anything, but people have suspicions, as you can imagine."

This wasn't helping him. He paced, the hardwood floor creaking softly under his feet. "When my ghost takes control, there's always a specific problem I'm working on. I need to know why I did this."

"You didn't say much while you were working on me. At first I didn't understand what you were doing. Sedating me, cutting into my muscles and bones, stitching me back together. Operating on my brain and feeding me hormones. It hurt, Henry. I'm grateful for it now. But it hurt so much."

He thought again of his sheets, blood-soaked. The dark stains crusted under his fingernails. He groped through the fog of memory, trying again to latch on to the last moment, the last few days before his ghost took him, body and mind. Frustrated, he spoke directly to the silent ghost lying cold at the bottom of him, putting the problem into terms it would understand. *How are memories stored?*

The ghost barely moved at so simple a question, but it gave him something. A whirlwind of images. Henry in the kitchen while his sister washed dishes and listened to the radio. The lot behind the cafeteria where his father balanced on the edge of the dumpster. Henry in the attic, watching an old man fix a VCR, not knowing until much later that the man was a ghost. Memory was spatial, strongly activated by place.

"Is everything okay, Henry?"

"I need to visit the plant."

"That can be arranged." The pig man rumbled in his throat, sounding pained. "Henry, there was another reason I called you. Everything is so confusing and different now. I have questions."

"Okay."

In the quiet of the yearbook room, with all the teachers and students gone for the day, Hogboss began to ask, "What are chocolate Swiss rolls? How are they butchered? Are there pigs everywhere, or only here? Can I get inside the television? Can people in the television get out? Where do ghosts come from?"

"Cake is made, not butchered," Henry said.

"Like I was made? Does that mean I can't be butchered?"

"I don't know. Pigs are different from cake."

"Do butchered pigs have ghosts?"

"I don't think so. I'm not sure."

"Does it hurt the pigs when they're butchered? Is it okay for a pig to eat another pig? Are only pigs for butchering, or other things as well? What about people? Are they ever butchered?"

Henry did his best to answer, his head heavy and throbbing. They talked this way for almost an hour, at the end Henry just repeating, "Sorry. I don't know."

The game was poorly attended. The home side of the bleachers was so full of ghosts that it was unusable. They weren't strong spirits, their attachment tenuous, the sort that would vanish during the day. But this late in the evening, they rose in the stands, a forest of overlapping bodies and waving arms. Voicelessly, they called out the names of family and friends who had left Swine Hill long ago.

On the visiting team side, there was only one ghost. The specter of a girl sat far in the back corner, holding her knees and muttering. If anyone had come close to her, they would have heard her threatening to kill herself in front of everybody. Her pain rooted her so firmly to the town that she didn't remember that she'd made good on her threat years ago. Far below the ghost girl, a few students and parents sat with the small crowd of visitors, maybe fifteen people all told. There were more players on the court than were in the stands, the gym quiet except for the squeak of sneakers, the hollow drum of the ball thumping the floor, and the static hum of the ghosts.

Henry sat, waiting for his sister to come and take him home. He kept dropping into sleep and then starting awake when he fell sideways across the bench. Every time he opened his eyes, Bethany had the ball. She pounded down the court and dodged between the defending team members, untouchable as wind. He closed his eyes and heard the swish of the ball dropping through the net four, five, six times before he opened them again.

The scoreboard maxed out for the home team at 999 points. Bethany kept making baskets, and the coach pulled out pen and paper to keep up with her. Her teammates got bored and stopped chasing her up and down the court. They sat down under the opposing team's basket while Bethany went one on five.

The parents shook their heads and whispered to one another, glaring hate at the unbeatable girl. It didn't matter if the Ortiz family had lived in town for two generations. People still considered Bethany an outsider, wanted her to go away to wherever it was they thought she belonged. They hadn't come tonight to watch their children be outshined by someone like her.

Henry was about to text his sister, wondering what was keeping her, when he saw Jane standing near the doors to the gym. There was a guy with her, dressed in a bulky white jumpsuit. Jane said something, and the guy smiled shyly, keeping his eyes down.

Even from this far away, he could feel a chill coming from the boy. The floor under his boots was frosted white. Few ghosts were strong enough to warp reality that way. Jane wrapped her arms around herself while she talked to him. Henry knew that her ghost loved secrets and scandal. It had drawn her to bad men before, endlessly scrutinizing their every terrible motive. For Jane's ghost, to be in pain was better than to be bored.

He texted her. *He's going to be just like the last one. You're going to get hurt.*

Jane looked at her phone and put it back in her pocket.

Henry texted her again. *If you can't handle Mom's ghost, how are you going to deal with his?*

The visiting team kept rotating out players, keeping them fresh, trying everything to get the ball and score even one basket. They lunged for Bethany, trying to foul her. Winded and pouring sweat, they eventually sat down with Bethany's team. Some of the players went for their backpacks and started doing homework.

Bethany picked up the ball and hurled it into the middle of them. It cracked the baseboard in front of the stands, rebounding hard and scattering the sitting players. "Get up," she yelled. "At least try."

The referee called a technical foul on her, but the opposing team couldn't be bothered to take their free throw. Bethany threw the ball again, letting it disappear among the ghosts crowding the home side. The spirits made a breathy roar, moving what little air they could, and shouted the names of sons and daughters long gone. Bethany stormed out of the gym.

Henry followed her out. He made a point of pushing between his sister and the boy, opening space between them. The cold sank into his chest, making him go numb and stop breathing. The shock was like falling into a lake.

He found Bethany in the parking lot.

"You were great," he said. "They're just jealous."

Bethany started her car, the window down. "It doesn't matter how good I am if I'm stuck here."

"I'm sorry. I'll keep working on it, I promise. We'll figure out a way for you to leave."

"You already found a way. I just don't want it. I'm done with all of this. I'd have to leave the planet for anything to be different."

She drove off in her old car, taillights winking erratically. The parking lot was dark and almost empty, the utility lights having burned out years ago. Stars arced across the sky above him, the glow of distant planets falling toward their suns.

Jane pulled up beside Henry in her car, shivering. "Trigger's just a friend. We used to be in class together. Why are you so worried about him? Have you heard something?"

Henry got in and shut the door. "You already know what I'm thinking. Why ask?" His seat, the springs worn out like she'd been moving furniture, sank deeply.

She turned out of the school and the car drifted heavy and slow toward home. "You're thinking about stars and planets and math. What am I supposed to do with that?"

He was too tired to explain. Bethany said she wanted to leave the planet. He couldn't help but think about what that would take. The closest Earth-like planet was still very far away, and the human body couldn't handle a journey like that, not without major changes. In his head, he sifted through what little astronomical data he was familiar with, other stars and their necklaces of worlds with alphabetical names. A human would probably never be able to make the trip. You'd have to become something else.

His ghost awoke in him, filling his chest and spreading through his body like fire. "Shit. No. Not again." If he'd been more awake. If he had focused, had refused to let his mind wander . . . But it was too late now.

Jane looked over at him, eyebrow raised. "Henry, this is serious," she said. "I really like this guy. Trigger isn't anything like Mom."

Henry looked out the windshield at a field of stars. His ghost swallowed him up.

ORMALLY, JANE WOULD be working on a Saturday, but the owner of the grocery store was cutting hours. Jane lay across her bed, staring up at the rows of secondhand speakers, mixers, record tables, and CD players stacked along her back wall like a headboard. Nylon netting stretched across the equipment so that nothing would vibrate loose and fall on her head.

Jane's ghost reached out for her family and ferried their thoughts back to her. Her mother slept late after a night wandering the dim pool halls and bars dotting the highway south of town. Henry kneeled on the roof above, hammering and drilling together some contraption that only his ghost could understand. Last night, Jane had been in the middle of talking to him when she saw the pale blue shine stretch over his pupils, the ghost rising inside him and looking out through his eyes like windows. He'd abruptly stopped talking, grabbed an old pen from her console, and made furious calculations in a spiral-bound notebook.

Henry told her that he loved it, that the ghost made him feel brilliant and powerful. But Jane could see deeper, into the pores of his mind, the wispy truths he couldn't quite bring into focus. Henry worried that he wasn't really in control, that the inventions had nothing to do with him. And deeper than that, he worried that one day his ghost would make him do something he would regret.

She looked back over her texts from Trigger, wincing at the nickname. She had told him about her ghost, but he didn't seem bothered by it. Most people in town had one. She asked to go to his house that morning, but he said his dad didn't like company. No one but the two of them had stepped foot inside their house in years.

Is it company his dad doesn't like? her ghost asked. *Or is it you?*

Trigger had asked to come to her place instead, but Jane didn't trust her mother around anyone she cared about. A quick hug, a handshake, the lightest touch could burn and scar if her mother's ghost was feeling especially lonely, and it usually was. In the end, Trigger texted that he should catch up on sleep anyway, and their conversation ended.

Is that true? Is he really sleeping? Maybe he has other friends. Maybe he has a girlfriend.

Jane took a deep breath and put on some music. Her ghost needed something to chew on. If no one else was around, it would pick at Jane's insecurities, magnifying them and throwing them back at her. It had taken Jane a long time to understand, longer to ignore it. "Listen," she said to the restless spirit darting around like a bird inside her chest. "You like this song."

The singer's voice trickled down from the speakers looming over her. The woman sang with her mouth close to the microphone, and Jane could hear the wet pop of her lips parting, her tongue scraping the back of her teeth, the hot wind pushing out of her throat to sear the words into the melody. Jane's ghost could dredge up what the singer had been thinking just from a recording of her voice, the woman's secret thoughts scattered in the hollows between her words. The spirit raced over the notes, curled into the lyrics, flashing between Jane and the storm of sound falling down on her. The ghost cracked the songs open, reached through the clean narrative to pull out its messy tangles. The boyfriend in the song had been a girlfriend until the record company made the singer change it. The drug addict friend was the singer herself, too afraid of what her parents might think to sing the truth. Confronting a rival in a dance club — just a fantasy, something that had never happened.

Jane lay on her back in the sun coming in through her window, the music pressing down on her body and filling her ears, the ghost sending off firecrackers of synchronized feeling inside her head. She stayed like that for almost an hour.

Your mother is awake. She brought someone home late last night.

Jane turned the music up, softly singing along.

He's still here.

The ghost flooded Jane with sensation, inside her head and inescapable. No amount of music would block it out. In the bedroom downstairs, her mother felt tense, stretched like fence wire. The man lying next to her was a sea of pain. His body felt disconnected, liquid, vast with hurt. Burns in the shape of handprints, kisses, soft bites spread over his body. His breath was weak. Nearly dead, his mind was snared in a web of need. He only wanted to please her.

"Fuck off," Jane said. "I don't care."

Her mother's whole self was want. She wanted to feel loved. She wanted to be held and calm. She wanted not to hate herself so much. She had so much heat and need inside her, and pouring it onto someone else was her only relief. She loomed over the feverish man gasping in the dark. She rolled on top of him and kissed him hard. Took his tongue in her mouth. Pressed her palms hard to his cheekbones. Gripped his legs with her own. Fire rushed out of her and into him. He curled like paper kissing flame. Beneath her, he died.

Don't care? But you're crying, Jane. You care so much.

Her mother lay in bed next to the dead man for a while. Her ravenous ghost retreated within, and she ran her hands over her body, finding her skin cool. Soon she would be burning with fever again, but for now she could breathe.

Jane's mother was tired. The man had been kind. Like most of them, he really thought he could help her. The woman felt a knot of self-loathing in her throat and sat up in bed, reaching for a glass of water. She worried that Jane lying upstairs or Henry stomping around on the roof might have heard something. She was not a good mother. At most, she paid the bills. And with the pig man taking control of the plant, who could say how long she would continue being able to do that?

Jane surfaced from the rush of feeling, concentrating on her sagging mattress, the blast of music, the sunlight heating the skin of her legs. It didn't do any good to be angry with her ghost. There was no getting away from it, no storming out of the house and spending the night somewhere else, no blocking its calls, no locking the door. The ghost was wherever Jane was, and she could have no secrets from it.

She tried to remember when she stopped loving her mother. She had sympathy for her at first, when her mom came home burning to the touch. It was storming that night, and a woman had run in front of her car, shouting for help. Her mother never should have left the car, but the woman looked so sad, so completely alone. Jane's mother stepped into the downpour, looking for a wreck. She asked the woman what was wrong. The ghost took her hand and said, "Stay with me. Never let me go."

In the weeks after, her mother changed. She needed so much from Jane and Henry. Insisted that Jane sit on the couch and watch television with her for hours, or wanted to endlessly braid and unbraid her hair, needed to be told that she was loved every few moments. Her skin grew hotter and hotter, her hands leaving burns on anyone they touched. Jane and Henry started to keep their distance. They reminded themselves that it wasn't her fault, that she was haunted like so many others.

Her father took the brunt of it. Jane didn't have her ghost back then, couldn't feel her father's pain, but she could see it written on his skin. He blistered and burned, his body becoming overgrown with scars.

After Jane found her own ghost, her mind alive to the thoughts of everyone around her, she tried to help. Jane borrowed albums from friends and teachers, downloaded songs from the Internet, and burned CDs in her room. While her mother wept, begging her daughter to embrace her, Jane played track after track, the saddest and most broken songs she could find. She listened with her ghost, trying to find the moment when her mother's spirit would be tempted into some greater sadness. But her mother's ghost wouldn't budge. It couldn't let go of something until it was dead.

Jane picked up her phone, thinking about texting Trigger again. She wondered if Henry was right about him, if his ghost would be too much for her. Maybe she could help Trigger get rid of his ghost, find the one song in the world that would speak to its pain and loneliness better than anything else could. Or would it be like her mother's haunting, the spirit too deep in him to ever be ripped loose?

Downstairs, Jane heard her mother leave.

She'll be gone for a while, her ghost said. *Let's go see.*

Jane didn't want to see the dead man. Her mother had done this before. She brought home men she found in the ruins of rural towns dotting the interstate south of Swine Hill, and they died in her arms. It was a miracle that the police hadn't come for them years ago. Jane could hardly breathe when she thought about it, and wished she could abandon her mother and go somewhere else, if only leaving weren't so hard.

But the men who were drawn to their mother, someone so obviously haunted, rarely had anyone to miss them. Alone for too long, they knew they needed saving and thought this burning woman did too. They dared to hope that they could be what she needed, and like moths courting a candle, their hope killed them.

Henry said that he built the robot to take care of their mother, but Jane knew its real purpose was to clean up after her, to shampoo the carpets, wash the bedding, and hide the bodies in one of the infinite empty places surrounding the town.

Something pulled her downstairs to see. Was she curious, or was it only her ghost? Was there a difference? Jane got dressed and went to look.

The carpet in their house was stained and sandy with dirt. The drywall was nail-studded and cracked. Trim was missing, leaving gaps between the walls and ceilings. Some of the windows were cracked, held together with packing tape. The house was falling apart. It needed a lot of money and time, something that no one in her family had to give.

The robot was already in her mother's room, its heavy step making

the floorboards groan. She switched on the light in time to see it sliding a trash bag over the dead man's feet. The man was small and shriv-
eled, a mummified husk. The robot wrapped the corpse in bags, taped
him up, and hoisted him onto its shoulder.

"Why do you let her do this?" Jane asked.

The headlamps over the robot's eyes flickered. Was it annoyed? Her
ghost couldn't read its mechanical mind.

"If you really wanted to help her, you wouldn't let her bring anyone
inside this house."

She followed it downstairs to the garage, the robot weaving from
side to side on its stiff legs. The garage was mostly filled with her father's old tools, his clothes, bins of family photos that their mother
couldn't bear to look at. The robot wrested a shovel out of the mess,
raised the door, and headed down the street.

"It's the middle of the day. What if someone sees you?"

The robot didn't seem concerned. And why should it be? Even when
Jane was born, the street was half empty, and by the time she was a
kid, there was no one left for her to play with. Now they were the only
ones left in their neighborhood. Close as they were to downtown, people had been moving away for years. Jane couldn't remember someone ever moving in, the bright For Sale signs eventually sun-yellowed,
knocked over by wind, drowned in the grass.

The robot crossed the street and turned between two derelict houses,
pushing through the gate and into the backyard. Jane followed it across
an overgrown field, grass coming up to her knees. Sunlight glinted in
the bright scratches on the robot's bucket-shaped head. The bagged
body lay across its shoulder, unmoving with the jerky strides, as stiff
as kindling.

They came to the back of a three-story house, what must have been
a mansion once, now down on its knees among fallen columns and
tilted balconies. Jane knew that if she walked around to the front, she'd
be able to see the old bank, the boarded-up front of a restaurant, dust-
eaten clothing boutiques with their shattered windows. One street
over, vicious ghosts prowled even in the daylight, wanting to know

why their world had fallen apart. She was almost in the heart of downtown.

The only thing left in the city center was the police station, its offices and holding cells crowded with suspects and protesters long dead. Few officers remained. Those left screamed at the chains of spirits twining through the building like starling murmurations. They fought the ghosts inside their own skins, the bloody history they couldn't escape, the past more real to them than the present. Jane knew to stay away from that place.

In the windows of the house, spectral shapes moved. There was a popping, like distant gunfire or glass shattering. A quiet sob moved through the grass. Jane stepped away from it.

The lot behind the house was filled with dirt mounds, each rising a few feet. Most were old and grass-covered, but three were new. The robot started digging a pit. It didn't take much time, the machine being frighteningly strong. It made a hole and threw the body in, then covered it up and scraped earth from the soil nearby to mound on top of it. When it was done, the robot sank to its knees on the grave, cradling the shovel to its chest. The wind played with the shirt it had unevenly buttoned, the collar trembling. Her father's shirt.

You're sad for that murder machine?

"I think it loves her," Jane said. "But she needs more than a machine. I think it knows that. Look how heartbroken it is."

It has electricity, not feelings.

"Sure it does. Not like a person's feelings. But there's something there. A machine-kind-of-sad."

The ghost conjured images of construction cranes abandoned on muddy job sites, cars up on blocks and weeping rust, the shattered bones of a cell phone flattened in a parking lot.

"Yeah. Just like that."

It's broken. Let's go do something fun.

Jane didn't feel like fun. Too much of her mother's anguish and the robot's quiet mourning had gotten inside her head. She needed to do something, to think of things that weren't so hopeless. She pulled out her phone and was texting Trigger before she even realized what she was doing. *My mom won't be home for a few hours.*

His response was immediate. *Be right there.*

She left the robot to keep its strange vigil over the grave and went back through the field. When she came out from between the houses, a police car was parked on the street, blocking her way.

The car had rusted and been repainted poorly, the paint clotted and streaks of muddy brown breaking through to wander down its sides. The engine had an ugly, rasping idle. A rotten smell, like a carcass steaming on the road, came from the car.

Her chest tightened. Had the cop seen her? Did the police know about the dead body? This was it, her whole life about to unravel to threads in a moment.

Don't talk to him. He's looking for an excuse to do something.

Jane had been bothered by cops plenty of times before. She had learned not to linger, never to go out without a destination, always to work or school or home or the store. To always have a story. She was fanatical about stop signs, knew the speed limits even on streets where the signs had been missing for years. Still, she got stopped. It was tense every time. The police had left ghosts all over town.

Jane tried to go around the car, keeping close to the sides of the damp-smelling house. He turned on his lights, letting them flicker for a second, then chirped his siren once.

"Girl," he called. "Come here."

His hand is on his gun. His seatbelt is off. He wants you to run, because he will chase you, and he will catch you, and that will be all the reason he needs.

He knew. He must know. The earth was soft under Jane's shoes, her sneakers turning in the mud. She struggled not to fall, going down the slope to stand by his open window. The ghost fed her every flashing thought from the man's head. Little fantasies of violence licking out. The feeling of hands around a throat. The smell of gunpowder and rasp of a whetstone. The tension building in his chest like an oil well ripening to explode.

Now that she stood by his open window, Jane could see his face.

The officer's eyes were bloodshot and his lips cracked. He was balding, and his hands trembled on the steering wheel. A small trickle of blood curled from his ear, and she wondered for a moment if he was hurt. More blood issued from the corners of his eyes. Clotted around his fingernails. Leaked drop by drop from his nose and stained the beard around his mouth. She didn't need her ghost to tell her that the man was haunted.

Jane made herself smile, shoving her anger and fear down her throat. "Yes, sir?"

"That's your robot. I saw you with it." His tone was pleased and justi-fied, like he'd caught her doing something and knew she would deny it.

He doesn't know. But be careful. Don't contradict him.

She enunciated each syllable, speaking soft and clear, as proper as possible. "Did it do something wrong? If it did, I'll make it right."

The man's teeth were stained dark. "That's all I want. To make things right. It's not right to replace people with things."

"The robot just helps my mom around the house. Her ghost is really bad, so it's hard for her to take care of us."

He nodded. "I know something about bad ghosts. I've had mine a very long time."

"I'm sorry to hear that." Jane swallowed, waiting, but her ghost was silent. "Was it someone close to you?"

"A suspect. He ran. My gun went off." The officer gave a pained laugh, pressing a fist to the side of his head. "I tell it every day that I'm sorry. That it was an accident. Still, it's angry."

Jane hated the man for forcing her to talk to him, for making her sympathize with his pain when he was so ready to hurt her. She kept the rage off her face. "The robot is mostly junk. A lemon. It could never work a real job. My brother's always having to fix it."

"Your brother."

The man's anger shifted from her, finding a new target. Jane didn't know whether to be relieved or afraid. He wiped the blood pooling un-der his eyes, smearing it in two wide bands across his face.

"So he's the one responsible?"

"He's haunted pretty bad too," Jane said. "My whole family ended up that way. What we get for living around here. Sometimes his ghost takes over and makes him build things, like the robot. He can't help it."

"It's not his fault." The bleeding man sounded sincere. "It's not my fault when I have to hurt people. But somebody has to pay when things go wrong, and you can't wring blood out of a ghost, can you?"

There was no one else on the street. The sky was big and clear and achingly blue. It was hard to believe this man was in front of her, his hand resting on his gun. Her ghost waited, had nothing to say.

"You're right," Jane said. "You can't get blood from a ghost."

The officer buckled his seatbelt and put his cruiser in drive. "I'm glad you see it my way. Keep an eye on your brother. And that robot. Make sure they don't do anything stupid."

He drove away, Jane watching his car and unable to move. Her phone vibrated against her leg. Trigger was probably already at her door. She was on the precipice of collapsing or running away. Something inside her was close to breaking.

Just imagine, her ghost said. *What if he'd found your brother walking down the street alone? Henry would have said all the wrong things.*

6

JANE SANK DOWN against Trigger on the couch. His skin was like a sheet of ice, and sadness poured off him like fog. It helped her stop thinking about her mother, the robot burying the corpse, the bleeding man who might have killed her.

"I don't understand why you went downtown," Trigger said. "Or why you'd walk. You should know better."

He meant because of the ghosts. It hadn't occurred to him that there might be other reasons to be afraid. She would have been annoyed at his tone, the implication that she had done something wrong when it was the world that had wronged her, but her ghost opened his mind to her, full of desperate fear that she might have been hurt.

Above, her brother pounded a piece of metal, the sound echoing through the house. She wanted to climb to the roof and shake Henry, tell him that he'd almost gotten her killed. But there was no reaching him when his ghost had taken over.

"What's your brother doing up there?" Trigger asked. But he was thinking again about how Jane was still in Swine Hill, wondering what kept her here.

Her ghost pushed heavy against her chest, circling in silent irritation. It didn't like the thought of Jane leaving. If she ever left Swine Hill, taking the ghost far from the streets it knew, the memories that anchored it to the world, it would most likely vanish, going wherever it was the dead went. At least, that's what it had told her.

"Why are *you* still here?" Jane asked him.

He looked at her in surprise, realizing she'd been listening to his thoughts. He wondered if he even needed to speak or if she would just pull what she wanted out of him.

"No," Jane said, "I like to hear you say it. And the things people think and the things they say aren't always the same."

"My mom left a long time ago," Trigger said. "My dad is never going to leave that house, though. If I go, he'll be all alone."

There was another reason, a thought he was trying to hold back. Before he could think of something else, Jane caught it. His dead brother, the ghost that wrapped Trigger in winter. He felt guilty for his brother dying. He couldn't leave the ghost behind.

"What about you?" he asked.

She folded herself into him, his big arm draped over her back. "My mom doesn't think she'll find anything better than Pig City, so she's staying put. She's never really done anything else. Henry needs someone to look out for him. And my dad."

Jane couldn't finish the thought. She was the only one who even tried to look out for him. Her dad could die or disappear. Something awful could happen to him and she would never know.

Trigger leaned back and stared at the ceiling. "People think leaving will fix everything, but it doesn't. Everywhere has problems. And it takes a lot of money to start over in a new place."

He wasn't wrong. Still, people did it. Even if they had to leave parts of themselves behind. Jane felt him wondering what she would do once Henry graduated and inevitably left. She wondered herself.

"Come upstairs." Jane pulled Trigger up from the couch. "I have a song I want you to listen to."

• • •

Her old desktop computer booted up slowly, the fan purring and monitor flickering with ghosts. Jane opened a music app, where her songs
were sorted by artist and album, but also by emotion: mournful songs,
angry songs, gleeful songs. She made a playlist of every sad song she
had, everything from glossy radio hits to stripped-down indie bedroom recordings.

"Tell me if your ghost moves when I play any of these," she said.

Trigger sat on her bed, his eyes tracing the curve of her neck and
back. Her ghost told her how he lingered over her, how he imagined
slipping his hands around her stomach and pulling her to him. For the
first time in a while, she felt in control, all the pieces falling where she
wanted.

Except that he knew Jane was trying to lure his ghost away, and he
wasn't sure he wanted that. It was exciting for him to imagine being
free, but the thought made him feel guilty. Icy fog spread from his cold
skin to coalesce along the floor of her bedroom.

Jane kept cycling through songs. It didn't matter if he wanted to keep
his ghost. Some were benevolent, even useful, like hers. Others ruined
people's lives. He was too deep in his own haunting to see how happy
he would be without it. She would show him.

A thick, winding bunch of cables carried sound from the desk by
her window over the dirty floor to the wall of speakers. Music came
like wind. There were songs hard-bitten and rural, full of barbed wire
and bite, hoarse women singing through cigarette smoke about lovers who hurt them. There were nasal-voiced boys playing electronic
dirges, the absurd weight of the universe settling across their teenage
shoulders. There were machine-gun-mouthed MCs strafing the wide,
unfair world with their words. There were strings and soaring vocals,
things old and weathered and as melancholy as a grave. There were
voices that raged like storms over the trickling guitar and thunder of
the drums, anger made myth.

Trigger lay across the bed, listening. He didn't say anything, but
Jane's ghost told her what she wanted to know. Sad alone wouldn't do
it. His ghost craved crashing anger, full orchestra requiems, a labyrinth

of pain. She found a track with few words, an obscure math metal band that squealed with dissonance, its melody sharp to the touch, time signature folding into complex patterns. It was a maze of furious sound, a deep, dark forest to get lost in. Trigger's ghost sat up and paid attention.

Trigger reached down and unplugged the cables, his hands leaving them white with frost. "I think I need a break."

Jane started burning a CD of the tracks that had worked best. She went to the bed and leaned over him, her ghost telling her how badly he wanted to touch her. He noticed how much darker she was than him, wondered if it was okay to notice, hoped that she hadn't read his thoughts. He felt naked before her, ceding all power, eyes wide and waiting. Jane let the moment of stillness settle around them like a pool, and then she bent and kissed him.

His breath was sharp. His arms folded around her, and Jane's skin burned with cold to be so close to him. She remembered what Henry had said, that Trigger was like their mother, that he needed more than she could give. Defiant, Jane pressed deep against his mouth.

After a few minutes, the CD tray slid out of the computer, offering the disc. Jane pulled away, her lips chapped from cold. "Promise me you'll listen to it."

He closed his eyes. "I'm all my brother has left. What would happen to him if he didn't have me to carry him?"

Who would you be? Would you recognize yourself without me?

Jane sat next to him on the bed again, their fingers twining. "He's already dead. You don't have to feel guilty for being alive."

He feels guilty because he's the one who killed his brother.

The ghost had to be lying, just trying to get a reaction out of her. Still, Jane pulled her hand away from his.

It was an accident. But that doesn't mean it wasn't his fault. How do you think he got that nickname? Trigger fingers. Trigger happy. Get rid of his ghost if you want. He's never going to get past what he did.

"Shut up," Jane said. "You're not helping."

Trigger raised an eyebrow.

"My ghost," Jane said. "She's a bitch sometimes."

"Have you ever tried to get rid of yours?"

Her ghost swelled with anger, making Jane dizzy.

"We fight sometimes, but she's my best friend. She doesn't hurt me."

Jane lay back on the bed, and Trigger lay down beside her. She draped her arm over his chest.

He had been in her bedroom long enough for it to feel like a different place. The temperature fell into winter cold. The window had iced over. Blood-smeared leaves were scattered over the floor.

"How did you get your ghost?" she asked.

Trigger said nothing for a while. Her ghost pulled feelings, images, impressions out of him. There were the shadows of sounds, strange and distant noises that she couldn't make out. Men walking through snow. The barrel of a shotgun breaking open with a metal snap. Plastic shells clicking into place. A foot catching on fallen branches, feet slipping, an explosion of sound. And then quiet, the smell of gunpowder cutting the air like a sword.

"Sorry," Trigger said. "I don't really talk about it."

He tightened his brow and thought hard of his job at the plant, holding everything in like a dam. He'd already learned how to pull back, how to hide things from her ghost. He was better at it than Henry.

Jane pulled a blanket over herself, making a wall between them. She shouldn't have tried to pull it out of him. She couldn't help it, though. People got uncomfortable that her ghost knew what they were thinking. They couldn't imagine what it was like for her, to have no private thoughts, every idea she'd ever had open to judgment and mockery.

"What about you?" he asked. "How did you get yours?"

Jane was nine when she became possessed.

It was summer, and their last close neighbor had just moved away. Her mother had been wrestling with her own ghost for the past year. Henry was five and often left to play alone with his toys. Her father was still himself, trying to be strong enough to endure their mother's need. He worked as a roadside mechanic, gone at all hours of the day to rescue people stranded on the highway.

Her mother's ghost made the house a suffocating place. She didn't touch Jane often for fear that she would burn her, but she always wanted the girl near. "Tell me you love me," she would say. "Tell me I'm pretty." She would make Jane come with her on outings to the town's dying boutiques, trying on clothes that they couldn't afford to buy. Jane felt pent up and restless. She wanted school to start again. She wanted a friend.

In the mornings, she sneaked out of the house and explored the neighborhood's streets. She walked through backyards and courted stray dogs with bread and lunchmeat. She stood on their quiet road and drew patterns in chalk. One day, a girl sat down beside her, picked up one of Jane's chalk sticks, and started writing.

The girl was white, and Jane hadn't seen her before. Her dress was dirty, and she didn't have shoes. Her hair hung loose and messy past her shoulders. But she had an open, eager face. She asked Jane where she lived, what grade she was in, if she had a sister or a brother. Jane told her everything.

Where Jane drew people, figures walking and holding hands, the other girl drew a halo of words around their heads. Now Jane's smiling couples bickered, argued, said hateful and cutting things. There was a thrill to it, the pleasure of doing something that would make her parents and teachers upset.

"Come," the girl said. "I want to show you something."

She took Jane by the hand, leading her deep into a tangle of streets where she hadn't gone before. The grass stood high in the yards, the pavement pocked and stained. They climbed onto a dark porch, the stairs long rotted away, and pushed through the door. "Look," the girl said.

Whoever had lived here left the house in a hurry. Stuffed animals, photos, and VCR tapes were scattered over the floor. There were clothes heaped against the walls. The house was hot, the air still, and the heavy buzz of a wasp nest resonated from a corner of the room. A dog had gotten in the house at some point, leaving clumps of shit at the foot of the stairs and down the hallway.

"This way." The girl's hand in hers was insistent, pulling Jane up the stairwell. There was a quick, fearful moment when they stepped into the dark and Jane couldn't see anything, her feet finding the steps by feel. The curl of stairs was as dark as the inside of an ear, plunging Jane into a world of smells: mildew and rot, water and old wood.

They emerged into sunlight. The girl took her to an upstairs bedroom overlooking the fields behind the house. There was a pair of binoculars on the floor by the window, one of the lenses cracked. The girl put them over Jane's eyes and directed her gaze toward the window of a house across the way. "Watch."

The other house wasn't abandoned. Curtains fluttered clean and pink at the edges of the window. Lawn chairs stood in the backyard. A woman passed in front of the window. A man took her by the shoulders and pushed her down onto the bed.

Jane watched him shed his shirt and kick off his pants. The woman dropped her clothes over the side of the bed. Jane adjusted the focus of the binoculars when the man bent over the bed, grabbed the woman by her heels, and dragged her to him. Jane was young enough that she only half understood what she saw, both repulsed and fascinated.

"They do it a lot," the girl said. "Almost every day."

The rest of the week, Jane waited until her mother wasn't paying attention to go meet the girl. Sometimes they watched the couple through the window. Other times, the girl dressed her in the stained clothes littering the floor of the abandoned house, or found pens for them to write on the walls.

At some point, Jane realized she was playing in the house alone. She looked out the window by herself. She wrote vicious things on the walls and picked through the cast-off clothes and toys for what she wanted. The girl was still with her, but inside. When the sky darkened and Jane went home to avoid the thickening ghosts, the girl came too.

At home, the ghost brought her mother's burning loneliness right into Jane's head. Her father spoke his fear and pain without saying a word. Her parents circled each other, afraid to touch but unable to stay apart. Henry sat in front of the television, eating stale cereal, feeling forgotten.

Jane went into the living room and brought down an old game box, setting it between them. "Let's play something."

Henry picked up a deck of cards and spilled them across the floor. "How do you play?"

"I don't know." She put paper and pencils in front of him, found some dice, an abandoned game board. "Why don't you make something up?"

Something kindled in his mind, and her baby brother went through the parts in front of him. Her ghost told her everything he was thinking, helping her follow the convoluted rules of the board game he was inventing. While Henry flipped through the cards and made notes, Jane decided she would have to take better care of him. Her ghost settled into her ear. It spoke and spoke and spoke.

Trigger got up to open the door and window, to let out some of the cold.

"That must have been scary," he said. "To have a complete stranger get inside you like that. With my brother haunting me, at least I know who he is."

"We know each other better than anyone." Jane wasn't sure if the defensiveness in her voice was her ghost's or her own.

Trigger stepped into the hallway. "You know each other now. But you didn't at first."

"I don't think that matters. I know exactly what my mom is thinking, but that doesn't mean I understand her. Half the time she feels like a stranger to me."

He shrugged. "I guess you can't really know anyone."

"I know my ghost. Why are you smiling? What are you thinking?" She got off the bed and went to him.

Her ghost refused to tell Jane, withholding his thoughts for the pleasure of it.

"I'm hungry," Trigger said. "Let's go eat something."

"Tell me what you're thinking." Jane wasn't used to not knowing, didn't like feeling unsure of herself.

This is why you need me, her ghost said. *I'm the only one who will be honest with you.*

"I think that you wish you could haunt me. You want to be my ghost. Then you'd know everything."

Jane smiled and said nothing, unused to someone so clearly seeing into her mind.

7

ENRY LAY ACROSS the peak of the roof, the shingles rough under his cheek. It was night. His clothes were damp, and mucus plugged his nose and coated his throat. He shivered in his thin shirt. When he sat up, his head spun. He felt weak and hungry. His old gnawing headache was still with him, a clenching squeeze like his head was gripped in the jaws of a dog.

A few feet away, a box was nailed to the roof. A bundle of wires ran from the attic to feed the machine's guts: a circuit board, a set of motors, and an array of metal cylinders thicker than his arm. It fired a spray of red laser pulses into the sky. Henry looked up and saw fingers of red light braiding through the clouds, a spear of information fired into space as far and fast as light could go. Still, given the vastness of what lay over his head, he'd be dead long before the light reached anywhere interesting. If his ghost was trying to help Bethany leave Earth, this seemed like a poor way to do it.

He ran his hands over the box. The laser array was small. His ghost probably hadn't taken control of him for more than a day. Jane would worry that it might be dangerous. It would be easy to destroy it. Henry could bury the head of a hammer in it, or he could rip out the wires trailing from its side. But nothing about it seemed dangerous. Maybe he'd leave it for a while and see what happened.

His bedroom's dormer window had been left open to the rain. Henry lowered himself inside, his carpet and school papers soaked. His clock read three in the morning.

He trudged down to the kitchen and poured himself a bowl of cereal. The robot was spreading soapy water over the tile with a ratty mop. The washing machine and dishwasher were both running. His mother must be home. The robot only cleaned when she was asleep, staying close by her side when she was awake in case she might need something.

"Your corrosion is getting bad," Henry said. "And I've seen you dragging your left leg. Is that why you're wearing clothes? To hide the damage? You should come to me when you need repairs."

The robot swiveled its head and narrowed the shutters on its headlamp eyes, slicing him with a thin sliver of murky orange light. Its stance seemed to say, *You made me wrong. Fix something that matters.*

Henry put his bowl in the sink. "You do her a lot of good. It's just hard to see it."

He pulled on his shoes and walked outside, his head aching and a sweet film coating his mouth. Over his head, the laser array made its red scar across the galaxy's edge. He dug his cell phone out of the pocket of his jeans, the battery almost dead. Hogboss answered on the third ring.

"I was worried about you, Henry. You never answered my texts."

"Are you working tonight? Want to show me the plant?"

"Nights are best." His voice was harsh and well-deep, like iron warping. "The workers get concerned if they see me too often during the day. They worry that something bad is going to happen."

"*Is* something bad going to happen?" At the edges of Henry's vision, a blue shimmer moved in the house across the street. Some ghost still gnawing away at whatever had obsessed it in life. He kept his eye on it.

"I don't know why people ask me questions like that," Hogboss said. "I've only been a man for a few months. I just learned how to turn on the news. Give me fifteen minutes, Henry. I'll be right there."

Henry had fallen asleep sitting on the porch by the time Hogboss pulled up, his head resting on his knees. Careless of him. Ghosts didn't always make noise. One could have slipped up and walked right inside him, like he was an unlocked room. Henry stood and climbed into the passenger side of the Pig City truck.

It was too dark for him to get a good look at the pig man. He was an immense shape, featureless and huge, a mountain. Hogboss's breath made the cab hot, and there was a bloody, almost sterile smell, like the meat counter of a supermarket. Even without being able to see him, only feeling the vibrations of his throat rumble through the truck, Henry was crushed by his size and inhumanity. He remembered seeing a lion at the zoo as a child, how when it yawned he could have lain inside its jaws.

"You want to find out why you made me," Hogboss said.

"People are nervous. If I knew why I did it, I could tell them that there's no reason to worry." Henry was glad Jane wasn't there — her ghost was always eager to unearth his secret fears. There were things it was best not to think about. "Why do you think I made you?"

"To butcher pigs. And you should know, Henry, I take a lot of pride in my work."

In the road, wisps of fog coalesced into the shapes of men and women and children, the barest shadows of ghosts. They drove through, Hogboss turning his windshield wipers on as if the spirits were rain. The pig man adjusted his mirror, catching sight of the lights battering the sky behind them.

"What's that on top of your house?" Hogboss asked.

"My ghost made it. Just like he made the robot. And you."

"Do you know why he made it?"

"I can't talk to my ghost. It's not like Jane's."

"How did you get haunted?"

They were still several minutes away from the pork-processing plant, shining with light on the plateau over the town. There was time, and as strange as it was, no one had ever asked Henry before. The pig man had caught him off-guard with simple kindness.

"It was my sister's fault," Henry said. "She was supposed to be watching me."

Henry was ten when he first saw the stranger in the house.

His father had left years before, and his mother was at work that day. Jane mostly raised him, making sure he had dinner and was woken up for school, but her ghost was getting tired of Henry. It craved something messy and complicated. There was an older boy who lived a few streets over, and it coaxed Jane out of the house to meet him.

"You'll be fine by yourself for a few hours," she had said. "Just stay inside and don't open the door."

Henry got bored watching TV alone and started to pace. He found the attic stairs had been left folded down, wondered if his mother had been putting things away. He wasn't allowed up there. The people who had lived in the house decades ago had left behind furniture, photos, tools that even his father hadn't known what to do with. His parents worried some of it might be possessed by spirits, though Jane said she couldn't hear any. There was an entire lost life in the attic, and they had been sorting through it and throwing it out, piece by piece, for years.

The attic steps were steep and narrow, swaying when Henry put his foot on them. He climbed up with hands and feet, going slow to listen for his mother coming home, and stuck his head through the hole in the ceiling. The air was hot. He waited for his eyes to adjust.

There was a man sitting on the floor at the other end of the attic. He had a lean face and small, round glasses with thin frames. He was dark-skinned and lanky, his shirt and pants baggy around his bony limbs. The man held an old cassette and was winding the ribbon of film back into it, carefully untangling its shining snarls.

"Who are you?" Henry asked.

The man looked up at him, frowned, and was gone.

Henry stayed on the steps for a long time, staring at the spot where the man had been. It was a ghost. Their house was haunted.

By the time Jane came home, he was in tears. She went up to the attic to look herself, then went through every room. "There's no one, Henry. My ghost would hear if there was."

She took him into the attic and made him look with her. The cassette was still there, lying beside an old box of books, VCR tapes, and photos. Jane pulled one of the photos out, a badly faded picture of a family eating together. The daughter wore a ballet dress and tights. The man Henry had seen sat in the middle of them, ignoring his family to probe a wristwatch with a jeweler's screwdriver.

"You probably just imagined it," Jane said.

She could read the bright flame of anger in his mind, his frustration that she'd left. Sometimes he didn't even speak, just projected his raw feelings at her without words.

"I watch you all the time," Jane said. "And I deserve to have friends. You better not say anything to Mom about me leaving."

In the weeks after, Henry saw the stranger again. In the garage, he found the man staring into the engine of his father's old truck, there and gone as soon as Henry laid eyes on him. After a power surge knocked out one of the electrical sockets, Henry found the stranger bent over, removing the socket cover.

One afternoon, Jane brought him a broken handheld game she'd found in an old house. The screen was cracked and it wouldn't turn on, not even with new batteries. While Jane went to make dinner, Henry got some of his father's tools from the garage and began taking the game apart. He arranged the pieces beside him on the floor, uncovering the green of the circuit board. He didn't know what he was doing or what to look for, but he was curious. How could something made of metal and plastic just die? Could he make it live again?

In his periphery, the stranger went through the screws and plastic debris at his elbow. Henry was careful not to look at him.

The long fingers pointed and guided. Henry cleaned the battery terminals, glued back a broken piece, spliced together a frayed wire, shook dirt out of the case. When he had it all back together, he flipped the game over in his hands and snapped on the power button. The screen lit up green and music came out of the speakers. What a miracle, resurrecting this broken machine. Watching the sprites make their pixelated crawl between his hands, Henry felt that there was nothing he couldn't do.

"Henry? Did you get it to work?"

As Jane walked into the room, the stranger grabbed Henry by the arms and stepped inside him. He felt something heavy and cold push through his chest. The weight pressed against his lungs and knocked the air out of him, leaving him sprawled on the floor. It moved deeper, into his bones. When he got his wind back and sat up, he felt heavy, off balance.

His sister leaned over him, shouting. "Henry! Are you okay?"

He blinked. Shapes blurred together, out of focus. His sister's face was a smear of color, featureless. The carpet and ceiling bled together in a pale field.

"I can't see."

He groped around on the floor, and his hands brushed metal. A pair of old glasses — the stranger's glasses — lay beside him. He put them on, and the world grew sharp and clear again. "The ghost is inside me," he said. "What does it want?"

"I don't know." Jane angled her head toward him, like she was listening. "My ghost can't hear anything. Is it talking to you? What's it saying?"

As shocked as he was, afraid of the spirit that had stepped into him like he was a closet, Henry had one secret thrill: Jane, who knew his every thought, didn't know this.

"It's not saying anything," Henry said. "It's just waiting."

Hogboss's truck climbed the steep and winding road up to the gates of the plant compound. There were streetlights here, their white glare spearing through the ghostly fog.

"Does that mean the stranger made me?" Hogboss asked.

Henry wasn't sure if the pig man was angry or grateful. "You can't separate us. It's a part of me."

"It must be hard to share yourself," Hogboss said. "Your ghost could use you to do anything."

Henry wanted to say that the ghost only helped with what he wanted to do. His mind and his hands animated it. But part of him would always worry about what it did when he was sleeping. He didn't know who actually had control. He tried not to think about it.

They drove through the gate, the guard catching sight of Hogboss and waving him through without checking his ID. The forest was dense around them, trees climbing the sides of the plateau and falling away into deep valleys of green. Rounding a corner, they arrived.

The white tin buildings looked like they were on fire. A roiling, cloudy haze swept over the walls and reached up from the roof, poured from the door seams, and made tidal gasps along the ground. It swallowed up the few people coming and going in their blue jumpsuits and headlamps. Huge plumes of white floated over the high-ceilinged pig houses. Smoky and indistinct shapes, flailing like men, fell from the windows of the concrete butchery. Little puffs of what seemed to be steam twirled from cracks in the asphalt. Henry covered his mouth, held his breath involuntarily.

But there was no fire. The heavy haze was only the dead; Pig City drowning in spirits like the river Styx.

Hogboss came around and opened Henry's door. "They won't hurt you. Pig City's ghosts are here to work. They're quite content."

As they walked to the door of the closest building, though, Henry saw faces rise out of the fog and stare. Insubstantial mouths opened and wispy hands reached out to point. The ghosts understood that a pig was working at the plant and they didn't like it.

Decades before, those hands belonged to the living. They pointed not at the pig man but at the few black workers brave enough to fight for jobs here. Afraid of losing some future they couldn't quite see, resentful that anyone different would have something they were so assured was theirs, the men closed ranks to keep the plant jobs for their kith and kin. They started fights in the parking lot, spread rumors to bosses, insisted people be fired, and got their black coworkers sidelined to the most dangerous and worst-paying jobs until finally there were only a few black faces in the whole sprawling body of the plant.

Still, black ghosts did wander the factory. For those who had spent years seeing the lights of the plant shining on the hill over the town, a star cold and unreachable, it was no surprise their desperate ghosts would at last find their way here.

Hogboss gave him a tour, taking Henry past the time clock and into a dressing room where workers put on vinyl smocks, plastic gloves, and elastic boot covers. The floors and walls were tiled over in green squares that had been bleached almost gray. There were few people at the plant this late at night. Mostly janitors and repairmen. The workers were thin-haired, their faces acid-scarred or chapped red from cleaning agents. They moved slowly and stiffly, carrying weariness in their backs. They seemed like old trees, wind-stripped and thunder-struck, half toppled over and barely clinging to the earth. When they finally died, would their ghosts even know? Or would they show up to work, punch their phantom time cards, tongue their old sores, and continue to dread the day cancer or a heart attack would finally knock them down?

The workers stared openly, mirroring the faces of the ghosts leering up from the fog. Henry didn't need Jane to tell him that no one wanted Henry or the pig man there.

Hogboss put his arm around Henry and continued the tour, not sensing the animosity. He identified workers by name and told Henry what they did. He showed Henry the deep vents where cold air blew through the plant, and rattled off a list of numbers — pounds of meat, boxes shipped, stores serviced — completely oblivious to the tension building around them.

While they walked the hallways, ghosts moved thickly past. They hurried with screwdrivers or cleavers in their hands, off on some errand decades done. Occasionally, workers tracked dark chains of blood over the tile, lines leading to violence happening just out of sight.

"Does it bother you? Slaughtering pigs?" Henry kept his voice low, not wanting anyone to overhear.

Hogboss furrowed his brow. "I don't know. Do you think it should?"

"I don't want it to bother you. Maybe I made you so that you don't care."

"I care about everything I do here, Henry. This is my livelihood."

As Hogboss led him from room to room, talking about every stage of the production process, Henry's eyes lingered over the mangled bodies of the workers and the shattered ghosts they had left behind. Everyone had scars. Some were missing limbs. People were exhausted, their clothes worn thin. Through the parade of ghosts and their descendants, Henry saw the brutality of the plant stretching back for generations.

The problem assembled itself piece by piece in Henry's mind with every horrible thing he saw. Tired people made mistakes. Unhappy people lashed out, destroyed property, committed violence on one another. Poor people got sick and stayed sick. Everyone here was one unlucky moment away from a life-changing mistake. One sleepless night from losing their temper and taking it out on someone they loved. The place was explosive, a volcano of misery, but it was the best game in town. Worker satisfaction was what he'd been sent to work on. People were unhappy here. So he solved the problem.

He made pigs to work here instead.

Henry slumped against the wall and sat down.

"The floor isn't for sitting," Hogboss told him. "Someone could trip. We have rigorous safety codes."

"People are right to be afraid. It's exactly what they think."

The pig man looked at him blankly, twitching his ears.

"There have to be more of you somewhere. It wouldn't change anything to make just one."

Hogboss extended a massive hand.

Henry studied the scars covering it, how he had surgically reshaped and grafted together this new limb. Why create something so amazing just to make it bleed?

"Come with me," Hogboss said. "I'll show you the others."

HOGBOSS LED HIM down a long stairwell into a storage basement. Here, relics of Pig City's long past lay heaped against the wall. There were wooden butcher blocks, iron hooks, whetstones. Porcelain basins sat heavily in the middle of the room, the dry dust of blood still crusting their rims. The broad mouth of a fireplace, long bricked up, gaped from the back wall.

They passed through a long tunnel, the lights out in most places, before climbing another set of stairs. Henry stepped carefully around the old equipment, the rusty teeth of bone saw blades catching on his jeans.

"I hadn't planned on showing them to you today," Hogboss said. "They aren't ready yet."

Hogboss took Henry to an iron door, so dusty and soot-covered that it was almost invisible against the wall. He unlocked it, carefully holding the key in his big hand, hesitating before opening the door.

"They aren't as disciplined as I am," Hogboss said. "But I'm working with them. They'll be ready when the time comes."

Henry wondered how many pig people there were, if it would be possible to somehow undo what he had done. "Show me."

Hogboss opened the door and ushered Henry inside, locking it behind them.

They came out in one of the pig houses, a tin warehouse honeycombed with pens. The doors to the pens had been removed, and inside them, the pigs sat at desks or lay on twin beds. Most were dressed in army surplus brown shirts and camo pants cut into shorts. Some already wore the uniform of the plant. On the walls, there were posters of superheroes, Hollywood actors, musicians. Clusters of pigs grouped around televisions, singing along with educational videos. On the screens, cartoon letters and numbers bounced: *ABC. 123.*

In one corner, a group of them sat on the floor and watched an instructor pig show them how to cut up meat, pack it in plastic, and prepare it for shipping. He passed the knife around, and the pigs held their quivering snouts over the blade.

"There are *hundreds* of them," Henry said. "How could I have made so many?"

"You only made me," Hogboss said. "I was the prototype. Once I had been built and Corporate saw what was possible, they sent you a full lab and team. These other pigs were modified before they were ever born. Gene-splicing, engineered viruses that affected their development in the womb, growth hormones and steroids. You did something marvelous, Henry. And soon we'll be able to show the world."

"When?"

"There are a few pig families in town already. I had them move into abandoned neighborhoods. I've been buying groceries for them, but they're getting restless. If people in the town haven't noticed yet, they will soon."

Henry looked around the space. "What happened to the lab equipment? The team? There must be files or notes."

"Corporate moved all of that off-site. They're waiting to see how things develop here before any more modified pigs are made."

There would be no taking it back, no stopping it. His work, the creation of his own hands, would spread over every little pig-raising town in the country. In a few years, there would be pig people running farms globally. He had always wanted to make a big change in the world. Now he had.

What would happen to all the people working here? Their lives, already so hard, were about to get worse. They would be angry, and they would find someone to blame.

Henry had an idea where they might start.

And the pig people, owned body and blood by the company they worked for, just corporate property, high-tech slaves. What would their lives be like — the pork plant their shelter, trade, and temple? What would it mean for the pigs themselves, fully aware that the factory owned them, able to see themselves in the faces of the animals they killed? He felt sick, lightheaded with the implications.

"Eventually," said Hogboss, "our goal is for all pigs to be self-slaughtering pigs."

This was bigger than him or his family, bigger than the shattered little town curling around the plateau where the factory stood. The town would fold. Once the plant stopped hiring, Swine Hill would finally die. But all Henry could think of was his mother, so full of need that she scorched anyone she touched. What would she do when there was no longer a job for her at the plant? When she couldn't make payments on the house, where would they go? Their extended family out of state wouldn't take them in. They blamed his mother for what had happened to Henry's father, were afraid that she would ruin their lives too. He imagined the doomed town as still as a cemetery and on fire with its ghosts, his father walking through the ruins, the only living person left.

A young pig boy in a black hoodie and jeans walked over to them. "Hey, Dad," he said to Hogboss. "Who's your friend?"

"Dennis, this is Henry. He's the one who made us."

Dennis tilted his snout up, sniffing, taking Henry in. The pig boy had freckles running down his snout and breaking over his cheeks. He was the same height as Henry, looked to be about the same age. Henry reminded himself that the pig boy could only be, at most, a couple of months old. Had he ever even been outside?

"Do you think there might be other things pigs can do?" Dennis asked. "I don't want to be a butcher."

Hogboss snorted and flicked his head to the side. "Dennis spends too much time on the Internet. Thinks he's a vegetarian." He pronounced the word slowly, tripping over the many syllables, as if it was an alien spore that had landed on his tongue.

"I want to go to school," Dennis said.

Hogboss gestured to the walls surrounding them. "There's nothing I can't teach you right here."

"Is your mom here too?" Henry asked.

The two pig men were quiet, looking at each other and considering their answer.

"My mate was slaughtered shortly after Dennis was born," Hogboss said. "She wasn't a modified pig, just the regular kind."

Henry felt small and stupid, not knowing what to say. "I'm sorry."

Hogboss waved him off, closing his eyes. "It's nothing. That's what she was born for, and I like to think she did a good job. I'm not upset over it."

If only Jane had been there. Her ghost could see past his big-toothed smile, past his furrowed brow and dark eyes, through the keyhole of his mind. Did Hogboss remember his slaughtered mate, her scent, the feel of her bulk against his? Was he really okay that she had been killed? Had someone else butchered her, or had the pig man been made to do it himself?

"I'm ready to go home," Henry said.

When they left the building and came into the parking lot, it was almost light out. The ghosts were fading with the coming of the sun, only the smallest wisps of them left clinging to the ground. Cars streamed into the compound, workers in rumpled blue jumpsuits rushing to clock in. The morning shift gave Hogboss and Henry a lot of space, gathering in their knots and whispering.

Parked next to them, Trigger and his father leaned against their truck, pulling off their masks and stripping off their heavy suits. They had rolls of hoses in the truck bed and bulky canister backpacks filled with a cleaning agent. White foam clung to their suits and oozed out of the mouth of the sprayer nozzle. It was cold near them, the asphalt salted with ice.

Trigger's father rested an arm on the side of his truck bed, his hand missing two fingers. He coughed hard and stretched the straps of his mask, complaining that it didn't fit. Trigger smoked a cigarette, coughing a little himself, the stream of smoke coming from his mouth thick and white in the chill air.

"Henry?" Trigger asked. "What are you doing here?"

"Nothing. I'm leaving." He didn't want to get in the truck with the pig man, not with Trigger, his father, and a cluster of workers staring. But there was nowhere else to go. Henry stepped into the cab and buckled his seatbelt.

Trigger knocked on his window, his breath painting the glass white.

Henry rolled it down, and Trigger handed him something wrapped in paper.

"Can you give this to Jane? Tell her that it didn't work."

Henry unfolded the paper and found a CD, the paper annotated with songs and artists. "Aren't you going to see her again soon?"

"I thought you could just give it to her now."

Trigger went back to help his father finish taking off his suit, leaving Henry with the CD.

Hogboss yawned, two short tusks almost protruding from his mouth. "Let's get you home."

He drove them down from the plant. There was no traffic in their lane, every car climbing up to start the day's work at Pig City. The trail of cars stretched on and on, as far as Henry could see, like everyone in the world worked there.

"Did you figure out what you needed to?" Hogboss asked.

"What if a person did something really bad, but they didn't mean to? What if they didn't even know they were doing it, but then it's too late? It happened. And it's going to hurt a lot of people. Is it really their fault?"

Hogboss awkwardly patted his shoulder. "I'm sorry, Henry. I can't be a father to you. *You* made *me*, remember?"

When Hogboss dropped him off at his house, it was almost eight in the morning. Jane's car and his mother's were both gone. The house stood quiet, lights off, yolk-yellow sunlight running over its shingles.

Bethany stood on the sidewalk in front of his house, staring up at the laser array dimly lacerating the sky.

Henry crossed the street to stand next to her. He was so tired he could barely stand. The implications of what he had done looped in his head, repercussions and fears colliding like asteroids circling the sun. His ghost lay deep at the bottom of him, satisfied and silent.

"You were with the pig man," Bethany said. "That's what you were doing for the last few months? Are you the reason he's here?"

"Yeah," Henry said. "I think so."

The curtains moved in the living room, and the robot looked out at them, its eyes telescoping wide. It stared at the driveway, waiting for Henry's mother to come home.

"Don't worry," Bethany said. "Your inventions never work all that well anyway."

"You running before school?" Henry asked. "I didn't know you came this far."

"If I get up early enough I can make it all the way across town and back. I saw the red lights and wanted to see what it was. What does it do?" She seemed mesmerized by it, the light reflected in her eyes.

"I'm not sure yet. I should probably take it apart, just to be safe. Especially after the pig man."

"It doesn't look dangerous."

That was the problem, Henry thought. The most dangerous things never did.

"Aren't you worried about running across town so early? There are still a lot of ghosts out. Especially around here."

"I'm always picking up a few more." She shrugged. "Usually I don't even notice. Not unless I try to leave."

People still talked about the last time Bethany got on a bus to go to an away game. At the edge of Swine Hill, an army of spirits had come boiling out of the girl and started tearing the engine apart. It looked like a car accident: pieces of rent steel and broken car parts littering the asphalt. And when Bethany walked out of the mess and down the road, ready to leave it all behind, those long, airy hands stretched out and gathered her back.

Henry pointed to the garage. "I've got a flat basketball and a trash can. Want to lose some games to me? You might be able to get rid of all of them."

She laughed. "I'm not throwing a game. Not even trash basketball. Not even for you."

"Have your ghosts ever made you do something that you regretted?"

She shook her head. "Everyone worries that a ghost will get inside them and make them do something awful. But ghosts can't haunt you unless they see themselves in you. Whatever happens when you're haunted, you wanted it. At the end of the day, you're still you."

Henry sighed. Bethany wasn't always the easiest person to talk to. She saw the world in black and white, wins and losses. How to explain to her his strange relationship with his ghost? It made him do things he didn't even know he wanted to do yet. It was amazing. But his ghost didn't understand the difference between should and shouldn't. It changed the world without concern for consequences, leaving Henry to deal with the fallout.

"I should go to sleep," he said. "I feel like I've been awake for months."

Bethany nodded, but she kept staring at the light. Henry went inside.

He stumbled upstairs and fell into bed. His body was lead, sinking into the mattress, and his head hurt from exhaustion. But his mind spun and spun, couldn't shut down, couldn't stop analyzing everything that was wrong. Guilt and consequence. Right and wrong. Exactly the kind of problem his ghost wasn't interested in helping him solve.

He still had Jane's CD in his hand. He rolled over and dropped it into the tray of a CD player and switched it on. The music was mournful, complicated, the perfect soundtrack for the pain he would soon bring to Swine Hill and his family. The density of it, layer on layer of instruments weaving together, stacked like variables in an equation.

This problem couldn't be smashed with a hammer or taken apart with a screwdriver. The pig people were here now. He was responsible for them, just like he was responsible for the hurt they would cause.

The drums laid down walls inside walls, a maze of sound. Vocals scraped over the back-and-forth gunfight of the guitars. The world collapsed into a knot. The music flooded into his body, not distracting him from his pain, but submerging him in it. He felt like Jane had made the CD just for him, just for this moment. He fell asleep listening to it, all the space in his head taken up by one harsh song, this bloody-voiced herald of some new day to come.

9

ALL MORNING AT the grocery store, people had been thinking about the pigs. Night-crew workers from the plant came in wearing their jumpsuits, dark with pig blood or bleached pale from cleaning agents. *That boy was there again*, they thought. *The one who made the robot. Why is he at the plant?*

A lawn crew came down Jane's lane, their hair sweat-damp under faded ball caps. They smelled of cut grass and gasoline, buying bottles of Gatorade and packaged sandwiches from the deli. *Pigs trimming hedges*, they thought. *Pigs planting flowers. Pigs checking the mail.*

All the secret things they believed about people who were different they believed about the pigs, too. In the minds of her customers, the one or two pigs they had seen multiplied. People imagined houses full of them, lounging on dirty mattresses on the floor, sleeping six to a room. Pigs stealing gas cans or bicycles right off the porch. Pigs crowding the line at the unemployment office or, worse, asking for jobs at the plant. Pigs closing in around the town and all it had left, pushing everyone back into their dim houses where only television newscasters came to speak to them, the news never good.

It was around noon when Jane's shift ended. Instead of going straight home, she drove around, braving the edges of downtown. On a street corner, she saw the top half of a ghost hanging in the air, wispy hands reaching out to her. She blew through the stop sign, not slowing down enough for it to be able to approach her car.

Driving past an old park — the hulks of unused playground equipment vine-covered and cancerous with rust, beer bottles smote upon the hard ground — she saw her father.

His jacket hung in pieces and his bald, scarred head gleamed in the sun. He was her name, was skin and blood of her, alone and out of his mind and living like a stray in the ruins of the town. She and her family had failed him utterly. It made Jane ache with shame.

Her father reached into the bushes with both hands, trying to get at something deep among the thorns.

Jane parked and went to him. He looked up, startled for a moment, but when he saw that it was only her, he went back to his work. Jane was the only person he wouldn't run from. He ripped away the briars, leaving bits of leaf and stalk on the ground. Fine cuts wrapped his hands like lace.

"Dad, what are you doing? Are you trying to find food? Are you hungry?"

Her ghost was no help with him. It wouldn't have known her father was there if Jane hadn't told it. His mind had changed, retreating too far into memory and pain, a locked room that no ghost or person had the key to.

"I'm going to get you something to eat. Stay here."

He didn't acknowledge her. Jane got back in her car and went to a drive-through not far away. When she got back, her father was still there. He had made some progress with the vines, opening up a hollow big enough to step inside. What was he doing?

Her ghost, unable to get into her father's mind, dug in to Jane's instead. It dragged up memories from when he'd been himself. Flying a kite in a grassy lot behind a closed-down general store. Cooking to the radio while Jane did dishes at his side. A music shop manager telling Jane not to touch anything before taking a cassette away from her, and her father taking it away from the man and putting it back in her hands. He had been such a big piece of their lives once.

When she handed her father a burger, he turned away from the vines and sat on the ground to eat. She kicked the briars out of the way and sat with him. Sharing a meal was the closest thing she had to having a relationship with him anymore, the only way Jane could show that she cared. She didn't know if he understood.

It was hard to look at him and not hate her mother. Her mom's lips were pressed into his arms and neck. Her handprints on his head. Everywhere she had touched, he was burned, layers of scar tissue built up over years. No wonder he hadn't been able to stay.

"You should be home," Jane said. "It's not safe for you to be out here. Cops might pick you up. Or you could hurt yourself. You could get sick. Being ghost-proof doesn't make you invincible."

You might as well be talking to yourself.

He finished the food she'd given him and went back to tearing away the vines. He had almost reached the fence behind it. Jane was about to give up, to leave him to his strange work, when, deep in the thorns, he pulled something free and turned around, showing it to her.

It was a soot-colored bird, dead a long time but still faintly smelling of decay. It had landed too hard and impaled its throat on a long, woody thorn. Its feathers were dark around its neck. It was half rotten, the head mostly skull and beak, eyeless, its clawed feet still tucked under its tail.

Her father took this small dead thing, patted it on the head, and tucked it into his pocket as if he had saved it. Then he left, disappearing into the shattered warehouses across the street, as always, without a word.

Jane went back to her car and sat down. She wiped her eyes and rested her head on the steering wheel. It was nothing, her father rescuing a bird that was already dead. Still, seeing him cup his hands around it, seeing him put it inside his coat like he could protect it, made her hope that her father still lived deep within himself. For a few moments, she let herself think that everything might be okay.

Pulling into her driveway, Jane heard the scream of a power saw from a few houses away. She was so stunned to hear a sound like that on her empty street that she left her car door open and walked toward it. A few homes down, there was an old house with a sagging roof and boarded-up windows. But the grass was cut for the first time that Jane could remember. The sawing came from the backyard, and from somewhere on the roof she heard shingles being ripped loose.

Behind the house, she saw a pig man stripped to the waist, his pink gut hanging over a pair of jeans with suspenders. He was smaller than Hogboss, only about the size of a man, and his skin was smooth and unscarred. He laid boards across a sawhorse and cut them, stacking them on the ground. Younger pig men, lean and paint-splattered, picked up the boards and carried them inside. From the open door, Jane could smell fresh paint.

The house's spirits are gone. Her ghost sounded disappointed, angry.

"I didn't know there were ghosts here," Jane said.

Only a murmur of them, a collection of memories stirred together. They roosted in the attic like birds. Not anymore, though. The pigs changed the house, and they didn't have anything to hold on to.

Jane walked a few blocks down to the old house where she had played as a girl, the green-smelling place where her ghost had haunted her. Pig City work trucks, their beds filled with new drywall and lumber, sat in the driveway. A pig girl read a book in the newly hung porch swing. All the old curtains, rotted to yellowed strips over the years, had been replaced clean and white.

"I'm sorry about your house," she said to her ghost.

Her ghost circled wide inside of her, then collapsed tightly around Jane's heart and made it race, like an embrace or a threat.

It's fine. As long as I'm with you, I'll always have a home.

Walking back, Jane saw more cars than usual on her street. People

crept down the road with their windows rolled down, their eyes darting from house to house.

They heard that more pigs moved in. They've come to see.

Trigger texted her to say that he was awake. Jane ignored it. She
needed to eat something. She walked back home and opened the door
to the sound of the robot vacuuming. From upstairs, Henry played sad
music. The song was familiar, but she couldn't remember why.

Trigger texted again. *My dad had to run some errands. He'll be out of
the house for a few hours, if you wanted to come over.*

Jane grabbed a granola bar from the kitchen and ran back to her car.
She'd asked to go to his house before, but he said his dad wouldn't like
it. He shared so little of himself, was so guarded. Even her ghost had
a hard time getting to the bottom of him. There were things Trigger
just wouldn't think about, or wouldn't think about when Jane and her
ghost were around. She'd been hoping that if she went to his house,
then she might really know him.

Text me your address, she wrote.

It's not a good place, he wrote back. *I'm letting you come so you'll understand.*

Trigger lived on the outskirts of Swine Hill, his house close to the forest surrounding the plant. A dirt track cut steeply back and forth to
where his house sat on a hill. The yard was tangled with briars and
wild blackberries. Old bits of trash, Styrofoam cups and rain-washed
paper, hung in the thorns. The house was small, sitting up on concrete blocks. There was no truck in the driveway. A dirt path led to the
door.

Jane stopped with her hand on the doorknob. "Are there ghosts inside?"

Just one. But, oh, Jane, it's enough.

She went in without knocking.

It was dark and cold. Above her head, branches knit together, pressing their thin fingers against a bloated moon. The floor was thick with
pine needles, fallen branches, and dead scrub, all of it clotted with ice.

Leaves lay stacked, their brown edges frozen, like stars dead and fallen to earth. Through the elephantine trunks, wind pushed endless and heavy and sobbing like a train.

It took her a moment to find the furniture, to see the couch facing a busted television, the kitchen table piled high with snow. She moved aside leaves and found dirty carpet, frayed and hair-covered. Low animals crept in the corners of the rooms. Black squirrels and birds moving in and out of the branches. Rabbits, heads down, beggaring their way over the floor. From the hallway, a deer stared at her.

The only bright things in the dim were flares of blood, red-black and heavy as jewels, dotting the floor. Gunpowder and smoke hung so thick in the air that they coated her tongue. There was a hum, a ringing needle of sound that seemed almost on the verge of fading but never did.

Trigger was behind her, slipping a hoodie over her shoulders and rubbing her skin through the fabric. "You don't have to stay," he said. "We can go whenever you want."

"There's a whole memory in this house. It's not just the ghost of a person. It's the ghost of a place and time. It's the ghost of something that happened."

Jane's ghost brought her fragments from Trigger, something he was trying to suppress. *I am what happened. This place is me.*

She pulled him against her. "Why would you stay here? Why punish yourself?"

Trigger didn't say anything. He couldn't get the words out, not knowing where to start. Everything in him was a snarl of self-loathing and anger. But he let himself feel everything, didn't try to hide it from her. Jane's greedy ghost drank it up.

The house isn't haunted. He is. This is the same ghost he carries everywhere.

"Show me," Jane said. "I want to know what happened."

He took her hand and led her down the hall. The walls shimmered in and out, one second brown paneling, the next a stand of dark trees. There were pictures hanging, though frost obscured most of them. She brushed away the ice from the glass and saw a family portrait, his father, mother, brother, and him.

The beads of blood grew thicker down the hall, giving way to a violent slick of black. Dark blood. Heart's blood, still steaming in the cold. He waved her toward the bedroom alone and went to his room to wait.

He can't look at it again. He'll be waiting for you when you're done.

Jane pushed open the door, cobwebs stretching wide and tearing. No one had been in here in a long time. His mother's clothes still lay bundled in a hamper. On the dresser top, a scattering of leaves covered a set of porcelain boxes. Jane brushed the dirt and ice away, her fingers stinging with cold. She found a jewelry cabinet, a few simple rings stacked together within. And she found a music box, the brass key on the bottom caked with tarnish. She turned the key and held the box to her ear, but there was nothing. She slipped it into the deep pocket of the hoodie.

You would trust Henry with something so important?

"Maybe Trigger would like to have it fixed. Maybe it would give him a piece of his mother back."

When has Henry ever made anything better?

Jane ignored her ghost. Blood sank deeply into the carpet, a trail leading to the closet. Inside its dark mouth, dresses hung, as silent and pale as ghosts. Jane walked through them, into darkness and wind, coming out in a little clearing under the moon. It was night, and winter, and years ago. Branches hung down to catch in her hair. A family of deer startled and crashed away, leaving a circle of flattened grass and the steaming trails of their breath.

Here, in the hollow where the deer had slept, a child lay on the grass. A bullet wound lanced through his small chest. Blood stuck his shirt and orange vest to his body. The rifle shot rang loudly here, like it was right inside her head. The child, so obviously dead, turned to look at Jane.

He says that you should go, her ghost said. *He says that Trigger did this, and it's only fair that Trigger remembers. Nothing will ever change that.*

Jane stared into his dark, hateful eyes. "I'm going to bury you."

Is he wrong? her ghost asked.

Jane went into Trigger's room and found him lying in bed. She shrugged her hoodie off and lay next to him, stroking his back.

"You should probably go soon," he said. "My dad will be angry if he finds you here."

"You were really young when it happened."

"Yeah."

"And it was an accident."

He started to cry, but her ghost pulled images and memories out of him, all the things he couldn't say. His father had taken them on a hunting trip. Trigger had insisted on carrying the rifle. Said he would be careful. He'd seen some shape move in the woods and switched his safety off. He darted forward, got his feet tangled around a fallen branch in the dark. He twisted and fell. The gun went off in his arms, his baby brother standing cold and afraid only a few feet away. His father had run the bleeding boy back toward the truck, through the fallen leaves, and into the dark, blood pouring out of him. "Goddamn you, Trigger Fingers," his father had shouted. "Look what you did."

"He only said that because he felt guilty," Jane said. "Your dad blames you so he doesn't have to blame himself."

"My brother blames me," Trigger said. "I'm the one he haunted."

"He's a child. All these years later, he can't be anything but what he was."

Her ghost moved darkly in her, feeling rebuked.

Trigger turned to face Jane. She took his face in her hands and kissed his eyes, smearing the salty wet over his cheeks. He pulled her hard against him, so close that she could feel his sad heart beating through his chest.

"My mother left after that. She couldn't stand to look at me."

"Then she failed you," Jane said. "It sounds like a lot of people have."

His mind butterflied open, grateful and guilty and vulnerable. She saw deep into him, sinking into the frozen lake of his mind. She knew all of him, knew him better than she'd ever known anyone. His thoughts and feelings collided with her own, Jane feeling like she was two people in one skin. She drank him up.

Jane pulled off his jeans and her own, their pant legs twining together on the floor. They were still wearing their shirts, the blanket pulled close around her shoulders. His mind focused completely on Jane, her eyes staring into his eyes, her breath against his neck. He felt nothing but her, and she took the feeling back, feeling herself through him. For a short while, he didn't hate who he was.

While they lay together, skin on skin, a layer of ice and leaves collected on top of the blanket. Jane's phone kept buzzing in her pants pocket on the floor. Worried something might have happened to her father, she shook free of the blanket and stood to get dressed.

When she pulled Trigger's hoodie back on, the weight of the music box thumped against her side. He felt stunned and happy, watching her dress in simple adoration. It was nice to have her ghost bring her something sweet for once.

She flipped open her phone and read a string of messages from her brother.

Jane? It's gone. Jane, where are you? I can't feel my ghost anymore. The CD you made for Trigger stole it.

"You gave Henry the CD I made for you?"

Trigger sat up and started pulling on his clothes. "He was at the plant last night. I told him the CD didn't work and asked him to give it back."

"Did you listen to it?"

He tried to think of something else, but couldn't focus. Guilt flared in him again, and a quiet, stubborn anger.

"You didn't. What the fuck is wrong with you?"

"My brother doesn't have anyone else but me."

"Neither does mine. And your brother is a ghost. You aren't responsible for him anymore."

"I'm *more* responsible for him. It's my fault he's dead. You have a ghost. You should understand."

"My ghost doesn't hurt me. If it did, I'd get rid of it."

There was a spike of shock from her ghost, but Jane ignored it.

"Why are you so mad about this?" Trigger asked.

"Henry listened to the CD and lost his ghost somehow," Jane said. "He's freaking out. I have to go."

Trigger wouldn't meet her eyes. "He should be happy, right? Maybe we'd all be happier without our ghosts." He didn't believe it, though. At the bottom of him, he felt that he deserved to be haunted. He wondered what Jane was thinking, what she wanted from him, how he could make things right.

She walked out of the room, glad that he couldn't read her mind. "I have to go."

Trigger's father, Mason, opened the door and found the two of them standing in the living room. The older man held his keys oddly in his mangled hand, tweezing them between thumb and ring finger. Jane and Trigger looked at each other, confused and cold, like lost hunters in the woods.

"You aren't supposed to have company," Mason said.

He didn't look at Jane, but his mind was full of her. She was a stain to him. A blemish in his house, a thing that didn't belong. She had seen the ugliness of their run-down home, and he was ashamed to be made so low in her eyes. Her being here made him feel like less, and feeling so made him hate her. He wanted her and everyone like her cast from the earth.

"I was on my way out," Jane said. "We'll talk soon, Trigger. I'm not letting this go."

She closed the door and went back to her car, mouth dry and shoulders tight from seeing herself through Mason's eyes. Her hands trembled badly enough that she almost dropped her keys.

They're fighting, her ghost said.

Jane put the car in gear. "Don't tell me."

His father pushed him. They're screaming. I think Mason might hit him. Her ghost rolled in the feeling, finding its own anticipation delicious.

Jane pulled out of the driveway, not wanting to stay long enough for her ghost to tell her what happened. She turned up her music and sped down the road. Whatever wrath Mason took out on his son, was that her fault too, for staying and trying to make things better when she knew nothing could? She felt sick, but she couldn't deal with that right now. She had to go face her brother after taking away the thing that mattered to him most.

10

HENRY SAT ON Jane's bed listening to the CD in her stereo, the volume cranked up loud enough to rattle the windows and send sonic booms of bass slapping the walls.

"I'm sorry!" Jane shouted over the sound. "You weren't supposed to listen to it."

He ignored her, focusing on the music. There had to be some moment, some change in the melody or dizzying pile-up of instrumental patterns, some seam his ghost had fallen into. If he could find that moment in one of the songs, maybe he could get it back. He'd listened to the CD four times through already.

The last track ended. His ears throbbed. What was he missing? He picked up a guitar in the corner of Jane's room and tried to play, his fingers tripping over the strings. If only he could play something that would draw the ghost back into him. The strings made stuttering, self-conscious ripples of noise. He threw the guitar down.

"You listen to it," Henry said. "Find out what song he's stuck in."

Jane looked afraid, no doubt thinking of her own ghost, imagining what it would be like to lose it. "I *have* listened to it. I can't hear a ghost in there."

Henry paced back and forth, squeezing his head in his hands. "Why did you make this CD? Why didn't you warn me?"

"I was trying to get rid of Trigger's ghost. I didn't think it would work for anyone but him."

The ghost had been a piece of Henry. Everything he saw, touched, or thought about, the spirit had been there, ready to help him remake the world. The school counselor had made it clear that no matter how smart Henry was, no one in Swine Hill would ever see anything good in him. Only the ghost would help him escape the town and find the life he wanted. Losing it was like having the sky taken away, the world folding flat and suffocating around him. He sank to the floor.

Jane sat down beside him and gave him a hug. He held himself rigid, looking out the window. Where was it? How could he get it back?

"I don't think your ghost is inside the disc," Jane said. "I should be able to hear it."

"You couldn't hear it when we were kids. It was right inside the house, and you never knew."

"What if it's gone because it made the pig people? What if it did everything it had left to do, and now it's at rest?"

Henry shrugged her off and stood. "What did it do? Mom was lonely, so it made a shitty robot that breaks the dishes. Bethany wanted to get away, so it made a light show. Everyone in town is miserable, so it made pig people to be miserable with them. How the hell could it have done everything it meant to do? What has it even done?"

"Things are different now. The pigs are changing everything. I'm worried."

"Worry about getting my ghost back. Worry about fixing what you screwed up."

He left Jane's room and went down the hall. The path leading to his room was narrowed by heaps of broken appliances and bins of spare parts. A busted AC unit, its fins dark with grime, sat dead on the floor. The skeleton of a vacuum cleaner twisted beside it. Even without his ghost, he might be able to fix them. Pour enough money, time, pain into something, and he might see power flash through it again, hear the compressor groan to life.

But with his ghost, he could have made them sit up and speak, could have taken trash and transformed it into living machines. Never again would he take ruin and bend it into the impossible, effortlessly making things that had never been before. He shoved one of the bins over, sending a rain of nuts and bolts sloshing down the stairs.

In his bedroom, the robot sat on Henry's bed, its weight almost folding the mattress in half. Deep in its motors and circuits, the robot was eaten through with ghosts, too many and too small for even Jane to hear them. Wanting nothing to do with spirits, the robot couldn't shed them. Wanting only to be possessed, Henry couldn't make his one shy ghost stay.

"Not a good time," Henry told it.

His computer scrolled with information, some program he'd forgotten that he was running. It looked like a data feed for the laser array on the roof. There were columns for distance, for wavelength, for pulse frequency. He hadn't even known it was collecting information. The dataset might contain the secrets of free energy or faster than light travel. He might never know, might never be able to interpret what was right in front of him.

The robot made a crackle of static from the bed. Henry turned and took a closer look at it, his heart sinking.

The machine looked like it had been hit by a car. Its chest was dented in, the front panel bent and swinging open. Sparks flashed inside its body. One of its thin legs was crushed. The floor was scraped where it had dragged itself into the room. It held out its long-fingered hands, the palms caked with dirt. *Please help me,* it seemed to say.

"My ghost left," Henry said. "I'm not sure I can repair you now. I'd probably just make things worse."

The robot struggled to climb up from the sagging bed, Henry's blanket getting tangled around it like a shroud. It dropped to the floor and crawled away, fans and drives moaning within its hull.

. . .

The robot had retreated to a corner of the living room downstairs, hiding like a spider behind the recliner. It glared at anyone who came into the room. Henry made himself breakfast before school. He kept getting distracted thinking of all the things he would never be able to do, burning his eggs hard to the bottom of the pan. He scraped the mess onto a plate.

His mother poured coffee into a thermos, her makeup already blurring in her own heat. She breathed through her mouth, looking like a woman dying of thirst, and wrung her hands.

"You should be grateful," she said. "Jane tried to get rid of my ghost for years, but it wouldn't budge. Now you can be yourself without the dead weighing you down."

He didn't want to be himself. He was nothing — a kid smarter than most, but not special enough to impress anyone who mattered. He had thought he would leave the town in a couple of years, attend a robotics program in a major city, build fantastic machines that would change the lives of everyone in the world.

But without his ghost, he might never go anywhere at all. He was a prodigy by Swine Hill standards, but he'd done enough research to know what he was up against: a lifetime of money, personal tutors, private schools, summer camps, everything he'd never had. He would stay here, pinned by the town's awful gravity, his only friends the strange pig people he had made.

His mother gave him a quick, tight hug, kissing him on the temple. It hurt, like he'd touched his forehead to a hot skillet. Even through his shirt, her touch spread like a sunburn. He tried not to flinch, but couldn't help it.

She dropped her arms and stepped back, ashamed to have hurt him. It must be hard for her, Henry thought, to watch things fall apart and only be able to make it worse.

"Where's your sister?" she asked. "Isn't she taking you to school?"

"I'm riding the bus."

After his mom left, Henry sat on his front steps. It was cool out, and he rubbed the chill from his arms. Pale shapes moved in the house across the street. He wished his ghost would come walking out of that house and step back inside him. Hadn't he been important to it? Didn't it need his hands as much as he needed it?

His phone buzzed, a message from a number he didn't know.

Hey, Henry. Jane gave me your number. I'm really sorry about giving you the CD. I didn't know this would happen.

He was about to text Trigger back, say thanks and tell him that it would be okay, even though it would never be okay, when Trigger texted again.

You probably don't want to hear this, but you're lucky. I don't think my ghost will ever leave. This is the best thing that could have happened to you.

He slammed the face of his phone against the steps. No, he wasn't lucky. He was lost. Worse than losing a friend or relative, he had lost a piece of himself. He was less than he'd been before. Why couldn't everyone understand that?

The bus pulled up and sighed to a stop. Henry climbed on, walking between seats ripped open and vomiting foam. Whorls of graffiti covered every surface, even the windows. Only a scattering of kids rode it, most of them young. There was no driver. The haunted old thing kept dragging itself along the same route it always had, propelled by spirits alone.

A few days ago, he might have wondered how a machine could draw power from the grief of the dead. His ghost might have taken control of him, and days or weeks later he would have woken up and beheld some ghostly engine that burned spirits like coal. Now he could only imagine such a thing. Henry went to the back without looking at anyone.

"Henry? Hey, it's you. Come sit by me." The pig boy from the plant lounged across a seat in the back. He had pierced the edges of his thin ears, and heavy rings weighed them down against his cheek. He wore a T-shirt two sizes too big, the logo of some band Henry had never heard of splashed across it. Dark eye shadow masked his eyes in wide bands.

Henry sat in the adjacent seat. "You shouldn't be here, Dennis. People aren't going to like it."

"Dad said that you'd look out for me."

Henry stared into the pig boy's face and started running through the variables. Hundreds of students and faculty, almost none of them comfortable with pigs being in town. Quiet nooks, dark rooms, dead ends, and narrow corridors in a place without enough adults to keep track of everyone. Angry kids who felt like the world was unfair and getting worse all the time, no outlet for their anger. People who saw any difference as a criticism or a threat. A pig boy, alone. Even with his ghost, this wasn't solvable. Henry's heart raced with all the terrible things that could happen.

"Go home, Dennis."

"I'm good at making friends," the pig boy said. "Just wait and see."

Henry skipped first period to follow Dennis. The pig boy unfolded a schedule and pointed to his first class: physical education in the gym. Henry pulled Dennis's hood over his ears and motioned for him to follow. "Let's go around the long way."

Twenty minutes later, Dennis was dressed out in basketball shorts and a tank-top, struggling to dribble the ball in his clumsy hands. Henry sat in the bleachers, his skin prickling, waiting for something bad to happen. Even if he had still been haunted, this wasn't the kind of problem his ghost had been good at dealing with. People didn't act rationally. They would do things against their own interest, out of boredom or spite. Better to get them out of the equation all together.

On the court, Dennis smiled and said something to one of the girls next to him. She laughed, though whether it was from what he said or from the novelty of having a conversation with a pig, Henry couldn't tell. The girl's boyfriend pulled her away. The floor of the court was slightly off-level, as the soft earth under the school had sunk and turned slowly over the past few decades, the very ground rising up to bury the town. Whenever Dennis fumbled the ball, it went rolling away. Henry watched him drop and chase it for an hour.

After gym, Dennis didn't come out of the locker room for a long time. The other boys walked out and grinned at Henry, their smiles knife-sharp, wanting him to know that something had happened.

Henry plunged in. The room was steamy from the showers and had a wet and fungal smell. The walls were textured with mold, the lights half burned out. In the close, dark space, old ghosts sat on the floor and muttered to one another, reliving some horrible thing that had happened years ago. If the ground did swallow up the school one day, Henry wondered if they would still be down here, whispering in each other's dead ears, not knowing that the earth had closed over their heads.

Dennis sat in the corner, staring at his jeans. He held them up so Henry could see: someone had cut a hole in the back. The pig boy stuck his finger through.

"Get dressed," Henry said. If the boys came back, they'd both be trapped here. Anything could happen.

"My tail will hang out. Everyone will see."

"People already know you're a pig. You might as well be comfortable. Maybe this is a good thing."

He sounded like his mother or like Trigger, telling Dennis what was good for him, how best to be himself, that his pain didn't matter. Henry bounced his fist against the wall, impatient, wanting to get back to looking for his ghost.

"When we were playing basketball, that girl was missing all her shots too. I told her that we had something in common." Dennis gave Henry a sad smile. "I guess they wanted to remind me that we're not the same."

Henry sighed, annoyed at how raw the pig boy was, how little Dennis understood. Once after school, a group of upperclassmen had caught Henry walking alone and thrown bricks at him in the parking lot. Once, he smiled at the wrong time, and the principal thought he was laughing at her. Someone's wallet went missing and Henry was blamed. He was chewed out by teachers for talking too much or not talking enough. Whatever he did, it was wrong. He was different, so people thought anything they did to him was okay. When he came home after, the rage and unfairness of it sitting heavy in his mind, Jane would hug him and nod and say that she knew.

"You aren't the same," Henry told the pig boy. "Try to remember."

Henry shadowed Dennis all morning. No one asked what he was doing out of class. They were used to his ghost taking over and making him do odd things, and honestly, Henry knew they didn't think he was worth their trouble. He stared blankly ahead, not speaking to anyone, staying close to Dennis like he was monitoring an experiment. Every time he thought of his ghost, wondering where it might be and how to find it, he would catch someone staring at Dennis and it would break his concentration.

He pulled out his phone and texted Hogboss. *I don't think it's safe for Dennis to be at school. He's drawing too much attention.*

Hogboss's response was slow in coming. Henry imagined him punching in the letters with his big, blunt fingers. *People will get used to us eventually. I can't keep Dennis home. He asks me upsetting questions.*

Dennis's tail stuck out from the back of his jeans, twitching while he listened to the teacher.

At lunch, Henry pulled Dennis to the back of the cafeteria, a broken table with few seats. Dennis had a plate full of green peas, the only vegetable they were serving today. The cafeteria steamed with the sweet, salty smell of barbecued pork.

"They're afraid that pigs will take their jobs," Dennis said.

Henry shushed him, hoping no one heard.

"But I don't even want to work at Pig City. I'm going to college. I'm going to travel. I think you made me for more than this."

"I wish you'd go home. You'd learn more on the Internet than you would here anyway."

"You did make us for more, didn't you? You can tell me. What's your plan?"

At the best of times, Henry didn't know what his ghost was trying to do, and that was when it had been right inside his head. It was highly likely that Dennis had been created to be a plant worker, to be torn up and underpaid, to worry over an underwater mortgage and fight with his kids so that the people of the town wouldn't have to. And after his sad and brutal work was done, he would be fed into the meat grinders and processed into sausage like any other pig.

"My ghost left me. Whatever plan it had is done now. Tell your dad that I can't help you."

A group of senior boys came over and sat on the edge of Henry's table, their long legs touching the floor. They all had the tired eyes and scraped, ropey arms of evening plant workers. One of them wore his Pig City uniform, the cartoon pig logo giving a toothy smile.

"We're done," Henry said. "You guys can have the table."

"You look familiar," one of the boys said to Dennis.

Dennis tossed his head from side to side, nervous. "I don't think we've met before."

"No, I know you," the boy said. He reached out and grabbed Dennis through his jeans, squeezing his hip. "That's ham."

Another boy grabbed the base of Dennis's neck. "Pork shoulder." He dug in his fingers, shaking the pig boy's flesh. "Lot of good meat there."

They surrounded Dennis, grabbing his body while he asked them to stop. "Spareribs. Loin. Chop. Hock." One of them punched him in the stomach, knocking the wind out of the pig boy and folding him over the table. "Pork belly."

Henry watched, paralyzed. He wanted to stop them. He wanted to say something, to do something. He felt so small, so weak without his ghost. The boys were huge and dangerous, and there were so many of them. The teacher on duty was Ms. Miller, the yearbook crone. She watched the boys put their hands on Dennis, pretending nothing was wrong.

Dennis pulled away from them, knocking over his plate of peas. He fled the cafeteria. Henry kept eating, head down and silent, until the boys drifted away. Then he followed, feeling ashamed but also relieved. Maybe now Dennis would go home.

H ENRY LOOKED ALL over campus for the pig boy. He saw the silhouette of someone walking on the abandoned third floor of the classroom building and slipped up the stairs, finding Dennis in the old drama room. Dennis stood on stage, dancing slowly with the ghost girl. She led him through the steps, spinning him in her strong, airy hands. His eyes were swollen from crying.

"What are you doing?" Henry asked. "You didn't get killed by the living, so now you're trying your luck with the dead? Can't you feel how dangerous that ghost is?"

Dennis sniffed, his flat snout glistening. "She played music so I would find her. She wants to be my friend."

"*She* is a ghost. An *it*. And it doesn't care who you are, so long as you give it what it wants."

The ghost girl laughed, grabbing Dennis by both hands and twirling him in circles while the piano played faster. "Henry was half ghost himself once," she said. "Now he's not even half. What kind of friend has he been to you?"

"He just wants to get rid of me," Dennis said.

The dancing girl pulled Dennis against her, resting his head against her shoulder. Few ghosts were so solid and present, especially in the middle of the day. Whatever the ghost wanted, she wanted badly.

"That's what he does. He makes things and abandons them." The ghost's voice cut through Henry, like she knew things about him that even he didn't know. "There are dark rooms full of things he made and forgot about. But the people he hurt, they won't forget."

"Wait," Henry said. "Are you talking about me or my ghost? You knew him, didn't you? Do you know where he is?"

The ghost girl's hair swung out behind her, floating on the air like spider silk.

"I tried to get Henry to dance with me before," the ghost girl said. "He wouldn't even hold my hand."

Dennis narrowed his eyes. "He's a coward. He wants to run, and he wants me to run too. But I won't."

"Then you're going to get hurt," Henry said. "Even if I had my ghost, what was I supposed to do?"

"I would have helped you," Dennis said. "I would have found a way."

It was stupid. The pig boy didn't know what he was talking about. He didn't know how anything worked here. But his words cut Henry. It was true. He *had* been a coward. But what else could he be?

Dennis started sobbing, sitting down on the stage. The ghost girl bent and put her arms around him. Henry came closer, started to apologize, but she waved him away. She looked past him when she spoke, reliving some memory. "You only made things worse. Just like always. Leave. You only care about your machines anyway."

Henry walked out of the school and headed down the cracked and trash-blown streets of downtown. The deeper he pressed into those shattered buildings, the more things moved in the windows or raced thin and eel-like over the ground.

He had just watched while the boys hurt Dennis. He had left the pig boy alone on stage with the ghost girl. He wasn't brave enough to help when people needed him, and he wasn't brilliant enough to reshape the world into what it needed to be. He was trapped by his own limitations. Losing his ghost had shown him what he really was: nothing. If he wanted to be more than himself, he would need to be haunted again.

An old brick building faced him, its windows blown out and staring like the hollows of a skull. Henry tried the door, but it was nailed shut. He lifted himself up on the ledge, cutting his hands on broken glass, and climbed inside. He trembled, his breath fast and legs heavy, unwilling to walk deeper into the dark. But he had to. He would find a ghost, any ghost that would have him. He had to protect Dennis and the other pigs, had to somehow fix what he had done, and he couldn't do that alone.

Something big moved in the dark, crawling up a flight of stairs and knocking things over on the next floor. Henry followed the sound, barely able to see. The stairs were littered with old clothes smelling of sweat and cat piss.

The second floor was ringed in windows, and here Henry could see dim shapes of ghosts hovering over the floor. They shoved and screamed silently at one another. As the light faded outside, they would grow thicker, put on flesh, come roaring back into the world. Henry sat down on the carpet and waited for night to come.

His sister texted him after a while, asking if he needed a ride. A few hours later, she texted again, wondering where he was. He ran a finger over the phone's cracked face and turned it off.

As the light died, the room awakened. Ghosts pulled themselves up from the floor and went shouting down the stairs. They threw things from the windows. One grabbed Henry and pushed him hard against the wall, demanding to know where its wife was. The room was a riot of half-formed shapes begging and crying, tearing at the walls and casting rubble around them. They tugged at his clothes and screamed in his ears. Henry covered his head and let it roll over him like a storm.

Night deepened and the shapes took on definition and weight. In the corner of the room, a woman stepped out from the wall. She stood over a broken machine. She passed her hands over it, and the metal lifted to meet her. Tiny hammers raised. Pulleys squealed. An arm moved back and forth, dragging a tattered skein of thread behind the point of a needle. She plunged her hands into its guts, ripping out gears and metal rods, shredding her flesh to destroy it.

A low black shape came crawling up the stairs and sniffed him out, baring teeth and pinning Henry against the wall in the dark. It was a dog, its side ripped open by a car. It wasn't dead yet, or not completely. Its eyes shone blue with ghost-light, and it spoke with a dog's tongue through broken teeth.

"You're lost," it said. "Let me help you."

"I came to find a ghost."

"You found one." The dog's flanks heaved with fast, feverish breath.

Henry leaned back from the sour mouth. "I made the pig people. They'll take over the plant eventually and lay everyone off. The whole town's going to collapse. I need a ghost to help me fix things."

The ripple of a snarl passed over its muzzle. It bobbed toward him and away, like it was struggling to hold itself back. "I'm always looking for a new body to carry me around. I go through them so fast."

Henry could barely speak, desperate and scared, his chest heaving. This was a mistake. But what else could he do?

"If you want me, you can have me," he said. "Any ghost would be better than none."

The dog sat back on its flank and lolled its tongue, seeming to laugh. "I'll need a way in. Show me that you can be who I need you to be."

"What do I have to do?" Henry asked.

"You have to kill," the ghost said. "You have to fight and hurt. Show me you can do that, and I'll make you strong."

It lay down in front of him, turning the gash in its side toward Henry.

"Kill," the ghost said, "and eat."

Henry was disgusted, horrified that he was even talking to this thing. But the ghost was already washing over him. It swarmed, hot and angry, through his head. The world had taken everything from him. Shouldn't he take something back? Shouldn't he hurt something, be strong for once? He pressed his hands to the dog's wound, digging his fingers into its side.

The dog leapt at him, snapped its jaws around his arm. Blood washed over its snout.

Henry screamed and hit it with his free hand, his glasses tumbling to the floor.

"Good," the ghost said. It was somewhere near his ear now, not in him but not in the dog, either. It was close. "Earn me."

The dog had been nearly dead, only the presence of the ghost keeping it on its feet. It bit into his arm with the last of its strength, and died. Henry tore out a piece of meat from its wound. It stank of rot and blood. He opened his mouth, ready to receive the ghost like communion, to be transformed —

Someone slapped the meat out of his hand and lifted him up. He fought back, terrified but also angry, the ghost lingering on his shoulders furious at having been interrupted. The figure twisted his injured arm, bringing tears to his eyes. Henry was dragged downstairs and rolled out the window, jerked up from the pavement and pulled along dark streets.

Outside in the moonlight, he saw that it was his scarred father who held him. Henry's arm burned where the dog had bitten him, was probably getting infected. The last traces of the ghost's influence faded like smoke leaving his lungs.

"I almost ate that. I almost let that thing inside me. I was so stupid. Why did I come here?"

His father looked straight ahead, not giving any indication that Henry was there. But he held his son's arm, keeping him close.

All the fear of the last two days passed over Henry — waking up without his ghost, seeing the boys grab Dennis in the cafeteria, the ghost girl saying that he had done horrible things, the violent ghost that he'd almost let inside his body, this unknowable person dragging him down the stairs in the dark. He pressed the fist of his good hand into his mouth and bit down on it, closed his eyes, and let his father lead him. He walked mechanically, focusing on his hand so that he wouldn't collapse.

· · ·

I'm okay, he texted his sister. *Dad found me. We're almost home.*

They were only a few blocks away. This late at night, the streets boiled with ghosts, a river flowing up to the plant. Shapes half formed of flesh and fog went along the roads on their strange errands. His father held Henry against his side, and the ghosts passed without noticing them. A rusted police cruiser drifted shark-like down the road. Henry didn't know if it was living or dead.

At home, Jane stood framed in the light of the open doorway. She ran out and hugged Henry. Their father started to back away into the dark, but Jane grabbed his hand.

"Come inside," she said. "Please. Just for a minute."

Henry followed the two of them in, grateful that his sister would be too distracted with their father to ask him what he had been doing. She glanced back at him, her withering look letting Henry know that she had read his mind. Above their heads, the laser array sliced open the sky.

In the living room, their mother sat on the couch. The robot lay at her feet, eyes boring into Henry's father. The man stood just inside the room, his eyes flickering to take in the familiar space. He held himself tense, up on the balls of his feet, like he might run at any moment.

"What's he doing here?" their mother asked. Brutal heat came off of her, making the air shimmer.

Jane squeezed her father's hand. "Henry was an idiot and almost got himself killed. Dad saved him."

Henry looked at the floor. She'd already pulled the whole story out of his head. He was relieved at least that there was nothing left to talk about.

"Your father won't stay," their mother said.

"He might," Jane said. "He remembers us. This proves it." She wouldn't let go of his hand, though.

Outside, there was a roaring as if a plane flew overhead. Henry pulled aside the curtains and looked out the front window.

Something fell through the sky. It burned hot and scintillating, flashing white and blue. It looked like it was falling toward them, into the cradle of red laser light. Whatever his ghost's device had been signaling, it had finally arrived.

"We need to get out of the house," Henry said.

Jane came to stand beside him. "What is it?"

The light streaked toward the ground in an arc. It left a crackling tail behind it. Something about radiation and exotic matter teased at the corners of Henry's mind. It was hard to estimate the object's size. They should leave, but Henry knew that it was already too late.

On the road outside, Bethany came jogging by the house. She stopped in front of their yard, looking up. The laser array painted her skin red.

"Bethany!" Henry yelled. "Run away!"

The roar of the falling light drowned him out. The frenetic array painted the world crimson, drenching the houses and lawns bloody. Above, the sun-bright sphere curved down like a scythe, its coming a wail that split the sky. They could only stare up and wait, the glow burning their eyes and making phantom copies multiply in reds and pinks and blues across their peripheral vision.

The wind from its fall rippled Bethany's hair and shirt. The alien spark was basketball-sized, the sound of it shattering, like lightning sliding across lightning. Bethany stared up as it fell. While Henry called to her from the window, waiting for the impact that would surely annihilate them in a tidal wave of heat and light, Bethany did what she had always done when a ball fell within reach of her hands. She raised her arms and caught it.

PART II

THE FALLING ALIEN glow lit up the yard like an electric sun. Jane's ghost blew around the room, drinking up the family's terror and wonder. Outside, Bethany stood on the rippling grass, circles of light and shadow ringing her like a target. They all shouted for her to run. Instead, she raised her arms to the sky.

In the moment the alien glow slammed into her, Jane's ghost was with Bethany. It was over in an instant. The street went dark again, and the air turned warm and still. Jane blinked, unable to see after the wash of intense light. The house hadn't been harmed. They were alive. Everything was fine.

Her ghost returned to Jane with everything that Bethany had felt in her moment of contact. The girl looking up to see light shining red through her raised hands, like she was made of glass. Her skin tightening with the sudden shock of heat. The alien sphere spinning as fast as the blade of a saw against her palms.

But Bethany had not been afraid. It had not occurred to her that this was impossible. She leapt for the alien light like it was hers, snatching it out of the air, her muscles and skin straining against it. Between Bethany's ribs, an amphitheater of spirits roared, their hands raised with hers, animated by their belief that there was nothing this girl couldn't do.

The light had crashed down through Bethany's arms like a comet, cratering itself in her chest, breaking up and leaving fragments of heat and light all through her. Bethany looked down at her hands and found that she was whole.

Jane ran outside with her family to make sure that Bethany wasn't hurt. The light was gone, but Bethany's hands still glowed white. Henry's machine had brought this, whatever it was. Her ghost probed his mind, wanting to know what he'd been trying to do. As usual, he wasn't sure himself.

She isn't haunted, Jane's ghost said. *Well, not any more than usual. The falling light wasn't a ghost.*

Bethany stretched her arms, took a deep breath, bounced on her toes. "I feel fine. My hands are a little warm, but they don't hurt." She held out her palms, the alien light bleeding away until her hands were empty and clean.

"Was it an alien?" Jane asked. "Or some kind of satellite?"

Henry didn't look at her. He was tired, ashamed. Worried he might have hurt his best friend.

Their mother went inside with the robot. Their father was gone, vanishing just as the wash of light had descended. Jane walked to the edge of the yard, looking up and down the street, but there was no sign of him.

"Can we give her a ride home?" Henry asked his sister.

"I'm fine," Bethany said. "I need to finish my run."

"You should go to the doctor," Jane said.

Bethany shook her head. "I don't really get sick. Whatever that was, I'll be fine. I'll see you at school, Henry." She turned and started jogging home.

Jane could feel that Bethany was disappointed. When she had reached up for the ball of light, spinning so hot and fast, she had hoped that it would somehow transport her far from Swine Hill. Or, if it left her behind, that its hot light might burn away her weight of ghosts. The alien had come like destiny, and Bethany had expected it to change her. Instead, nothing. Jane was in awe of how reckless — how confident — the girl was.

Henry stared after Bethany, listening to her feet pound the asphalt. Ghosts rose pale and thick along the sides of the streets, but Bethany didn't fear them. At the end of the street, she was illuminated for a moment by the porch light from one of the pigs' houses. As she turned the corner, Jane saw Bethany stumble for just a moment. She recovered and kept going, but Henry had noticed. Terror spread through his chest, rising high within him like a storm. What had he done?

Last night, Jane had pushed Henry's junk aside to put down a stack of blankets beside his bed. The floor was hard under her, and she woke up with pain in her back and neck. A busted air-conditioning unit pressed against her arm, and a dead vacuum cleaner lay at her feet. Her ghost could feel the pulsing of spirits inside those machines, walking the endless roads of copper coil looped around the motors. The spirits didn't know how small and lost they'd become. The ghost swelled in her, aching for them, fearing for itself.

Henry had woken up before Jane. He sat at his desk, a screwdriver flashing in his hand. He bounced its tip on the wood, frustrated.

Jane asked her ghost why it hadn't woken her up.

He wasn't thinking about hurting himself. You needed sleep. And sometimes I like to be alone.

Her ghost wanting to be alone was so ridiculous that Jane laughed. Henry turned in his chair to frown at her. The spirit never wanted to be alone. It was always talking, always listening, a manic and fast-burning bird of fire swooping through her mind. It barely let her think.

When you're asleep, it's easier to hear other ghosts. Especially the ones that have almost faded away. If I don't listen to them, who will?

"You don't have to sleep in my room," Henry said. "We're both too old for that. It's gross."

Jane sat up, her limbs sore. "You're just afraid I'll hear you thinking about perverted things. It's not like I haven't before."

Henry focused on the problem in front of him. He listed the parts in his mind, trying to solve the puzzle of them. *Pin drum. Fan fly. Comb. Chain pulley.*

"When I'm sure you aren't going to hurt yourself, I'll sleep in my room again."

Henry put down his screwdriver and tensed. Jane's ghost brought her a stream of images. The dark stairwell. The dog with broken teeth. Some invisible and heavy thing winding around his shoulders, speaking into his ear. His hands full of rotting meat.

"I wasn't trying to hurt myself. I didn't want to die."

He's lying. Whether he knows it or not.

"Why else would you go downtown? Into the most haunted place you could find?"

"I didn't want to be me. I needed to be more than that. But I guess this is all I have."

His bloody hands, the smell of the dog's breath, his stomach clenching when he realized what he'd almost done. *He's horrified. He can't believe he was so stupid, but he also can't believe he was such a coward. It's tearing him apart.*

"You don't have to enjoy it so much," Jane said.

Henry raised an eyebrow.

"Talking to my ghost."

"At least you still have one."

Their mother pulled into the driveway. The trunk popped open, and Jane went to the window with Henry, watching their mom unload a wheelchair and take it inside.

She got it for the robot. So he can get around better.

"Glad to see she cares about someone in this house," Jane said.

Does she? If you only love things that love you back, do you really love anyone but yourself?

There was a twinkling melody, tiny chimes playing a sad tune. Henry opened his hands and revealed the music box, pink flowers garlanding the porcelain.

"You fixed it. See, you didn't even need a ghost."

"It was just dirty and old. I cleaned the case and tightened some screws. Not exactly a miracle."

"Still, that's something. You don't have to save the world."

"Bethany texted me this morning. Says she feels a little off. She's coming over so we can do some tests."

He's thinking about radiation, damaged DNA, exotic matter, cancer. He has no idea what's coming, and he's afraid.

"This is Bethany we're talking about," Jane said. "Whatever it is, she'll beat it."

The laser array on top of the house had shut down after the alien light fell. It stuck out from the roof, lightless and dead, no doubt swimming with ghosts. Jane watched Bethany do sprints in their yard while Henry made notes.

Bethany dug in to her run, shoulders forward and head down. She moved slowly, like she stood at the bottom of a lake. And she ran at a slant, as if the ground under her wasn't level. She gritted her teeth and sweat, ripping up chunks of grass in a pair of running cleats, her ponderous steps throwing turf into the air.

"Did something happen to her ghosts?" Jane asked.

They're the same as always. Just like her. Obsessed with reps and weights and protein powders. They haven't gone anywhere. They are frustrated, though. They aren't used to things being this hard.

Henry had her run sprints, blow bubbles through a straw until she felt lightheaded, and throw darts at a target with one eye closed. He had her hold a compass, and complete a low voltage circuit with her fingertip, and he measured the strength of cell phone signals near her body. She did pushups and crunches, and though she could do just as many as always, she said that it felt harder now. Still, he couldn't find anything wrong.

Every time Bethany asked him a question, he looked at the ground and said, "I'm not sure" or "I don't know yet" or "We'll figure it out."

Jane's phone buzzed, and she wondered if it would be Trigger. She still didn't know what to say to him. She understood why he hadn't listened to the CD. Her ghost made sure that she understood other people's feelings. But knowing why he was afraid to lose his ghost didn't make her any less angry with him.

The buzzing was only her alarm, letting her know that it was time to leave for work.

She asked her ghost what Bethany was thinking. Was she secretly excited, thrilled for some new obstacle to throw herself against, ready to prove that she could beat even an alien?

No. She's wondering if this is what losing feels like.

"Henry, I'll be back after work. Don't do anything dumb."

His mind flickered with the pigs working in the factory, the alien light falling, Dennis and the dancing girl, the warehouse full of violent ghosts.

He sighed and a wave of regret rippled through him. "Well. We both know I won't be doing anything smart."

13

JANE HAD NEVER seen so many cars at the grocery store. They filled all the available parking spaces and made new spots at the ends of rows. People parked off the street nearby and walked. The vehicles were rust-spotted, had different-colored fenders and hoods, sat unevenly on mismatched tires. Jane parked around by the dumpster and walked in through the back of the store.

There were people in the storeroom, digging through the produce cooler for heads of cabbage or sacks of fruit. When Jane walked through the vinyl flaps and into the fluorescent glow of the store, the tile was covered with torn boxes and spilled breakfast cereal. People grabbed armloads of packages and dropped them into overflowing carts. Some shepherded two or three carts at a time.

She could feel her ghost's glee, how it knew something Jane didn't and was holding back to savor the secret.

"I give up," Jane said. "What the hell is going on?"

The owner ran ads in the paper. He's closing the store. Selling off everything at a huge discount. After today, there won't be a grocery store in Swine Hill.

"He didn't tell me. What about my job?"

Her ghost wasn't paying attention. She fed Jane a stream of anxiety and panic. The closest grocery store was more than forty minutes east on the highway. Some people didn't have cars. They'd be shopping at gas stations or the tiny drugstore from now on.

Down one of the aisles, Hogboss pushed a train of five carts. Stray cans and boxes slipped from their mounded tops and left a trail behind him. People got out of his way, some because they were afraid of his size and some because they were repulsed by him.

They blame him for the store closing.

"That's stupid."

Is it? The owner thinks the pigs came here for him. The ghosts of pork roast and tenderloin. He has nightmares about dead animals clawing up from the meat coolers to kill him. He thinks about it all the time. So now he's leaving.

"He's afraid of everything. Even me."

At the front, lines backed up in every checking lane. There were no more bags, so the cashiers just put the groceries loosely in shopping carts. Thought after flashing thought cut through Jane's mind. She'd never been around so many people at once before. She could track Hogboss through the store by how the thoughts shifted. An invisible thunderhead, a spot of pressure and violence, followed him.

"Aren't you going to help?" asked Kathryn, one of the day checkers. She was possessed by the ghost of her dead husband, Jerry, and talked to herself all the time. She wore his nametag instead of her own.

"Why?" Jane asked. "Tomorrow, none of us will have a job. Maybe we should be stocking up on groceries too."

Kathryn and her husband started arguing about it, and Jane walked away, wanting the couple's thoughts out of her head.

When Hogboss came back to the front, Jane waved him over to the manager's booth and checked him out there. He held up a package of sandwich cookies. "Dennis says that he's a vegetarian now. He won't eat anything I cook for him. Do you think he'll eat this?"

He's talking about his son, a pig boy who goes to school with Henry. Hogboss actually thinks your brother will keep him safe. Isn't that sad?

Jane made a note to ask her brother about Dennis, then looked at the ingredients on the cookies. "I don't think there are any animal by-products in this. Not a lot of plants in it either. Just trash."

Hogboss seemed relieved.

After he paid with his Pig City charge account, Jane helped him push the overflowing carts outside. Customers watched her go. *Special treatment for the pigs,* they thought. *What about us? What will we do without a grocery? Will that girl finally leave? Better take her broken little family with her when she goes.*

Jane and Hogboss dumped the groceries in the back of his truck bed, almost filling it.

"Thank you for being so kind," Hogboss said. "We don't have many friends in town. People still haven't gotten used to us."

People will never get used to them. He knows that, deep down.

"I'm sorry to ask, but I need a favor. The store's closing. Everywhere in town is cutting jobs."

Hogboss put his hands in his pockets, the denim stretching around his broad fingers. "Corporate doesn't want us hiring. We have so many pigs working now and more starting every day."

"Maybe you have something temporary?"

He shook his head, but he wasn't thinking about her question. Something else was on his mind, a mosaic of smells and memories from the pig houses, his earliest memories before Henry had reshaped his mind.

"I've been watching the pigpens," he said. "How we manage the animals. You know, I might never have met my son. There's no reason to introduce a boar to its offspring. I read that in the wild a boar might even kill his own piglets so the sow will go back into heat. Without Henry, I wouldn't know Dennis. Isn't that amazing?"

Don't turn around. Don't meet his eyes.

Jane could hear the police car slipping up behind them, could feel the fist-pounding anger of the officer watching her talk to the pig man.

Of course, he recognized her. He would blame all of them, her whole family. The store closing was just further proof.

Hogboss kept speaking, unaware of the danger they were in. "I suppose I owe your brother a lot," he said. "Hop in the truck and ride with me up to the plant. Maybe I do have a job for you."

"I had wanted Henry to help me with this," Hogboss said. "But he said that he doesn't know how to speak to machines anymore."

He showed Jane into a dusty and claustrophobic room with a bank of security monitors. The screens had error messages. Some trembled with static. Jane could feel the ghosts of old plant workers caught in the equipment. A tired spirit, wandering back and forth across one of the monitors as a flicker of light, wanted desperately to go home.

He's been in there for years.

"I'm too clumsy for this sort of work," Hogboss said. He held up one of his dinner-plate hands, blunt fingers splayed apart.

Jane crawled under the desk and unhooked some of the ghost-fouled cables. "Do you have more of these somewhere? Or could you get more?"

Hogboss took them away.

She cobbled together enough working parts to get one of the video feeds working again. It showed a corner of one of the pig houses. People came to give the pigs shots, to open sacks of feed, and to hose out the stalls. They took the biggest ones away for slaughter.

Jane connected the same feed to all of the monitors so she could pick out which screens were still working. Pigpens covered the wall in front of her. She rewound the tape, watching a day's worth of work speed by. A woman sat on the floor by one of the pens and stayed too long. It was Jane's mother. She fed the pigs from her hands, like they were pets.

She misses being able to touch someone without hurting them. At least the pigs don't flinch from her.

Jane felt ashamed and angry, wishing she could hide the feeling from her ghost, but she had no privacy from it.

Hogboss came back into the room carrying a bundle of new cables.

"I'm pretty much done," Jane said. "Too bad it only took me an afternoon. Did you have anything else you needed me to do?"

"I talked to HR," Hogboss said. "We can keep you on for a few months at least. You'll monitor plant operations from here and let me know if you see anything strange."

Before Jane could thank him, Hogboss pointed at the video feeds, the image of the kneeling woman repeated ten times.

"I remember her," he said. "From before Henry worked on me." He touched one of the screens, and the image shattered into static until he took his hand away.

"That's my mom," Jane said. "She isn't always this nice. Honestly, she's a bit hard to live with."

"Your mother? Wait here." Hogboss left the office again.

"What was that about?" Jane asked.

He was thinking about a field behind the factory. There are wildflowers growing in the waste runoff there.

"Flowers? Why?" Jane turned back to the video, trying to understand. The picture was grainy, but it looked like her mother was talking to the pigs. She let her arm hang in the pen, scratching their heads. They pressed their soft snouts into her palm.

Hogboss came back holding a bouquet of flowers he'd just picked. They had a faint chemical smell from the ditch behind the factory, and gray dirt still clung to their roots. "Please," Hogboss said, "give these to your mother. Tell her that I — Tell her that we all appreciate her very much."

He left wiping his eyes and leaving Jane holding the flowers.

Oh, the big dumb pig, her ghost said. *I think he's in love with her.*

Back home, Jane put the flowers in a vase and left them on the kitchen table. The robot sat tall in the secondhand wheelchair, narrowing its glowing eyes at her. She could feel her mother lying in bed and watching TV and Bethany holding in her anger while Henry tried to help her.

When Jane went upstairs, she heard Bethany say, "You're looking at the Wikipedia page for acute radiation syndrome. Even without a ghost, you can do better than this."

Jane found the music box on her dresser. She wound the key and let it play, making sure that it worked before she put it in her pocket.

He might hate you. This could be how you lose him.

She ignored her ghost and went back outside to where Trigger waited in his work truck. He'd given her a ride back from the plant after Hogboss stranded her without her car. It was growing dark out, but Trigger had the night off. Like most other people, his hours were being cut.

He drove her back toward the store to pick up her car, not saying much. More people than usual sat on their porches or drove aimlessly, full of nervous energy, nothing to do and nowhere to go. Swine Hill was trembling, on the verge of something violent.

The truck was cold. Trigger concentrated on the road so that she couldn't read his thoughts, but her ghost caught fragments. Guilt, anger, and desire. He wanted her, kept thinking about the afternoon spent in his bed, but he was afraid he'd already ruined things. His self-loathing was the skeleton the rest of him hung on.

The grocery store was dark. Jane's car was the only one in the lot. Inky shapes stepped through the locked doors and windows, ghosts flooding the empty store, full of anger that another piece of the town had crumbled. By the front door, the murky figure of the ghost who had been shot lay in front of the doors, still crying out for help. At the corner of the building, Jane thought she saw her father for a moment, just a glimmer of motion and then gone. Trigger pulled up beside her car and waited, unsure what would happen next.

He'll take you there, her ghost said. *If you ask him. He'd do anything for you right now.*

"Where did it happen?" Jane asked. "The place where your brother died?"

The inside of the cab sparkled with frost under the console's glow. He ran the heat to keep the windshield clear, but every time he exhaled, it was like winter itself came pouring out of his mouth. Jane clenched her teeth and held herself for warmth.

"Oh." He gestured south of the town, toward the freeway that carried Pig City meats into the world. "Less than an hour away. Not far."

"Do you ever go back there?"

"I used to. I'm not sure why. That place is always near." He picked up a star of leaves stuck together with ice that had grown in the space between them.

"I'd like to see it. Maybe it would help me understand."

Her ghost expanded in her, wide and smiling like the moon. It loved when Jane told a lie.

"Okay." Trigger put the truck in drive and pulled out of the lot. "If you think it would help."

The sun went down, and ghosts rose hissing and thick out of the wreckage of the city. Trigger drove away from town. Spirits on their way to work at the pork-processing plant bloomed in the headlights like fog. As soon as they joined the highway, the cloud of ghosts vanished.

They passed through a small town where billboards had faded to white. The old brick buildings had been gutted and stripped down to their foundation. They passed through the whole thing — a scattering of houses, some churches, a school — in less than a minute. A green sign, choked with ivy, read, WELCOME TO DALEVILLE: CITY OF PROGRESS.

"Are there any ghosts here?" Jane asked. She pulled her legs against her chest, rubbing them with her hands.

"Just the ones we bring with us," Trigger said.

There are a few. Deep in the oldest buildings. In houses sunken into the woods. Every place has its hauntings.

Soon they were out in the country, following asphalt that slowly disintegrated into gravel. Trees closed in tall and dark on both sides. The road plunged down into a wooded valley, and the stars were swept away by the long-fingered hands of trees.

They turned down an old logging track, the truck rocking back and forth over the uneven dirt. Tall weeds battered the front of the truck, tinkling like rain against the bumper. Inside the cab, the windows grew milky with ice, narrowing what they could see.

His ghost knows where we are. This is exactly what it wants, for Trigger to remember what he did.

Trigger took a flashlight out of the back of the truck and led Jane through the woods. The leaves died and whitened as they passed, and the air cut her skin. All around them, his ghost bent late spring back to winter.

There was no danger of them getting lost. Droplets of blood guided them between the trees. There were echoes of distant gunfire, a teasing at her ears like voices shouting far away. Animals crashed through the leaves nearby, fleeing the icy breath that blew into their dens. After being inside his house, Jane found this place familiar.

Trigger stopped in a clearing between the trees and gestured with his flashlight. The beam passed over weeds shrinking in the cold. There was a bloody patch of ground here. He tried to speak, but his voice broke. Taking a deep breath, he said, "Well. This is where I killed him."

His ghost is lonely. It wants to be held.

Jane nodded. She didn't think his ghost would be that complicated. Most spirits weren't.

There was a flare of outrage and disgust from Jane's ghost. *Just do what you're going to do.*

She pulled the music box out of her pocket. When Trigger's flashlight beam found its shape, the porcelain box looked like a ball of snow.

"That was my mom's," he said. "It's broken. Why do you have it?"

Jane wound the key and set the music box in his hand. Inside, a tiny brass drum turned. Teeth struck keys. Soft music rose from his palm.

Memories—whether from Trigger, his ghost, or both of them—washed through him like floodwaters. They swept away all sense of where he was, bringing him back years and years ago to when his family had been whole. He sank to his knees, cupping the box in both hands. His chest glowed with blue light.

Slowly, the ghostly face of his brother leaned out of Trigger's skin. Its eyes were wide and afraid, staring into the box. The ghost stretched its small arms out of Trigger and reached down. Serpent-like, it poured its body out of him and coiled into the porcelain.

Trigger dropped the box on the ground. It pulsed with cold, making the ground beneath it tighten and crack. A warm wind blew out of the trees and through the clearing, dispersing the chill air. Jane touched Trigger's shoulder, feeling heat in his skin.

"He left me," Trigger said.

"Wind the key. Keep it playing."

She used the heavy metal end of his flashlight to gouge out a hole in the spot where moments before the ground had been soaked with blood. Tiny roots crisscrossed like netting, making it slow and hard. She dug the hole as deep as she could. Beside her, Trigger unloaded his mind to her ghost, full of hope and fear.

Jane picked up the music box, wound its key one last time, and set it inside the hole. It was freezing to the touch, shocking her arm up to the shoulder. She kicked dirt back over the box and pressed the ground flat with her shoe.

"Come on." She pulled Trigger away through the trees, following the flashlight's tunnel of light. "In case it changes its mind."

Trigger was in pieces. Sweat bled out on his neck and under his arms, wetting his back. He wasn't used to heat. He was amped up, excited and free, but he was also angry. He didn't like that she could keep secrets while knowing everything about him. He didn't like that this choice had been hers instead of his.

The truck appeared ahead of them, and Jane walked Trigger around to the passenger side.

"The metal." He passed his hand over the lip of the truck bed. "It's so hot. I forgot what that felt like."

Jane got in the driver's side and moved the seat up. There wasn't room to turn around on the narrow track, so she backed out, watching the road behind her in the red glow of the truck's taillights.

Trigger rolled down the window, letting the air rush over his arm. "You should have told me what you were going to do."

Jane sighed. "You never would have said yes. Your ghost wouldn't have let you."

"I don't know how I'll tell my dad. He's going to feel like we abandoned my brother."

"It has your mother's memory to haunt. Maybe it needed to get away from you so that it could move on."

"What if it can't move on? What if it's just stuck there, alone with that memory?" And in his mind, *What if I can't move on either?*

Jane backed onto the main road and started for home. She squeezed his hand. "Things are going to be better now."

Her ghost circled behind her eyes, full of pity for Jane and Trigger both. *Do you believe that? Do you really think things are so easy?*

14

ENRY STAYED UP late with Bethany reading articles on his computer and sketching out ideas on a whiteboard. He swabbed the lip of her water bottle and magnified the saliva and stray cheek cells under his microscope. The cells looked like ragged eggs, a yolky nucleus lying at their center. And there, suspended in the nucleus, Henry saw a faint shimmer of light. The alien light Bethany had caught was still inside her, buried in every cell of her body.

Finally, he sent her home with a list of tests for the doctor to run tomorrow. She couldn't actually leave town to go to the hospital, but there was a walk-in clinic in Swine Hill. He wanted brain scans and radiation measurements, but he doubted they would be able to do much more than draw blood and send it off for testing. Still, it was better than nothing.

He tried to get a few hours of sleep, but his mind kept stumbling through the ruins of half-remembered equations. He watched the red numbers on the face of his clock count down the night. Finally, Henry sat up in bed and fumbled for his glasses — his ghost's glasses, worn by the spirit when it was alive. They were old with delicate metal frames, sitting loose on his face. He needed, more than anything, to find his ghost.

He went to the stairwell, grabbed the hanging string, and pulled down the attic stairs. He switched on the light and went to the farthest corner, where a pile of boxes from the house's old occupants sagged apart, spilling tongues of yellowed cloth and dingy photos. There was an old TV and VCR, a stack of family videos, their ribbons of tape too snarled to play. This was the first place he had seen the ghost, back when he was only a child.

He went through the boxes as he had many times before. There was a young girl in ballet tights. An older woman giving the camera a sad smile. In only a few did he see the man wearing his silver glasses, always looking down or away, his hands busy with some broken thing in his lap. Why had this strange man haunted him in the first place? And why had he left?

He fell asleep on the floor of the attic for a while. A soft thump against his cheek, quiet and regular, woke him. Something moved under the boards. He pressed his hand to the wood, feeling it rise to bump against his palm. At first he thought it might be an animal, a rat or squirrel lost inside the house. But it was too even, too regular. It sounded like a machine.

He went to the garage and dug around in his father's toolbox for a hammer. Henry had been the only one to use those tools for years, but he still thought of them as his father's. Through them, he could know something of the man who had left when he was so young. Henry went back up to the attic and pried up the wooden floor, finding a stack of papers hidden between the ceiling joists. He brushed them aside and uncovered the source of the vibration. It was a wooden box slightly bigger than a fist.

He pulled it out, the lid straining against its latch, and opened it. On a bed of green felt lay a human heart. It was brown and dry to the touch. The heart was covered in electrodes, their wires snaking off into the secret workings inside the box. The organ should have been long dead, but the small genius of the box had kept it alive. The heart beat slow but steady. Had Henry made the box? And who did the heart belong to?

He gathered up the heart box and as many of the papers as he could carry, taking them down to his room. Spreading them on the floor, he tried to make sense of it. The manuscript was typed, the ink half faded, and it was heavily annotated in pencil. The technical was mixed with the personal. The author's name — his ghost — was Neilson. Anecdotes about Neilson's two unhappy daughters were woven in with facts about pain tolerance, nerve signals, the relationship between psychological and physical pain. Exploded diagrams of machines covered page after page, factory-sized behemoths with thousands of numbered parts, most of it crossed out in frustration. Neilson had been trying to build something.

Long letters to himself, like diary entries, covered the back of Neilson's notes. He logged the times he had been asked to leave restaurants and hardware stores for causing a disturbance. The times his car broke down and police had stopped him walking to work. How the plant only employed him part-time, the hours chaotic, his pay always late. His inability to protect his daughters from illness, hunger, and violence. Neilson wrote about a helpless anger that smoldered for decades. He tried to turn it into numbers and degrees, to quantify his hate.

Henry skimmed the pages, a repeated phrase jumping out at him: *pain engine.* It didn't surprise him that Neilson had wanted to make a machine that ran off pain. Suffering had been more plentiful for the man than sunlight, could animate the world in ways that electricity never could. Still, the thought was chilling. Maybe it was best that the ghost wasn't lurking inside him anymore.

There was no mention of the strange heart in any of the notes. His alarm went off and he sighed. What was the point of going to school? His teachers hadn't taken him seriously even when he'd been haunted by the genius ghost. Now that he'd lost it, they might even be pleased, happy to see him sink to the low bar they'd set for him. No one there was going to do a thing to help him.

He got dressed and zipped up his backpack anyway. He might not want to be there, but he couldn't leave Dennis alone. Until he convinced the pig boy that the school wasn't safe, Henry would have to look out for him.

On his way out the door, Henry saw the robot slumped over in its wheelchair, like it was sleeping. He turned on the lamp and snapped his fingers in its face. It lifted one arm and moved one leg, trying to straighten itself. A spark of light flashed from the joints of its chest cavity. Most likely there was a short in its wiring, or some part of it was finally too haunted to work anymore. In his pocket, the heart thumped in its box. He wished he could put it inside the robot, let it feel the kind of pain that would make it enough for his mother. He wished he could do anything at all to help his shattered family.

"As soon as I get home, I'll fix you. I'll figure something out."

The robot grabbed one of its wheels with its working arm and turned itself around, facing away from him. Henry went out to wait for the bus, wondering how something he had made could hate him so much.

Henry climbed on the bus and saw Dennis sitting alone in the back. As usual, they were the oldest. As poor as the town was, most teenagers had a busted old car or access to a Pig City work truck. They'd rather pack themselves three and four deep across a truck cab than ride the bus like children. They drove without licenses or insurance, their vehicles worthless anyway, the police too understaffed and buried in their ghosts to care much about traffic violations.

The younger kids leered at Dennis over their seatbacks and pushed up the tips of their noses with grubby fingers, giving themselves snouts. The pig boy looked straight to the front like he didn't notice.

Henry started to sit next to the pig boy when he noticed Dennis wearing heavy eye shadow in ragged bands, his long ears drooping with piercings. He wasn't wearing a baggy shirt and jeans like usual. A dancer's leotard looped over his shoulders and stretched down his torso and legs, as tight as skin.

"Don't you know anything about high school?" Henry asked. "You stand out enough as it is. Are you trying to get killed?"

"Krystal — the ghost girl — she says I could be a dancer. She's going to teach me."

"That ghost is going to get you murdered."

"I'm not scared."

Henry sighed and pushed the sagging glasses up his nose. "There's nothing wrong with being scared. There's a lot to be afraid of."

Last week, the coach complained that Dennis's hands weren't the right shape for a basketball, so Dennis had been moved to the laughing room for first period. Henry didn't say so, but he thought it was probably for the best.

They entered the shrieking classroom and pulled headphones out of their bags to block out the ghostly laughter. Dennis stood in the back, stretching and doing dance exercises. The other students watched him all period, ghosts burning in their eyes.

When the girl who was always late floated into the room — Henry thought her name was Erica — she froze at the sight of Dennis doing toe touches in the back of the room. She stared at the pig boy, her eyes wide and bright. Something about the sharpness of her face, the thinness of her limbs, made Henry think of origami. She left, letting the door pull itself shut behind her.

Henry took his binder of Gifted problems from the teacher and sat down. He switched on the CD of music Jane had left for him, this one full of sad songs, regrets and apologies, her way of emphasizing how sorry she was.

He lost himself in the math for a while, pages thorny with dense differential equations, variables nested within variables. In the flat world of numbers and graphs, the answers were clear and he was in control. It was nice to remember that he was good at something, haunted or not.

He had no time for the English and philosophy questions, paragraphs asking him to reflect on power and responsibility. Why was it that people without power were always blamed for what was wrong? Thinking about it only made him feel helpless and tired.

He turned the pages over to their clean backs and started writing down everything he understood about Bethany and the alien. It came from a corner of space dark and swept clean of stars. It was made of heat and light, held together by a powerful magnetic force. It might be technology, or it might be a living thing. Whatever it was, it was inside her at a cellular level, so integrated with her body that it couldn't be surgically removed. At best, it was changing her. At worst, it was killing her. He had no idea why it had come, what it wanted, or how to make it leave. All he knew was that it was here because of him.

In his pocket, the heart throbbed against his thigh. The rhythm was two beats and a pause, over and over, like it was saying, *Your fault. Your fault. Your fault.*

Between classes, Henry shadowed Dennis, watching the long hallways for any sign that someone might be following them. People got bored, and there weren't enough teachers to keep an eye on everyone. If the wrong person noticed Dennis at the wrong time, he might get destroyed, shoved into a bathroom stall and beaten until he was numb, all of it too quick for him to even know who had done it. Henry was surprised someone hadn't jumped him already.

The pig boy was supposed to be in Algebra II, but Henry followed him to the old drama room, where the ghost girl was waiting for him on the stage. When Henry saw her, he remembered the girl in the attic photo. This was the ghost of Neilson's daughter. How unhappy their family must have been for so many of them to rise as ghosts, desperate to find someone to live out their unfulfilled dreams. Would the same happen to his family if they stayed in Swine Hill?

When she saw Dennis, the ghost girl smiled. Music played from the wreckage of the piano, bright and fast. Dennis stepped on stage and took her hand.

Henry watched the ghost lead the pig boy through the steps. There was a strange grace to Dennis, a lightness that he never would have expected. When Dennis first started coming to this room, Henry thought he had them both figured out. The pig boy, he imagined, must have a hopeless crush on the dead girl. And she must want him for his body, to haunt him, live through him, and accomplish whatever terrible purpose obsessed her. He wasn't sure now. They danced, rocking their shoulders with the music, laughing when Dennis mixed up a step. Maybe they were just lonely. What if all they wanted was this, to dance with each other? He wished Jane was here to read their minds and tell him.

Dennis came over and sat beside Henry, draining a bottle of water. The ghost girl came closer too. Henry drew away from her in spite of himself.

"There's no dance team or anything like that here, so we'll just dance together at prom," Dennis said. "That's about the best we'll be able to do."

Henry didn't go to things like prom. He didn't dance, didn't have money for nice clothes, and didn't want to spend any more time with his classmates than he had to. But if Dennis was going, then he would need to go too. Maybe he could invite Bethany, just as friends. It wasn't her kind of thing either, but maybe for just a night it would take her mind off the alien slowly killing her, the heavy chain of ghosts that tied her to the dying town, all the danger and frustration in Swine Hill that both of them had been living with for years.

"All you want is a dance?" Henry asked. "How long have you been practicing this routine? Years?"

"Decades," the ghost girl said.

Henry turned to Dennis. "Some ghosts are insatiable. They need something, but they can never get enough of it. My sister's ghost needs to know everyone's business. It could have every secret in the world and it would still want more. But other ghosts" — *like mine,* he thought — "they have one thing left to do, and once it's done, they're gone. They vanish."

Dennis looked up at the ghost girl, and she looked away.

"I just want you to know," Henry said. "Ghosts need things from you. They aren't here to be your friend. And sometimes when they get what they want, they leave."

Dennis shrugged. "That's okay. She's been a better friend to me than anyone."

"You remind me of him so much," the ghost girl said to Henry. "I can see why he haunted you. He was so frustrated with everything he couldn't change about himself, so he tried to fix other people. And like you, he only seemed to make things worse."

"What did Neilson do to you?" Henry asked. "Did he use you and your sister in his experiments?"

The ghost girl laughed. "See, Dennis? He says that he's looking out for you, that ghosts only care about themselves. But he's only here to find out why his ghost left."

Dennis gave a sad snort and kicked at the carpet. "I was wondering why you were hanging out with me so much."

"It's not like that," Henry said. "I need my ghost to help you. I need it to help all of the pig people, and now Bethany, too. This isn't about me."

The ghost girl stabbed him in the forehead with her index finger, giving him a jolt of hurt. Her ghostly fingertip slid a centimeter into his skull, teasing at his brain. Spasms of light broke across his eyes.

"Do you miss my father riding around in there?" the ghost asked. "You sad that he's gone? You'd be the first person to ever miss him."

Dennis stepped in between them.

The ghost girl backed away, looking rebuked, not meeting the pig boy's eyes. "My father thought pain was the most plentiful thing in the world," she said. "He wanted to build machines that ran off of it. Making me and my sister unhappy was a research project for him."

Henry felt sick. Maybe there was a reason all of his inventions caused pain. But it was more than just his ghost, wasn't it? The machines had also come from Henry, and he only wanted to help people. There was still so much good they could have done together.

"Do you know why he left me?" Henry's voice broke in spite of himself. It had hurt so much to be abandoned. He hadn't admitted that to anyone, not even Jane. He felt unworthy, stupid, small. He felt cast aside.

She gave him a hard smile. "He didn't care about his own daughters, and I doubt he ever cared about you. At best, you were a tool."

Henry didn't want to believe that, but of course he hadn't known Neilson better than his own daughter. He'd barely known the spirit at all. And the worst part of it — the accusation that his ghost would do what it wanted with no thought for anyone but itself — hadn't Henry been guilty of the same?

HENRY AND DENNIS waited outside for the buses to pull around, packed in with a bunch of underclassmen. The younger kids stared at Dennis, but it was the older ones, the ones who didn't look at Dennis but quietly talked about him, who worried Henry the most.

"I heard someone say that your dad is cutting hours at the plant," Henry said. "Is that true?"

Dennis shrugged. "He just does what Corporate tells him to do. It's not like he has any choice."

Bethany pushed through the crowd, her steps heavy and slow. She had cotton swabs taped to her arm where blood had been drawn. She handed Henry an envelope.

"That was fast," Henry said. "Maybe you should be at home getting some rest? Give your body a chance to recover?"

Her face and shoulders were slick with sweat. "Most of my lab results won't be back for a few days, but I had the doctor write down everything that seemed strange to her. We can start with that. I'm taking the bus to your place so we can keep working."

Henry put his hand to her forehead. Her skin was scorching hot, reminding him for a moment of his mother.

"A hundred and five degrees," Bethany said. "The doctor was surprised I could walk."

"Your immune system might be reacting to it like a virus," Henry said. "Or it might even be waste heat. Just a by-product of all the energy the alien is using to fuse with your body."

Bethany noticed Dennis, the pig boy, glancing awkwardly between them, waiting to be introduced.

"Who's the pig?" she asked. "Did you mess up his life too?"

Her tone was joking, but Henry winced.

Dennis brushed his ears down self-consciously, as if they were bangs. "I'm Dennis. Actually, I think I have a lot to thank Henry for. Sorry I never said that."

Henry looked around, hoping no one had overheard.

The buses pulled around. The three of them piled in the haunted old bus with no driver. They went to the back, each of them sitting sideways across an entire seat. The bus pulled onto the road, and Henry flipped through Bethany's results. He didn't know a lot about medicine and had to look up the values on his phone. There wasn't anything that pointed to a clear problem. Everything was just slightly outside of the normal range.

"You probably don't have old medical records for comparison," Henry said. "You've never been sick. For all we know, your numbers could just be weird because you're you. It might have nothing to do with the alien."

Bethany nodded.

Dennis listened, fascinated by aliens and contamination and things he'd only ever seen on TV. Fascinated too by Bethany, her sheer strength and presence, the closest thing to a mythic hero anyone would ever see. But then he looked to the front of the bus, and Henry saw his ears lift and face go pale.

A group of young men stood up from behind the seatbacks. It was the same group of boys who'd threatened Dennis in the cafeteria, all of them seniors wearing their Pig City coveralls. Henry hadn't been paying attention, hadn't noticed that the boys had followed them onto the bus. Grade school kids leaned over the seats and grinned, waiting to see what would happen next.

The bus picked up speed, in between stops for a few minutes. Bethany moved in front of Henry and Dennis, gesturing toward the emergency exit. "As soon as the bus slows down, jump out the back."

The older boys stepped into the aisle and started walking toward them. "Sit down, Bethany," one of them said. "We're here for the pig and the pig lover. Try to stop us and you'll get hurt."

They gave her knife-blade smiles. Henry didn't need Jane to tell him what they were thinking. Most of them were taller than her. There were more of them. She looked sick and exhausted, her shirt heavy with sweat. Likely, none of them had ever been to one of her games before, had never seen the way she could move. They were thinking that, for all her reputation, she was only a girl. They were thinking that they might enjoy getting their hands on her.

The first guy walked straight into her, putting his arm out like he would sweep her aside. The alien had made Bethany slow and heavy, but she was slow like a steamroller or the fist of a wrecking ball. She grabbed his arm and turned him around, palming his head in one wide hand like it was a basketball. She smashed his face against the bus window. He crumpled to the floor and she kicked him hard, folding him up. The windowpane dripped blood into the empty seat.

The others swarmed forward, tripping over themselves in the narrow aisle or climbing over the seats. The younger kids screamed and cried and laughed. From the front of the bus came murky and overlapping voices shouting, the remains of past bus drivers yelling for everyone to sit down and behave. And then up from the floor came more ghosts, children who had suffered something horrible between those seats, rising to wail their displeasure and fear.

Bethany struck out with her fists, breaking noses and smashing eyes, battering them back and away. The boys grabbed her arms and surrounded her, trying to pull her down, but it was like wrestling with steel. She dropped one after another, throwing her knees and elbows into them in the tight space. They spat blood and tried to stumble away, but the seats hemmed them in. Still, there were too many for Bethany to hold back. They shoved their friends into her and slipped past.

One of the boys grabbed Dennis by his ear, ripping out some of his piercings and making him squeal. Another hit Henry in the face, cracking his glasses against his forehead. A knife appeared in one boy's hand.

Bethany jerked the emergency release and threw the back door open. She shoved Henry and Dennis out of the bus. Henry tumbled through the air, watching the asphalt rise to meet him. He hit the street, the ground punching the wind out of him and scraping his arms and face. They rolled over the blacktop, eventually washing up against the curb.

Gasping, Henry looked up and saw the bus disappearing over a hill, Bethany's silhouette still fighting in the aisle. The boys tried to push through her, but she blocked the door with her body, striking them down and leaving them bleeding and heaped on the floor.

Dennis held his ear and limped to the sidewalk. "She's going to get hurt. We have to help her."

Henry's head rang. A bright flare of light cut through the center of his vision, sunlight catching in the crack of his glasses. By the time he'd caught his breath, Dennis was calling someone.

"Hello?" His voice shook. "Is this the Swine Hill Police Department? I need to report a crime. Some guys from school got on our bus and tried to kill me. They wanted to hurt me because I'm a pig. It was bus number six."

He paused for a moment, listening.

"This is Dennis Hogboss. Yes, Walter Hogboss is my father. Why?"

The heart box in Henry's pocket thumped faster and harder, distracting him, but there was something off about the conversation. Hadn't Jane told him that a police officer had stopped her not long ago? She had been shaken up by it.

"Where am I now?" Dennis looked around, searching for a street sign, though most had fallen down, rusted through, or been stolen.

Henry grabbed the phone out of his hand and turned it off.

"Why did you do that?"

"The cops might be worse than the guys on the bus."

He led Dennis down a side street that ran parallel to the main road. Soon, they saw a police cruiser approaching. Henry pulled Dennis behind an abandoned house, and they huddled under the eaves of the back door, waiting for the squad car to pass.

The hair stood up on the back of his neck. He wondered what he would say if the officer found them hiding here, crouched near a house that wasn't theirs. Would any answer he gave the man be good enough?

Someone had spray-painted a red X across the house's doorway. Dennis turned the doorknob and found that it was unlocked. "Maybe we should wait inside?"

The paint was still wet, dripping down the wood. It looked like a warning. "No," Henry said. "There might be ghosts inside."

Dennis slumped against the side of the house, licking spots of blood off his snout. "Everything is so beautiful outside the plant. But some days, it feels like the whole world wants to hurt me. I didn't think it would be this way."

Henry wondered what Dennis had expected, his first image of the outside world drawn by pharmaceutical commercials, nature documentaries, and cartoons. Around the broken neighborhood, a sea of waist-high grass grew right up to the doors, leafy vines reaching up to pull down the walls of abandoned houses. Henry tried to find the beauty in it, but all he could see was the dull boredom of empty streets, the danger of dark windows.

"Just survive it," Henry said. "When you get old enough, you can go somewhere else." He hoped he wasn't lying. He hoped the pig boy would have some say in his own future, that Hogboss and the plant would let him be what he wanted to be.

After they were sure the police cruiser was gone, the two of them started walking back toward Henry's house, since it was closer than Dennis's. Henry texted Bethany but didn't get an answer. He thought of the knife, the sheer number of them. Could even Bethany win against so many?

They walked for about twenty minutes, the sun bright and hot.

Henry took off his shirt. He'd tried texting Jane and his mother for a ride but had no luck. They were both working at the plant during the day now.

There was a metallic rattle, and the two of them dropped behind a bush. Henry looked through the leaves, searching for the sound. A few houses down, a man dressed in rags and covered in burns stood on the porch of an abandoned house and shook a nearly empty can of spray paint. The heart in Henry's pocket raced against his leg.

"Stay here," Henry said.

Dennis ignored him and followed, not wanting to be left alone. The closer Henry got to his father and the old house — its shattered windows billowing with the shreds of curtains, the inside of it dark and damp like a mouth — the harder the heart box beat in his pocket. His father sprayed an *X* over the door and dropped the can, moving on.

"I think he's marking houses where the ghosts are dangerous," Henry said. "He's trying to protect people."

"Who is he?" Dennis asked. "Do you know him?"

His father limped behind the houses and was gone again. Henry shook his head, burning with shame. "No, I don't know him. Just some homeless guy."

They were almost back to their neighborhood when, across the overgrown yard and between the sagging houses, Henry caught sight of a person walking beside the main road. She was stooped over, struggling to walk. Her hair, long and black, blew across her face like smoke.

"Bethany?"

They ran to catch up with her, looking to see if she was injured. Unlike the two of them — bleeding and arms scraped raw from falling on the road — Bethany was unscratched. Her knuckles and fingers were red with blood, but Henry didn't think it was hers.

Dennis threw his arms around her and thanked her, over and over, crying softly into her shoulder.

"You aren't safe yet," Bethany said. "They aren't going to stop, and I may not be there next time. Henry, you have to do something."

Henry only looked at the ground, ashamed. Everything that had gone wrong led back to him. "There aren't even that many pigs in town yet," he said. "Hundreds more are coming. What are people going to do when the plant lays off everyone human?"

"It's not our fault," Dennis said. "We didn't ask to be made. And we don't have anywhere else to go."

"I don't have my ghost," Henry said. "What am I supposed to do?"

"Try harder," Bethany said. "There's more to you than your ghost."

He nodded, wanting to believe her but terrified it wasn't true.

Henry took the two of them back to his house, hoping that someone would be home to give his friends a ride. Jane's car was gone, still at work, but his mother's car sat in the driveway.

Henry paused before opening the door. "My mom is haunted pretty bad. It's fine. I can't remember a time when she didn't have her ghost. Just don't try to hug her or shake her hand or anything. If she comes close to you, keep your hands in your pockets."

His mother wasn't downstairs. Henry thought he heard the shower running. He was soaked in sweat from the walk, and his legs burned. He limped into the kitchen and got them cold sodas from the fridge. When he came back, Dennis was bent over the robot.

"What's its name?" the pig boy asked.

Henry shrugged. "It's just the robot. I never named it."

Bethany checked her phone. "My parents are going to pick me up later. I would just jog back home, but I feel tired. And dizzy. Nothing looks the way it's supposed to."

"You're having trouble seeing?" Henry asked. "Did you get an eye exam?"

"Everything is clear." Bethany gestured to the window. "But it looks wrong. The colors are different. Sometimes I see buildings or streets that I don't remember being there."

Not knowing what to do about this problem — hallucinations or memory issues — Henry went to the garage for his dad's toolbox and some spare parts. While the other two watched, he opened the robot's chest and replaced lengths of wire and damaged servos. He guessed where ghosts might have accumulated in its systems, rebooting it and restarting processes to flush them out. When he was done, the robot sat up straight and moved both arms. It still couldn't walk, though. Its legs were badly damaged. It would take weeks of hard work to fix everything wrong there, if Henry was even capable of fixing it.

Someone knocked on the door. Henry tensed, wondering if it was the police, an angry neighbor who saw him bring Dennis home, or the group of boys from the bus. Bethany pulled the door open, and there stood Hogboss.

Rather than his usual Pig City work clothes, the pig man wore a pressed blue shirt tucked into black jeans. A tie, straining around his big neck, was looped into a tiny knot at the base of his throat.

"Are you here to give me a ride?" Dennis asked.

"Oh," Hogboss said. "Did you need one?"

Henry's mother came downstairs wearing a black cocktail dress. She froze on the edge of the stairs, looking at the crowd of people in her living room.

"Are you going out?" Henry asked. "Wait, what's going on?"

Bethany laughed, shaking her head. Henry didn't understand until the robot scraped its long fingers over the couch and spit a blast of static.

Since she could touch the pigs at work without hurting them, Henry wondered if she thought it would be safe to date Hogboss. He watched, waiting for his mother to touch the pig man's shoulder or squeeze his hand, waiting for him to flinch in pain. Hogboss held the door for her, and she got in without laying a finger on him. The pig man drove her away in his work truck.

"Should we be worried about this?" Dennis asked.

The robot wheeled itself over to the table and picked up the bouquet of flowers wilting in their vase. Before Henry could ask what it was doing, the machine dashed them against the floor, sending broken glass and water splashing over their shoes.

16

I T HAD BEEN a few days since Jane had taken Trigger's ghost away. Every time she texted him, he was either at work or having endless and circular conversations with his father. Mason asked him, *What happened to your brother? Why did he leave? Is he happy now? What are we supposed to do?* When Jane asked how Trigger felt, he said, "Different." She had hoped for more than that. He was supposed to be happy, to be moving past it. Hadn't years of suffering been enough?

She pulled into his driveway a couple of hours before she had to be at work at Pig City. Trigger and his father had just gotten home from their night shift. She'd texted, *Don't go to bed yet. I want to take you somewhere.*

Text me when you get here and I'll come out, he said. At least it wasn't a no.

Jane got out of her car. The world was golden with early-morning sun, damp and cool and dew-touched. Her ghost stirred within her. *Why doesn't he want you to come inside? Did he go back for the music box? Is there something he doesn't want you to see?*

"He wouldn't do that." Jane kicked at the gravel. Even so, there was no reason she should have to wait outside. She went to the door and knocked twice. When no one answered, she walked in.

The house was transformed. Gone were the howling dark and frost-glazed trees. Gone were the dark-furred animals, the bloody leaves, the cold and gunpowder smell. The house was small and close. Stains and tears fissured the green carpet. There were spiderwebs in the corners, and the furniture was thick with dust.

The two of them sat at the table eating eggs. Mason wiped his eyes, red and wet. Trigger gave her a look of irritation, gone so quick she might have imagined it. Still, it stung.

They're mourning, her ghost said. *As bad as things were, they never felt like he was really dead before now.*

"Hi," Jane said. She sat down in the living room and waited for them to finish eating.

The two of them chewed, swallowed, and clicked their forks against their plates, but they didn't talk with her there. Her ghost netted their thoughts. Trigger was annoyed with Jane for coming inside, but also grateful. He was worn out from talking to his father about this. Mason kept thinking of his dead son, pictured him still bleeding and cold, wondered where he had so suddenly gone after years of haunting. He barely thought of Jane at all, and that at least was a relief.

Trigger finished his food and headed for the door, motioning for Jane to follow. He wanted out of the house before his father got angry about him having company.

They got in the car and buckled their seatbelts without a word. Jane felt tired, wondering if she should have just left him alone. She knew exactly what was in his head, a snarl of frustration and blame, but knowing it only made things harder. She put in a CD of something slow and sad, the singer's voice burning higher and higher, a rocket of grief.

She felt her phone buzz and saw that there was a long message from Henry. She skimmed it. Some kids at school had started a fight with Dennis on the bus. Bethany was seeing things or forgetting things. Their father was marking haunted houses. Something about a heart.

Did you talk to Dad? she wrote back. *Does it seem like he's getting better?*

Trigger radiated frustration, so she put her phone down and pulled out of the driveway.

"Everything okay?" she asked.

"Can't you just read my mind? Don't you know already?"

"Sure, if you want. You don't like Hogboss being in charge of you at work. You're overwhelmed by how different everything feels without your ghost. You're exhausted from your dad asking you questions. And because you can't be angry at anyone else, you're being a dick to me. How's that?"

His frustration collapsed into guilt. Her ghost grinned huge inside her. Everything was mixed up in her head: the ghost's pleasure, Trigger's pain, Jane's love and hurt. She was glad he felt guilty. Trigger still didn't understand how much he had taken from Henry, and he'd been cold and thankless to Jane. It felt good to make him sting, even if she felt gross for enjoying it so much. She focused on the music, trying to separate the ghost's feelings from her own.

"It's fine," Jane said. "It must be really hard to have everything change."

"I'm grateful. I promise I am. It's just a lot to get used to. I never thought I deserved a second chance."

His mind buzzed with self-loathing, a swarm of winged and fast-beating thoughts that covered up her own image of him — shy and careful, eyes down and smiling, cautious like he might scare her away. Having to see him as he saw himself made it harder to love him. She was irritated with him for being sad, and angry at herself for feeling so. Her ghost spread as wide as night in the space between them.

"You're getting a second chance anyway," Jane said.

She drove them a little south of downtown. On the way, they passed the gray shell of the grocery store. One of the front windows was shattered. Someone must have broken in to scavenge whatever canned and boxed goods hadn't sold.

Trigger squeezed her leg in apology. "Where are we going?"

"To get you fitted for a tux."

He's wondering if someone died.

Jane let him wonder.

At a rundown strip mall, Jane parked in front of Rae's Bridal, between a taxidermist shop that had closed years ago and a hardware store only open on the weekends.

Trigger followed her to the door, eyeing the white dresses stretched over the yellowed mannequins in the window. "Are we getting married?"

"Is *that* your proposal?"

He struggled to speak, terrified that she knew what he was thinking as soon as he did.

She kissed him, laughing softly into his neck. "No, we're not getting married. Let's hurry. Hogboss gave me a shift this afternoon, and I can't miss it."

The shop was narrow and dark. Aside from the owner sitting behind the register, it was only the two of them in the store, but it felt crowded. Old mannequins missing limbs and scuffed of paint stood along the wall and between the racks of clothes, all of them in tuxedos and gowns. It was like they had walked into a silent party, as formal and still as a cemetery.

"He needs to be measured for a rental tux," Jane said. "We're going to prom."

The owner came around to measure him. Trigger stood stiffly, arms out. "Aren't we too old for that?" he asked.

"The school wants me to DJ again this year. You can help me carry speakers and set up. We might even have time for a dance."

The ghost brought her a sunburst of joy from Trigger. Even he didn't know why the idea made him so happy.

Mirrors covered the walls, but the light was bad, making everything murky and dark. Jane held a blue gown against her chest and stepped right up to the mirror, but the face that looked back wasn't hers. The girl in the mirror was white-skinned, blue-eyed, smirking.

The ghost of a young girl had gotten trapped in the mirrors of the bridal shop. When Jane tried to look at herself, she saw the reflection of the ghost instead, wearing her clothes and posing as she did.

"What a needy little thing," Jane said.

The owner frowned at her, and Jane wondered if the ghost was a relative. It must be, otherwise the woman would have smashed the mirrors to be rid of it by now. She stared into the ghost girl's eyes and watched it clutch the dress tighter, pulling it back into the depths of the mirror. Jane felt the dress tighten in her hands, like something was trying to take it from her. She stepped away from the reflection.

The owner rang them up. The dress she wanted — not a rental, but Jane planned on returning it — was more expensive than she had realized. Jane opened her wallet and saw that she was ten short. The plant still hadn't processed her first paycheck, and who knew if she would ever get her last check from the grocery store. Her mother would need money for bills, and there was always something wrong with the car. She stared into her wallet, wondering if there was a cheaper dress or if she could just make do with something she had at home.

Trigger counted out the bills and paid for them both.

"Sorry," she said. "I'll pay you back."

"It's fine." He shrugged. "It's not like I'm going anywhere."

She felt something go tight in her chest, not wanting to say it but feeling like she had to. "You could, though. Now that your ghost is gone, I mean. You could get out of Swine Hill and find somewhere better."

He took the suit from the clerk, glancing toward the dusty windows and the rundown neighborhood outside. "Maybe someday. I still have people I care about here, though. I can't just leave them."

Jane nodded, neither of them looking at each other. It wasn't the best thing for him, but she was glad he was staying. She wanted to go eventually, but for now, so many things tied her to the town. Just getting the money to leave felt almost impossible. When Henry graduated. When her father came back to himself. Maybe then. At least while she waited, she would have Trigger. She squeezed his hand.

He's not just staying for you.

Jane tried to keep the irritation off her face. She knew that. His father was here. Maybe he had other family in town, aunts and uncles. She still didn't know him as well as she wanted to. It was hard to imagine him sitting down with relatives at Thanksgiving, harder to imagine her sitting beside him. What kind of future did they really have here?

You still don't understand. He won't go because he thinks his brother's ghost might come back.

As they left, Jane looked back to see the owner staring into a hand mirror and combing her hair, no doubt looking into the eyes of some lost sister or daughter or friend. Jane felt her own ghost heavy around her neck. Trigger and Henry were both obsessed with spirits that had already left them. Across Swine Hill, the dead reached up from the earth, bony fingers tight around the ankles of everyone in town. What would it take to break their grip?

When she got to the plant, Jane went to the payroll office to pick up her check. It wasn't much, about the same as she had made at the grocery store, but better than not having a job at all. Looking over her pay stub, Jane saw that her job title was listed as "Pig." Hogboss had said they weren't hiring any new human workers. He must have lied on her paperwork so that Corporate would okay the job.

There were a dozen working screens in the security room now. Jane turned the lights off and swiveled back and forth in her chair, submerged in the glow of monitors. She'd found an old boom box and set it up under the desk, filling the room with crackling, tinny sound. Her ghost couldn't read people as clearly through the video feeds, but it could pick up a few things, worries and fears that were written right on their faces. It sent Jane an unending stream of heartache and bitterness, soaking up their secret thoughts.

There was a crew of boys who worked packing the cut meat with gloved hands and hairnets, shifting from leg to leg in the chill of the cooler. They were the ones who'd tried to hurt Henry and Dennis. Their faces were bruised and swollen, all of them marked from the fight. They were angry, wanted to get even with Bethany. As they grabbed bloody chunks of meat and slapped them down on Styrofoam trays, violent fantasies curled through them like thorns. They imagined Bethany on her knees, begging. When one of the pig workers walked through the room with a clipboard, they imagined throwing him down on the floor and hacking him to pieces. One of the boys thought of Jane's brother standing with Dennis at school. She changed the monitor to a different feed.

After flipping through cameras for a while, Jane rewound footage until she saw Trigger and his father, insulated in their heavy suits, spraying the empty workrooms of the plant down with corrosive foam. His father was hollowed out, struck with the new loss of his son, while Trigger was ashamed that he was so happy to have his ghost gone. Their minds blew about, as light and skeletal as dead leaves.

On another monitor, she saw night footage of a crowd of ghosts surrounding an antique grinder. A ghostly man had gotten caught in the machine up to his shoulder. The others stood around him, shouting and shoving, cigarettes falling from their mouths. She knew that they would argue and wail until the man's blood muddied their shoes, until he finally passed out. Then the ghosts would take their knives and cut him out of the machine. They would lay him down on the floor, and then the whole scene would dissolve into cigarette smoke and fog, waiting to repeat itself tomorrow.

Someone knocked on the door and wheeled in a stack of new monitors and cables. Jane spent a few hours hooking it all up, letting her ghost feel out whether there were spirits trapped in any piece of the equipment. Crawling around behind the desk, she fished out an old piece of coaxial cable with her hands and saw that it had been cut in half. Several cables had been severed, and a full bank of monitors smelled burned.

Your brother was here every day for months. He must have cut the cables so no one would know what he was doing. What else has he been hiding from you?

"His ghost had control of him."

His ghost helped him do what he wanted to do. The same as you and me.

Jane replaced the damaged parts and switched on the new bank of monitors. Security cameras in the farthest corners of the plant sent her their bright data. After a few moments of static, the screens cleared. Jane looked upon a world of pigs.

One entire warehouse was full of bunk beds and cubicle space. Hundreds of pig men, women, and children lounged or sat in circles on the floor, wrinkling their snouts at the stale air. Another feed showed her pig people working in a slaughterhouse, carving up meat and sending it down the line to be packed. A single wall separated the human packers from the pig butchers. Everyone knew that there were pigs living in town and working at the plant. At most, Jane thought there were a dozen families. But there were far more than anyone knew, packed into the cavernous spaces of the plant like refugees, watching from unlit catwalks, all of them waiting for their turn to emerge from the plant at night and find a home for themselves in the town below.

She texted Henry a picture of the monitor, asking, *Did you know?*
He didn't answer.

"Maybe he thinks that if they come down gradually, a few at a time, people will get used to it."

He's wrong.

She saw one of the pigs cut her hand and drop to the floor. A more senior pig came over and yelled at her, throwing a clipboard on the ground.

Hogboss won't let them leave until he's sure they're ready. Her mistake means that this group will spend another month here at least.

Jane watched the pigs for a while, as if watching some alternate reality where humans never existed. Looking back to the other monitors, she saw her mother in one of the pig houses. She was on her knees near one of the stalls, her arm draped over the side. The pigs clustered close, overfed and crusted in shit, nosing and nipping at her hand for treats.

Her mother's hair was sweat-damp and stuck to her face. Her skin glistened. Jane's ghost tapped into the raw need and loneliness she was feeling until Jane floated in it, as if her mother was in the same room. The other workers kept their distance, didn't make eye contact, did everything they could to keep from falling into her beautiful, burning arms.

"Why is she crying?" Jane asked. "What happened?"
She didn't think she could burn him.
"Him who?"

Her ghost didn't answer. Jane could feel it holding something back from her like a weight in her mind.

The pig woman still clutched her hurt hand on another screen. Jane leaned closer, trying to understand exactly what was going on. Finally, she called Hogboss to the security room.

When he arrived a few minutes later, he hesitated on the threshold, not entering the room.

He's thinking about his neck. He hopes you won't see.

"What?" She said it aloud, glancing at the edge of Hogboss's massive throat where it swooped down to meet his shoulder. There, in the twists of surgical scars from when her brother had molded the old pig into a man, her mother's bright handprint was seared tenderly into his skin.

"What the hell is that?" Jane asked.

He blushed and looked down at his work boots, trying and failing to meet her eyes. "You needed to see me about a security matter?"

"You have to stay away from my mom."

Jane couldn't keep the revulsion off her face. The thought of her mother tracing Hogboss's wormlike scars, her lips on his wet snout, her hands pulling at the hairy tail hidden in his work jeans. He was barely a person, if he was one at all.

Isn't that what Mason thinks when he sees you with his son?

"No more." Jane was so angry with her ghost that she almost shouted the words.

Hogboss frowned. "Adult love might seem gross to children, but when you're older, you'll understand."

It took Jane a moment to process that he thought of her as a child, this fusion of pig and man that couldn't have been walking upright and speaking for more than a few months. What could he possibly know about how complicated and hard it was to love another person?

Her ghost couldn't resist showing Jane everything he was thinking. Hogboss's mind was full of movie reel highlights, classic romance films in grainy black-and-white, chaste and simple and sweet. In the pig's mind, he envisioned Jane's mother as a woman in need of saving.

"Jesus, no. Stop." She covered her face with her hands. "You have to stay away from her because she'll kill you. She's killed every man she's dated since my dad."

"Maybe she just hasn't met someone strong enough for her."

"Are you listening to me? She will burn you to ash. She can't help herself."

"Her touch doesn't hurt me as much as it does others."

"But she still burned you. And it will only get worse, for both of you."

"Your mother is a wonderful and kind person. She deserves love no matter how terrible her ghost. You of all people should understand that."

"I didn't call you here so that you could lecture me about my own mother."

Jane gestured to the screens behind her. On one monitor, her mother draped herself over the side of the pen, fingers brushing the cement floor of the stall. On another, the pig woman still argued with her supervisor, the white tiles smeared with blood.

"One of the pig people hurt herself," Jane said. "In the secret warehouse you're hiding from everyone. You should probably do something about that."

Jane swiveled around in her chair, turning her back on him. Hogboss left at once, closing the door behind him. She watched the monitors, waiting for his massive shape to appear on her screens. The pig woman was helped into a chair, hand wrapped in a towel, her supervisor and colleagues still cursing her.

A few minutes later, Hogboss stepped into view, but not in the slaughterhouse. Instead, he approached Jane's mother and lifted her up from the floor, pulling her against him in a hug. There was a flash of light when she laid her head on his shoulder and her heat passed into him. Hogboss shuddered in pain but held on. The other workers stopped, pig antibiotics dripping from their fingers, and stared at the two of them.

Jane got up from her chair and walked out of the security room, not wanting to see any more. She hated Henry in that moment, absolutely hated him for making the pigs, for making Hogboss to fall in love with their mother.

You're worried he'll make her happy.

"After what she did to my dad, what she does to people all the time, she doesn't deserve happiness."

When Henry does something, it's his ghost's fault. But when your mother does something, you blame her?

It wasn't the same. Her brother didn't have control of his own body. And Henry had been haunted to begin with because he was curious, inventive, good with machines. Their mother, lonely and afraid that she wasn't really loved, had been possessed by something that sniffed out the worst parts of her. She might as well have invited the spirit in. How could Jane ever forgive her for that?

Her ghost didn't have to point out that she was being unfair. It sat smug in the back of her mind, gloating in the fact that Jane already knew.

17

J ANE GOT HOME and found a pile of bills in the mailbox. She put them on the counter for her mother along with what money she had. Henry was up late in his room, going over Bethany's lab results and talking to her on the phone. She only saw him for a moment, sunken-eyed when he stumbled into the kitchen to eat a bowl of cereal for dinner. Jane waited on the couch for her mother to come home, but she never did. The robot waited beside her, watching the door.

It began to rain outside, and Jane thought of her father wandering somewhere in the dark and wet. She hoped he found a dry place. She closed her eyes and drifted off to the soft sound of water whispering over the roof —

The front window of the living room exploded.

Jane started awake, bits of broken glass scattering across her lap. Long fangs of glass covered the carpet in front of her. The robot brushed shards from its shoulder. Their curtains stirred in the wind. Two red taillights burned on the road outside before a truck sped away.

They're angry, but they're mostly afraid.

"Who?"

They want you to be afraid too.

Henry came down the stairs and turned on the light. "What happened?"

In the midst of the broken glass, Jane found a brick. She picked it up. Someone had written *Pig Lovers* on all four sides of it.

"Who were they?" Jane asked her ghost. "Did you get their names?"

They were gone too fast.

Jane wondered for a moment if the spirit was lying to her, holding back some small piece of knowledge just for the thrill of keeping it from her. The ghost was silent in her mind, not deigning to respond.

The robot wheeled itself into the kitchen and came back with a broom and dustpan, but Jane stopped it. "Not yet. Leave it until the police come."

"I don't know if that's a good idea," Henry said.

Jane didn't either, but she didn't know what else to do. She was already dialing. A bored voice answered the phone, music playing somewhere in the background. "Is this the police department?" she asked. "Someone just threw a brick through my window."

Henry went upstairs to get dressed before the police came. Jane opened the door and looked outside, but her mother's car was still gone. She might have driven to a nearby town and hit up the bars after work. Her ghost had been burning hot. She'd want to find someone to release all of her heat. Or she might have gone home with Hogboss after her shift. Might be lying in bed with him now. Goddamn her brother. He should have invented something to get rid of her ghost, not something to feed it.

A few minutes later, strobing blue and red police lights descended on their driveway. They cut through the thin curtain and licked over the living room walls. Jane opened the door, blinking, the brick held out in her hand.

"I thought it would be you." The officer smiled at her, blood staining his teeth.

It was the same man who'd threatened her before. Blood dripped slowly from his ears, stained the hollows under his eyes, clotted in his mustache. It seeped from his scalp and collected thick in his wispy hair. Jane's ghost injected her with the man's tightly suppressed rage, flooding her with adrenaline.

"So this is where you live?" he said. He took in the torn carpet, the stained drywall, every broken and dirty thing. He already had imagined the sort of person Jane was. He hunted for things to confirm it.

She reached for her phone to text Henry or Trigger or her mother, but the officer took her by the arm and led her inside to the kitchen table, gesturing for her to sit. He sat beside her. When Henry pounded down the stairs a few minutes later, the officer's hand slipped down to his gun.

"Is anyone else at home?" the bleeding man asked.

"Just me and my brother," Jane said. The robot wheeled over to the table, its eyes widening and looking strangely concerned. "And the robot."

The officer pulled a pad of paper and pen from his pocket. Blood matted the pages together, oozing out from under his fingernails. "You consider the robot a person?" he asked.

"No. Not really."

"What about pigs?" the officer asked. "Are they persons?"

The brick lay in the center of the table, the words *Pig Lovers* facing her.

Jane could barely speak, looking at her brother for help. Henry had put on a button-down shirt over jeans, trying to look nice, proper, innocent. He was quiet, trusting her ghost to tell her the right thing to say. But her ghost was balled up deep in her stomach, as scared as she was.

"Some of them are," she said. "The ones who wear clothes and work and talk."

"Are there any pigs here now?"

"No," Henry said. "It's just us. What does this have to do with someone breaking our window?"

The cop turned to Henry, droplets of blood falling on the blond wood of the tabletop. "You never know what will end up being help-ful later on," he said. "How would you describe your relationship with the pigs?"

"We don't have a relationship with them," Jane said.

Don't contradict him. Her ghost was small and dim, a moth flitting in the back of her mind.

"You say that they're people." He flipped through his pad, peeling the dark pages apart. "Henry has a history of making strange things, like the robot here. He spent quite a bit of time at the plant before the pigs arrived. That little, funny-looking pig that hangs around the school, what's his name?"

"Dennis," Henry said.

"Dennis has spent some time here at your house, hasn't he? And your mother was seen getting drinks with Hogboss. So I'll ask you again. Tell me about your relationship with the pigs."

The bleeding man leaned toward her as he spoke, jaw quivering, and more stars of red struck the table until the blood began to pool and run in lines around him. Jane asked her ghost what to say, but it was quiet.

"We just work with them," Jane said. "My mom works for Hogboss. Henry worked for him for a while. We do our jobs. We're not any closer to the pigs than anyone else."

The officer picked up the brick and turned it over in his hands. "It looks like some people feel differently."

Henry opened his mouth, but Jane kicked him under the table be-fore he could say something that would get them both killed.

"People are worried the plant will stop hiring now that the pigs are here," Jane said. "We understand why they're upset. We're worried about it too."

The cop nodded. He stood, setting the brick back down. "There's a lot to worry about. The world just doesn't have much regard for people anymore. If the pigs say anything to you or if they do anything strange, be sure to call and let us know."

He walked out of the house, back to his car still spinning its lights in the driveway. He sat there for a long time. Jane worried that he was calling for backup, that other police cruisers would slide neon down their street and surround the house, taking her and Henry both away. Finally he backed into the street and drove off, leaving their living room and kitchen streaked with blood.

Henry got dishrags from under the sink and they scrubbed at the blood, but it stained everything it touched. It smelled dead. Jane's ghost rose up in her again. It gave her a quick window into Henry's thoughts: a ghost haunting a dog, the smell of death, violence, and teeth.

"Can you at least fix the fucking robot?" Jane asked. "So we'll have something to protect us in case they don't just throw a brick next time?"

"I'm trying. Everything is hard right now."

"Things are hard because of you. And don't tell me you're going to make it all better. We both know you can't."

Jane could feel her brother's shock, his chest tighten with hurt and betrayal. Hadn't she been the one to tell him that he was more than his ghost?

Before she could apologize, the front door burst open. Jane and Henry fell back against the table, their arms up to shield themselves.

Their father stood in the light. His clothes were soaked with rain. He seemed confused, like he'd walked into the wrong house.

"Dad?" Henry asked.

Jane almost ran to him, thinking he had finally remembered who he was, that he'd come home. But her ghost hadn't moved when he came in. It curled fetal at the bottom of her, not realizing that someone had walked into the house.

Their father looked over the two of them, the robot, the inside of the house. He didn't seem to recognize anything. He turned and walked back into the dark, leaving the door swinging open behind him.

They went to the door and watched his silhouette disappear into the night. Jane wanted to chase after him and make him stay, but she was exhausted and afraid. She didn't have space in her head to worry about him right now.

"What's he trying to do?" Henry asked.

"I don't know," Jane said. "If there's anything in him, my ghost can't hear it."

The spirit welled up in her, having found something heavy in Henry's mind. He knew more than he was saying. Their father saving him from ghosts. Their father marking houses. A strange heart throbbing in a box on Henry's desk upstairs. Henry thought he knew what was wrong with their dad, hoped he might even be able to fix him. He hurried upstairs.

Could he really help without his ghost? If Henry could lead their father out of the cave of his own mind, it would change everything. Her family could be together again. Maybe they could even find a way to help her mother.

Jane tried to remember the last time her whole family sat together at this table. Beside her, the robot swabbed at the blood, smearing it in a wide, sickle-shaped arc.

"Where did Henry get a heart?" Jane asked.

Her ghost stretched within her, listening to her brother working upstairs, every thought he couldn't hide trickling down to her.

He doesn't know where it came from. But he thinks it belongs to your father.

18

AFTER HIS FATHER left, Henry ran upstairs to his room. The heart knocked in its case on his desk. He opened his window and stepped onto the roof, holding the box out to the dark. It beat stronger, directing him like a compass. As he held it out in the direction of downtown, he could feel its frantic beats start to slow, like the footsteps of his father fading ever farther away.

He climbed back into his room and fell into bed, the heart box beside him on his mattress. It must belong to his father. It held all the man's pain and feeling, was the reason he had become invisible to ghosts. And if that was true, Henry must have been the one who had cut it out. He would have been only a child then, with a child's understanding of the world. He shuddered, wondering what else his ghost had made him do.

Maybe there would be a way to fix some of the harm he had done. If he could somehow get the heart back in his father's chest, maybe the man would remember who he was. He would come back home to them, and maybe his mother wouldn't need to love the pig man. It hardly mattered, though. Henry would never find a surgeon willing to implant the dried, beating heart. And without his ghost, how would he put the organ back into his father without doing more harm?

He fell asleep, thinking of the father he barely knew wandering the dark, the pigs sleeping amidst all the ghostly history and hate of the town, and Bethany slowly being crushed under the alien's heavy light.

Henry woke up to a message from Bethany: *Come over.*

He pulled on clothes and started downstairs, hoping someone would be home to give him a ride. There were voices in the kitchen. He froze on the stairwell, listening. His mother was talking, her voice reedy and cigarette-strained, pulling the listener in like a chain around their throat. The other voice was snarl and bass, a low thunder of sympathy. Hogboss was here. Henry sank down on the steps, listening like he was a child again.

"Jane and Henry keep bringing him home," his mother said. "They think they'll get their father back. But he died a long time ago. The man who looks like him is just an empty suit of clothes. He's not in there. I can't make them understand. It hurts me every time I have to see him."

"It's different for us," Hogboss said. "I can't remember much of her. I didn't have language then, so I only knew her by smell, taste, heat. And we were only together for a few days. Dennis remembers her a lot better than I do. It's why he won't eat pork. He's afraid part of her might still be out there, frozen in a butcher's cooler."

"It's hard losing someone," his mother said. "They never really go away."

Henry's phone buzzed: Bethany sent him an image. The loading icon on his phone slowly revolved. Finally, the picture spilled over the screen. It was an empty expanse of sky, a few wisps of clouds trailing across the edge of the image. Henry looked for something in all that blue but couldn't find anything.

Bethany texted, *There's a city above me. Can you see it?*

Henry pounded down the steps. Hogboss and his mother sat at the table while the robot viciously burned their lunch on the stove. "I need a ride," he said.

His mother pointed at the robot sitting in its wheelchair in front of the range, inky smoke rising from some small and black thing welded to the bottom of the skillet. "What's wrong with it? I thought you were going to fix it soon."

Hogboss scratched a floppy ear, his broad face and neck reddening. "I was just heading back to the plant. I could give you a ride on my way."

"I'm ready." Henry picked up his backpack from the hallway and shrugged it on, the straps straining from the weight of his junky old laptop and stacks of annotated medical printouts.

The pig man and his mother shared a long, warm look. Henry went outside and got in Hogboss's truck to wait. The vinyl seats burned his legs and back. Around him, the broken-down houses seemed to steam and sag in the summer heat. In the distance, he heard hammering and sawing.

After the pigs fixed this neighborhood and more came down from the factory, would they start rebuilding the rest of the town? Would there be a future Swine Hill where new lumber and paint pushed the ghosts farther and farther away until the town was no longer such a haunted place? It was hard to imagine that people here would ever let things change so much. They were as attached to memory as the ghosts who haunted them.

Hogboss got in the truck. "I'd be happy to teach you how to drive, Henry. It isn't hard."

Henry clenched his teeth. He had created the pig man, edited him down to his DNA. Now Hogboss wanted to teach him how to operate an internal combustion engine. He shouldn't be frustrated about it, but he was. Everything, the smallest kindness, was a reminder of how much he had lost.

"My problem isn't that I don't know how to drive. It's that we only have two cars: my mom's and Jane's. If I wanted, I would just build my own car. They're barely more complicated than a popcorn maker."

Henry regretted the boast immediately. He still hadn't adjusted to a world with limits. Maybe he never would.

"Oh?" The pig man looked at him. "Can you explain to me how it works? I've always wanted to know, but it seems so complicated."

Henry took a deep breath, ready to outline the various parts of the engine and how they functioned. But it wouldn't come together in his head. He couldn't remember the names for things. Without taking a look under the hood, he wasn't even sure what all was there. And he didn't know where to start. He began to speak several times, but finally said, "I'm too tired right now. Maybe later."

"Do you know what Dennis is doing today? He went out this morning."

He shouldn't have done that, Henry thought. "He's probably getting ready for prom tonight," he said.

"He's going to prom?" Hogboss's face split in a too-wide and tooth-filled smile. "Does he have a date?"

"Yeah. I guess so."

"That's wonderful."

Henry sighed. Let the pig man think that everything was fine, that people loved Dennis and that he had friends. What harm could it do?

Bethany's house rustled with a wind of the dead. A basketball hoop and board was nailed to an oak tree in her yard. The chain net splashed and chimed, moved by the warm, foggy shapes of ghosts rising to sink their phantom baskets. The branches of trees shook with ghosts climbing and swinging, and tracks were worn in the front lawn from spirits doing line drills and sprints. There was nothing dangerous about them. Like the shades who marched in to work at the plant every night, these ghosts had everything they wanted.

Her mother let Henry in the house, leading him down a long hallway lined with trophy cases. Ghostly hands, some solid as flesh but most only a shimmering in the air, wrapped their fingers around the statuettes or clinked fistfuls of medals in their hands. Henry saw a row of trophies for youth football and boy's youth basketball too.

When they were children, Bethany hated that she wasn't allowed to play boy sports. There weren't many teams for girls so young, especially in Swine Hill. Henry had cut her hair on the bus, the heavy black strands piling on the floor until she could pass as a shaggy-headed boy. Her parents didn't let her play with him for weeks after, but they did dress their daughter in baggy clothes and drive her to summer practices the next town over. Bethany went to school in a different district for two years so she could pose as a boy, until the weight of ghosts gathered within her and kept her from leaving Swine Hill.

Pull-up bars were mounted over every doorframe. Invisible ghosts rose and fell from them, sending tremors of wind across Henry's face. Instead of a couch or TV, the living room had barbells and exercise mats. Even in the middle of the day when the ghosts would be at their weakest, the weights trembled and rolled around the floor.

"I forget that she's so haunted," Henry said.

Her mother nodded. "It gets pretty loud at night, but they don't hurt anyone. They just want to be close to her. They want to remember what it feels like to win."

Ms. Ortiz gestured to the stairwell, lined with portraits of Bethany in athletic gear, her black hair sweat-stuck to her shoulders. Wisps of fog moved over the glass, as if ghosts had submerged themselves into the photos, trying to get inside these moments of victory.

"She's upstairs. Been resting a lot lately."

"She's really sick," Henry said.

The woman shrugged. "Don't worry about Bethany. Nothing is going to beat her. Not even illness. That's what I worry about. People need to lose every once in a while, don't they?"

"I lose a lot," Henry said. "I'm not sure it's helped me any."

"Maybe that's why you're her friend. To help her understand."

Henry didn't know if he liked thinking of himself that way. But he thanked Bethany's mom and headed upstairs. Ghosts sprinted up and down the steps like they were bleachers, their passing a blast of air.

Bethany sat in front of her window staring at an empty sheet of blue sky. When she heard Henry walk in, she pointed up. "What do you see?" she asked.

Henry wiped his glasses on his shirt and looked up, searching for a plane or cloud or kite. "Nothing. Just air."

"Sometimes — not all the time, but right now — I see a city. Like I'm in the sky looking down on it. It gives me vertigo."

Could the alien be affecting her mind? He wished he knew more about mental illness, delusions, people seeing things that weren't real. Should he tell her there was nothing or should he play along? What did she need?

"What does the city look like?" he asked.

"It's Swine Hill, but it's a different Swine Hill." She turned around, looking perfectly lucid and in control, but her hands gripped the sides of her chair as if she was afraid she might fall up into that other place.

"Are you sleeping okay?"

"No. I feel like I'm going to sink through my own bed. The world feels so thin and fragile. That's why I'm slower now. It's not that I'm weaker. It's that the world is less solid. I can't get any traction on it."

"We don't know how the alien is affecting your brain. We should get you back to the clinic, try to get you an MRI."

Bethany picked up a signed baseball from a shelf near her bed and threw it hard at the wall of her room.

Henry flinched, bracing himself for the sound of the ball cratering into the drywall. There was silence. He looked up, searching for broken glass or a crack in the wall, for the ball rolling across the floor. He looked at Bethany's hands, making sure she didn't still have it.

"Where did it go?" he asked.

"Somewhere else," Bethany said. "Some other Swine Hill."

Henry's mind raced, alternating with terror and excitement. "Wow. Okay. Let's try some things."

He pulled a microscope out of his backpack, taken from the science lab at school, and examined a skin cell from her arm. There were no longer glowing pinpricks of light inside the nucleus of the cells. Now the entire cell was limned with gold, as if it had absorbed whatever the alien was. As he watched, the cells slipped through the specimen glass and vanished.

He took more cell samples from her and tried everything he could think of to kill the strange light. He bathed them in acid, electrified them, iced them down as cold as he could get them, heated them up. He only succeeded in destroying the tissue. The alien light wasn't going anywhere.

Feeling inspired, he found some old antibiotics rattling around in the cabinet, went downstairs and scraped the mold off an orange, rubbed a smear of dirt from the paws of Bethany's cat, blew his runny nose directly onto a slide. He exposed her cells to every foreign thing he could think of, fungi and bacteria and viruses. If the alien was alive, he might be able to trigger an autoimmune response, let it overwhelm itself responding to the foreignness of their world. But after he'd worked for over an hour, dirtying all the slides he had brought and scraping Bethany's forearm red, nothing seemed promising.

Bethany stood at the window, staring out at the roofs of junked houses and the twisting smokestack of the plant looming over it all. "If I relax, I'll fall through the world. What will happen to me? Will I die?"

What was the problem he had been trying to solve, the riddle that had brought out his ghost? She had wanted to get as far away from Swine Hill as possible. Not just another planet. There were places much farther away than the other side of space.

"I don't think you would die," Henry said. "But I'm not sure you could come back. I think you're phasing into an alternate reality. Like a parallel dimension."

Bethany looked around her room at the snarl of jump ropes tangled on the floor, the hill of busted running shoes falling out of her closet, the stacks of college applications she had filled out but hadn't mailed. All around her whispered her hundreds of ghosts, rustling through the room like a breeze.

"Maybe this is a good thing," she said. "Maybe I'll end up somewhere better than this."

Her arms and shoulders looked real as stone or iron, solid and *here*.

It was hard to believe that she was slow, cautious, afraid that she would fall off the world like it was a tightrope. She went to her bedroom window and struggled to open it. Her hands kept slipping off the wood, like she was having trouble getting her hands on it. Finally she got it, letting in the sun and the breeze and the green smell of the cut lawn below.

"Maybe I should just take the jump. If it's inevitable, why waste time fighting it?"

"We don't know that it's inevitable. And you don't know anything about that other world. What if it breaks your atoms apart like confetti and you just disintegrate?"

She stared at him blankly, and, not for the first time, Henry wished that he could read minds like his sister.

"I can't catch a ball," she said. "I can barely walk, much less run. There wasn't much for me here before the alien came, and there's less for me now. Whatever reality I'm falling toward, at least I might be able to get my hands on it."

"What if you just need a little practice and time? Your parents think you'll beat this on your own. Maybe you will."

"I've always had to hold back. People try to stop me from doing what I want, tell me that I can't do it, and then ignore me when I do it anyway. Even if I learn to control this and stay, why would I want to?"

"Promise me you won't go jumping into that other universe until we learn more. This is dangerous. It could hurt you." Like all of his inventions, Henry thought.

Bethany sighed. "Fine. You should probably head to school soon. You need to keep an eye on Dennis so nothing happens to him."

He had forgotten about prom already. With everything happening, it was the last thing on his mind. Henry wasn't really dressed for it, just wearing jeans and an oversized T-shirt.

"I was going to invite you," Henry said.

Bethany raised an eyebrow.

"Not like that. You're graduating soon, and I don't know what will happen after that. I thought it would be fun to go as friends. But then everything changed."

"I probably would have said no," she said. "But thanks. You're a good friend, Henry."

She stared at the sky through her window, eyes wide with horror or wonder. Too ashamed to know what else to say, Henry texted his sister to come pick him up.

TRIGGER WAS IN the passenger seat, looking uncomfortable in his too-tight rental tux. He kept clawing at the collar and raising his arms to keep from sweating. Henry's sister wore a dress with the tag still on, hanging out of the collar like a flag of surrender. No doubt she'd return it to the store tomorrow. But it fit her well, as pale as snow against her arms and legs. He didn't often think of his sister as beautiful, or pretty, even — but she was. She smiled at him, and he rolled his eyes, knowing she'd been listening in.

"Can you drive already?" Henry asked. "I'm dying back here."

They'd wedged him in with all of the speakers, mixers, and amplifiers. His cheek pressed against the window, equipment resting against his shoulder. Jane's air conditioner had just gone out, and Henry was soaked with sweat. For a moment, he had a dark wish that Trigger's ghost would come back just to cool them off, but he quickly buried it before his sister could catch what he was thinking.

They were about two hours early so Jane could set up. Only a few cars were in the parking lot. Henry helped his sister and Trigger cart the stereo equipment into the band room. It was a cavernous space with ratty gray carpet and no windows. The art teacher had covered the walls and floor with black tissue paper, stringing up white Christmas lights to try to make the space less depressing.

Along one wall, there was a giant mirror. Its edges were cloudy and its surface scraped. Henry walked up to it, wondering what strange world Bethany would see behind its glass if she were here. The mirror was haunted, reflecting the room from years before, new and beautifully decorated. People long dead danced in the reflection. This was the version of Swine Hill people preferred to remember, back when the town was still prosperous.

No students were here yet, but there were already some ghosts. Over the decades, a few people had died in car accidents on their way to prom. Every year, they came in their bloodied finery to dance through the evening. While Jane and Trigger set up the DJ table, the ghosts made silent circles on the floor. Jane put on an oldies playlist, letting them have this first hour to themselves.

Henry propped against the wall, sneaking shy looks at upperclassmen girls laughing with their friends. They were like a completely different species. For all the things his ghost had helped him understand, he'd never been able to flirt.

Dennis still hadn't arrived. The room was filling with people. Jane's music rained down from speakers mounted in the corners, the sound shaggy and huge and thundering, making the hair rise on the back of Henry's neck.

Henry stayed close to the mirror, watching how it reflected another time and space. He wondered if Bethany would one day be able to walk through history like that, or if she would have no control, falling back through the past until she arrived at the beginning of time. The faces in the mirror were all white, the black kids first forbidden and then discouraged for years from attending the official prom. Henry wondered where their ghosts danced tonight.

The door opened and Dennis walked in alone. He held his arms up, pirouetting into the room. He took the hands of anyone near and spun them, pulled them close, twirled away. People laughed, nervous, as he uncoupled them from their dates for a moment and used them like islands to dance across the room. Henry caught sight of his eyes, blue with ghost-light, and understood that he wasn't alone after all. The ghost girl was in him now, making Dennis dance for her.

The pig boy, in a powder blue sequined coat and white shoes, spun and leapt his way in front of the mirror, dancing right against the edge of it. From within the glass, a ghost surfaced, pressing her tear-streaked face against it from the other side. Dennis laid a four-fingered hand on the glass, and from the other side, the ghost pressed its palm to his.

The ghost of the dancing girl slipped in and out of Dennis's body, her hand rising from his hand, her leg extending from his leg. Once, she leaned out of him and tried to embrace the ghost girl in the mirror, but the glass kept them apart. The three of them danced — the mirror ghost with the pig boy, the dancing girl with Dennis, Dennis with the eyes of the room — but none of them could have what they wanted most.

The pig boy's eyes were wet. Henry wondered if he only now realized that the person the ghost girl wanted to dance with had never been him, had always been this shade trapped in the mirror. Or maybe he did know and Dennis had given her this dance because she had been kind to him, letting her have his eyes for an evening so that she could weep?

The song ended and a new one didn't start. The room fell to silence, the swishing of hems and shoe soles against the paper floor, the soft murmur of voices. Away from the DJ booth, Jane danced with Trigger. They looked like photographic negatives, Jane with her dark skin and white dress, Trigger with his pale skin and black suit, their arms holding tight to each other. The room turned to watch them, the only ones without baby fat in their cheeks, sharp and sad and mysteriously adult.

A girl, weaving between dancing couples and crossing her arms tight over her chest, came to stand a few feet from Henry. She walked up on her toes and took long steps, like she was tiptoeing over the surface of the moon. When she leaned back against the wall, Henry could hear her body crinkle and crush inward, settling like paper.

"I've seen you before," Henry said. "You're always late to the laughing room. Erica?"

She nodded, but stayed an arm's length away. Whenever one of the other couples moved close, she shrank back. Henry stepped in front of her, making a barrier between the girl and the rest of the room. She smiled. He had to go pee but didn't want to leave her, so he held it.

"You don't like people?" he asked.

"I have to be careful."

She folded her arm against itself, then folded it again, her limb flattening and bending like something two-dimensional. She shook it out and smoothed it with a papery rasp, her arm taking on roundness again. Her ghost had made her into an origami girl.

"If someone bumps into me, I could tear," she said.

"What if you get caught in the rain?"

She shook her head, eyes huge and lunar bright. "I would never go out in the rain."

He wanted to tell her about his ghost, how it used to take control of him but now he'd do anything to get it back. Her problems seemed worse, though, to be in fear of an accidental touch or a splash of water.

"How did you get such a strange ghost?" he asked.

She started talking, but her voice was so soft and whispery that Henry could barely make out what she was saying. He leaned a little closer, and she shrank back.

"I'm sorry," he said. "It's really loud in here."

She looked around to make sure that no one else was near and motioned for him to stand back against the wall. "Hold still," she said.

Erica lay against his shoulder, the whole weight of her barely any pressure on his skin. She spoke into his ear with her papery tongue and lips. Henry stood very still and listened.

Her family didn't have much money, so she didn't have the kinds of toys that other kids did. When she was a girl, her mother bought her a book of cutout paper dolls from a garage sale. Erica snipped out the women and their dozens of outfits, stacking them on the floor beside her bed and moving them around with her hands, telling their stories.

Even flat, they seemed prettier and wealthier and more interesting than she was. The paper women had more clothes than she did, nicer houses, cars and pets and vacations. She wanted to be like them.

There must have been some lingering ghost in the book and paper cutouts, some strange spirit that remembered only the magic of lightness and folding. It sank into her and made her paper-light. She'd almost died several times: a rainstorm that she spent months recovering from, a bad tear when her brother stumbled into her, a tiny hole in her neck from a friend who'd thrown a rock at her. She'd spent the last ten years in the laughing room, seated far away from everyone else.

"That's awful," he said. "Have you tried leaving? Maybe if you lived somewhere else for a while?"

"I don't think it would help. I'd have to stop being afraid of everything. It's easy to want to be a different kind of person, but it's a lot harder to actually change."

Henry nodded. He could understand that.

"It's not so bad," she said. "I move slow. I'm careful. But your ghost . . ." She shook her head, moon eyes wide. "I watched from the back of the room how your ghost took control of you, saw the things it made you build."

"It was just trying to help. It liked solving problems. I miss it."

She gestured to Dennis, spinning in front of the mirror, arms in the air. "Why did you make the pig people?"

"You think I made him?"

She grasped his arm with both hands, her touch feather-light but insistent. "Don't lie to me. Everyone knows you made the pigs. They make me nervous."

He tensed, hyperaware of her hands on his skin, suddenly unable to tell her anything but the truth. "I was only trying to help. I know people are worried about jobs at the plant, but that's not the pigs' fault. You shouldn't be afraid of them. They're just like anybody else."

"What about the one who runs the plant? He has tusks. He's bigger than anyone I've ever seen. If he breathed too hard, he could rip me in half."

"He's the most gentle person I've ever met. I promise."

She studied Henry for a moment. "And what about you? Are you a gentle person?"

He thought about it, unsure how to respond at first, but knowing this was a kind of test. "I want to be."

She looked into his face for a moment, considering him. "Do you want to dance?" she asked.

Henry froze, not sure how to tell her that he didn't know how, and not wanting to move too suddenly.

"You'll have to stay perfectly still," she said.

He nodded, relieved, and pressed himself flat against the wall.

The paper girl fell against him and moved from side to side with the music. She slid her hands over his chest, down his sides. It was the closest he'd ever been to a girl. He listened to the strange rustle of her, concentrating on her light weight against him. He took deep breaths, and she rode the rise and fall of his chest like they were really dancing together, keeping her silvery eyes locked on his.

"It's good that you don't have your ghost anymore," she said. "If you did, I would be too afraid to kiss you."

"You want to kiss me?"

"Close your mouth." She cupped his face in her hands. "Don't even breathe."

Her face met his lightly, then crushed forward against his lips. He wanted to wrap his arms around her slight back and pull her against him, but he held still.

Ms. White, the history teacher, reached between them. Erica shied back.

"Too close," the woman said.

Erica sulked back against the wall, waiting for her to go away.

Henry closed his eyes and remembered Erica's strange touch. He wanted to take her away into the quiet and dark of the empty school. He wanted her to kiss him like that again.

"I have to go to the bathroom," Henry said. His stomach hurt from holding it in. "I'll be right back. Will you still be here?"

She nodded.

Henry left the band hall, into the quiet and dark hallway. A few students milled around out here, faces lit by their phone screens. The restroom was at the end of the hall and stank like piss. His shoes stuck to the floor.

Henry stepped into a stall. The door was broken off its hinges. He unzipped his pants and closed his eyes, still imagining Erica's impossibly soft hands on his face.

Someone came into the stall behind him.

"Occupied," he said.

The person wrapped their arms around Henry and grabbed his face roughly in their hands. They were holding something hard and metal, pressing it against his cheek. Henry's hands were still holding himself while he urinated, the walls of the bathroom stall penning him in on three sides.

"What the fuck?" He could barely speak around their hands on his face. "Get away from me!"

The boy grabbed the tip of Henry's nose and tilted his head up. "Fucking pig lover. Now you'll look like one."

The metal object pressed against his skin, right under his nose. By the time Henry realized what it was, it was too late.

There was a flash of pain unlike anything he'd ever felt before, a red current that sheared through his whole body. He raised his hands to his face and screamed.

He heard something fall with a soft splash into the toilet. A bloody piece of flesh — *his fucking nose* — spun in the toilet bowl. Henry reached for it, but the boy kicked out and hit the toilet handle with his shoe, flushing it.

Henry found himself bent over the toilet, blood pouring into the empty bowl, holding nothing. The door to the bathroom opened and closed, and the boy was gone. The world blurred, his face burning with pain and eyes brimming over. There was a long, low whine coming from somewhere. It took him a minute to realize that it was coming from him.

He pulled his shirt up and pressed it against his face, but it barely held the bleeding in check. He thought for a moment about going to find a teacher, to ask his sister for help, but he remembered what Erica had said about being afraid of the pigs. *Now you'll look like one,* the boy had said. He couldn't go anywhere near her now. He sank to the floor and struggled to keep pressure on his face. The world spun around him.

STUDENTS PILED AROUND Jane's table, leaning into the river of sound and letting their drink cups vibrate on the speaker tops, hoarsely shouting for her to play their favorite songs. Trigger watched from the plastic chair beside her, a sad smile on his face. She had a hard time focusing on his thoughts with so many people around.

Her ghost rolled in the psychic noise, ferreting out teenage crushes and vendettas. It floated on their lust and longing, the innocent electric thrill of their hands and eyes moving over each other's skin. Jane tried to keep her eye on Dennis and her brother, the two of them looming clear then suddenly lost again in the swirl of faces flashing through the dark of the room.

The dance started winding down early like it always did, kids slipping away in twos and threes to old barns or abandoned farmhouses where they would get drunk and have sex on the outskirts of town. Dennis, his face shining with sweat, walked out with a group of others after hours of dancing with the mirror. Jane couldn't tell if they were his friends, her ghost distracted by a couple arguing against the wall.

She hoped Dennis had a ride home, that his father or some friend was picking him up. Maybe she was overreacting to worry about him. He didn't seem so unlike the other students, just as careful and shy in his rented clothes. Just as full of want and heartache as anyone else. Hardly different at all.

You're not so different, either. Did they ever let you forget it?

"Aren't you supposed to be helping me watch Henry?" Jane asked.

But her ghost was already distracted again, finding a secret sitting loaded and ready to fall from someone's lips, a bomb that would incinerate a decade-long friendship. The spirit gathered the two of them close, an invisible witness to the hurt they were about to inflict on each other.

Jane ignored it and looked for her brother. Henry had spent most of the night standing against the wall, talking to some slight, nervous girl Jane didn't know. One moment, the girl leaned against her brother's chest, whispering in his ear. The next, they were gone.

She texted Henry, but he didn't answer. Had he actually gone home with the girl? Was her skinny, awkward little brother out there losing his virginity tonight? Her ghost flashed back into her mind, disgusted and thrilled.

Someone had been thinking of a song all evening, a stuttering and half-remembered melody. Finally, Jane realized it was Trigger. He stared off into space, thinking of the song. It looped, the sound slowly sawing at him no matter how hard he tried to ignore it.

Jane leaned over and squeezed his hand. "Is that from something I played tonight? Do you want to hear it again?"

Trigger looked surprised and shrugged her question away, standing up.

"I have to go to the bathroom," he said.

The room was almost empty now. The chaperones picked up plastic cups and turned on the lights. The last few students sat on the floor and talked arm in arm. Even the ghostly prom in the mirror was slowing down. Around the edges of the room, spirits still held tight to one another and danced. The hems of their translucent dresses and jackets silently spun. They would hang on until morning.

Jane switched off the music, the bubble of sound and emotion collapsing back into stillness. As the building emptied, her ghost ranged farther down the halls, already feeling bored. It found Trigger, and by the time Jane felt his shock, she could already hear him shouting her name.

There was an image in his mind. Dingy white tile brushed with dark red. A pile of wet clothes curled in on themselves. Two hands — her brother's slender hands — covering his face. Henry lay in front of a toilet, his shirt mashed against his mouth, haloed in blood.

Jane ran into the hallway, but Trigger was already coming out of the bathroom carrying Henry in his arms. Her brother seemed smaller, as limp as a doll and sticky with blood. He breathed weakly and stared without focusing on anything, his hands trembling to keep pressure on his face.

"Just take me home," Henry said, his mouth hardly able to form the words. His mind teetered on the edge of consciousness.

Everything that had happened to him was right on the surface of his mind. The hand grabbing his nose and jerking his head up. *Fucking pig lover.* The boy's palms so rough after the light touch from the paper girl. The hot, wet lick of the knife, and then the heavy plop of his flesh in the toilet bowl. *Now you'll look like one.*

"Get him in my car," Jane said. "We're taking him to the hospital."

One of the teachers fluttered nearby, grossly fascinated. "I'll call an ambulance."

"No," Jane said, thinking of the bleeding officer who would surely come if they called for help. "We'll take him." The ambulance wasn't close, and the hospital was even farther away. People had died in Swine Hill waiting for someone to come save them.

The parking lot was mostly empty. Bright embers of weak spirits, barely holding on to the world of the living, streaked back and forth through the dark. A clump of students boldly shared a pack of cigarettes under a utility light, watching them carry Henry out.

Jane wanted to hold the teenagers down and scream at them, to let her ghost drill deep into their minds and pull out everything they knew, to ask who had hurt her brother and why. But there wasn't time for that now.

She made space in her back seat, throwing out some of Henry's junky old machine parts and a busted subwoofer. Trigger bent and laid Henry across the seat like something that could shatter.

"Should I drive?" Trigger asked. The tune still cut back and forth through his head.

"No," Jane said. "Just get in."

The town was empty but for the ghosts hauling their shaggy bodies down the roads or whirling like lanterns through the sky. There was no moon out, and the sky with its needling stars felt heavy as a cast iron lid. Jane stomped down on the gas, and her clanking car fishtailed over the cracked pavement.

They hit the highway and crossed out of Swine Hill. Many of the ghosts clinging to her car started to fall away, the road holding no memories they could see themselves in. It glided more smoothly, shedding ghost-weight, metal and rubber parts moving more easily. A stubborn ghost that had lodged itself into her CD player broke loose, and the disc fell into place, shocking them with an eruption of music.

Jane turned it down and talked to Henry, telling him that they would be there soon, that everything would be okay, her words braiding together like a long rope lowered into a dark place. Henry let it wash over him, dizzy and only half understanding. Lines of pain burned hot on his face, and he traced that sigil in his mind, drawing a triangle.

Their headlights ripped across the trees lining the sides of the road. Here and there, a homemade cross was stuck in the grass along the shoulder, a ghost standing over it to pace the spot where it had died. If her brother died in her car, would he return to her? Would his spirit fold itself across her back seat, cradling its pain and waiting forever for her to save him?

Jane's ghost strained to listen for waiting cops or people turning onto the highway, letting Jane know when to slow down and when she could push the engine to its limits.

There's no one for miles. Go, go, go.

Trigger carried Henry into the emergency room. Her brother kept pressure on his nose, not wanting anyone to see it. Dizzy from loss of blood, his mind spun hallucinations. He imagined that the pass of the knife had carved him into a pig. He thought of Hogboss's skin rippling with stitches and scars. If only he held himself together, he could be a person still, safe from slaughter.

The drywall was stained and cracked, the bands of fluorescent lights flickering. There were floor tiles missing, exposing the almost black grout beneath, and the waiting room seats were heavily duct-taped. There were spirits here, though not so many as in Swine Hill. In the corner of the waiting room, a dark-eyed ghost woman stared ahead, waiting for someone long dead to return to her.

Two Pig City workers sat together with bandaged hands. They'd each severed their right index finger, and carried both digits in the same plastic bag. One of the men held the bag up to the light, trying to tell which of the fingers was his own, worried he wouldn't know when the time came.

There were others: a girl who couldn't turn her neck after a car accident; a man with tightness blooming through his chest; a grandmother with a child who'd swallowed floor cleaner. They didn't think about their pain, instead fixating on the cost. They resented doctors the same way they did mechanics, experts who discovered a problem and then made them pay for it.

Trigger helped Henry stand, Jane steadying him. His head hung limp, clothes matted dark and wet. The nurse took him back right away, handing Jane a stack of insurance paperwork. They didn't have insurance. Whatever Henry needed, she knew they couldn't pay for it. She studied the forms and wrote down her name, waiting until the staff wasn't paying attention to set them aside.

Trigger leaned back into the seat beside her, squeezing her hand. "I wish I could read your mind," he said. "Are you okay?"

"I thought I could keep him safe," Jane said. "But I was right there. I didn't even know."

"We'll figure out who did this." Violent thoughts roosted in his mind. He felt out of control, guilty for abandoning his ghost and worried that he was making Jane unhappy. He wanted things to be simple, to find Henry's attacker and to hurt him.

"It doesn't matter who did it. Everyone might as well have. I'm leaving Swine Hill and taking Henry with me. We should have left years ago."

He had been expecting this the entire drive to the hospital, his shoulders tense the whole time at the thought of losing her. "Where will you go?" he asked.

Jane didn't have an answer. She barely had any money. Even if she asked Hogboss for her pay early, it still wouldn't be enough. She didn't know if she could get her father into a car and make him come with her. She couldn't wait any longer, though. She would have to make it work. Looking around the aging waiting room, almost an hour away from Swine Hill and just as poor and rundown, she wondered how far she would have to go to find something better.

You won't find anything better, her ghost said. *Every other place is just like this, but without the people who love you.*

Jane shrugged the ghost's words away. It needed her to believe that, was selfishly trying to keep Jane where she was so that it wouldn't lose its hold on her. She had to get her brother out before something worse happened. Her mother and father would come or they wouldn't. A sad, sinking part of her already knew that Trigger wouldn't leave with her.

"I finally recognized the tune stuck in your head." Jane hummed it quietly, watching his face fall. "You've been thinking of the song from your mom's music box all night. Why?"

His mental defenses collapsed, letting her see into his mind as clearly as if his head was made of glass. Jane saw his father sitting at the table, staring off into space and whistling the tune. Mason had a bad cough from smoking, and it seemed like he hadn't whistled in a long time. But he licked his lips, tapped along with his three-fingered hand, and practiced for hours. It was badly off, too slow, halting. But he was getting closer. He was about halfway there.

Trigger wondered what to say, not sure how much she already knew. "My dad keeps asking me what happened to my brother's ghost. I think he might have found the music box."

Trigger told his father what you buried.

Anger flooded her, Jane's ghost riding it like a wave. "Henry lost everything he cared about because I helped you. That thing isn't your brother anymore. It's poison."

"You've never lost anyone," Trigger said. "You don't know what it's like."

She could tell that he regretted saying it, that he was already shrinking from her, but she was too angry to care. "Have you met my father?" she asked. "No? Ever think there might be a reason for that?"

He sighed, not looking her in the face. "Even with my brother's ghost gone, my dad won't ever leave that house. He's staying in Swine Hill, and I can't leave him behind. I'm the only family he has left. If you leave, I'm not coming. I'm sorry."

"I don't want you to. We're done." Her words, sharp and hot, cut through him just as she'd intended. He'd all but resurrected the ghost that had ruined his life. How could he be so stupid? Why did he feel the need to be such a martyr?

He smiled sadly, looking down at his shoes and drawing his hand back from her armrest. "Thanks for the dance, Jane. Things were nice. I'll miss it."

You still have me. You always will.

Jane recoiled from the spirit. What she wanted was to be alone, to crawl into bed with the lights off and know that no one was there. But the ghost was always with her, always awake and listening, even to her dreams.

Henry stumbled out, a nurse leading him by the arm, his face wrapped in bandages. The woman said that there wasn't any more the doctor would do until they had insurance on file. Jane handed her the blank clipboard of forms, put her arm around Henry, and took him to the elevator. By the time the nurses realized she was leaving, not just stepping out to make a call or go to the bathroom, they would already be gone. Trigger followed, exhausted and heavy, his heart a millstone of regret.

Henry's thoughts were an inventory of violence. A burning house with the door chained shut. The cold weight of a gun and a pocket full of brass-jacketed bullets. A car hurtling toward someone standing in the road. He couldn't keep it up, though. He wasn't the kind of person to hurt people, to see them bleed and bruise under his hands. He didn't understand thoughtless, pointless cruelty like that. He wanted to save himself from it, to be wrapped in a big robot or suit of armor. To fold glass and steel around himself and burn off across the horizon, pulling away from Earth's orbit. But his ghost had floated away, leaving him in the ruins of its brilliance.

He's afraid people will see his piggy snout.

"Stop being such a *bitch*," Jane said.

She could feel the spirit smile in her mind, pleased to have gotten a rise out of her. *He's right, though. People already associate him with the pigs. Things will only get worse.*

21

FOR HOURS, JANE lay awake, seeing her brother's bandaged face. She remembered how Trigger had found him, blood seeping through his fingers on the floor of the bathroom. And then she thought of Trigger telling his father about the music box, throwing away everything she'd done for him. With no one else to be angry with, she tossed in her bed, arguing with her ghost.

I didn't know. The bathroom was on the other side of the building, and there were a lot of people between us. I couldn't listen to everyone at once.

"You've kept things from me before."

Her ghost was wounded, its voice strained and heavy. *Not things like this.*

Jane had an early shift at the plant. A few minutes before her alarm would have sounded, she turned it off and got dressed. Henry's door was closed. She could feel him sleeping, his mind flickering with panic, fists balled in his sheets.

When she had brought Henry home, her mom made Jane explain how Henry had gotten hurt over and over again, as if telling the story a different way might change what had happened. When Jane walked past her mother's bedroom, she could feel a rush of heat blowing out from under the door. Soon, her mom would get up and find someone to unleash her need on. Jane hoped that it wouldn't be Hogboss.

It was raining softly, the world gray and dim. Jane drove through the neighborhood, seeing rows of old houses that had been pulled up straight and square with new siding and shingles. Pig people sat on the porches wearing hats and drinking coffee, snuffling their snouts at the smell of rain.

When she reached the road to Pig City, it was backed up with vehicles. She held her foot on the brake, waiting for the car in front of her to inch forward. There were always a lot of people coming and going from the plant, but she'd never seen traffic stopped on the road before.

"What's going on?" Jane asked her ghost. "Was there an accident or something?"

The spirit was silent, sulking in the back of her mind. Jane sighed and closed her eyes, wishing she had slept. She went back through the faces from the dance, the kids who mobbed the DJ booth, the ones standing along the walls. Henry had texted her something about kids trying to jump him on the bus a few days before. How many people in that room had known what was going to happen?

She thought of Trigger — her fury with him for telling his father where the music box was buried, but also the feel of his arms around her — and she almost started to cry. A few feet at a time, her car made the climb up the narrow, winding road. Rain beat across the windshield. She shuffled through song after song on her CD player, but nothing felt right.

At the top of the road, a group of pig security guards in rain ponchos stood in front of the gates to the plant. The gates were chained shut. The pigs waved cars to turn around and head back down the road.

Jane rolled down her window, rain drenching her arm and shoulder. "What's going on?" she asked.

The pig woman gave her a strained smile from under her hood. "The plant is temporarily closed for maintenance. Please turn around."

Her ghost swam to the front of her mind. *She's lying.*

"What kind of maintenance?" Jane asked. "Will it be open tomorrow?"

"No, not tomorrow. But soon. The plant manager will make an announcement."

Something happened. Hogboss is angry. He closed the plant as punishment.

The ghost sent her a barrage of images. Hogboss crying at his kitchen table. A photograph of Dennis. A group of police standing in the light of their sirens, the bleeding man among them with a mad grin on his face.

"Could I speak to Hogboss?"

The pig woman stepped away from her car and waved for her to turn around. The car behind her honked.

Drive slowly back down, her ghost said. *Some of them know why. They're thinking about it.*

Jane passed car after car waiting to go to work. She stared at the faces of the drivers. They looked down at their steering wheels or talked on their phones. Their faces were worried, tired, guilty.

They've heard rumors. They knew someone who was there. Their kids saw something. They have suspicions. The ghost pulled fragments of what happened out of their minds, building a story in Jane's head. She came down from the ridge and drove aimlessly through town, letting her ghost reach into the houses around her.

A group of kids saw Dennis waiting in the parking lot after the dance was over. His blue suit looked white under the glare of the sodium lights. He said he was going to get a ride home with a friend.

There was a bright-eyed girl, holding her arms close and keeping her distance from other people. A fragile, tissue-paper girl. She was afraid of the loud boys in the big truck who followed her in the parking lot, who offered her a ride home wedged between them with the gearshift between her legs.

"He needs a ride," the girl had said, pointing at Dennis. "Take him."

Why had Dennis gotten into the truck? Maybe he knew the paper girl was afraid. Maybe he did it so that they would go away and leave her alone.

In the truck, the boys took Dennis joyriding on the back roads and dirt tracks around Swine Hill, crashing through potholes and pushing down grass-strangled alleys. They had a bottle of vodka and made him drink, watching him wince with their laughing eyes.

"Take me home," he had said.

"Soon. Real soon," they had replied.

They took Dennis to an old barn in the woods where other kids had gathered to drink and lie around a bonfire. They clinked beers and drunkenly pawed one another in the dark. A girl tried to make out with Dennis, but kept bumping into his snout. She fell backwards, laughing.

"What does it even look like?" she snorted. "How big is a pig dick?"

Dennis slurred that he wanted to go home. He rolled around on the dead grass, his shirt unbuttoned, trying to get up.

"First, you have to show us," one of the boys said. "We won't take you home until you do."

They stripped his clothes off, throwing his suit jacket, pants, shirt, and underwear into the bonfire one by one. The garments caught fast and flared up, turning to ash and floating embers. Dennis stood in the firelight's glow, trying to cover himself and looking painfully like a human boy.

"Why'd you burn his clothes?" the girl asked. There was a note of sympathy in her voice now, a gnawing worry. Only now had she realized something bad was going to happen to the shy pig boy, that things were too far along for her to stop it. She blinked, buzzed and bleary-eyed, telling them to stop.

"We're going to take him back to the farm," they said.

Someone slipped a coarse rope around Dennis's neck. They kicked his knees out from under him, making him get down on all fours. The boys led him to the truck, and there, they threw him over the tailgate and tied him wrists to ankles. They drove away from the party, the girl watching their taillights fade and wondering what to do but not doing anything at all.

The boys talked about him as they drove. How much they hated seeing pigs in their town. The pig boy wasn't one of them. He didn't deserve to walk around their school on two legs. They would make him remember what he was.

What had Dennis been thinking, bent double and tied in the dark? Did he remember a few hours before when he moved so light and fast up on his feet, his suit coat trailing him like wings, that it was like he flew? Was the ghost of the dancing girl with him in the back of the truck, or had she already passed on?

The boys drove around town for a while, not knowing what to do with the pig boy, but knowing they weren't done with him yet. People saw them stopped at a traffic light, or getting gas, or coming too fast around a bend in the road. They spied Dennis tied and naked in the back of the truck. They ignored it. Pretended he was only an animal when they knew otherwise. Got their coffee and went to work, busy with their own problems. What did it matter to them what happened to one of the pigs?

Drunk and not paying attention, the boys took a wrong turn and drove into the dark heart of downtown with its army of sad ghosts. The vicious shades came out of the boarded-up doors and surrounded them. The ghosts saw a violence and hate in the boys that reflected their own, and they flowed into the cab of the truck and filled them up like venom.

The haunted boys went into the shattered buildings for knives and saws. Weeping with living eyes over everything they had lost, the ghosts dragged Dennis onto the tailgate, and they killed him in the dark. They carved up his body, butchering him like the pig carcasses they had handled while alive. And then, bloody-handed and shivering with pain, they wandered back into the buildings they'd come from. The police found the abandoned truck and Dennis's remains a few hours later. The boys stared out at them from the ruins, their eyes gone blue with the dead. The cops left them there.

Jane turned away, not wanting to let her ghost lead her into downtown to the spot where it had happened. She had already seen the bloody asphalt in her mind, and she didn't need to see it again.

Henry would blame himself for this, too.

Shouldn't he? You can't blame everything on the dead.

Jane went home, pulling into the driveway just as her mother was coming out the door in her Pig City uniform.

"Henry is still sleeping," her mother said. She was shaky, sweat running down her face. "Can you stay with him today? Someone should be here."

Her mom worried that Swine Hill had broken Henry, that he would retreat into himself and vanish just like their father.

"Have you heard from Hogboss?" Jane asked.

Her mother shook her head. "I'm supposed to see him at work later."

"Something bad happened to Dennis. The plant's closed. You should just stay home."

Her mother hesitated in the driveway, caught between love for her son and love for Hogboss. But both of her children had flinched from her. Both of them resented her for the ghost that burned in her breast. She couldn't talk to them the way she could with the pig man. Walter had only ever been kind, had never blamed her for anything. He made her feel like she wasn't her ghost, and no one had made her feel that way in a long time.

Stunned by her mother's depth of feeling for Hogboss, Jane watched her get into her car and drive away.

F OR THREE DAYS, Henry's phone lit up with messages from Hogboss. *I thought you were going to keep him safe. I thought he had friends. Was I wrong to let him leave the plant? When will it stop hurting to think of him?*

Henry didn't write back. He lay in bed, the bandages tight around his face, the scar of his nose burning with pain no matter how many pain relievers he took. Finally, Hogboss texted him the time and place for the funeral.

Bethany texted him too. She might have found a way to beat the alien light, but it meant she had to move slowly, to stay very still. A sprint down the court or a leap to catch a ball might send her flying through the fabric of the world. But as long as she sat and concentrated on breathing, she could keep her balance. Henry had told her the same things months before when she was trying to overcome her ghosts. Give up. Quit trying to win. To survive the alien, she would have to stop being who she was.

Maybe it's for the best, she wrote. *I'll finally be able to leave Swine Hill.* Henry felt like he might as well have killed her, too.

Jane came to sit on the edge of the mattress and talk to him. She was sorry that her ghost hadn't seen this coming. She was leaving Swine Hill as soon as she could, insisted that he come with her. Dennis's funeral was in the morning. Jane would take him. Her words fell over him like rain as he drifted in and out of sleep. Everything was so wrong that just thinking about anything exhausted him.

In the middle of the night, he heard someone crying. He touched his eyes to see if it had been himself. Henry rolled over, expecting to see Jane or his mother, and came face-to-face with the ghost of the dancing girl.

The pale burn of his computer background illuminated her face, her dark hair, the hollows of her eyes. Instead of reflecting light, her body was shot through with it, like a piece of glass. He saw the matted bedsheets and blankets beneath her. The girl was far less solid than she had been before. *It, not she,* he reminded himself. A ghost was a thing, never a person.

"Why are you here?" It was the first he'd spoken in days.

She moved closer, her anger radiating into him. "It was my house before it was yours."

"That's not what I meant." He reached for her, surprised that her shoulder felt solid under his hand. Her skin was cold and crawled with electricity. He pulled his hand away. "I thought your spirit would have moved on. You got what you wanted, didn't you? You finally had your dance."

He didn't say it with accusation. He didn't feel up to judging anyone just now. He was only confused. The ghost girl shouldn't be here.

"Dennis changed me. The world was so new for him, and he loved all of it. If a moth flew into the drama room, he would stare at it for an hour. He asked me the strangest questions: 'Why did it fly here? Can we help it? Do you know its name?' The more time I spent with him, the more I wanted to show him things. I didn't get to live for long, but I had so much more than he ever did."

"He's dead now. After the dance."

More anger from her, a physical wave that needled his skin. "I know.

I was inside Dennis while they killed him. He kept asking me why they were hurting him. How do you answer a question like that?"

"Because they're stupid and cruel. They're fighting for everything to stay the same, even if that means nothing will ever get better. They deserve Pig City. I hope it grinds them up."

"Pig City is gone now. Hogboss closed down the plant."

Henry got up and staggered to the window, his head heavy. There was no plume of white smoke illuminated by the lights of the plant. The ridge was indistinguishable from the forest around it, lightless and black. No headlights of cars moved through the streets. The town held its breath.

"What did your father think he was doing when he helped me make the pigs?" Henry asked. "Is this what he wanted?"

"He wanted to build a machine that would run on pain," the ghost girl said. "He thought he could power the world with it. Dennis was more than that, though. It's good that your ghost left, Henry. He could have made you do much worse."

He accidentally tried to breathe through his nose, and his face caught fire. He held the edge of his desk, lightheaded. It was hard to imagine how he could have screwed things up for everyone much worse than he already had. Wasn't the town itself an engine of pain, its people cylinders under pressure, moved by anger and hurt? He had hoped that the pig people were somehow a solution for everything wrong with the world, some missing variable that he didn't understand yet. But they weren't. They were just people, caught in the same machine as everyone else. It would shatter them, too.

He got back into his bed. Dawn was coming, the sky lightening outside. The dancing girl's ghost grew wispy and blurred along with the dark.

"Why are ghosts stronger at night?" Henry asked. "I've never understood."

"To hold on, we have to remember what things used to be like. It's hard to do that when so many new people are walking down our streets, sleeping in our rooms, sitting at our desks. If a ghost has a strong enough attachment, it doesn't matter. But at night, it's quieter. It's harder to tell that the world has left us behind.

"Henry." Her voice was faint. She moved closer to him. "I'm passing on. I won't be back after tonight."

"Are you afraid?"

"Can I stay here for a little while? Just until morning?"

He nodded.

"At the old bridal shop, there's a ghost. She haunts mirrors. If you find her, tell her that she won't see me again. Tell her that I love her and that she needs to move on if she can."

Henry thought again of Dennis dancing with the mirror at prom. It sent a wave of grief through him. He told the dancing girl that he would deliver her message.

She rolled over to face the coming light, its rays shooting through her skin and erasing her, minute by minute. Henry sat up on his elbow, watching until she fully disappeared. Somehow, only now, it felt like Dennis was really gone, blown away like smoke with the dancing girl. Henry held everything in until a moth floated over his bed and landed on the wall, flexing its drab wings. Then he curled up and wept until Jane came to wake him for the funeral.

White shirt tucked into his darkest jeans. A stained tie of his father's. And Trigger's rented tuxedo jacket.

He'd left it in the seat of Jane's car, and she insisted Henry wear it even though it was far too big. A tremor of emotion passed over her face when she put it over his shoulders, but she squeezed her eyes tight and fled the room. Henry turned to the mirror and saw himself: the worn-out clothes, the coat hanging limp over his back, the dark bandages still covering his nose.

In the garage, he threw open bins and boxes, scattering tools amidst the dust, until he found an old painting mask. It had a plastic shield for the wearer's eyes and a respirator that covered the entire bottom half of the face. It looked like a gas mask. Henry wiped it off, finding it stained with red paint, and strapped it on.

When Jane saw him, she suddenly laughed. "People are only going to stare at you more if you wear that."

Henry watched her through the plastic guard, not moving to take it off. He didn't want anyone to see the bandages, especially not whoever had cut him. It was bad enough that he had to leave the house at all. Finally, Jane picked up her keys.

The church was on the outer edges of Swine Hill, away from the roiling ghosts of downtown and the now silent factory. A cemetery curled around the sides of the church, the graves well maintained and marching away in gray rows. How strange, Henry thought, that here was a place full of the dead but empty of ghosts. No spirit had an attachment to the empty lot near the church. They were all haunting elsewhere.

Cars stacked down the roadside, filling fields and massing on the shoulders. It felt like the whole town was here. Not that any of these people had been good friends of Dennis or his family. They wanted spectacle, and they hoped for mercy. In the distance, the sky over the pork-processing plant was clean of smoke.

Inside, the pews were full of people wearing Pig City uniforms. Their blue coveralls were stained black with pig blood. Henry wondered what they were trying to say. Was it supposed to be a gesture of support? A threat? He wanted to ask Jane, but she was distant, preoccupied with her own thoughts. Occasionally, she would whisper something to herself, arguing with her ghost.

A group of kids from the high school crowded together in the back. They murmured in one another's ears, smiling and joking even here, even after everything. When Henry walked in, several of them looked up and met eyes with him.

Someone made a low noise, almost a cough. Then others echoed it, raising their hands to cover their mouths. They were quiet, careful that only Henry and Jane could hear it as they walked by. A grunt. A pig noise. They were making it at him. Henry's neck and shoulders locked tense, a hot and metallic feeling floating through his blood. He hated them. He hadn't known he could hate someone so much.

Jane put her arm around him and led him toward the front. "Just be glad you can't hear what they're thinking," she said. "There are worse words than *pig*."

He looked around for someone he knew, hoping Bethany would be here. She hadn't answered his texts that morning. In the front, a group of pigs stood together, all of them sweating in too-tight suits. Hogboss stood with them, long-faced and hollow-eyed. When the pig man noticed Henry and his sister, he motioned to an empty space beside him, right at the front of the church.

Their mother was already there, sitting with Hogboss in the front row. She wore a yellow floral dress. Her forehead and arms were slick with heat, her cheeks glistening. Unable to hug Henry or Jane, she gave them a small wave.

"Have you seen him yet?" Hogboss gestured to the casket at the front. "Go see what they did."

Jane sat near their mother, leaving Henry to walk up alone. There was a short line. People streamed by, covering their mouths to hide disgust or thrill. He reached the head of the line and looked down, not understanding at first what was in front of him.

There was no body. At least, no whole body. There were parts. Pieces stripped of skin and bone and wrapped in cellophane against Styrofoam plates. A head. A piece of leg. Hooved feet. Dennis's skin had been washed pale and bloodless. The brutal ghosts of Swine Hill and the vicious men who animated them had processed Dennis like an ordinary pig. He had been carved up and packaged for a grocery store shelf.

Henry stood over the mess for several minutes, too shocked to move. Something cold trickled onto his foot. There was a bed of ice in the bottom of the casket, melting and pooling on the floor.

He sat back down by Hogboss, the pig man huge and straight-backed, scarred hands folded in his lap. "Did you see what they did to my sweet boy?"

"Maybe we should close the casket." Henry's voice was hollow through the mask, strange and unreal.

"I want everyone to see," Hogboss said. "They think the plant being

closed is cruel. Let them see what cruelty looks like. Let all of them ask
what hand they had in this."

Henry looked over his shoulder. "Some of them are laughing."

Jane squeezed his shoulder, keeping him from saying more.

Hogboss gave him a tight smile, made more human for the malice
written in his lips and teeth. "They won't be laughing for very long."

A few people came to Hogboss, shaking his hand and offering con-
dolences. One man lingered afterward, the palest hint of ghost-shine
behind his eyes. He cleared his throat to speak.

"Mr. Hogboss, you can count on us to run the plant for you while
you get through this. There's no need to leave it shut down. You can
take as much time as you need."

"The plant won't be reopening," Hogboss said.

The ghost-light in the man's eyes bloomed and deepened, the spirit
almost pushing out of his body. "For how long?"

"It will never reopen. Corporate wants to start the self-slaughtering
pig project at other plants out of state. There won't be any need for the
Swine Hill location."

The man walked away, his hands spasming and limbs moving erratically. He fell back into his pew and told the other workers around
him. A hissing, vicious whisper spread through the group, eyes glowing with their raging ghosts. They stared at Henry, faces full of accusation. He turned back to the front, wishing he hadn't sat next to the pigs,
but he could still feel their eyes on him.

Jane flinched and reflexively covered her ears, like she stood in the
middle of a shouting crowd.

Henry tried to run the numbers on how the plant's closing would af-
fect the town. Home values were already low. His mother had told him
that they owed more on their house than it was worth. But without the
plant, their house and everyone else's would be worthless. The last few
businesses would fold. The town would crumble and fall apart. For the
people left behind, no money and no possessions of any value, what
would they do?

"What about all the pig people?" Henry asked.

"Corporate will move us wherever it needs. We lived here and we tried to make a good life for ourselves, but Swine Hill was never ours. Our houses, our trucks, even our appliances. It all belongs to Pig City. I tried to tell Dennis that, to make him understand that the world wasn't his."

"You told them to close the plant," Jane said. "To punish people. Do you know what that will do to the town?"

"I have an idea," Hogboss said.

Henry tried to imagine his family putting all their belongings in two cars, locking up the house, and going somewhere else. His paranoid, mute father tied up in the back seat. His mother sucking on a cup of ice and blasting herself with the air conditioner. The robot, its legs still broken, hanging out of the open trunk. And Henry, wearing his painting mask and facing the road ahead.

They had family out of state, his uncle, cousins, and grandparents. But Henry had barely spoken to them in years, didn't even know what town they lived in. They had escaped Swine Hill and its clinging ghosts a long time ago. They wouldn't risk Henry's family bringing all that past and pain back to haunt their door.

The preacher stepped behind the altar and spoke platitudes. He did not know Dennis or any of the pigs. It was still an open question in the churches scattered through Swine Hill whether God could love a walking, talking animal, whether salvation was for the pig people, whether it was a sin even to harm a pig. But the preacher put all of that aside. He talked about Dennis being in a richer place, read verses from Revelation about streets paved with gold, and spoke of building prosperity on Earth. Under the Bible verses and talk of Heaven, his appeal to Hogboss — *Reopen the plant* — was nakedly clear.

They sang hymns at the end, and the pigs raised their rough, scalpel-made voices to scrape through songs of love and forgiveness. But they were united with Hogboss, the first of them, the one who'd lost so much. They had no forgiveness for Swine Hill.

Hogboss pulled Henry aside after the service. People were already leaving, the lines of cars dissolving and heading home before Dennis was lowered into the dirt. "There are things you never told me," Hogboss said.

Henry thought of the guys at school who harassed Dennis. The pig boy's friendship with a ghost. His own nose being cut off for having spent time with the pigs. Yes, there was a lot Henry had kept from him.

"After you made me," Hogboss said, "you taught me what I needed to know to work and live."

"I don't remember any of it."

"You taught me to keep my hands away from fire. You taught me that knives could hurt, but I remembered that from when you made me. You taught me the taste of poison, how electricity could grab me, what could break a bone. But Dennis isn't even here, and he hurts me so much. You never told me anything about this."

Henry hugged him, his facemask rubbing painfully against the pig man's side. Hogboss laid a massive arm over his back.

"I'm sorry," Henry said. "You're right. I should have told you."

THE CAR'S ENGINE moaned, and the steering column shook whenever Jane had to slow down or stop. Even to Henry, the car felt full of spirits. They burrowed into its metal like mold, drifting viral through the veins of gas lines and electrical wiring. Everything about it felt heavy and slow.

Breathing through his nose still burned. Henry looked at himself in the car's dash mirror, readjusting the painting mask. It was hot and cut angry lines across his neck and face. Still, it was better than seeing the bandages, the flatness where the end of his nose had been. He was afraid of the day when the bandages would be ready to come off.

Jane took him to the bridal shop to return Trigger's tuxedo jacket and her dress.

"You can stay in the car if you want," she said. "It should only take a few minutes."

After the funeral, Henry just wanted to be alone. He didn't want to feel strangers staring, to wonder if another attacker was slipping up behind him. But he had told the dancing girl that he would say goodbye to the ghost in the mirror.

"I'll come," he said. "Are you feeling okay? You know. About him."

Jane got out of the car. "Let's hurry. It's too hot to sit in the car and talk."

A bell chimed when they walked in. The store was cramped, surrounded by mirrors along the walls. There were two pig boys inside, trying to explain to the owner how they had stained and torn their tuxedos. Henry didn't remember seeing them at prom. They must have had their own dance, maybe at the factory. So strange that he could have made them but knew so little about their lives. For a moment, he felt a rush of happiness. All his life, he'd wanted to do something great, to solve a problem that mattered or do something that would make his name famous. His ghost had left him, and he wasn't sure anymore if he was as brilliant as he'd always believed. But he'd made the pigs, and somewhere a few nights ago they had danced. That was worth something, wasn't it?

While Jane returned the dress and jacket and the pigs tried to talk the owner out of charging them extra, Henry walked through the racks of clothes, dresses as satiny and soft and cool as milk running along his arms as he passed. At the back wall, he stood in front of one of the giant mirrors, its surface cloudy with dust.

His hair was messy and needed to be cut, and the mask was bulky and strange. He looked like a survivor of the end of the world. He supposed he was. Behind his reflection, he could just make out the image of a ghost deep in the glass. She looked like she stood in the middle of the bridal shop, but she was only inside the mirror. She held a red gown in her arms and danced with it, crushing the fabric against her breast and wrapping its sleeve around her hand. Henry tapped on the glass to get her attention, wanted to tell her what the dancing girl had said, but she wouldn't come closer. Maybe she already knew.

The pig boys walked out of the shop. Jane gave the owner Trigger's legal name — "Riley Mason." Hearing the name reminded him of losing his ghost. Such a small, stupid accident. Henry felt helpless and furious all over again. He had known the boy would be trouble when he first saw him, had known Jane was making a mistake. He tried to stomp down the feeling, to think of something else before his sister read his mind.

Henry knocked harder on the mirror, but the ghost wouldn't acknowledge him.

"Krystal wants you to move on," he said. "She loves you, but it's time for you to go."

But the spirit trapped in the glass was far away and dancing, twirling with the dress in her arms like she would never stop.

Bethany finally texted him back. Her parents had packed everything and were leaving in the morning. Both of them worked at the plant. With it closing, there was no reason for them to stay. Bethany was on her way over to say goodbye. Now that she had been so utterly defeated by something, her ghosts would surely relax their grip.

He should have been happy for her. Bethany was getting out of Swine Hill. She could go anywhere now, could *be* anything. But Henry couldn't find anything to celebrate in this. His mouth was sour with the unfairness of it all.

He sat on the roof outside his window to wait for her, watching the sky grow dark and spirits rise from the pavement. They were oblivious to the plant being closed, eternally flowing up to the steel doors to take on form and toil with the past. When everything else in the town was gone, the dead would still be here.

Bethany pulled up in the driveway. Henry waved to her from the rooftop. She walked slowly to the door, testing her weight one foot at a time. When she came upstairs, Henry started to come back inside, but Bethany held a hand up to stop him. She climbed through the window, placing her feet carefully on the shingles, face tight with concentration. Bethany moved like the world under her was made of thin ice, ready to shatter and drop away. It made Henry burn with shame to see what he'd done to her.

She didn't ask him about any more tests. They both knew that he couldn't reverse what he had done. Whether she let go and fell into another reality or managed to hang on was entirely dependent on her. Strangely, it was easier for both of them that way.

"Do you see anything up there?" Henry pointed at the sky, dark clouds spreading in the fading light.

"Yeah," Bethany said. "It's a little hard to look at. Like a city made of light."

Henry wondered if, somewhere in the infinite universe, there was a Swine Hill where he hadn't made everything so much worse. Maybe there was a place where he was the kind of person he had always wanted to be.

From inside the house, Henry could hear Jane arguing with their mother. She had been trying to get him to clean up his room and pack all day, but it was hopeless. How could you plan to leave when you didn't even know where you were going? How could you decide what to bring when there was no room to bring much of anything at all?

Their mother insisted that Hogboss would reopen the plant. She was talking to him about it. She said everything was going to be okay, but when had things here ever been okay?

The moon was heavy and bright over their heads. More ghosts surged up the hill, capping it in white like it was covered in snow. Beneath it, the town lay dark and still. Most streetlights were long burned out. Few cars cut the dark with their beams. Everything waited.

"When do the bandages come off?" Bethany asked.

Henry turned away, the mask bulky, his own breath warm on his face. "I don't know. I'll probably just keep wearing the mask anyway."

"Build yourself a better nose. Make it out of brass or gold or something. That's what the Henry I know would do."

He couldn't tell if she was joking or not. "You should hate me," Henry said. "Why are we still friends?"

She shifted on the roof, balancing with both hands. "I know you didn't mean for this to happen. And I was the one who caught the ball of light. I could have just watched it fall. But I've always thought that I could do anything. Sooner or later, I had to find out that wasn't true."

Henry sighed. "It *was* true, though. Until me."

Her hands tensed on the roof, like she'd almost lost her balance. "I dream about swimming. I worry that I'll make a sudden move in my sleep, and then I'll fall through the world. And then, what if I never land? What if I just keep falling?"

Henry struggled to find something to say. He'd broken so much. After Dennis was killed, did the pig boy's consciousness just slip through the world? Did he fall forever, or might he have arrived in the city of light only Bethany could see? Not even the ghosts knew what was next. Maybe it was only a starless nothing, an absolute silence, the fear that made ghosts cling so tightly to the world.

"Don't worry about me," Bethany said. "Maybe I can go to college now. My life was already going to change, whether I wanted it to or not. And being still is a kind of game. I can be good at that too."

There was a stroke of lightning in the distance. Rain started to fall, a few drops striking the plastic screen of Henry's mask. He waited for Bethany to go inside, then followed.

In the hallway, Jane sat in a circle of her own clothes, throwing things into boxes. She argued with her ghost, blurting out half sentences and staring ahead like she could see it. The spirit wanted her to stay. Jane was risking her own ghost, her best friend, to get Henry out of Swine Hill.

The lights flickered, steadied, and then went out completely. Darkness and quiet fell over them. Henry led Bethany downstairs, using his phone as a flashlight. His family gathered in the living room. Wind tossed branches against the windows, and the floor shook with thunder. The rain wrapped its big hands around the house.

Henry's mother pulled candles out of the hall closet, but her skin was so hot that the wax deformed and wept in her palms, sliding apart. The robot wheeled over and tried to pick up the mess from the floor, wax dripping and hardening in long strings from its hands.

Bethany sat on the stairwell, arms crossed and head down, no doubt concentrating on not falling through the world. Henry wanted to say something to her, about how strong he thought she was or how much her friendship had meant to him. How much he would miss her when she left. How sorry he was that he'd changed things for her. He didn't know where to start.

Jane came over and put her arm around his shoulder, hearing everything he couldn't say.

Headlights cut across their curtains. A car pulled up in their driveway.

Henry thought maybe it was Bethany's parents coming to claim her, but when he looked through the window, a scattering of old vehicles were parked in the street outside. A truck sat blocking Jane's car in the driveway.

"They were at the funeral," Jane said. "They're angry about the plant being closed."

Henry watched people get out of their trucks. They wore Pig City work clothes — coveralls, hairnets, facemasks, gloves. Many of them were haunted, trembling with ghosts. Their eyes burned blue in the dark and they murmured senselessly, the crowd of souls inside their bodies fighting to speak past one another. But just as many weren't haunted at all, their eyes dull and hard, possessed only by their own resentment and need to lash out.

One of the men saw Henry peeking between the curtains and shouted. "We've come for you. We're taking back what's ours."

"We have to leave," Henry said. "*Now.* Let's go out the back."

Jane tilted her head, listening to the storm of violent thoughts only she could hear. "People are in the backyard, too. They're all around the house."

Their mother threw open the curtains and looked out. A lightning flash illuminated the yard and the crowd closing in on them. "What do they want?" she asked.

"They want us," Jane said. She turned to Henry, squeezing his hand. "But mostly, they want you."

The door bounced in its frame and cracked as something slammed into it from the other side. Shining eyes stared through the splintered boards, their voices a murmur, so many ghosts trying to move one tongue. "We had nothing," they said, "and you took it away."

"Save us," Henry told the robot. "Get rid of them."

The robot shook its head in irritation. It thrust its arms through the cracked door and parted it like cloth. Rain blew in around it, lightning striking again and again in the distance, revealing the yard in sudden bursts. The machine rolled into the men, pressing them back with its weight and flailing its metal fists.

The robot smashed someone hard in the chest, and the man dropped. The robot wheeled forward, arms up and threatening anyone to come within reach. Wind and rain blew over it, the machine glinting in the storm light. For a moment, Henry thought the robot would drive the mob away. But water seeped into its damaged legs, and arcs of electricity snapped across its chest. The machine already struggled with the colony of spirits chewing their way through its metal hull — water flooding its delicate electronics was too much. Its arms drooped. It lost its balance and tipped over in its chair.

The men grabbed bricks from the garden and fell on the robot, smashing in its bucket-like head and denting its metal body. It shuddered and raised its arms, trying to fight them off. It turned its head to look back through the door at Henry, and the light inside of it died.

The plant workers came marching into the house, rainwater pebbling on their beards and sluicing down their faces. They reached out with scarred hands, ready to take out their anger and helplessness on anyone they could catch.

Bethany herded everyone back, shoving Henry, Jane, and their mother toward the kitchen door. "Get to your car," she said.

Henry wanted to argue with her or find some better plan, but the mob was coming for him. He fell back to the kitchen door, dragged by his sister's tight hand around his arm and his mother's scorching palm on the back of his neck. As they ran into the dark and rain of the backyard, Bethany stood in the doorway, trying to keep the men from following.

Through water beading on his facemask, Henry watched Bethany fight. She dipped low, lunging like a boxer, spinning — untouchable. But her face was blank with shock, like she'd just tumbled off a ledge and found she couldn't fly. She sank inch by inch through the floor tiles.

A woman swung at her face. Bethany grabbed her arm and punched out, knocking the woman down. For a second, Henry saw Bethany's shoe sink through the floor, out of this reality, but she balanced on her other leg and concentrated, pulling her foot back up.

"If we can't butcher pigs, we'll butcher pig lovers," one of the men shouted. He wasn't haunted, his face merely human in its thrill to hurt. The man raised a cleaver, its blade catching the storm light, and chopped down at Bethany's shoulder.

She stepped inside his reach, the knife cutting only air, and grabbed him under his arms. Bending her legs, Bethany jumped up and twisted to the side, throwing the man toward the wall. Instead of smashing against the paneling, she shoved him through a seam in reality, his heavy body vanishing into the air. She almost went with him, her upper body disappearing for a moment before she pulled herself back into the world.

The haunted and unhaunted alike fell on Bethany en masse, battering her face and clawing at her arms, trying to drag her to the floor. She shoulder-checked them, swept their legs, knocked them off the thin beam of this world while trying to keep her own balance. They dropped into oblivion with their cargo of ghosts as if they had never existed. As she fought them, her foot would slip below for a moment, then her whole leg, then her body up to her hips. She jumped back up, struggling to stay afloat. The more she moved, the deeper she fell.

In the yard, Henry pulled away from his mother, the back of his neck bubbling up from her burning hand. A few people made it past Bethany and ran for him, separating him from his family. Jane ran around the side of the house with their mother and Henry sprinted the other way, his feet slipping in the mud.

The man chasing Henry spoke through his teeth, his strange words giving voice to the dead within him: "We still have hands to give. Our flesh was made for cutting. Where will our sons bleed now?"

Henry got around the man and ran to the front yard. His sister and mother were already in the car. There were too many people between them, though. He looked to the open doorway, past the wreck of the robot, and saw Bethany still struggling inside. She threw another person through reality, her face bruised and flushed from the fight. Maybe she could win even when the world was dissolving under her feet. Maybe she was as unstoppable as she had always believed.

Three people rushed Bethany. Her feet went out from under her. She stuck an arm out to catch herself, but her hand passed through the floor. Her eyes met Henry's for just a moment, and then she fell through the world—

And was gone.

The ghost-eyed mob came for Henry then, knives clutched in their hands. His mask fogged, making it hard to see, and Henry ran through the rain, looking for someone who could help. Blue and red lights cut through the dark. Henry turned and ran toward a police car. Jane honked her horn and yelled something out her window, but he couldn't hear what she said. He opened the cop's passenger door and fell inside, slamming it behind him.

The cop, blood running from his eyes and ears and trickling from the corners of his mouth, threw out a startled arm in the dark.

"I've got you," the officer shouted. "I've got you."

The same thing Henry's father had once said when Henry had climbed into a tree as a boy, one of his few clear memories of the man. *Jump into my arms. I've got you.*

Henry reached for him in the dark, ghosts gathering around them, and waited to be saved.

PART III

24

JANE SHOUTED FOR her brother from the window of her car, her voice swallowed in the storm. Henry ran toward a parked police cruiser, its spinning lights soaking the front of their house in oceanic blues. She could feel the bleeding man sitting inside, his violent pleasure unrolling warm and wet and full with itself.

The men closed around Jane's car, blocking her view. Some were driven by bitter ghosts, but just as many were possessed only by their own hate and anger. In the passenger seat, her mother begged her to drive away. Jane was right inside Henry's mind, could feel him become scared and small, like a child again. He threw himself forward, crying out to be saved.

And then, he was gone like a light switching off, his mind too far away for her to hear him anymore.

Had Henry gotten away? Run too far for her ghost to hear him? Or had he been knocked unconscious? She asked her ghost where Henry was, but it was quiet, swollen with something it didn't want to say.

"No," Jane said. "You don't know that."

She hesitated for a moment, her foot holding down the brake. The crowd pressed against her car, their hands covering the windows and reaching across the windshield. Jane could hear their raucous thoughts, the voices of the living mixing with the dead. She couldn't see anything through their interlocking fingers. It was like the town had come to bury them under its weight.

A fist smashed into her window, cracking the glass.

Jane let her foot off the brake, and the car lurched forward across the front lawn, shrugging off the weight of the mob. She drove through the backyard, scraped over the curb, and came out onto the street on the other side.

She drove fast in the rain, her car exploding through potholes and sliding around curves, circling the neighborhood for any sign of her brother. But she couldn't feel Henry's mind. There was no sign of the police cruiser, either, the bleeding man gone like an eel into the dark.

Jane, her ghost pleaded. *What if Henry isn't here to find? I don't want you to get hurt trying to save what can't be saved.*

The ghost was only doing what it always did. Digging into her insecurities. Finding some fear to feed itself on. It had no idea if Henry was alive or not. But it wanted Jane to feel alone, needed her to need it.

You do *need me,* it said. *Now more than ever.*

Jane ignored it, focusing on her brother. She had already let him get hurt once. That she might have failed him again, failed him completely and unforgivably, was too much for her to process. She turned her high beams on and watched for the silhouette of a boy running between the houses.

Her mother sobbed in the seat beside her, thinking about all that she had already lost.

Jane checked her rearview mirror, but none of the haunted plant workers followed them. They'd swarmed over the spot where Bethany had vanished, tearing apart the floor to try to find her. Jane wondered what had happened to the girl, if she was alive or dead or something worse.

At the memory of Bethany falling out of the world, the ghost pressed deeply into Jane's muscles and bones, sending pain shooting through her limbs. Whatever waited outside this world, the spirit was terrified of it.

They drove around for over an hour. Finally her mother said, "Go to Walter's house. He'll help us."

She was like a furnace next to Jane, the seats tacky and plastic from heat. Did her mom really think the pig man's house was safe? Or did she only want to be comforted, to let out her fire on someone?

Why shouldn't she be comforted? What else is left?

"Hogboss is the reason those people came," Jane said. "What if they come for him next?"

But she turned the car around, threading through the empty neighborhoods to where most of the pigs lived. She didn't know where else to go.

The pig man lived on the other side of downtown, under the ridge where Pig City stood. Jane skirted the outer edges of the haunted middle of Swine Hill, but they were close enough to hear the wails of ghosts breaking glass and howling in the dark. Decades' worth of hate and need lay beneath brick and concrete, deep as the sea.

The pig man's work truck wasn't in his driveway. Jane's mother took out her keys and opened the door, waving her inside. She had a key. Jane wasn't sure why that made her so angry, but it did. The house was small with old paneling, scuffed linoleum, and sagging furniture. At the funeral, Hogboss had told Henry that nothing the pigs had was theirs. Standing in Hogboss's living room was as good as standing in the plant itself. Pig City owned him.

Evidence of Jane's mother was everywhere: hairbrushes, lip balm, and bar coasters were scattered over the tables. A pair of her jeans, some shirts, a stray bra lying on the floor. Burn marks on the countertops. On the carpet and back of the couch. On the posts of his bed.

"We'll stay here tonight," her mother said. "Tomorrow, I'll call the police station. Walter will go down there and clear this up for us. Ghosts don't usually bother the pigs. We'll tell them that Henry didn't have anything to do with those people damaging property and breaking into houses."

Jane didn't know what to say to her. How could her mother not understand? The bleeding man hadn't come to stop the violence; he'd come as part of it. Jane watched her go into Hogboss's kitchen and pour herself a drink. Her mother trembled, full of fear. But she wasn't worried that Henry was in pain, wasn't worried that he might already be dead. Her mother worried that Hogboss would leave the town and abandon her with it, that Jane didn't really love her, that if something did happen to Henry, she could end up alone. Jane knew it was the ghost burning through her, that it kindled her mother's worst fears and obsessions, but Jane needed more from her right now. She'd been carrying all of them for years.

Exhausted and needing a place to be alone, Jane walked into Dennis's room. Unlike the rest of the house, the pig boy's bedroom was a riot of color and mess. Posters covered his walls, a mix of emo and goth rock musicians, but also drag queens, ballet dancers in costume, Cirque du Soleil performers. He had been fascinated with painted faces, pomp and style, transformations of any kind. She wondered what he had wanted to make himself into.

Past his tangled bedding, there was a desk in the corner with a letter on it from Pig City's corporate offices. It was a notice that Dennis was being sent to oversee a plant out west. Management had decided that he would follow in the footsteps of his father.

Jane took a pair of headphones and an MP3 player off his desk, filling herself up with Dennis's music. She had never spoken to the pig boy, but she had come to know him through the memories within the townspeople, through Henry's needling worry for him, and now through his room and what he had left behind.

It made her think of Henry's room, the broken machine parts covering the floor, his notebooks filled with diagrams and smeared calculations. If only she hadn't made the CD that stole his ghost, or if only she had kept him closer, or if she had found a way to get him out of town years ago, how might things have been different?

Jane numbly watched the clock, her mind circling the question she couldn't answer. She listened for the sound of trucks outside, afraid that the haunted men would break through the door and grab her in their rough hands, that they would carve her apart like they had Dennis.

Hogboss still wasn't home. Outside, she could hear the roar of diesel engines and the beep of machines from up the ridge at Pig City. Through the window, the plant's lights blazed down. Jane left her mother on the couch and got in her car. She didn't know what she would say to Hogboss, but she needed to say something.

With Dennis's music shrieking in her ears, she drove up to the plant. The song was whispery and crawling, alternating from ear to ear in the headphones. It was sad and strange, raising the hair on the back of her neck. She focused on the road ahead of her, the ghost lying silent and heavy in her head.

The road was choked with spirits staggering up to their jobs. Their faces stretched across her windshield, silently screaming and full of fear. Whatever the pigs were doing, the ghosts didn't like it. Normally the plant spirits were so content in their haunting that they were airy, little more than wind. But now Jane felt them knock and jostle her car, clattering against the doors like hail. She slowly nosed through them, approaching the wall of light ahead.

They're about to lose everything, and they know it.

The gates of the plant were chained shut, but pig people and their trucks swarmed through the parking lot. Jane pulled up to the gate and got out to stand on the hood of her car, holding on to the chain-link fence. Rising above the fog of ghosts and shouts of pig people, the long neck of a crane pierced the sky. It was already moving, the pigs falling back to the fence or taking cover in Pig City trucks. Jane watched the arm swing forward, bringing an iron ball to crash through the side of the main slaughterhouse. The sound shook the world, sending vibrations through the steel of Jane's car and shivering the trees in the dark. Hunks of concrete and steel bounced down the slope and opened a hollow in the forest below.

The pigs cheered, and Jane's ghost brought her their ragged, desperate thoughts. This was bigger than Dennis, bigger than just their need to punish the town for the heartache it had brought them. Pig City owned them, would send them across the country and scatter their families. It controlled where they lived, when they got up and went to bed, what they were allowed to buy in the grocery store. Tearing down the old factory was a small rebellion against Pig City too, the only one they might have before they were sent off to train more pig people, to go back to processing pigs, and to one day lie down and be slaughtered themselves.

She wished that Henry was here to see this, to help her understand what he had done. What would her brother think of the pigs he created tearing down the decades-old heart of the town? Jane couldn't blame them. She felt a guilty satisfaction watching the pigs tear it apart, knowing this meant the end of Swine Hill.

The dead howled noiselessly and chased broken chunks of concrete spinning across the parking lot, trying to gather their world back together in their gossamer hands. Jane stared without pity.

Her own ghost was quiet, not wanting to draw her anger. But Jane knew it stung. It never liked when she got angry at spirits. It was afraid she would blame it, too, that she might want to pull it out of her like a tick, crush it, and cast it away. But she couldn't comfort it now. She felt shredded, torn up with worry for her brother.

She watched into the early morning as the wrecking ball brought the plant buildings down to a hill of rubble. In the distance, Hogboss climbed into the seat of a bulldozer and pushed the remaining pieces of the factory off the side of the cliff. Columns of dust rose from the edge of the plateau. Someone cut an electrical line, and the lights around the factory died. The pigs turned on the lights of their trucks and kept going, scraping the surface of the ridge clean, as if the factory had never been.

Jane shouted to the closest pig. "I need to talk to Hogboss!"

The pigs ignored her, loading everything that had been worth taking from the empty plant into semi trucks to be shipped off to other meatpacking facilities.

"Please," she said. "Henry is missing."

They can't hear you over the machines. And even if they could, they wouldn't care. They have their own heartbreak to deal with.

From the edge of the plateau where Hogboss had pushed away the wreckage of the plant, spirits whipped through the air and swarmed like hornets. The ghosts around Jane were taking on substance and form. Their outlines became more solid, and they struggled to untangle their wispy limbs from one another. They were changing, becoming like the brutal ghosts of downtown who had lost everything. Jane got back in her car.

Hurry, her ghost said. *They'll be looking for some reminder of what they've lost.*

Jane headed back to Hogboss's house, but a tide of spirits flowed down from the destroyed plant and swept over the surrounding neighborhoods. Lights in the houses around her went dark, the electronics saturated with spirits. She turned around and drove away from it, trying to find a way back to her mother, to a bed where she could sleep and forget for a few hours everything that had happened.

Your mother will be safe. The ghosts don't like the pig neighborhoods. Not enough memories for them there.

Jane's ghost guided her away, keeping always a street between her and them. She felt the ghosts fall on sleeping families and burrow into them like worms. People awoke to five or six warring ghosts within them, demanding they get up and work, desperate to finish all that they'd left undone. When a ghost didn't have enough in common with someone to haunt them, it burrowed into their joints or organs, doubling them up with pain. Objects inside flew around and crashed into walls. So many years of pain, so many crises and lost causes, all erupted at once.

Jane found herself driving to Trigger's house. It was down a rough

gravel road on the outskirts of town, a place the flood of ghosts probably wouldn't reach. He would let her spend the night there. As angry
as she was with him, she needed to tell someone that Henry had been
taken, that he might be dead. Whatever else had gone wrong between
them, she knew that Trigger would listen.

I T WAS STORMING again when she reached Trigger's house, the rain coming down in sheets and battering the top of her car. The work truck Trigger and his father used was in the driveway, but no lights were on. Her stereo clock read 4:00 a.m. With the plant closing, there would be no reason for them to be awake.

Jane texted Trigger that she was outside, hoping his phone wasn't on silent. *I don't have anywhere else to go,* she wrote. *Please, can I stay here tonight?*

Driving among the surge of angry spirits had left her mind coated in the hot, stinging anger of the town. She felt bruised from contact with them. It reminded her of when Dennis had died, how she relived his death through the guilty memories of everyone involved. Or of the mob who had descended on their house, their need to retaliate against Henry for taking something from them. Even her mother had been too much, the woman a black hole of emotion. Jane wanted space, somewhere quiet to figure out what she would do. Inside her mind, her ghost was like a full moon, bright-shining and full. She wanted away from it too.

Tired of waiting, Jane got out of the car. The rain drenched her instantly, but it was midsummer, and the damp wasn't cold. The pure physical shock of the downpour was good, took her out of her head for a moment. But then she thought of the police lights again, her brother disappearing into the dark.

Trigger might be angry if you just show up and pound on the door. You know his father doesn't like you.

It was true. He might be angry. But something evil had happened to her family, and Jane needed a friend. Surely he would understand.

There was no porch, just a shallow ledge over the door. She leaned against the wood, knocking hard, her back and legs getting soaked. No one answered. There was no sound from inside. She tried the door handle, and it was unlocked.

It will be morning soon, her ghost said. *Just sleep in your car and then go back to Hogboss's house.*

Jane froze with her hand on the door. "You know something. What is it?"

The ghost twisted and flinched within her, not wanting to say. *Please, Jane. I love you. Don't go in that house.*

Jane opened the door and stepped inside. Immediately, she felt the heavy anger of ghosts. She didn't understand. The wave of spirits from the plant couldn't have spread this far. Stepping forward, she found herself in the woods on a dark winter morning. Then she understood.

Trigger's ghost, that hateful winter child, had found its way home.

Jane turned, looking for the door, but there was no door or house or walls. She was in a clearing. The rain was gone, and sharp wind cut across the grass, prickling her arms. The ground was darker in the gloom at her feet, and she reached down, finding it bloody.

"Trigger!" she yelled. "Riley! Where are you?"

Go back. Find the door.

Jane walked into the woods and pressed her hands against the tree trunks. They were solid and rough. She closed her eyes and felt around her: dead leaves, icy branches, hard ground. The dense forest pressed in. "How did I get here?"

Don't let the ghost confuse you.

Her ghost flooded her with images caught from the spirit that enveloped them. She saw Mason cupping the dirt-covered music box in his maimed hands, whistling to it. The porcelain iced over. A hissing tongue of fog rose out of it and took up all the space in the house. They were inside the ghost, its haunting on their skin and in their lungs.

"My poor son," Mason had said, full of gratitude. "Where did you go?"

She saw Trigger and his father lost in the house, pacing in the endless trees and cold, trying to understand what had happened. The ghost put a name in Mason, like dropping a coin into a well. *Jane.*

Mason had left in a fury, Jane's face rolling through his mind. When the house saw him return hours later, back into its frozen mouth, he was eaten up with ghosts, their lights burning deep in his eyes like the torches of explorers lost in the dark.

The man took an old hunting rifle out of its cabinet, the gun that had killed his youngest child and hadn't been fired since. Years of spiderwebs wrapped the barrel like gauze. Mason sat at their table cleaning it, his eyes pale and gleaming. He spoke with a child's voice, listing all the things that had been taken from him. Long, copper-wrapped shells rolled across the table.

Trigger pleaded with his brother's ghost inside his father. He said that everything was his fault and he was sorry for forgetting. He apologized for bringing Jane to the house. He said that he would send her away and never talk to her again. "Please," he said. "Put the gun down. Come back where you belong."

Mason stood and leveled the gun at him. He spoke in the voice of the dead. "I'm not coming to you. You're coming to me."

The rifle shot cut through her like a lance. Jane could feel it, the memory so strong and sharp that she collapsed, holding her stomach. The afterimage of Trigger fell to the ground beside her. Jane rolled toward him, shouting his name, and found only a pile of leaves under her.

"Oh, God." Jane lurched up and ran from the past. "Trigger's dead."

The presence of the winter ghost was all around her, its rasp of wind and bone-aching cold, the sharp drops of ice that fell like knives from the trees above. Branches dragged across her face, and frozen weeds tangled around her legs. The forest made her feel small. She was in pieces, her body reduced to gasping breath, two pounding feet, the heavy punch of her heart.

Where are you going?

"I have to find the logging road. I have to get out of the woods."

You're not in the woods, Jane. You're in a house.

It was raining just outside the windows, she reminded herself. It was summer. There were four walls around her, old furniture, stained carpet under her feet. But the wind and cold felt so real. The branches clattered in the wind like chimes, and ice fell and broke on the hard ground.

Animal shapes rose from the loam and leaf rot. Deer and rabbits and squirrels, soot black and staring, trapped here the same as her. Out of the dark and cold, a shape pushed through the leaves and came to her, a child in an orange hunting vest.

"This is your fault," said the boy.

"You took him away," Jane said. "You tortured him for years, and now you killed him."

"I was alone," the boy said. "He was all I had. You tricked me and buried me in the ground."

Jane, no. Be careful.

"You're dead!" she shouted. "You're supposed to be in the ground."

The boy grabbed her arm, his touch so cold that it burned and left ashen streaks on her skin. "You have a ghost too," he said. "Are you going to bury it?"

"Trigger was sorry for what happened. Why did you kill him? He was a good person."

"You didn't want him," the ghost said. "But I did. He was my family. He should be here with me. Why should he be alive if I'm not?"

Jane held her aching arm and cried, the tears icing down her cheek. The tune from the music box began to play, sweeping through the forest with the wind and growing louder until it sounded like the trees were hung with chimes. The ghost boy dropped a shovel on the dirt in front of her.

"You want to be with my brother?" he asked. "Then dig. Make a hole and get inside."

Her mouth was dry from fear. Her ghost sank deep within her, heavy and distant, like a stone falling through water. It couldn't save her, and it was afraid that it would fade too, losing the one thing that tethered it to the world.

Jane stood and picked up the shovel, not knowing what else to do but dig. She couldn't find her way out of the haunted house. She was in the dead boy's winter kingdom, and he would do what he wanted with her.

She pushed the tip of the shovel into the frozen ground. Her hands were chapped with cold, sticking to the handle and scraped raw. The earth was stony and hard, tiny roots spiraling through the dirt, bright with ice. The boy watched her, and she dug. If this was all only a haunting, if the shovel and the frozen earth and the dark woods weren't real, why did everything hurt so much?

A white shape stepped between the trees in front of her. A man, tall and wide-shouldered, standing in a bulky hazmat suit. He had a tank of cleaning solution on his back, a metal pump and hose in his hand. Through his facemask, he looked at Jane with Trigger's broad, young face, his eyes full of longing. Trigger had come back as a ghost. He too was lost in his brother's sad dream.

Her ghost rose in her again. *Don't talk to him. You don't know what he wants.*

Jane dropped the shovel, her hands numb with cold. The ghost boy had disappeared when his brother had come, but her ghost could still feel him watching.

"Trigger? Do you remember me? Can you help me get out?"

Trigger's face was empty of expression behind the mask. He didn't speak. But he came and put his arm around her, the barrier of the suit making the embrace feel strange, and led her into the trees.

"I'm so sorry for what happened to you," Jane said. "I wanted you to be happy. I was trying to help."

He isn't the same, her ghost said. *Be careful. He wants to show you something.*

Ahead of her, Jane heard rain. She felt heat. She was almost free. The ghost flit through her mind, afraid but not saying why, its presence as light as insect wings.

The front door and living room came back into focus through the trees. Trigger's ghost brought her to the couch where Mason lay shaking with fever. A whir of gnashing thoughts swarmed over him, his ghosts a hive. He held the music box, dirty and split in half. He muttered to himself, quick and clipped sounds, no meaning to them apart from accusation, blame, anger. His eyes blazed, motes of light dancing like arcs of lightning.

A dozen ghosts pressed their lips to his ears and spoke to him. Their dead hands fought for control of his body, and they poured their grief and hate through his blood. More spirits, fragments small and sharp like fiberglass, itched in his muscles and bones, making him flinch and kick.

He obsessed over the last few days. The gates of Pig City shut for the first time that he'd been alive. A funeral for a pig. The rumor that the plant would never open again. He knew who was responsible, who had encouraged the pigs, who had come into his home and taken something private away from him. A warped, ugly version of Jane and her family crawled through his mind. It was their fault, he had decided.

Mason had gone into the ruins of downtown with a few others from the plant. They had found vicious ghosts and let the spirits fill them up. Loaded full, the ghosts packed into them like bullets in a gun, Mason and the others had driven to Jane's house in the dark. He'd come to wreak violence on her family, not because he thought it would make anything better for him, but because he wanted to take whatever he could from her.

Mason shouldn't be alone, Jane knew. Trigger wouldn't want his father abandoned in that haunted house, shivering with the poison inside of him. She had gotten ghosts out of people before. There was every chance she could save him. But she wasn't going to try. Whatever was inside of him he had invited in. Let it burrow down until it filled even his bones.

The door was in front of her. With a crash of sound and damp, Jane was back in the rain. Behind her sat the house, its door swinging open. Inside, the forest stretched deep and covered in ice. Warmth moved through her limbs. Trigger's ghost still held her arm, still looked at her with his flat dead eyes. He was solid and real, as if he were alive. But he was wrong, too, less than he'd been before.

"What can I do?" Jane asked. "What do you need?"

He spoke, his voice expanding in her mind like a cloud of smoke. *To be with you,* Trigger said. *To haunt you.*

She backed toward her car. Trigger's ghost watched her go, the early-morning light blurring his edges. Jane locked her doors, knowing it wouldn't keep him out if he tried to follow, and spun her tires pulling out of the driveway. His pale shape grew smaller in her mirror.

"Is he following me?" Jane asked.

Not yet.

She should be ashamed to have left him there, to have abandoned him like everyone else had. But Jane didn't want his ghost living inside her, filling her up with his old pain. Emptied of all feeling, she drove back to her house.

Through her windshield, the sun swelled over the town of the dead.

ENRY WOKE FROM a heavy, dreamless sleep. He sat up and found himself on the haunted school bus. It groaned and lurched forward, dragging itself through the ruins of Swine Hill.

The seats and aisles were crowded with jostling ghosts, mostly children screaming that they wanted to go home. But they had no home left to go to. Something was missing or different. Their parents were gone. New families had moved into their old houses. The smallest change — a missing stop sign, a porch torn down after storm damage, an overgrown lawn, an empty house — might keep them on the bus, not seeing a place where they belonged outside the rows of ripped seats and rubber floor.

How had he gotten here? The last thing Henry remembered was rain. The pale ghost-light in the eyes of the men who chased him, their teeth clenched so hard that blood ran from their gums. His sister shouting from their mom's car, backing out of the driveway. Over them all, the ridge above the town burning with light again, like Hogboss had decided to reopen the plant and spare Swine Hill.

He remembered the cop car, its handle crusted with something like rust, and how he had thrown open the door and fallen inside. It was the bleeding man's cruiser. In the dark, the man's face was drowned in shadow and the red glow from his console. His sparse hair was matted and streaked, his hands dark. Henry never would have run to him for help, not if he'd had anywhere else to go. His best friend was gone, fallen out of reality. Violent men were coming for him. He needed the safety of a locked door. Henry shouted wordlessly, hands out and pleading.

I've got you. The cop's raised arm, like he might shield Henry. And then the dark mouth of the gun, its blue-black shine, and a world-shattering sound in the close space of the car.

What happened after? Henry looked up and saw his reflection in the bus driver's wide mirror.

He had his nose again. Henry reached up and felt its soft bulge, the scars and bandages gone. Had his ghost come back? Had it saved him, rebuilt his nose, and left him here? It was the only thing that made sense.

There were gaps in his memory again. He couldn't remember how his ghost had returned or what it had done with him when it came back. He couldn't remember how it fixed his nose or rescued him from the mob.

It was early morning. Henry looked out the window, trying to understand how much time had passed, and saw that Swine Hill had changed. Power was out at every gas station, house, and convenience store. People sat on their front steps or lay in their yards muttering to themselves, shivering from the cold things that had slithered inside them. They twitched and trembled, their eyes blazing with light. Henry didn't need Jane to tell him that they were haunted.

He wasn't the same either. His haunting felt different. Whatever ghost power was in him, it was closer to the surface. He had a certainty about things that he'd never had before. His mind burned electric. On the window, he traced equations with his fingertip, inventing formulae as he needed, translating everything around him into a language of numbers and functions. He could almost reach out and grab the world, spin it like a globe in his hands. He'd never felt so brilliant, so in control.

After the alien light merged with Bethany, she'd said that the world seemed thinner, like she might pass right through it. Henry could see that now. Beyond the foam seats and metal hull of the bus, past the overgrown yards and falling houses, the world was paper-thin. He could see through its glassy edges into some other place beyond.

Beyond the horizon and outside of reality, Henry saw a great, yawning nothing. It pulled at him like wind on his back and water rushing over his feet. If he didn't find some way to anchor himself, he knew that he would be dragged away.

Far out in that dark place, there was a single point of brightness. It was the unmistakable glow of the alien, the strange light that had become a part of Bethany. Henry tried to look away from it, but the geometry of the void curled through and around Swine Hill. No matter which way he turned, he could see Bethany's light burning in the deep.

He had thought that when his ghost came back, he would know how to save her. But looking into that sea of emptiness, he felt small and cold. Even with his ghost, he wouldn't be able to help. It should have devastated him, but he didn't feel guilty about the past anymore. His mind only had room for the present. Everything seemed possible again. He was going to right as many of his wrongs as he could. He was going to mend his broken family.

The bus let him off in front of his house. The other homes on their street, long empty of people, boiled with ghosts cut loose from the plant. Henry could hear them in the groan of boards swaying in the wind, could see their bright eyes moving through the dark windows. Even during the day, they paced and raved, ready to make someone hurt for all that they had lost.

Their yard was churned up from the heavy boots of the mob. The robot lay blighted across the driveway, its body crushed and battery dead. The head tilted toward him, the lenses of its eyes cracked and one of its arms stretched out, palm open. Its lanky frame wore the tatters of his father's old clothes, rippling in the wind.

Before, Henry had always wanted to fix it. But now, with his mind leaping electric again, Henry understood. There was use in broken things. The robot, lying dead across the front walk, was exactly what he needed to help his mother. He felt like a fool for not understanding before. So many things were perfectly clear now. He stepped over the machine and went inside the house.

The downstairs was trashed from Bethany's battle with the plant workers. Picture frames had fallen to the floor, their faces spider-webbed with cracks. The couch was upside down, spilling foam and splintered wood. Holes were constellated across the drywall, and the hardwood floor was sagging and cracked from whatever Bethany had done when she'd hurled people out of the universe.

He went through the house looking for something, but he didn't know what he needed. It was like he'd lost his keys or his wallet, some small and essential thing that he couldn't go on without. What he wanted, he realized, was to find something that reminded him of himself.

At the base of the stairwell, one of his father's metal toolboxes was hinged open. Henry had left it out weeks ago when he'd needed to tighten a loose leg on the kitchen table. The toolbox was softly dimpled, its latch broken, and the red paint was scuffed through in places, showing its gray metal skin. He kneeled on the floor and stared at the tools for a while. The scrambled socket set looked like a series of tunnels. He imagined himself walking through them, pressing his hands against their smooth sides. The pile of wrenches, pliers, and screwdrivers looked like a city folded in on itself. For a moment, he felt vertigo, like he might fall inside and become lost.

With effort, Henry pulled himself away from the toolbox and went upstairs.

He found Jane lying in his bed. She had one of his old shirts balled up in her hands, and the skin under her eyes was swollen. She looked more tired than he'd ever seen her. When he stepped into the doorway, Jane covered her mouth with her hands, suppressing a scream.

"Are you okay?" he asked. "Where's Mom?"

He went to his desk where a clutter of old school papers was mixed with the notes he had taken on Bethany. He winced to see his thinking written out, how shallow and simple it all was. None of this could have helped her. He glanced over the stack of papers, finding Neilson's pain engine notes. He knew as soon as he touched them that they weren't what he needed.

Jane pulled her knees to her chest, staring wide-eyed at Henry. She still hadn't spoken. Her clothes were dirty and wrinkled, her hands scraped and shoes muddy. She looked shattered.

"Did Mom get hurt? Did something happen?" he asked.

Jane swallowed and spoke very softly. "What do you want?"

At one time, that might have been a hard question for him to answer. He had wanted to invent or discover something amazing, to be respected and remembered. But he had never really known what that something might be. He had wanted to go to a good college because he was supposed to and he thought he might like it. He had wanted to leave Swine Hill because it was such a small and suffocating place. But those were vague wants, undefined, more a wanting not to fail than a want for anything in particular.

But now he knew exactly what he wanted. It was the only thing he wanted, and it was clear and sharp and drove his every thought. He had no plans beyond satisfying this desire. It was all of him.

"I'm going to fix my mistakes," he said.

Jane started to cry. Henry sat on the bed, thinking, for some reason, of the dancing girl who had spent her last night next to him. Did she get pulled into the darkness beyond the world? When he thought of it, he could see Bethany's bright star again.

"What's wrong?" he asked.

Jane struggled to catch her breath. "They butchered Dennis, and I felt every bit of it. Bethany is gone. Trigger was murdered, and his brother's ghost almost killed me, too. They tried to kill all of us. Our own neighbors. People we grew up with. Everything is wrong, but I kept hoping you were alive. God, Henry. I'm so sorry."

For the first time since his ghost had returned, he felt a dissonance in himself. It bothered him that she thought he had died. Why would she say that?

He could see something familiar on her face. Jane had regrets. Everything was so broken, and she wanted to make it right. Maybe his sister was what he had been looking for. They could rebuild the world together. He started to sit down on the bed, his arms out to pull her close. He had the same feeling as when he stared into the toolbox, a feeling that he was growing small.

Jane backed away from him.

"I didn't know about Trigger," he said. "He was a good guy. I might have died in the school bathroom if he hadn't found me. I'm sorry, Jane. As soon as I make things better here, we're going to leave, just like you always wanted."

It felt odd to say that he was going to leave. For some reason, he couldn't imagine what lay beyond Swine Hill. He tried to think of somewhere else — a city or country or university — but couldn't name a single place. He didn't dwell on it, though. He had too much to worry about here.

Jane shook her head, looking at Henry like she didn't recognize him. "I don't know where Dad is. My car is dead with ghosts. I don't have anyone left. I'm going to die here just like everyone else."

These were problems he could solve. It was all he wanted to do, to make right the things he had left undone. Waiting was unbearable. He got up and went to his desk, gesturing to the slowly beating heart in its box.

"Take this," he said. "It will help you find Dad."

Jane waited until Henry backed away before she would approach the desk. She picked up the box and opened it, grimacing in disgust. She cried silently, her voice soft. "You made this? A heart?"

"I didn't make it," Henry said. "I took it years ago. It's Dad's heart. Can you find him and give it back for me?"

Jane watched the heart's slow beat. "You took it?"

"My ghost must have thought it was helping. I did a lot of things I didn't mean to. But everything is different now. I have control. Just wait. I'll fix your car. I'll put our family back together. I'll even fix Swine Hill."

"What about the pigs you made?" Jane asked.

"What's wrong with the pigs?" He tried to remember if there was some flaw with the pig people, but he couldn't think of any. He'd built them to work at the plant, and they did it beautifully. He thought of Hogboss — his skill in managing the plant, his strength, his honesty and kindness. The pig man and his kin were maybe the only good thing Henry had ever done.

"Pig City owns them," Jane said. "They're being shipped all over the country to train the next generation of pig people. You made slaves, Henry. And when they start working and more people get laid off, everywhere will be just like Swine Hill."

Had he made them for that, to be owned heart and hoof by the Pig City Corporation? Was this Neilson's pain engine, the pig people made to overturn the world? Henry couldn't remember. He didn't like it, though. They did their work, but they also loved and hurt and learned. They had already changed so much about Swine Hill. People were asking questions they had never asked before: what it meant to be a person, what the world owed them, if they could escape the past. Henry thought of the philosophy and ethics questions in his binder, the hard problems he had never liked to think about. The pigs forced those questions. They would change how humans saw the world. Dennis believed that Henry had made the pigs for more. He must have.

"You're right. I need to fix that too. I'll get it done."

He could tell by her face that she didn't believe him. She was afraid. He didn't blame her. He had been making everything worse for a long time, the ghost in him wrecking whatever it touched. But everything was different now. She would see.

"Pack your things," Henry told her. "We're leaving."

H ENRY FOUND HIMSELF in Hogboss's house. His ghost must
have brought him. His mother's things were scattered everywhere. He found her sleeping in Hogboss's bed, though the pig
man wasn't with her. Henry turned on the light.

"Henry?" His mother sat up and rubbed her eyes. "Your
nose is back! Are you okay? Where have you been?"

He could see the ghost seething inside her. It rose out of her like a
bonfire, a shapeless and burning cloud of need. Finally, after years of
watching her suffer, he could help.

"Come with me, Mom. I have to show you something."

He tried to pull her up from the bed, but his mother drew away. He
put a hand on her shoulder. The contact didn't burn him.

"You don't have to worry," he said. "My ghost can protect me."

Her face fell. She wrapped her arms around him, sobbing into his
shoulder. "Oh, God," she said. "Not you, too."

His mother's ghost ballooned up huge, seeming to fill the room. It
wanted love and touch. It wanted to know it wouldn't be abandoned.
Henry had nothing it needed.

"Let's go home, Mom."

"I don't have a home," she cried. "I had one, but I killed it. Jane is the only one I have left, and she'll never forgive me. My baby. I'm so sorry, my poor baby boy."

"Come on, Mom," Henry said. "You don't have anything to be sorry for. I need you to follow me."

He led her into the morning light, telling her that everything would soon be okay.

Henry was careful to steer her around those streets and houses where powerful ghosts prowled for someone to haunt or hurt. Swine Hill had become a labyrinth of spirits. Henry could see them now, the layers of brick and wood thin to his eyes, the lurking ghosts bright as fire behind them.

His mother blamed herself. Said that it was her fault she'd lost her family. She wondered where Hogboss had gone, if he had left her too. Henry urged her along faster. He should have dealt with her ghost a long time ago.

It took an hour to walk across town back to their house. When they finally arrived, his mother was drenched in sweat. She trembled with fever and gasped, mouth dry with heat. From the window upstairs, Jane looked down at them.

Henry took his mother down the walk to stand over the robot. It was rusted dark, the gleam gone from its metal body. It looked skeletal in his father's baggy clothes.

His mother's ghost looked down on the dying machine and saw something that spoke to it more than any sad song ever could. The robot had never been in love with Henry's mother. It had always been in love with her ghost, had loved the spirit with a pathetic and hungry want that mirrored the ghost's own. They were made for each other, but the robot had never been broken and full of need enough for the ghost to notice it before. Lying shattered and abandoned on the grass, the machine was everything his mother's ghost feared it would become.

His mother clutched her chest as the ghost forced itself out of her, unwinding its limbs from her own and stepping free. It was a woman-shaped shadow with long-fingered hands and hair that dragged the ground, the air shimmering hot around it. For ten years it had made his mother fear being abandoned. Now it cast her aside without looking back.

The burning spirit fell down on the robot and sent soaring blue light shooting through its chassis and pouring from its eyes. The spirit haunted its battery and motherboard, moving like a storm through its programming. Machine and ghost became one. They held each other, wanting never to let go.

The robot's new ghost forced out the fragments of spirits fouling up its servos and wiring. It stood, a haunted machine, powered by its own want. It wrapped its arms around itself and spoke for the first time. Its voice was hollow and sharp, a warping of metal.

"I am love," the robot said.

Jane came outside and ran to her mother, hugging her tight for the first time since she'd been a girl. The robot smiled down at them, completely content with itself. Something was still wrong, though. His mother didn't say anything. Jane wouldn't meet his eyes.

"See," Henry said. "I got rid of Mom's ghost. Why aren't you happy?"

Jane's face was tight with grief. "I should have protected you. I should have gotten you out of Swine Hill sooner. If I hadn't been such a coward, we could have left."

"We will leave," Henry said.

"No," Jane said. "You can't. You'll be stuck in Swine Hill until you do whatever it is you need to do, but you won't ever be able to come with us."

The world felt thinner suddenly, the void closer, the sun somehow less bright.

"But I want to go with you," he said.

"I want you to come with me too," Jane said. "But you can't. You're dead, Henry."

"No, I'm not." Henry looked at his hands, his shoes, the sidewalk under his feet. "I'm right here."

"Your ghost didn't come back." Jane bit her lip and closed her eyes, fighting to keep her voice steady. "You *are* the ghost. I'm going to miss you. I'm sorry I didn't tell you how much you meant to me when you were alive."

"Get in Mom's car," Henry said. "The robot can push you back to Hogboss's house. I'll meet you there."

"Don't go looking for someone to haunt," Jane said. "Don't use someone like your ghost used you."

Henry almost screamed. He didn't want to hear that they thought he was dead. He didn't want to think that he might be a ghost. He had work to do. He was going to make things better. Why couldn't she see that? His body dissolved into smoke. He ran from them like a gust of wind.

Henry was downtown, walking between the old brick buildings a few blocks away from the school. He didn't have time to argue with Jane. He had to help the pigs. Certain that nothing could hurt him, he plunged into the dark of a haunted warehouse.

The ghosts inside shrank from him. It was the middle of the day, sunlight cutting in through the broken windows to expose everything for what it was: dead insects and trash, scattered bricks, fallen boards. Whatever this place had meant to the spirits before, it wasn't the same now. They just barely clung to it, desperate to remember the lives they had lost.

Henry found a dog in the corner, shivering with fever. It was covered in sores, its ears in tatters from fighting. This was a different dog, but the violent ghost inside it was the same, the feral and hungry thing that had wanted to haunt him when he was at his weakest.

"I'm not afraid of you," Henry said.

"Of course you're not," the haunted animal said. "Why would you be?"

It was mocking him, but he didn't understand why.

"You're going to come with me," Henry said.

"I can't haunt you," it said. "You missed your chance."

"I have something else for you to haunt. Something hungry and swift as light. Something with a million tiny teeth."

The dog staggered to its feet, panting past curling fangs. "I'll go and see what you have. But just because I can't haunt you doesn't mean I can't hurt you, little boy. Night will be here eventually. You might remember fear then."

The dog came with him, limping its way down the sinking stairs. Henry seemed to fly over the road, the dog running along behind him. What had the spirit meant, that he had missed his chance? His mind felt strange, too singular. He couldn't puzzle it out right now, couldn't be bothered to think about it. He had to help the pigs. He had to help his family. He had to save the town from its toxic haunting. Nothing else was worth a thought.

He was back in his room, waiting for the robot to return. He needed to use his computer. He knew what he wanted to do, but for some reason he couldn't do it himself. He needed another set of hands. Henry stared out the window, frustrated, while the haunted dog grinned from his bed.

Finally the robot came walking back down the street. The burning ghost rolled through its limbs and body. To Henry, now able to see ghosts as easily as he could see anything else, the robot looked like it was on fire. It came upstairs, and Henry motioned for it to sit in front of his computer.

He leaned close to the machine, explaining what he wanted it to do. The robot's blunt fingertips battered the keyboard, making keystrokes as quickly as Henry could bring them to mind. After a while, he realized he was inside the robot's head, looking down at his monitor through its staring yellow eyes. He could feel the burning ghost curled in its gut, jealous and wanting Henry to leave the robot alone. The laughing dog watched and grew larger as the day waned.

At some point, Henry found himself drifting through a maze. Walls of metal and silicone surrounded him. He wandered for a long time, the sound of the robot's fingers booming on the keyboard somewhere far away, like thunderheads or falling bombs. He caught chains of electricity and flashed through the labyrinth. Where was his body? In a wave of panic, he realized that he was somehow inside one of the robot's microchips. He wrenched himself free.

Like waking from a dream, he found himself standing over the robot again, directing its work. This wasn't anything unusual, he told himself. When his ghost had taken control of him before, he always lost time. Still, he tried not to think about the tiny architecture inside of the machine.

Using the robot's hands, Henry built a computer virus, something ravenous and multiplying. It would sweep through Pig City's corporate systems and destroy every bit of data about the self-slaughtering pigs. There would be no record of Hogboss, of Dennis, of any of the pig people. The genetic information, surgical enhancements, and hormone regimens Henry had invented would be consumed.

He needed to be sure that his virus could slip easily through any firewall, could lie unseen on hard drives and snap up the data Pig City's scientists and managers thought most safe. He gestured for the haunted dog to come closer. "Look. See how hungry this is? Does it remind you of anyone?"

The dog sniffed the computer, ghost-light blazing in its nose and mouth. "It does have a million tiny teeth," it said. "It is hungry. It understands what I am."

The ghost crawled out of the mouth of the dog and poured itself into the computer, nestling into the ragged lines of code Henry had written. The monitor darkened to gray, the colors draining out of it. The animal, unhaunted and afraid, ran downstairs and back into the sun.

The robot opened Henry's email, attached the virus to a new message, and sent it to every corporate manager at Pig City. They knew his name. They remembered how much money he had made them the last time he sent them something. There was no chance they wouldn't open that file to see what new wonder he'd created.

The haunted lines of code would burn hungry through their databases, blacken their drives, consume every piece of information they had. When it was done, their corrupted files would be only a pile of bones, the viral ghost lounging atop them like a wolf. It might escape Pig City, Henry knew, might find its way into other corporate systems. It would eat and eat, unstoppable, until it became so lost in the digital wilderness that it finally faded away, taking his failings along with it.

Henry's operating system crashed, ragged error messages multiplying over the screen. The hard drive whined and spun. From somewhere within the computer came a dead smell. The robot backed away, afraid for its own systems.

There wasn't much left now. Henry had helped his mother and the pigs. Now he would find a way to help the town. He tried to imagine what he would do after that, but nothing came. The limits of his imagination were starting to worry him. Beyond the walls of his room, the hungry dark waited.

Why would Jane say that he was dead? If he was, wouldn't he know it?

HOGBOSS FINALLY CAME back from supervising the pigs, finding Jane and her mother taking shelter in his house. With the world falling apart around them and her burning ghost gone, Hogboss and Jane's mother spent an entire day in his bed. They drank wine out of a bottle and wept, kissing sloppy and drunk.

"What are you doing?" Jane wanted to scream. "When will we leave?" The town grew more haunted and dangerous by the day. But Hogboss and her mother didn't want to do anything but hold each other and grieve their lost children. The pig man said that Corporate would send word when it was time for them to move. Until then, he and the other pigs would wait.

After everything her mother had been through, she deserved some comfort. But Jane hated having to be around them, hated the way they seemed to hear or see only each other. She felt like a ghost in the house, the past more real to her than the present, grasping for things she had already lost.

Jane could feel Trigger's ghost outside, circling in the dark. It hovered against the sky, daring her to come out and look up, to see it framed against the stars. She was afraid to leave the house, to look up and see a white hazmat suit. She didn't want to meet Trigger's familiar, defeated eyes. To have his ghost ask why she had abandoned him and not know what to say. Most of all, she was afraid of what he wanted from her.

Swine Hill hardly existed anymore. Power was out most places. Anyone who had a working car had already escaped. Those left were entwined with decades of bitter ghosts. Hogboss's neighborhood had been mostly spared. The pigs had done enough renovation while they were here, had thrown out enough of the old things and put up enough new paint, that the ghosts had trouble entering their houses. It was too different, too new, all wrong. The ghosts didn't like it.

But nothing would stop another mob from breaking the windows and climbing inside. Nothing would keep back the bleeding man when he decided to come for them. Jane couldn't sleep, waiting for a brick to come through the window again, for men with shining eyes to tear down the door, for Trigger's ghost to fall over her shoulders and cover her like a shroud.

Jane lay in Dennis's twin bed, her feet hanging off the end of it. The light was off. Her ghost darted through the walls and back, bringing her flashes of joy from her mother and sudden spikes of rage from the ghosts passing by outside.

I can hear Bethany, her ghost said.

"Here? She came back?"

Jane pulled open the curtains of Dennis's old room. Outside, a trio of pig men leaned under the hood of a truck, trying to get it running. In the darkness beyond them, the air was phosphorescent with spirits.

She's drowning in light, her ghost said. *She is trying not to fall.*

It showed her Bethany caught between sheer cliff walls, clinging with bloody fingers to bare rock, pushing herself up and up through a sea of black. A golden light coated her skin like mercury, heavy and filling her throat. Bethany struggled to breathe around it, struggled not to let the alien light sweep away the person she was.

"Where is she?"

Where ghosts go when they can't hold on anymore.

Jane imagined Henry being pulled into that crushing dark. She shuddered. "What's going to happen to her?"

Bethany is watching. She can see everything from where she is. She's trying to climb back, but she's fallen very deep. No one ever comes back from that place. Eventually, she'll fade too.

Her mother laughed somewhere in the house, cutting into the small space of Dennis's bedroom. Jane turned on Dennis's stereo. His spooky-sad music swelled to fill the room. Eerie wings of electronic sound floated up the walls. The singer's voice skittered and crawled. A song like this would have been armor for the pig boy, assurance that no matter how frightening the world, he could be strange enough to beat it.

Jane pulled the box Henry had given her out of her pocket. Her father's heart throbbed slowly, so slowly. Why had her brother given it to her? Not her brother, she insisted. Only a ghost. Only a thing.

Am I just a thing to you?

She didn't bother to answer, lying back on the bed and letting grief batter her again. Worse than not having Henry at all was knowing that his ghost haunted the town. It looked like him and acted like him. It was almost her brother, but only part of what he had been. She would never cook dinner with him again. She would never tease him about needing a haircut or give him advice about girls. His ghost couldn't grow or change. When Jane left, it wouldn't come with her. What did her brother's ghost think she would do with an old heart? How was it supposed to make any of this better?

The bed trembled. She wiped her eyes and looked down at the little box. The heart inside flexed and beat faster. Did that mean her father was close? Jane went to the window again, but it was so dark out that she couldn't see anything. The ghosts would be strong now. It would be stupid for her to go.

"Is Trigger out there?"

He's not far. He's angry, Jane. Don't let him find you.

If Trigger wasn't able to haunt her, would he be pulled into the same crushing dark that held Bethany? Or would he spend forever amidst the crumbling wreck of his father's house? Jane didn't know which was worse. She wanted something better for him, but not enough to let him possess her. She didn't want to live his pain.

Afraid her mother might try to stop her, Jane quietly opened the window and dropped to the grass outside. The heart held before her like a compass, she followed its frantic beats, hoping her dad wasn't too far away.

He's never going to be what you remember.

The ghost pulled something out of her memory, a time before hauntings. The house had flooded. Jane sat on the floor as a girl, the water lapping against her legs, holding her baby brother in her arms. Her father had stopped his work, bringing her a boat made of folded paper. He set it on the rippling skin of water, the jade tile underneath like a sea. He got down on his hands and knees in the water and blew hard into the paper sail, gliding the boat across the room.

You'll never have that again. Even if your father remembers who he is, that time is gone. He can't be that person. It's the same as Henry's ghost. Nothing you do will bring him back.

Jane felt something in her swell and drop. She didn't have an answer. The ghost was right that everything was different now. Her family was broken, scattered, changed. But she would hold the pieces as tight to herself as she could. She would save what was left. Even if it felt like her bones were being pulled out of her, she had to walk away from Henry. She had to abandon Trigger to his vicious hate. She would leave the town of the dead with all its memory and pain behind, but she would take her father with her. She had failed her brother. She wouldn't fail their father, too.

The ghost swirled within her, its heavy ball of fear making Jane feel unsteady and sick. It knew that if she could give up Henry and Trigger, that meant she could cast it aside too.

Jane left the safety of the pig neighborhood and followed the heartbeat into the ghost-dark. Fragments of spirits swarmed through the air, glowing and whispering over her skin. They had lost their anchor to the world, were looking for something to hold on to. She focused on her need to leave, her rejection of Swine Hill, not wanting to give any of them a door to haunt her.

The heart beat faster as she moved across downtown, in the direction of the school. Her ghost listened for the heavy, psychic tread of spirits and told Jane when to turn away from the dark doorway of a house, when to duck into a lightless alley between old buildings, when to keep still until something hungry had passed. It was desperate to prove how much she needed it.

Jane had a hard time trying to follow the heart and letting her ghost guide her at the same time. The beating slowed. She lost ground, her father slipping invisibly through the empty city. She felt something watching her. The night was warm and humid, but a crawling cold touched the back of her neck. Something slipped along behind her in the sky. Jane was afraid to turn and look at it, afraid that if she did it would fall onto her.

The buildings around her were dark. Loose teeth of glass hung in window frames and flared with light as she passed. But there was sound. Over her head, the night sky murmured and groaned, the lost voices overlapping in a song of grief. The old brick buildings of downtown were a riot of noise and motion. The ghosts seemed frantic, boisterous as drunks, shouting and shoving one another through the walls. The stores shuddered with their hundreds of feather-light touches, exhaling plumes of dust.

The end of the street swam with red and blue light. A police cruiser turned the corner, scarred and pale as an old shark. Jane stepped into an alley and pressed against the wall. The car's pulsing lights caught the cracks of windows, spills of bottle glass, and broken metal, making the street glisten and grin. Finally it passed.

In her pocket, the heart jumped. She followed it.

The haunted men are close, her ghost said. *They're still looking for you.*

Eyes shined far off in the dark. A crowd of people came from both ends of the street and would stumble across her soon. They weren't so much haunted as they were hollow. Ghosts had reduced these people to smoking embers of themselves, just hate and resentment driven forward by the needs of the past. She thought of Mason, eaten through with spirits, barely a person anymore. She hadn't known ghosts could so completely erase someone.

They invited the spirits inside. They made themselves exactly who the ghosts needed them to be.

The hollow men dragged metal chains and lengths of pipe. Several voices poured from each mouth, the dead shouting over one another to speak. They remembered decades of violence long forgotten, thought of themselves as heroes for bringing it back. They would kill Jane and the pigs, tear down their houses, bring Swine Hill to rubble. They would burn down the world to show that it belonged to them.

With nowhere else to go, Jane stepped into an abandoned warehouse, pressing the door closed behind her. She waited for a moment, feeling the heavy press of ghosts move deep within the building.

They saw you. They're coming.

Jane ran into the dark of the building, throwing herself among its ghosts. She crashed into old worktables and pillars in the dark, overturned carts of wood scraps and fallen insulation. She tripped over chains and hulks of metal, falling to the floor and scraping her shins. The noise of her flight was covered by the shouts of spirits, lifting and dropping tools, tearing into the walls, still doing work that hadn't mattered for decades.

She found a closet with a heavy door and hid inside. Spirits trickled down on her like spores, too weak and thoughtless for her ghost to know what they wanted. They seared into her skin. Jane covered her mouth to keep from crying out, feeling bee stings lance into her arms and legs. Ghosts twisted down into her muscles and bones, tightening into knots, rising as bruises, making her arms and legs ache. Every part of her hurt. She raised a shaky arm to open the door and flee.

If you go now, they'll find you, her ghost said.

Her arm spasmed, making a chopping motion like it held a cleaver. Her feet twitched and pressed the floor as if she was pedaling a treadle sewing machine. The ghosts moved through her, making her body ripple with pain, begging for the old work motions that would remind them of their sad, hard lives.

Finally her ghost told her that the hollow men had moved on. But the heart box lay still in her pocket now, her father out of range. Jane moved through the warehouse, careful to stay back from the angry spirits her ghost warned her about. She felt frantic and afraid, hunted. But she found her way out via the back of the warehouse and saw she was in front of the high school.

Henry is inside.

Jane crossed the street and pushed open the chain-link fence, her body heavy and burning with its weight of spirits. The ghosts at the school were tamer. As long as the buildings stood, they had what they needed. She wondered what Henry was doing here. She wanted to see him again, as much as seeing him would hurt.

From the sky, a tattered shape fell to the ground and slipped into the building behind her. Jane looked straight ahead, feeling dead eyes on her back. She thought of all the mistakes she had made, the ways that she had failed her family. She tried to forgive herself as if her life depended on it.

J ANE FOUND HER brother and the love-drunk robot in the yearbook room. The machine had opened boxes of old photos and spread them across the floor. Henry walked between them, staring down into the town's past.

In the images, Jane saw the death of the city center, the flight of people and industry, the way grass and eventually trees covered over the crumbling edges of the town. But no matter when the photos were taken, no matter what blow struck Swine Hill, the meatpacking plant always stood on the horizon, beating life into the town like an iron heart. It had taken Henry to finally destroy that.

Jane watched him for a while, lost in his work. Was he so different from when he'd been alive? She wished she knew what to say. She was sorry he had died, sorry that he was never going to experience a thousand wonderful things about being alive, that he would never find friends and love and a better home somewhere else. She felt guilty for wanting to leave him, but she couldn't stay. The town would kill her, too. Why had she come? What would it do but hurt?

Jane touched a grainy photo showing wagons spilling over with peaches. SWAIN HILL FARMS was painted on their sides. "Where's Swain Hill?" she asked.

"We're in it," Henry said. "People only started calling this Swine Hill when everything but the pig plant shut down."

Jane sighed. "What are you looking for, Henry? How are these pictures supposed to help you?"

"Why would you say that to me?" he asked. "Why would you tell me that I'm dead?"

"Because you are. You should know why this is so hard for me and Mom."

The robot held up a large framed photo showing acres of orchards and barns, workers with ladders deep in the trees, a place that was only a memory of ghosts now. Her brother leaned close to it, like it was a window into another world.

"It doesn't change anything for me," Henry said. "So I'm dead. I still have work to do."

"You don't have to do anything. Just let go and move on."

"It's not fair. I'm still here." He seemed to shrink, his edges as wispy as fog.

"I know." Jane's throat was tight. She couldn't look at him. "I'm sorry I told you. Maybe that was selfish of me. I wanted you to understand how I feel."

"I don't blame you. I don't want to think about it, though. I just want to fix everything that's wrong. When that's done, maybe I'll move on. Maybe then I'll feel like a dead boy."

"This isn't like a broken machine where you just switch out a part. Some things can't be put back together."

But the robot sat right in front of her, trails of ghost-light showing through its joints and cracks, illuminating it from within. Her mother's ravenous spirit had been transformed through union with the machine. Now it only burned with love for the metal arms that held it. Maybe Jane was wrong to tell Henry what he couldn't fix.

"Everything is going to be fine," he said. "You'll see."

Henry had thought a lot of himself when he was alive, but he'd also been full of doubt. He felt bad about the problems the strange spirit haunting him had caused. He worried and didn't know what to do. This dead version of Henry might hurt like him, might have the same obsessions, but her brother never had this unreasonable, mechanical certainty. She had never been afraid of her brother, but she was afraid of this ghost. Whatever it was going to do, there would be no way to stop it.

Trigger is in the school. You can't outrun him.

"A ghost is following me," Jane said. "Trigger. I'm afraid."

"Do you know what he wants?"

"Me."

Henry frowned. "He can't haunt you unless he sees some of himself in you."

A few weeks ago, she wouldn't have thought she was anything like Trigger. She'd never understood his need to carry so much blame on his shoulders. But after her brother's nose had been cut off, she couldn't stop wondering why she hadn't left town that day, taken Henry out of Swine Hill immediately. Wasn't he dead because of her? Even before then, hadn't she known that something was wrong? Henry had texted her about the boys jumping him on the bus. She'd seen every frustration and fear he'd carried for years. If only she had been braver. If only she had taken responsibility for him. If only.

"I think he might have a way in," Jane said.

Henry isn't paying attention. He's thinking about how no one wants his ghost. Even the robot doesn't want him. His sister is afraid of being haunted by him. He's scattering like smoke, and he just wants something to hold on to.

Jane backed toward the door. She already shared herself with one ghost. She didn't want another, not Henry's and not Trigger's. She didn't want to become like the hollow men, her mind torn to pieces by warring spirits. Bethany was the only person she knew who could handle so many ghosts inside of her, all of them aligned perfectly with her iron will.

Henry looked at the pictures scattered in front of him like he was searching for the right screw or tool, the right piece to a puzzle.

"I'll have your car fixed soon. Then you can get far away from Swine Hill."

That wouldn't help her now. Trigger's presence moved closer, its rage expanding storm-like in her mind. Henry's ghost vanished, and the robot lumbered out of the room, off on some errand of its own. Jane ran out of the room and through the halls, looking for somewhere to hide.

The laughing room, its ghosts hissing and boiling with glee, beckoned Jane inside. The spirits surged and rebounded from the walls, their shrieks serpentine and coiling. They promised Jane escape. If she listened to them, if she understood their jokes and laughed, she would be swept away. They promised that if she was chained together in the river of them, Trigger would never find her.

She ignored them and sank to the floor. He was almost here, and there was nothing to do now but wait. Maybe she could still reason with him. Maybe there was enough of the boy she had loved left inside the ghost.

The temperature dropped. The door opened and Trigger walked into the room in a white hazmat suit. He looked down at the floor, sandy hair falling over his eyes. Despite the width of his shoulders, his thick limbs, and deep chest, there was something timid about him, as skittish as a beaten dog.

He looked the same as the first day she'd seen him in the grocery store. Seeing him that way, knowing that he was gone now, made her ache to hold him again. She was breaking a rule, she knew. Ghosts were things, not people. But she couldn't see his shape and not remember what he had been to her.

Thoughts whipped off him like wind, cutting and cold. A long, scraping song blew over her: *your fault, your fault, your fault.* He blamed himself, he blamed the town, and he blamed Jane. Judgment was all he had left.

Trigger knelt down beside her. Before, he had looked at her with worship, astonished that she could care about him, full of gratitude. But now he saw Jane the way his father might. Dark and unfamiliar. A thief who'd stolen the music box and chased away his brother's ghost, selfish and smirking and careless. He thought punishment was what she needed, mixing up violence and love.

He grabbed Jane, and cold shocked her arms. He brought his face close, features blurry, mouth open and scrambling words like static. When he leaned in, she thought he might try to kiss her with his dead mouth.

Silence exploded in her head. Something leapt away from her, making her feel cored out. The thoughts of the laughing ghosts went away. Trigger's thoughts of blame and anger faded. For the first time in years, Jane couldn't hear what anyone else was thinking. Her ghost had left her.

"No," she said, speaking to her ghost and to Trigger. "No, please, don't."

Trigger hovered over her, wrapping her limbs like frost, his mouth on her mouth. He kissed her, his ghostly lips passing in and out of her skin like he was gnashing her open. Insubstantial, he was still heavy, and he pinned her to the floor. It felt like a storm cloud embraced her, drenching her with rain and cold, its lightning spearing her body, its words thundering in her ears.

"I'm dead because of you," he said, voice flat.

It wasn't true. Mason had been storing away anger for years. He might have killed his son anyway. But for a moment, Jane believed it. A seam opened in her mind, and Trigger forced himself in.

She drowned in him, sinking into dark and ice, the huge beasts within his mind brushing against her as she spiraled deeper. Trigger had killed his own brother. He brought Jane into their home, held her hand, loved her in his bed as if he deserved to be happy. He had lost his brother's ghost, and then he let spirits devour his father. Everything that had happened was his fault, and everything that had happened was Jane's fault, too.

He shook her in his dead hands, screamed his wordless pain into her ear, anointed her with his self-loathing. At the bottom of him, he thought that he still loved her. This was best for her, he had told himself. She deserved to be punished. Better it came from him. It was what she needed. He stroked her face, kissed her cheek. He told her that she had failed him.

Jane rolled away from his phantom arms and threw up on the floor. She spat until her mouth tasted clean, and tried to crawl away from him. But he was in her and through her, his weight on her back. She begged him to let go.

She didn't deserve this, Jane told herself. She had made mistakes, but so had everyone. She didn't want to carry Trigger's pain. There was no reason he should need her to.

There is every reason. He spoke within her mind, from the place where her ghost always sat. He filled her, put pressure on her skull. Jane thought her head would burst.

The river of laughing spirits still murmured along the ceiling. Jane looked around the room, hoping Henry would come back, that someone would help her.

She saw a little girl crouched behind the teacher's desk.

The girl wasn't older than ten. White, dirty hair hung limp over her ears. She wore an oversized dress with a frayed hem. Jane hadn't seen her in years, but she recognized her at once, as familiar as a sister.

Her ghost.

It watched Jane wrestle with Trigger, face partly covered by thin, translucent fingers. Jane had seen this same look on its face when she had been a girl, when it gave her a pair of binoculars to watch the couple through the window. It was horrified, but it was fascinated, too.

Feeling herself grow angry and knowing Trigger would use it against her, Jane turned, struggling to push him away, but her hands slipped right through him. She tried to sit up, but he pulled her back down to the floor.

You will feel sorry for what you've done.

"I am sorry," Jane said. "I'm sorry you're still here. I'm sorry you have to punish yourself for things that were never your fault."

He collapsed like a shutting eye, his hold loosening.

Jane stood and limped for the door, not bothering to see if the girl's ghost followed. The lost spirits that had found their way into her muscles radiated pain through her legs.

Trigger threw himself against her again, his probing mind looking for a way in. He reached deep into her memory and pulled up every glistening regret she had. Her father filthy and thin, crouching under a tree to get out of the rain. Her brother coming home bruised and bleeding, and Jane telling him only not to go out alone again, like it was his fault. Her mother crying into her hands because she thought no one loved her, and Jane not comforting her because she wasn't sure if she loved her mother either. Henry's severed nose. Dennis carved apart in the casket. Henry's naive ghost, thinking it could glue the whole broken world back together.

You understand me.

She tried to remember that she had taken care of her family the best she could, that she loved Henry, that she couldn't blame herself for what other people had done. But thinking so felt small in the face of all that had happened.

I can't haunt you yet, but I will, Trigger said. *I will help you change. You will believe that you deserve me.*

The ghost lifted from her. The floor was hard against her face. Desks circled her like a herd of animals in the dark. Jane sobbed so hard she couldn't breathe, choking on her own breath. What if he was right?

Her ears rang with laughter. She could almost hear what the ghosts said, the embarrassment that caused them so much mirth. If she listened a little closer, she would understand, and the voices would carry her away.

Soft footsteps came to her. Two slender arms wrapped around Jane. The ghost of a girl leaned over her.

"I'm sorry," the ghost said, the first time she'd heard its voice outside her mind in over a decade. "I didn't want you to be pulled apart, so I left. I knew he wouldn't be able to keep you."

Jane wanted to tell the ghost to blow away and be forgotten, wanted to lash out at it for not being strong enough to save her. Was that how she really felt? Or was it only a bruise that Trigger had left on her mind? Maybe he had already changed her.

There was a hollow place at the center of her, and her ghost stepped inside. *I'm here. No one can take me away from you.* But even her ghost didn't know if that was true.

30

I T WAS MORNING, and golden light filled the town. The streets were empty of cars. People stayed inside, hungry and tired, recovering from the night before. The storm of spirits had ebbed. Ghosts settled to the bottom of things, fading to shadows on the wall or a knocking in the attic. A vicious few still prowled the darkest hollows of the town, but they had already found anyone who was close enough for them to hurt.

The robot walked, languid and bright, down the middle of the empty street. Its eyes were wide, taking in the day, and it swung its long limbs easily. It was love-struck and happy, its whole world new. The passionate ghost within the machine chased the other spirits out of its gears and kept its battery hot.

Henry floated alongside it, his shape ragged, just a spray of oily smoke. He found the robot's joy tedious. And while the machine still let Henry give it orders and use its metal hands, neither it nor its jealous ghost would let Henry haunt the robot for long. They just didn't want the things he wanted.

"Hurry up," he said. "Are you going to help me or not?"

There wasn't much left for Henry to do. He could feel his tie to the world growing tenuous and thin. He would make sure that Jane had a way to leave. He would make sure that the pigs were free to become whatever they wanted. He would draw the poison out of Swine Hill.

Bethany still hung beyond the edge of the world in every direction he looked, defying geometry and space. He was losing time, having trouble keeping himself solid. Unless he found a person to haunt, someone whose desires would focus and feed his own, he would soon fade away. There was no one in town like him, but even if there was, he didn't want to become like Neilson's ghost. He wouldn't force someone to make all of his old mistakes. Jane had been right about that.

From their windows, people watched the robot stroll down the empty street. A man came out of a dark house and stood in their way. His hair and clothes were dirty, his eyes milky bright. He spoke with the voices of three ghosts, a rasping, overlapping hiss.

"You took everything from us," he said. "You gave it all to the pigs. What about the people who still live here? What are we supposed to do?"

Henry felt bad for the man, but he didn't know how to help. He wanted to scrape the living out of the dead shell of the town. It was true that they had been plundered—ground up by the town's brutal industries and then left behind with only debt and sickness and a faceless blame. There would be no justice for them. It wasn't the fault of pigs or machines or people like Henry. They would have to go new places, learn new things, change if they wanted to survive.

But how to reason with a ghost? How to convince someone that couldn't change, who was still trapped in a past that didn't exist, that had maybe never existed outside of their own belief? Even after Jane had told Henry that he was dead, that nothing he did mattered now, he still couldn't be anything but what he was.

"I'll try to help you," Henry said. "I only have a little time left, but I'll do what I can."

"Give back what you took," the man said.

Spirits wrapped the man and lay over his shoulders like a coat. Henry was surprised to find that he felt jealous. He wanted a home, some anchor to the world. But his family didn't want him, and he didn't want to wander lost through an old toolbox or computer processor until it turned to sand. There was nothing to be done but finish what he had started and then let himself be swept away.

"The plant's gone," Henry said. "Even if I could rebuild it, that wouldn't solve your problems."

We're already dead, Henry wanted to say. Everyone here might as well be, whether they know it or not.

"What are you going to do?" the man asked.

The robot stepped forward on long legs, its shadow falling over the man. It bent and put its arms around him, hugging him against its gleaming chest. "I will love you," the machine said.

The man struggled and shouted for them to get out of his town. He said he would break every machine, kill every pig, burn out every stranger and newcomer who didn't belong here. Finally the robot let him go, and the haunted man fled back to his house.

Henry led the robot deep into downtown, the streets cataclysmic with potholes, broken traffic cones, and burst sacks of garbage. Outside the police station, the bleeding man's cruiser idled. Like the haunted school bus and the robot, a powerful spirit had fused with the car, shrieking through its fuel lines and shaking its cylinders with dead hands. It had survived the tide of ghosts that had passed over the town and fouled the other cars beyond starting, jealously chasing all other spirits out of its engine.

Henry pointed at the car. "If you can take a break from being in love with the world," he said to the robot, "I need that engine."

The bleeding man watched Henry from the station window. Thick, dark blood gummed up his eyes, and he kept wiping them as if what he was seeing wasn't real. Once before, a man the officer had killed had returned to haunt him. He was afraid that Henry had come to do the same. He sweated blood thickly down his face and neck, keeping his eyes on them, but stayed inside.

Henry billowed over the pavement and kept his eyes on the cop. This was the man who had killed him, who would have killed his mother and sister. Already dead, Henry wasn't angry about it. He was astonished. Everything he might have been, all of it taken away by a man whose name he didn't know, for no reason at all. He understood how the ghost outside the grocery store could lie in the same spot for decades, holding its stomach wound and asking everyone it saw "Why?"

The robot ripped open the hood of the cruiser and started tearing out bolts and hoses, getting its thin arms under the engine and hoisting it up from the car. Black smoke roiling with the bright eyes of embers poured out of the haunted machine. Lifting the block of metal out of the car chassis and onto its shoulder, the robot turned and then followed Henry back the way they had come. The bleeding man watched until they were out of sight, not daring to follow.

It took the robot a couple of hours to lurch back across town, swaying with the weight of the engine on its shoulder. Back at their house, Jane's car sat dead as a stone in the driveway, its engine finally too full of ghosts to start.

"I won't be around much longer," Henry said to the robot. "You'll have to be Jane's brother when I'm gone."

"I will love Jane," it said, its metal throat whining and stretching out the "o."

He wondered where his sister would go, who she would become. There was so much ahead of her, decades of future when Swine Hill would be just a bad memory. No matter how much he did to help her on her way, he would only see her beginning.

It would have to be enough.

While the robot worked on Jane's car, Henry floated near the homes of the pig people. Other ghosts couldn't enter their houses, finding the pigs too strange, but Henry knew them intimately. He drifted through their ductwork and peered out from vents, listening in on their conversations.

They were worried. The Pig City Corporation had been hit by some kind of cyberattack. Paychecks weren't going out. Shipping schedules, deliveries, personnel changes, all were in disarray. No one knew what was happening or what needed to happen. The pigs called, and while management knew about the self-slaughtering pig project, no one had any record of it. "Just wait for someone to contact you," the people on the phone said. But it was clearer by the hour that no one was coming for them.

The pigs met in Hogboss's garage around a pool table. They found themselves free. They could do whatever they wanted. But they didn't have much money, and Swine Hill was falling apart. They were excited, but they were also afraid. What would they do?

Hogboss was in Dennis's old room, sitting on his dead son's bed and staring brokenhearted and bewildered at the posters. Henry pushed through the wall, boiling out of a Marilyn Manson print. It was still day, and Henry was having trouble holding his shape together. He was a smear of smoke with glowing eyes. He hoped the pig man wouldn't be frightened.

Hogboss stood and sniffed at the cloud, passing one of his thick hands through it. "You smell like iron and blood and smoke," he said. "You smell like the plant."

"I need you to come with me," Henry said. His voice was a soft rush of air, like wind through tall grass. "I want to show you something."

"I'm sorry I didn't understand you better," the pig man said. "I've been trying. I listen to your music and watch your movies. I'm doing my best to know who you were."

The old pig thought he was Dennis. Henry didn't know whether he should tell him the truth, but Hogboss kept talking. He had so much to say, as if he'd been waiting on that bed for days, as if he had been sure his son would return. Henry kept quiet. He could be Dennis if the pig man needed him to be.

Henry drifted outside, Hogboss walking beside him and telling him everything.

"There is so much I have to apologize for," Hogboss said. "I acted like I couldn't remember your mother, like I didn't miss her. I didn't want to make people any more uncomfortable than they already were. But I do miss her. I remember. I'm sorry I didn't tell you that."

Behind Hogboss's house, the tree line began. The forest wrapped the ridge and collared the town, years and years' worth of Swine Hill's secrets lying forgotten inside. Now the wreckage of Pig City lay within it, still humming with a few stubborn ghosts sunken so deep into its concrete and tile that they didn't even know it had been destroyed. Henry led him under the trees.

He had never thought about what Hogboss might remember from before he had become a self-slaughtering pig. Hogboss seemed to have come into the world already a plant manager, fully formed. But of course he had a past, a time before the ghost's knife had reshaped him, before he'd staggered up on two legs and before language had stained his tongue.

"I'm sorry I was going to make you work at Pig City," Hogboss said. "They owned us. I thought it was the only way. Henry must have done something, because they don't want us anymore. I don't know what to do with myself now. You would have been ready for this."

They passed through a row of trees that had swallowed up an old cow fence, the barbed wire sunken deep into the bark and stretched tight between branches. The pig man snapped limbs and furrowed a trail with his passing, the woods dense and still around them.

"I shouldn't have insisted that you be a plant manager like me. But I was excited. There were so many things I wanted to share with you. The smell of a burned-out light bulb. The taste of the brine we use to package cuts, and which cuts are good to eat raw. How heavy and right a knife can feel in your hands. The way the pigs in the pens look at you, like you're one of them. That factory was my whole world. I was good at what I did. I thought you could be good at it too."

They passed through a strange grove of trees that had been painted with graffiti, looping red words that dripped and smeared to the point of being unreadable. Old cars had been junked out here, trees splitting them open and vines wrapping their hoods. Sometimes Hogboss's boot found a piece of glass or an old board in the dirt, snapping it under his weight.

"You let me go to school," Henry said. "I got to have friends. I danced. You were a good father. I wouldn't have wanted you to be any different."

"I wish, so much, that I could have seen you dancing with your girl.

Henry told me you had a date. People must have liked you. At least, some of them must have."

"They did," Henry said. "I was happy." He wanted it to be true, hoped that it was. Either way, this was the story Hogboss needed to hear.

"I'm sorry I wasn't there to protect you." Hogboss stumbled, catching himself on a branch. He made a low grunt deep in his throat. "I'm so sorry I let them hurt you."

"There wasn't anything you could have done."

"If I had known," Hogboss said, "I would have killed them first. It wouldn't have been any different to me, butchering a man."

"Tell me something good that you remember," Henry said. He wanted to steer Hogboss away from thinking about murder and revenge.

The pig man sucked in a shuddering breath. "I remember how small you were when you first started walking, down on all fours. You chewed on everything, and you couldn't talk. I got a television from a pawnshop and set it up in the warehouse. I thought it would help. You remember, I wasn't around much then. I was so busy managing the plant. And the gene treatments and hormones were making you grow so fast.

"I came back from the slaughterhouse and hooked up the TV for you. I don't remember what video I put on. But you sat right in front of it, your hand on the screen. You couldn't watch anything without touching it. I was worried about you then. I knew you were going to want more than what the plant could give."

Hunchbacked pines with their sparse needles and green-crowned oaks fell away. They walked into a deep grove of peach trees, bushy and fruit-full. Wheelbarrows and ladders, chained to the ground by ivy, lay among them. Baskets had rotted into the dirt. In the middle of the grove, the leaning peak of a storage barn, its walls gapped with missing boards, stood over the trees.

The trees themselves were haunted by the ghosts of the families who'd tended the peach orchard. After a fire destroyed the farm and it went up for sale, after the woods swallowed up the fields and it never sold, the spirits had brought the trees back from blackened stalks. The earth was stony with peach pits, the grass green and thick. The scent of overripe peaches was overwhelming, unpicked and rotting in their skins.

"It's beautiful." Hogboss sniffed deeply. "Whose is it?"

"It's yours," Henry said. "If you want it."

Hogboss plucked a piece of fruit and ate it whole. He sat down in the shade, his back against a tree.

"People in town have forgotten about the orchard," Henry said. "The ghosts in the trees aren't dangerous. You and the other pig people can hide here."

Hogboss frowned. "We don't want to hide."

"What do you want?"

"We want to rest. To be safe. We want a home."

"Then make this your home."

Hogboss looked around, inhaling the scent of the place. His ears were up, intrigued.

Henry wouldn't last much longer, and the pigs would have to make their way without him. The world was such a cruel place, but if they could shelter somewhere until they learned to navigate it, they might have a chance. Henry imagined them having children and building communities of their own, joining with humankind, making people rethink everything about what it meant to be a person. It spiraled away from him, a messy and multivariable equation that he couldn't solve. He was in awe of what he had made.

"I have to go," Henry said. "I love you. You were good to me."

Hogboss lurched to his feet and ran forward, grabbing at Henry to stop him, to keep him near a little longer. But night was coming on soon, and with it Henry would sharpen, taking on his old form. He didn't want the pig man to know the truth. He broke apart like smoke in Hogboss's arms and let the wind carry him away. Behind him, the sky darkened over the orchard.

The trees shook with ghosts.

• • •

Night fell, and Henry grew solid and quick. He went back to his house, finding the robot oil-smeared and surrounded by car parts in the driveway. Jane's car growled low and throaty, idling on the concrete. The robot had both arms inside the cab, taking the dash apart and fixing her CD changer.

"Is that necessary?" Henry asked. "We have a lot to do."

The robot groaned, deep in conversation with the ghost that lived within it. While it worked, Henry checked the robot's servos and battery cells, the dozens of feet of wiring inside. Everything seemed fine. It needed to last Jane a long time. One day it would be damaged or something in it would break loose. Maybe its ghost would be so at peace that it would fade away, erasing the robot's code as it went. When that day came, his sister would remember losing Henry all over again. He hoped it would last her until she found friends and family, people to care about her in whatever new place she made for herself.

As the robot finished its task, Henry looked up at the laser array that had called down the alien light. It sat still and dark on the roof. All he had to do was use the robot's hands to write a new program, and then it would paint the sky again.

"Hurry," Henry told it. "I'm blowing away."

31

ALL NIGHT AND into the next day, Trigger came for her.

He hovered over Jane and battered her with his need, probed into her mind, desperate to haunt her. She tried reasoning with him, explaining that he was too hard on himself. She tried to comfort him, telling him that it was okay he had failed, that his suffering was over now. Finally she screamed at him, agreeing with him, telling him that he deserved all of this so that he might vanish and leave her alone. No matter what she said, he only drew closer to her. He asked Jane to remember all the times she had failed, everything she deserved to suffer for.

She did feel guilty. Henry had gone up to the plant every day for months and she never tried to stop him, never asked what his ghost might be doing. He had his nose cut off while she was in the same building as him. And he died a few dozen feet from her while she drove away in her mother's car. Even now, with Henry's mournful ghost roaming the town and trying to undo the harm he had done, Jane could only think of getting away.

Trigger's onslaught was fracturing her. Soon she would break apart and he would curl inside her. A reptile sliding back into its egg. The opposite of birth, an ending.

At the height of day, Trigger's ghost weakened. He floated up through the walls of the building, but she could still feel him close.

Dennis's MP3 player was in her pocket, and she pushed the headphones into her ears. His bass-heavy, ethereal music crashed into her head, blocking out the world for a little while. The heart was heavy in her pocket, barely beating at all. She slept for a time.

When she woke up, the sun was weak through the windows. It would be night again soon. Jane's arms and legs ached from the cloud of ghosts that had nestled into her muscles. Her lungs burned with them, making it hard to breathe. Her stomach clenched with hunger. She got up from the floor, the ghosts in the laughing room roaring around her. She staggered out of the classroom and left the building, going back into the warm summer air.

He's following you, her ghost said. *He's never far.*

"I can't run away from him. He isn't attached to a place; he's attached to me. If I leave town, he'll just follow."

You need to make him stay here. The ghost curled around Jane's thoughts, watching her ideas form. *You need to find someone for him to haunt.*

Jane thought of the officer sitting at her kitchen table, blood foaming between his clenched teeth. "Trigger is obsessed with me. He blames me for what happened to him and wants me to suffer for it. Who does that remind you of?"

Oh, Jane. Her ghost moved as heavily as the tongue of a grandfather clock in her breast. *This is dangerous. Maybe I could share you with him. I would be quiet, just listening. It wouldn't have to hurt.*

Jane remembered the hollow men, crushed under so many spirits, their identities burned out of them. If Jane could have shoved the ghost out of her head, she would have. "I'm not letting him in."

The bleeding man will kill you.

Her ghost circled, full of concern. It knew she was really leaving this time, that Jane would choose dying if that's what it took. Jane wasn't the same person she had been a few weeks ago. The ghost's attachment to her was tenuous. It wasn't sure it could hang on.

And for the first time in years, Jane wasn't sure if she needed it anymore.

The school wasn't far from the old center of town with its courthouse and police station. Jane hurried, trying to get there before the phantoms grew solid and filled the streets. She listened with her ghost, staying far from even the weakest embers of spirits. If she walked through another swarm of them by accident, they could paralyze her.

The lost ghosts of the Pig City plant had salted themselves across the town. They gathered in transformers and power lines, craving heat and violence. They filled the skins of those left behind, pounding in their chests, pinching deep inside their flesh. In the metal bodies of cars, they found steel walls to wrap themselves in. As she listened with her ears, the town was silent. But when she listened with her ghost, Jane heard it wail and beg, crying out that everything had been taken from it. Every place was just as haunted as downtown now.

The buildings in the city center looked like monuments or tombs. Their brick was crumbling and faded of paint. The names on the old signboards were unfamiliar. In the two decades she had lived here, none of these stores had been open. The center of town had been a festering wound for as long as she could remember.

With every step, she could feel Trigger pulled along behind her like a kite. Ravenous and inexorable, he fell closer. She only had a little time left before he descended on her again. She didn't think she would be strong enough to resist him much longer.

At one corner of the square, the edifice of the police station rose before her. Its steps were strewn with trash, rain-sticky wrappers and old newspapers clotted to the concrete. From the window in the second story, the bleeding man stared down at her.

He won't come outside. He's afraid. Somehow he knows that another ghost wants to possess him.

"Why would he think that?"

Because he deserves it.

Jane held the railing and climbed the steps. She didn't have any problem with that. He had killed her brother, had wanted to kill her whole family because they were close to the pigs. If he needed to punish himself for the sins he had committed, she would let him. She only hoped that Trigger's ghost would see a mirror of itself in him, would be willing to take the bleeding man instead of her. If not, one of them would kill her. If that happened, she hoped that she wouldn't come back as a ghost.

If you did, I would hold on to you. I would stay with you even if we were only lights in the sky.

To the ghost, it didn't matter if Jane was living or dead, host to dozens of spirits or only itself. It just didn't want to be left alone. It wanted to care about her, believed that it did, but its first love would always be itself.

Jane walked into the police station, Trigger's spirit cold and invisible and close behind her. In its wind, she could smell Trigger's hair, his sweat, the faint antiseptic and rubber scent always clinging to him from his work at the plant. It made her remember the afternoon she'd spent in his bed before everything fell apart. She had loved him. That was what made all of this so hard.

The police station was dim inside and coppery with the odor of blood. Dark stains bloomed over the backs of chairs, matted papers together, dripped in constellations over the white tile floors.

The building was full of ghosts. They darted, birdlike and afraid, under desks and behind furniture. They slipped in and out of cracks in the walls.

These ghosts were all people that the bleeding man tracked down, locked in his cells, and killed. Being afraid of him is all they have. You're lucky Henry didn't become one of these. Imagine him lost in here with all the rest, startling at shadows for years and years?

The thought made her wince, and the ghost knew it. Let it say what it wanted. It only had a little time left. She turned her music up louder until it filled her head. The ghost thrashed desperate and sour beneath her ribs.

There were no other police here, no deputies or assistants. The station had been understaffed before, but with the new flood of ghosts come down from Pig City, shutting off power and stopping cars on the roads, most people had left. Only someone like the bleeding man, someone who consumed pain like it was bread, would return to the most haunted part of downtown amidst the most vicious ghosts. Jane was surprised that he only had one ghost within him, that in all this time he'd never encountered another spirit that felt as he did.

But most spirits were tied to their work. A lifetime of labor had worn a deep groove in them, and they startled awake from death like waking up to an alarm clock for an early shift. They did what they had always done, taking purpose from their work even if it made them unhappy. Most of them didn't mean to hurt people. That happened by accident.

With the power out, Jane climbed the stairs to the second floor. The pain of spirits threaded through her muscles made her brace her hands against the tops of her thighs. Halfway up, she smelled coffee. The smell startled her, making her think of the kitchen at home, her mom getting ready for work in the morning.

On the top floor, a hallway led to an office with a window overlooking the street. The bleeding man waited for her inside. She could smell him, a dark, adrenal, wounded animal scent. Would this be where she died? Would this smell, coffee mixed with blood, be the last thing she knew? Trigger's ghost was close behind.

Jane went to meet her fate.

On his desk, the bleeding man had a metal coffeepot sitting on a tiny camping stove. Beside it lay his gun. The only other item on the table was a plastic bag full of pale dust. The bleeding man stood with the desk between them, strangely fearful of her. Bright lines of blood ran from his ears, eyes, and the corners of his mouth, matting his collar to his neck.

Small shadows played over the ceiling and blew around like shreds of paper over the floor. The bleeding man's ghostly victims could feel that he was afraid. They had come to see him suffer.

He was thinking of how he had become haunted. He had tried to stop someone, a shuffling and suspicious man, his body too big, clothes baggy, eyes downcast. The man had pretended not to hear the officer at first, and then he had run. The officer chased him to his house, the neighbors hanging their faded laundry in the sun.

The officer had believed somehow that people like this were the reason Swine Hill was poor and unhealthy and full of ghosts. They took more than their share, he believed. They made every place worse. He would see them fined, in jail, forced out of town.

The man ran into a dim house, and the officer followed him into the hot rooms. His heart raced, and he was afraid. Not afraid that the man might be dangerous, but that he might be innocent. The officer feared he was mistaken, his chase an embarrassment.

To be who he thought he was, the officer needed the runner to be guilty.

In the living room, children stopped their play to stare. He saw himself as they must see him, the pressed uniform and raised gun. They were afraid, and he liked it, wanted them to remember this moment, wanted his feet to stain the floors so they would never forget that he could go where he wanted and do as he pleased.

The suspect locked himself in the bedroom. The officer crashed into the door, splitting the hollow wood, and found himself tangled up with the man who'd been leaning against it from the other side. Arm in arm for a moment. Shoulder to shoulder and chest to chest. The man's wide eyes inches from his. The officer squeezed the trigger over and over, separating himself from this other person with sound and heat and shooting stars of steel and lead.

At the inquiry afterward, the ghost of the man he had killed followed him wherever he went. It watched when he was interviewed by the local chief of police, when he sat with a lawyer, when his fellow cops turned away reporters and family. The officer was terrified that he would have to answer the unanswerable — Why did you chase him? Why did you shoot? — but no one asked him this. None of them was confused about why he found the man threatening.

The ghost went everywhere with him. Riding in his car. Lying next to him in bed. Sitting on his desk at work. Furious that it would have no justice, it believed in the same things as the officer. It wanted to punish, to pass judgment, to make the officer pay for his wrongs. So it climbed inside him one night and forced blood up through his pores, making him hurt for all that he had done.

The pain broke his skin and twisted through him like screws. It taught him to hate himself, to understand that he was wrong and deserved to hurt. His knowing was what kept his ghost welded so tightly to him. He needed punishment, and he would have it.

The brutal story of his haunting washed over Jane in an instant. The bleeding man gestured to the bag on the table. "Here are your brother's remains," he said.

Ashes, Jane realized.

"That's what you came for, isn't it?" he asked.

Trigger's ghost lay along her back like a cloak. If the bleeding man couldn't see him, surely he must feel the chill, the stormy friction in the small room, the way the meager light from the cook stove and the fading sun outside the window had suddenly grown weaker.

Take the ashes and leave, her ghost said. *He's too afraid to hurt you for now. Go before he changes his mind.*

She didn't want to be here with the man who had killed her brother. She could leave the station and find some alley where Trigger could fall on her in the dark. It would be the easiest thing to just surrender.

"Do you remember the first time we met?" Jane asked him.

The bleeding man didn't answer her. He picked up his gun again, rolling the chamber open with his thumb and spinning it. He could feel the ghost in the room, was afraid it was Henry. His stomach clenched with fear. He thought about killing her.

Her ghost wanted her to run. It made her remember how the boys had killed Dennis, how her brother had been brutalized and mocked and then switched off like a light. It pulled every fearful thing out of her, slinging them against the walls of her mind. She held the desk to steady herself.

The circling spirits knit together, wrapping them in dark. They jumped in and out of one another and hummed, locusts hungry and ready to fall.

Jane swallowed and steadied her voice. "You told me that some-body has to pay when things go wrong," she said. "Do you still believe that?"

"I do." He didn't just say it. He felt it, deep in his gut. He felt it so hard that it had made him lift his gun and kill a sixteen-year-old kid. There was so much wrong in the world, and he had been born to come down on it like a wide, flat hand. He thrashed in bed at night, his ghost tearing him apart, and knew that his suffering was just.

He had no pity for anyone, not even himself.

Trigger's ghost stepped into the room, gathering heaviness and ethe-real flesh. The bleeding man's need to punish called to Trigger like his own name. He had come to haunt someone, to take on skin and blood, and he wouldn't leave until he had it.

The bleeding man rested his palm on his gun, wondering who this new ghost was, wondering if he should fire a bullet through Jane or himself. The flickering shadows of spirits covered his hand, waiting to see what he would do.

Trigger turned from the bleeding man and stepped behind Jane, tak-ing her in his arms like they were dancing again. Her ghost fled, and Trigger pushed into her mind.

You want me to hurt the bleeding man because of what he's done. You understand that some people need pain.

He tried to push into her body. Jane remembered the ghost of the old man that had haunted her brother, how it just walked into him as if through an open door. She had to close herself or Trigger would take her and have her forever.

"I am angry at you," she said. "I'm angry at both of you so much. I *hate* you. But I don't want to see you tortured. I don't want to see you anymore at all."

What about all the ways you failed your family?

She felt like he was stretching her lungs, shouldering his way inside.

"I did fail them. But I loved them too. They wouldn't want me to suf-fer." Jane felt the weight of responsibility that she'd been carrying, and she set it down. "I forgive myself."

The bleeding man raised his gun toward Jane and pulled the trigger. The quick motes of the people he had killed gathered in the gun like iron filings drawn to a magnet. They held the hammer in place, welded the bullet to its chamber, locked the gun down like a prisoner in a cell.

It didn't fire.

Trigger threw Jane against the wall, pulling himself away from her. She didn't have what he needed. His last lingering thought when he'd been entwined with her was disappointment and fear. He surged across the room toward the bleeding man.

The officer put down his gun, heavy with phantoms who had willed that it would never fire again. A high, sad cry rose from his mouth as Trigger crashed into him.

Jane's ghost returned to her, and she felt Trigger spiral into the officer's body like a parasite. The pain was so intense that she held herself. The bleeding man looked at her for help, weeping blood that spread over his cheeks like wings.

Echoes of ghosts jumped from the walls and floors, piling on top of him, gnawing their way into him too, responding to his fear with their own. The bleeding man fell and writhed on the floor, his eyes sun bright. Jane couldn't feel the cop or Trigger as distinct things anymore. The bleeding man was suddenly *honeycombed with ghosts,* an entire city of the dead. The spirits built a hell inside his heart.

Jane left Henry's ashes on the desk. That wasn't her brother any more than his ghost was. She fled the police station on her aching legs, letting her ghost guide her as it grew dark.

Do you feel bad for abandoning him like that? After everyone else left Trigger, now you left him too.

"He wanted to hurt me. And Trigger's dead. That was only a ghost."

That's a lie. He was more than an it *to you. You need to believe that Trigger and Henry aren't people. Otherwise, you'd hate yourself. Even when he was alive, Trigger had that same anger and obsession. That ghost was the boy you loved, and you left him.*

Her ghost was right. It was necessary for Jane to believe that the spirits were something else, that they weren't the people she had lost. Otherwise, she never would have been able to walk away from them. How much of a person was left in a ghost? It didn't matter. If she was going to survive this place, she needed to let Henry and Trigger go.

The spirit within her quieted, but Jane could feel its grief. Knowing that she would soon leave it behind, the ghost brought to mind fragments of all the sad songs it loved.

In the quiet room of Jane's chest, it sang and mourned itself.

I T WAS FULLY dark when Jane left the police station. Once she got far enough from downtown, Jane could feel Bethany again. Somewhere beyond their world, all around her and nowhere at all, Bethany rose up from the nothing that swallowed lost ghosts.

They watched her climb, astonished. Spirits never came back from that place. It was real death, the forever kind. Bethany seemed to be only inches away from their world, but she was tired. She was close to letting go and falling into the abyss. Jane and her ghost waited, wondering if Bethany would make it.

She walked toward Hogboss's house, but she could smell smoke and see the glow of flames far before she reached his street. Jane didn't need her ghost to tell her that the hollow men had burned the pig neighborhood to the ground. She wondered if the pigs had been dragged from their homes and killed in the streets, butchered the same as Dennis. She wondered if her mother had been caught or if she had escaped. Would she be spared, or would they treat her the same as the pigs?

The heart box throbbed against her leg. Jane pulled it from her pocket and held it out in front of her like a lamp, the pulse and flex of its beat straining against her fingers. Her sullen ghost warned her of spirits roaming the neighborhood. Jane stepped into empty houses, circled behind buildings, stayed clear of the road. The fragmented ghosts still coiled hard as shells in her arms and legs. Every step was pain.

Your brother is close. He's planning some new machine.

Her ghost wanted her to look for Henry, to try to stop him or help him move on. It made the suggestion, more in images than words, that she could find her brother's ghost a person to haunt and then she would have him back. Or they could figure out a way to help Bethany before it was too late. Anything would do, so long as Jane stayed in Swine Hill, tangled in its problems and wrestling with its spirits a little longer.

She left the tomblike closeness of downtown and came into the open, crossing a field of high grass that rose into dense brush and trees. The light of the moon fell on her like a spotlight. From the dark windows of nearby buildings, men called out to her.

Pinpricks of light turned to face her from the windows. The hollow men threw themselves down to the street, no concern for pain or injury, and rushed toward her. There were dozens of them.

Jane pushed on into the forest, following the racing heart. Her father was close. Her ghost sank deep within her, so quiet and still that Jane could hardly feel that it was there. It hadn't warned her about the hollow men. Had it not heard them? Or would it rather see Jane die than abandon it?

A slash of paint marked the trees ahead of her. The bark was stained with overlapping red Xs. She followed them, a long band of trees that seemed to wrap the town. She remembered something Henry had told her, how he had seen their father marking houses with dangerous ghosts. After the town flooded with spirits, her dad must have decided that all of Swine Hill was dangerous. He was doing his best to ring the town with warnings, to tell anyone who might stumble upon it to stay away.

Branches broke behind her. The hollow men were still coming. She tried to make herself go faster, her legs burning, unable to shake free the spirits that wrapped her muscles like barbed wire.

The heart box flared warm in her hand. At her feet, a gaunt figure lay wrapped in a torn coat, sleeping in the hollow of a tree. Jane was too exhausted and in pain to go any farther. The haunted would find her soon. She could feel them gathering around.

She lay next to her father, and his arms reflexively tightened around her, wrapping her in his coat. He smelled of sour sweat, rain, and earth. His face and chest were a thick map of scars: her mother's hands, lips, teeth, even her breath cutting riverlike channels across him.

The hollow men came under the tree and looked down at her. But they were so full of ghosts, the life within them so crushed under the weight of the dead, that they couldn't see her father in front of them. Held by him, the ghosts couldn't see Jane, either. And so they passed, shaking branches and trying to flush her out, but eventually they gave up and headed back into the town.

Her father awoke next to her and looked around, fumbling for his paint can.

Jane didn't know if her mother was alive. She and her father might be the last members of their family, the only ones the town hadn't yet killed. She had his heart, kicking like a trapped bird in its case. But he still wasn't himself, and he probably never would be. She had no way of getting the heart back into his body. She didn't know how she would take care of him. Maybe she had been a fool for thinking she could. Despair bloomed inside her, and Jane hung her head, holding tightly to her father's arm.

Bethany is drowning, her ghost said.

Through her ghost, Jane saw the girl struggle. Alien light coated Bethany's body and swept down her throat. She couldn't breathe or move. She dug in her fingers until they bled, trying not to fall. Bethany grew calm, and Jane waited for her to finally give up. Wasn't that all that was left to do?

Bethany tensed her muscles and screamed until the alien light dissolved in her throat. She forced the alien glow back down into her cells.

She made her brutal climb up the cliff face, scraping her hands and feet raw. Bethany would never be rid of the alien. It haunted her like her storm of ghosts. But it would learn what those spirits had learned. She was not the alien's prisoner. It was hers.

A blade of light rent the ground at Jane's feet. Her father started to stand, but Jane held on to his coat, keeping him from disappearing into the night. Bethany shoved her arms up into the world from some other place and, straining, lifted herself back into their reality.

Jane wondered for a moment if Bethany was dead and just didn't know it yet. But she seemed more solid and real than Jane herself. Her skin was shot through with the alien light. Her nails were broken and her arms and shoulders bruised. She gasped, taking in deep breaths, her arms spread like wings. She looked like someone who had forced her way through a wall of rock with her bare hands.

All of her spirits are still with her, Jane's ghost said.

Jane could see them, sitting inside Bethany's curved ribs like a stadium. They cheered for her, this girl who had beaten everyone, beaten the alien, even beaten death just as they'd known she would.

"Give me the heart," Bethany said.

Jane put it in her hands, Bethany's skin searing hot and as hard as metal. Bethany reached inside Jane's father like he was a pool of water. She pulled out something, a fist-sized lump of metal and rubber, and dropped it on the ground. Jane's father staggered, holding his chest, but Bethany held him up, then took the heart from its box and nestled it inside him, pinching the arteries back together afterward.

Somehow, Henry had trapped their father's wants and needs and hurt, most of who he was, inside this small lump of flesh. When Bethany gave it back to him, his mind came blazing back with it. He remembered who he was. Her ghost spooled his every raw thought across Jane's mind, letting her know how cold and afraid and guilty he was.

He didn't recognize his daughter at first, squinting and touching her face. His voice was coarse and paper-soft. "*Jane?* Did you already grow up?" He put his hands over his chest, the heart's rhythms unfamiliar and overwhelming, raw emotion pumping through his body. "Oh. I hadn't meant to be gone so long."

Jane held him. She had so much to say, didn't know where to start. Henry had given her exactly what she'd needed. Bethany had saved her.

No matter what else happened, she had her father back.

Jane spoke into her father's shoulder. "Henry's dead. The town is almost gone. I'm leaving as soon as I can."

Her father stiffened in her arms, struggling to process this new world he'd come home to, a world without his son.

"I've been watching Henry," Bethany said. "I can't stay long or I'll wear a hole in the world. But I'll take care of him before I go."

Jane didn't know what that meant, and her ghost didn't want to tell her. It was terrified of Bethany. She was untethered from the world, fading out of the universe like the dead.

Bethany left Jane and her father to get to know each other again. She walked through the woods back into town, searching for Henry's ghost. Her body burned with light, and Jane could see her even through the branches and trees between them. The world seemed more fragile, less solid and real, than Bethany Ortiz.

Her father sat on the ground and started to cry. He held his hands over his ears and drew his knees up to his chest. Jane hung on to him, telling him that everything would be okay. She didn't know if that was true. She didn't know what would happen next.

He hasn't felt anything in years. The wind is too cold. The trees are too loud. He has sores on his feet, pain in his mouth. He doesn't know how to be a person anymore.

The moon was a silver plate behind the grasping fingers of tree branches. There was a sweet smell on the wind, a rush of overripe fruit. Jane's stomach hurt. It had been so long since she had eaten anything. Her head burned with how tired she was, but she was happy, overflowing with gratitude. Even if her father struggled with the shock of consciousness and all its pain, at least she had him. Whatever came next, she wouldn't be alone.

There are people out here, her ghost said. *Or maybe pigs. I could never tell the difference.*

There was smoke in the wind. Through the trees, a tongue of fire lapped along a broken branch. A rough chorus moved through the woods. When her father had caught his breath, Jane pulled him to his feet and guided him toward the sound and light, one hand out to shield her face from branches in the dark.

The density of the forest fell away. Suddenly they were in a grove of low, bushy trees. Pig people had come here in the hundreds, sitting around small fires and stretching tarps over frames of rough wood. Jane could feel her mother somewhere among them. The hollow men hadn't hurt them after all. Her mother had been right about Hogboss keeping her safe.

But the orchard was haunted. Ghosts of those who had lived and worked here filled the trunks and spreading arms of the trees, making peaches swell and fall from their heavy branches. Spirits flew through the grass and chased one another invisibly through the grove, coiling and kissing in the dark. They circled the bonfires of the pigs, remembering night fires of their own. The ghosts barely noticed the pig people, so caught up in their own decades' long love of each other and this place. Swine Hill had forgotten that the orchard had ever existed, but for the spirits who haunted it, this place was the entire world.

Ahead, Hogboss spoke in his cavernous voice. Jane's mother stood next to him, her dress billowing in the wind. They were arm in arm with the other pigs, all of them gathered in a circle. Jane strained to hear, catching only a few words. "Here are the things I'm thankful to Henry for," one of them began.

Her father shied away from the mass of people, but Jane kept her arm around him, leading him closer. He seemed too small to her. But what had she expected? Had she thought that when he remembered himself, she would become a little girl again?

They joined the ring of mourners, listening to the pigs say a few words about Henry, the creator most of them had barely known. Her father stared at Jane's mother from across the circle, wondering if it was really her, but she didn't look back.

Your brother's ghost is close. He's keeping himself hidden, but he's in the trees, listening. This is the first time he's truly felt dead. He hurts.

Jane felt the ghost's sympathy for him, an unusual feeling for the spirit. It must be remembering its own funeral, the first time it knew what it was. She let herself have a moment of love for it, feeling it wrapped by her body. She didn't know if it was a person — or something more or something less — but she knew that she would miss it when it was gone.

It was hard to focus on what the pigs had to say about Henry. Jane's mind kept wandering to Trigger, his angry ghost finding in the bleeding man a whipping boy for everything he hated about himself. Was that better than his spirit wandering aimlessly, adrift from everyone he had ever loved? She wanted to believe that, given enough time, Trigger could forgive himself and feel some measure of peace. But he hadn't been able to let his mistakes go when he was alive. She was afraid, now that he was dead, he'd cling to them forever, devouring himself until the end of time.

After the ceremony was over, after the pigs sang together one last time and then went back to their campfires and tents, Jane brought her father to meet her mother. He was afraid to see her. He felt that he had left her behind and run out on their family. Jane's mother felt the same. It was wrong, Jane knew. That wasn't what had happened at all. Neither of them had done anything but what they had to do. But there would be no convincing them of that.

Hogboss looked back and forth from Jane's burned father to her hard-eyed mother. Understanding, he let go of her hand and stepped away from her. He looked down at the earth, his ears flopping over his face in a way that made Jane think of Dennis. Hogboss wasn't angry. He was prepared to let this woman go if that was best for her. He held his disappointment in, well acquainted with how it felt to be alone.

"Is he himself again?" her mother asked.

"I am," her father answered. He stood, waiting for her to forgive him.

Jane's mother crossed her arms. "I'm glad," she said. "I'm sorry about everything that happened."

He took a step closer, reaching for her, but Jane's mother backed away.

"I never wanted to hurt anyone," she said. "But I don't love you anymore. I hope you understand."

The words were like a hammer hitting Jane in the chest. She had done so much to bring the pieces of her family back together. She had been prepared to forgive everything, to let them start over as best they could. This was their chance to be a family again. She watched her mother move closer to Hogboss and twine her fingers in his. Jane, knowing it was unfair of her, couldn't help but hate her mother a little, couldn't help but resent the spark of joy that flared up in the pig man.

Is your happiness more important than everyone else's? What did you think was going to happen, Jane? You don't want to live in the past, but the future is hard. It won't be anything you expect.

She mentally pushed the ghost away, not needing it to tell her what she already knew.

"That's okay," her father said. "You look good. Happy. I'm glad." He turned to Jane, wiping his eyes. "It's very loud out here. Can we go somewhere quiet?"

"We're leaving Swine Hill now," Jane told her mother. "You could come with us if you want." She swallowed, finally looking at Hogboss. "You could both come."

Her mother dug through her pockets, finding a slender wallet with a little bit of money in it. She pulled out what bills she had and pressed them into Jane's hand, throwing her arms around her neck. "I'm going to stay here and help the pigs. And Henry's ghost might need me. I want to be close for him. You be safe. I'm proud of you."

Jane put the money in her pocket and led her father through the orchard, the light and sound of the pigs fading behind them. Somewhere in the windblown dark, she felt her brother's ghost watching. It was full of regret, wishing it could go with her. Jane wondered what Bethany would do with Henry when she found him.

She and her father went under a tree on the edge of the grove and pulled down new peaches. She ate and ate, like the fruit was pieces of the sun, like she could fill herself with light.

They walked across town back to her house. Jane was exhausted, had barely slept in days, but she didn't want to spend another moment in

Swine Hill. It would be morning soon. People stirred in the houses around her, as determined to stay as Jane was to go.

On the roof of her house, the robot worked on the laser array. Henry was already back, sunken into the robot's metal hands, using it to make a few final adjustments. Bethany was close by, but she waited, letting Jane say goodbye before she did whatever she needed to do.

Jane thought her car would still be dead with ghosts, had been planning to walk out of town if she had to, but she found it running in the driveway. There was something hideous under the hood, her ghost told her. Dead hands moved the pistons, their breath igniting the stale air in its fuel lines, making the car rattle and thrum and roar on nothing but the insistence of the spirits that moved it. Jane wondered if the car would slip loose from her control and carry her somewhere she didn't want to go. But as long as it got her far away from Swine Hill, she wasn't sure it mattered where it took her.

Her father went and waited in the car, sheltering from the immensity of the open sky with its light and sound and wind. She packed her clothes into trash bags and filled the trunk of the car. Her father's belongings were already boxed up in the garage, covered in years of dust. She raided the pantry for bottles of water and packaged food, taking the canned goods and even the can opener.

Where are you even going, Jane?

She didn't answer, but her ghost found her doubts anyway, uncovered her fears that she was heading from one bad place to another.

You could stay. There could be a new life for you here.

Everything in the town reminded her of the dead. Her house was full of memories of her family, how things had been before her mother had been haunted. The school made her think of her brother. Every curve in the road held some memory of Trigger riding in her car, how tense and urgent and hard loving him had been. Even the trees surrounding the town spoke to her of frost and the coming cold, of ghosts waiting in the wings for her to let her guard down.

No, she couldn't stay. The spirits needed Swine Hill because it made them animate with memory. But Jane needed to forget. She needed to get out from under the town's weight of history and trauma.

The robot came down from the roof, and Henry stood beside it. There was a low whine coming from the laser array, but no light. "I've done it," Henry said. "Everything's fixed now."

Jane laughed at how sure of himself he sounded. "Everything looks the same to me."

"Wait until tonight."

"I won't be around to see it." Jane reached for his shoulder, but her hand passed through him. Now that he'd done what he had set out to do, Henry was just a shadow in the air. "I've said goodbye to you so many times already. Why is it so hard to do it again?"

The robot got into the passenger side of her car, its metal head pressing against the ceiling. Her father was already curled up in the back seat, shivering through some nightmare.

"Since I can't leave," Henry said, "I asked the robot to go with you. This way you'll still have a family. You and Dad won't be alone."

"That's a weird family," Jane said. "I wish I could have my old one back."

The sun came over the edge of the house across the street, and rays of light cut through Henry. He started to say something, but his voice was gone. The light turned him glassy and drained him of color, until he was just a glint in the air.

Henry threw his arms around her and dissolved, gone like spider silk catching fire. Jane grabbed at the wisps of him, trying to cup him like smoke in her hands.

"Henry? Can you hear me? Thank you so much. For everything."

He's still here, but there's not much of him left. He'll be here for another night or so, but not much longer than that.

She was glad he would get to see his machine do whatever it was going to do.

"I love you, Henry. You took good care of Mom. You were a lot better to her than I was. Whatever's coming next, don't be afraid. You won't be alone."

Jane got into the car just as the sun rose. The air was cool, the last hot breath of summer guttering out, and the touch of fall already yellowing the treetops. Her father slept easier. The robot sat beatific beside her, its window down and long arm hanging out of the car. It stared directly into the coming sun, reaching out like it could grasp that coin of light in its metal hand.

Jane put the car in gear and let off the brake, the engine flying forward like an uncaged animal. She shot out of her neighborhood and raced out of town, passing the road that would have taken her to Trigger's house.

If Henry's machine worked and the ghosts were swept from the town, would Mason wake from his fever of ghosts and find himself alone? Would he walk through the quiet house and look at their photos, this temple to the family he had destroyed?

She let herself remember Trigger in her bed, watching her and wanting her, how incandescent Jane had looked through his eyes. Had the terrible shape of his ghost been inside him then . . . ? But no — she stopped herself and instead let him go, both halves of him, love and horror pulled out of her like an unwinding string with every mile.

The car dragged them down the road, hugging the corners tightly, and they broke onto the highway. A disc fell into place in the CD changer, and warm, frantic music came pounding out of her speakers. As the music filled her, Jane felt her ghost start to tear loose like a scab.

Her ghost's fingers, sunk so deeply into her, were loosening one by one. Jane didn't know how to feel. The ghost was cruel and selfish. It made her sad, forced her to dwell on the most awful things. It fought with her and made her feel small and weak. But it protected her too. And it had been there for so many years, living in her mind, her first and oldest friend.

Its voice was already quiet as they passed Daleville, heading west with the whole country laid out before them. *Who even are you without me?* the ghost asked her.

Jane's eyes burned hot, the road blurring in front of her. "Let's find out," she said.

The ghost rose from her body, half in her and half out so she could see its small face. Its grief rose in a pure, high tone like the striking and fading of a bell. Hadn't it been like a sister to her? How was it any less than anyone else she had loved? The ghost's face, eyes wide and lips parted, was streaked with an undeniably human hurt.

And then, the ghost was blown out of her.

Jane felt stillness. A loud silence inside, even with the music and the roar of the wind in her ears.

With a sad smile, she looked back at her father. She didn't know what strange dreams moved through the man's head. Neither could she feel the pain and violence of the haunted engine churning under the hood, and the invisible spirits burning alongside the road couldn't touch her with their grief anymore. She was alone in a way that she couldn't remember.

The music cut into her, the singer's voice husky and whip-fast, full of heat. The bass hit her in the chest. It sounded like a celebration or a feud. There was no ghost to tell her what anything meant, to unlock the secrets in the words. The singer rained down emotion and mystery. Jane surrendered to it, letting the song move her without knowing why.

Beside her, the robot shifted its weight and tilted its face to the bright sky, as if it could see beyond the universe and into wherever it was that Bethany would carry Henry. Its metal throat stretched and warped, and a moaning, lovesick call came echoing out of it like the reverberations of a gong.

H ENRY MOVED INVISIBLY among the pigs. He was wind
through tree branches, a gout of smoke from a fire, a chill at
someone's back, a black feather twisting through the night
sky.

The pigs circled and sang. Hogboss was there, Henry's mother at
the pig man's side. And Jane came to meet them, their father with her.
Henry felt a weight fall from him. Some small thing he had broken
was repaired.

The pigs stood in a circle around the fire. They sang and wiped their
eyes. Henry thought the ceremony might be for Dennis, but the pig
boy had already had his funeral. The pigs spoke and said what they
were thankful for.

"Without Henry, I never would have tasted spaghetti," one of them
said.

"Without Henry, I wouldn't have a sweater," said another.

They went around their circle, giving thanks for what Henry had
given them. They spoke of music videos, courtroom TV, and nature

documentaries. Of hot coffee, salted nuts, the bright orbs of wax-coated fruit. They named more abstract things — celebrity crushes, pet peeves, nicknames — and thanked him for these, too. One pig raised an arm to the sky and named the constellations, thanking Henry for each one, as though he had hung them himself.

"Without my son," his mother said, "I would have forgotten what it meant to be loved."

The ceremony ended. Below Henry, his parents reunited. For a moment, he wondered if they would go back into the old house, try to be the people they had been before. But his family, healed and whole, wasn't the same. His mother stayed with Hogboss in the forest; Jane and their father walked back toward home.

Henry floated over the city, racing ahead of his sister. He found the robot squatting on the roof and helped it finish the laser array. Jane arrived shortly before morning, coming into the house to pack for a future she couldn't imagine. She loaded the ghost-driven car.

In the pale half-light of early morning, Henry wanted to make his sister understand that he loved her. That he was sorry for what he had done to upset their lives. That what was in front of her was fathomless and unpredictable but as much hers as anyone else's. That she was powerful enough to face it.

But before he could say much of anything, the sun came up, shattering Henry and the words in his mouth. His sister called to him for a while. Finally she drove off to where Henry couldn't follow.

The world was thin and glassy, and behind it Henry could see an ocean of nothing waiting for him. Bethany's light no longer burned there. She had made it out or she had been dragged under. Henry stared into it, searching for the countless other Swine Hills that Bethany had seen. But there was only an inky dark.

It pulled at him like wind.

Night fell over Swine Hill, and Henry climbed out of the earth with the rest of the town's ghosts, living out his singular obsession. The toxic

spill of spirits from the destroyed plant would make the town unliv-
able for years to come. Ghosts had long memories. They would circle
the ruins until nature raised its green hands and pulled this broken
place deep under the earth. Henry needed to help them let go of the
world.

Using the robot, Henry had been able to adjust the laser array and
write new code. His computer would run the program on a timer, and
then his work would be done. Photos of the town from before its de-
cline were scattered around his room, one of them still sandwiched
into his scanner. Henry had to concentrate to keep himself solid. With
so much of his work finished, he was fading. There was little left to tie
him to the world now. He sat on his roof, waiting for the laser array to
do its work.

Bethany came jogging down his street, just like she had so many
weeks ago, before she had caught the alien and it had changed her. Her
face and arms were raw, her fingertips scabbed and broken. She looked
like a climber who'd fallen again and again, striking a shelf of rock, but
always dragging herself back up. Ghosts circled her like the rings of a
planet, shrieking and victorious. *She has beaten even this,* they seemed
to say. *She will keep fighting, and she will never fall.*

Henry sighed out his relief and felt himself become even less. He
didn't need to free her from the space between worlds, had probably
never been able to. There was nothing left now but to see what would
happen.

Bethany went inside and walked up to his room, coming to sit beside him on the roof. She was sharp and bright, lit from within by the
alien's nuclear glow. Henry's limbs were little more than smoke. He
thought of the dancing girl. She must have wanted her date with the
ghost behind the mirror intensely to have remained solid and whole
for so many years.

"What are we waiting for?" Bethany asked.

"To clear away the last of my mistakes," he said. "To help everyone
start again."

On the roof above them, the laser array hummed to life. The same machine that had scrawled its strange message into the cosmos now probed the sky with fingers of golden light. Finding the broad, flat belly of a cloud, it pulsed hundreds of times, painting an image in the sky. Using Ms. Miller's old photos as its model, the machine recreated the lights of the old town. The neat grid of neighborhoods and street-lights. The golden explosion of downtown with its banks, bars, pool halls, and tailors. The sparsely lit farms and mills ringing the town proper. And almost in the middle of town, alone in a circle of darkness, the blazing white of Pig City bloomed. The old city waited in the sky, gleaming like a map against the cloud bottoms.

From the lightless ruins of Swine Hill, there was a rush of warm air and a collective moan as hundreds of lost ghosts saw the city they had been looking for. They spread their shaggy arms and lifted from the earth like snow birds, a winding chain that seemed to move and breathe as one.

When the ghosts hit the city of light and cloud, looking for the world they had lost, the laser array shifted. It aimed its light at a clear patch of sky, and the rising river of ghosts turned with it. The city moved away from them fast, and the ghosts followed. They chased burning photons through the atmosphere and into the cold of space. The city of light lifted into the cosmos, and the ghosts followed the crackling motes. The light would race away from them for hundreds of years, the ghosts chasing this vision of their pasts until finally dispersing among frozen rock and bands of gas looping alien suns.

A few ghosts remained in the city. Some of those haunting people had already found the life they had lost, and they wouldn't easily let go. But the swarms of lost spirits that had flooded the town and made it unsafe, circulating through flesh and wood and wiring in frustration, had all been swept from the earth.

Everywhere in town, the power snapped back on. Microwaves chirped and refrigerators rumbled. Air-conditioning units flung their bent blades and stuttered to life again. People shrugged off their heavy coats of spirits. The hollow men awoke from fevers to find themselves lying in abandoned buildings far from their homes, guilty memories of hate and violence tunneling through them like worms. They walked into the open and looked up at the sky, seeing the city of light and its ghosts lift into the stars before vanishing forever.

Henry had done what he'd needed to do. What now? In his moment of satisfaction, everything around him became shadowy and soft. He felt heavy. At any moment, he could fall.

"I'm glad you're okay," Henry said to Bethany. "I wish I could have seen all the worlds that you saw. I don't think there's anything waiting for me after this."

Everything below him faded away. Henry dropped toward a pool of nothing, his horizon a rising ring of black. Lost in all that emptiness, would he even know if he was still falling?

Bethany caught the bleeding wisps of Henry and hauled him up. She spooled her hands in his spectral body like it was cotton candy, and dragged him toward her. In her palms, he was gathered back to himself, kept from passing on.

It hurt. He struck out at her, but he was smoke and Bethany was marble.

"What are you doing?" he asked.

"There are countless other worlds, Henry. Don't you want to see them?"

He struggled, tried to wriggle away into that soft night, but Bethany wouldn't let him go. She was as much a being of singular purpose as any ghost. He had to leave, but she had decided he would stay. She was his opponent, and she couldn't lose. For the first time, he was afraid of her.

"Henry is dead. I'm just his ghost."

"Not all ghosts are less than they were in life," she said. "My ghosts live through me. They do things they never could have done before. They feel just as strongly. The dead are worth caring about too."

"I don't want anything," he said. Every moment he stayed here without purpose sent knives through him.

"You aren't *trying* to want anything."

"I didn't want people to live with my mistakes. But I've already fixed everything I can. Why would you want to keep me around? I hurt my whole family. I took away the world from you."

"You did." She looked sad for a moment, but her hand didn't relax on his arm. "This wasn't a good place for me, though. And it wasn't a good place for you, either. We're going to find somewhere better. But first you have to want something. What about before you became a ghost? What did you want then?"

It was hard to think. What was left now? His life had ended.

"I wanted to invent something no one had ever seen before," he said. "I wanted to make the world better. But I think the pig people are going to do that. I don't know how. But they'll help us be more than what we are."

Her face loomed over him, pitiless and stern. She had climbed so far, had suffered so much to come back here. She had changed down to her cells, and she demanded a change from him, too. "The Henry I remember had more imagination than that," she said.

"You don't understand what it's like to be a ghost. Not being sure *hurts*. It's so hard to stay. I wish I had wanted more."

"*What else?*"

Uncertainty burned. Henry thought back over his short life, all the people he had been unkind to, everything he had put before his friends and family, all of the things he never understood. How he had flinched when his mother needed him. How he was too afraid to stand up for Dennis in the cafeteria. "I wish I had been a better person."

She shook him. "*More.*"

Henry considered it, let the idea sit with him. He felt himself grow more solid, starting to take on body. The pain of staying — the feeling that he was being torn away piece by piece and dragged into the void — lessened. He *did* want to be better. There were things about himself he didn't like. If he could live again, he would stop thinking he knew what people needed better than they did. He would be less of a coward. He would never let someone like Dennis get hurt if he could stop it.

It would be hard. Everyone wanted to be a better person than they were, and people always messed it up. What if he was aiming for something he could never have? Would Bethany ever let him stop chasing it, ever let him surrender and sleep? He didn't think so. It chilled him.

He was still just a spirit, though. A person only had one life, and he had spent his. Could he make a new body for himself? A Henry-machine that he could haunt, reborn in steel and electricity? Was that enough, wanting only to live again and live better?

But he didn't hurt anymore. He was full of purpose again, as whole as a ghost could be. He relaxed in Bethany's grasp and, seeing that she had won, the girl let him go. The roof felt solid beneath him, the world sharp and full of depth.

"I'm going to try to build myself a new body," Henry said. "I don't know how. I would need whole new technologies and sciences, things that haven't even been dreamed of yet."

"I can't stay here," Bethany said. "The alien light in me is too heavy. If I don't go, I'll tear this reality apart." She reached for his hand. "Come with me. We'll find what we need."

Henry let his mind circle the idea obsessively, dancing with it like the ghost girl had danced alone with her want for so long. He would write himself a new skeleton. He would wind it in tissue and fill it with blood. He would sink into it and suck breath into its new lungs. He would open his eyes from inside his new self, and he would be better than he had ever been before.

Henry felt solid and real, almost alive already. He *needed* something. And he wouldn't rest until he had it. He took her hand.

Together they plummeted through the thin fabric of reality. Henry saw only darkness in this place between living and death, a mouth that swallowed ghosts. The only light was Bethany, shining bright as a sun beside him.

"What do you see?" he asked.

"There are so many worlds around us," she said. "It's like staring into a kaleidoscope."

Bethany stretched out her arm and pointed toward something only she could see.

Henry closed his eyes and tried to imagine it, some new universe filled with strange people in strange towns, their pain and love familiar. A place where he could be new. He hoped it was real. He hoped there was something beyond the dark.

They fell face-first. The weight of all that they had lost fell away, and the heat and dust of the ruined town streamed away from them and scattered in their wake like wreckage from a storm.

Behind them, the comet's tail of Bethany's ghosts followed.

ACKNOWLEDGMENTS

First, I would like to thank my wife, Brenda Peynado, for reading draft after draft, always giving me her honest opinion, and pushing me to do the best work that I could. This book wouldn't exist without her.

I would also like to thank the early readers who gave me such great feedback on this novel as it developed: Robert Barton Bland, Billy Hallal, John Jarrett, Tabitha Lowery, Emily Rainey, and Laura Smith.

I owe a lot to the creative writing program at Florida State University, particularly the professors who helped me with this book: Julianna Baggott, Diane Roberts, Robert Romanchuk, Elizabeth Stuckey-French, and Mark Winegardner.

My agent, Kerry D'Agostino, has been such an amazing champion of my work. I want to thank her for loving this novel so much through all its many drafts and revisions.

Thanks to John Joseph Adams for his sharp edits and insights, Chris Thornley for the beautiful cover, and to everyone at John Joseph Adams Books and Houghton Mifflin Harcourt for making all of this possible.

I also want to thank a few of my friends for their years of kindness and support: Kilby Allen, Garrett Ashley, Mikayla Ávila Vilá, Laura Bandy, Gabrielle Bellot, C. J. Bobo, David Bowen, Alicia Burdue, Julialicia Case, Leslee Chan, Emily Rose Cole, Marian Crotty, Jessie Curtis, John Deming, Eoin James Dockter, Okla Elliott, Brett Gaffney,

Brandi George, Jesse Goolsby, Liz Green, C. J. Hauser, Rochelle Hurt, Anna Claire Hodge, Daniel Kasper, Donika Kelly, Girwan Khadka, Gitanjali Shrestha Khadka, Sydney Kilgore-Manuel, Gwen Kirby, Katie Knoll, Julia Koets, Lindsey Kurz, Sara Bland Landaverde, Lucas Lowery, Joshua Manuel, Dyan Neary, Ashlie Rae Odom, Dan Paul, Ondřej Pazdírek, Daniel J. Pinney, Ellis Purdie, Misha Rai, Jessica Reidy, Sophie Rosenblum, Shannin Schroeder, Kimberly Shirey, Andrea Spofford, Lindsay Sproul, Kayla Henderson Thompson, Kristina Treadway, Dillon Tripp, Linda Tucker, Anne Valente, Anne VanderMeer, Jeff VanderMeer, Nathan Waddell, Josh Webster, Melinda Wilson, Michael Yoon, and Tina Raborn Zuniga.

Finally, thanks so much to my family for their unwavering belief in me and my writing: Billy Hicks, Melissa Hicks, Patience Hicks, Trevor Hicks, Bianca Peynado, Celia Peynado, Daniel Peynado, and Esteban Peynado.

THE BOOK OF NIGHTMARES

GALWAY KINNELL

An Imprint of HarperCollins Publishers

ecco

An Imprint of HarperCollins Publishers, registered in
the United States of America and/or other jurisdictions.

www.harpercollins.com

ISBN 0-395-12097-7
ISBN 0-395-12098-5 (pbk.)
Library of Congress Catalog Card Number 71-134312

Printed in the United States of America

22 23 24 25 26 LBC 6 5 4 3 2

Parts of this book first appeared in the following magazines: "Under
the Maud Moon," sections 1–3 in *The New Yorker*, sections 4–7 in
the *Iowa Review*; "The Hen Flower" in *Harper's*; "The Shoes of
Wandering," sections 1–4 and 7 in *Poetry*, sections 5 and 6 in the
Quarterly Review of Literature; "Dear Stranger Extant in Memory
by the Blue Juniata" in *kayak*; "In the Hotel of Lost Light" in *Field*;
"The Dead Shall Be Raised Incorruptible" in *Sumac*; "Lastness,"
sections 1–3 in *The New Yorker*, sections 4–7 in the *New American
Review*.

To

MAUD and FERGUS

> But this, though: death,
> the whole of death, — even before life's begun,
> to hold it all so gently, and be good:
> this is beyond description!
>
> —Rilke

CONTENTS

CONTENTS

I

UNDER THE MAUD MOON

1

On the path,
by this wet site
of old fires —
black ashes, black stones, where tramps
must have squatted down,
gnawing on stream water,
unhouseling themselves on cursed bread,
failing to get warm at a twigfire —

I stop,
gather wet wood,
cut dry shavings, and for her,
whose face
I held in my hands
a few hours, whom I gave back
only to keep holding the space where she was,

I light
a small fire in the rain.

The black
wood reddens, the deathwatches inside
begin running out of time, I can see
the dead, crossed limbs
longing again for the universe, I can hear
in the wet wood the snap
and re-snap of the same embrace being torn.

The raindrops trying
to put the fire out
fall into it and are
changed: the oath broken,
the oath sworn between earth and water, flesh and spirit, broken,
to be sworn again,
over and over, in the clouds, and to be broken again,
over and over, on earth.

2

I sit a moment
by the fire, in the rain, speak
a few words into its warmth —
stone saint smooth stone — and sing
one of the songs I used to croak
for my daughter, in her nightmares.

Somewhere out ahead of me
a black bear sits alone
on his hillside, nodding from side
to side. He sniffs
the blossom-smells, the rained earth,
finally he gets up,
eats a few flowers, trudges away,
his fur glistening
in the rain.

The singed grease streams
out of the words, the one
held note
remains — a love-note
twisting under my tongue, like the coyote's bark,
curving off, into a
howl.

3

A round-
cheeked girlchild comes awake
in her crib. The green
swaddlings tear open,
a filament or vestment
tears, the blue
flower opens.

And she who is born,
she who sings and cries,
she who begins the passage, her hair
sprouting out,
her gums budding for her first spring on earth,
the mist still clinging about
her face, puts
her hand
into her father's mouth, to take hold of
his song.

4

It is all over,
little one, the flipping
and overleaping, the watery
somersaulting alone in the oneness
under the hill, under
the old, lonely bellybutton
pushing forth again
in remembrance,
the drifting there furled in the dark,
pressing a knee or elbow
along a slippery wall, sculpting
the world with each thrash — the stream
of omphalos blood humming all about you.

5

5

Her head
enters the headhold
which starts sucking her forth: being itself
closes down all over her, gives her
into the shuddering
grip of departure, the slow,
agonized clenches making
the last molds of her life in the dark.

6

The black eye
opens, the pupil
droozed with black hairs
stops, the chakra
on top of the brain throbs a long moment in world light,

and she skids out on her face into light,
this peck
of stunned flesh
clotted with celestial cheesiness, glowing
with the astral violet
of the underlife. And as they cut

her tie to the darkness
she dies
a moment, turns blue as a coal,
the limbs shaking
as the memories rush out of them. When

they hang her up
by the feet, she sucks
air, screams
her first song — and turns rose,

the slow,
beating, featherless arms
already clutching at the emptiness.

7

When it was cold
on our hillside, and you cried
in the crib rocking
through the darkness, on wood
knifed down to the curve of the smile, a sadness
stranger than ours, all of it
flowing from the other world,

I used to come to you
and sit by you
and sing to you. You did not know,
and yet you will remember,
in the silent zones
of the brain, a specter, descendant
of the ghostly forefathers, singing
to you in the nighttime —
not the songs
of light said to wave
through the bright hair of angels,
but a blacker
rasping flowering on that tongue.

For when the Maud moon
glimmered in those first nights,
and the Archer lay
sucking the icy biestings of the cosmos,
in his crib of stars,

I had crept down
to riverbanks, their long rustle
of being and perishing, down to marshes

where the earth oozes up
in cold streaks, touching the world
with the underglimmer
of the beginning,
and there learned my only song.

And in the days
when you find yourself orphaned,
emptied
of all wind-singing, of light,
the pieces of cursed bread on your tongue,

may there come back to you
a voice,
spectral, calling you
sister!
from everything that dies.

And then
you shall open
this book, even if it is the book of nightmares.

II

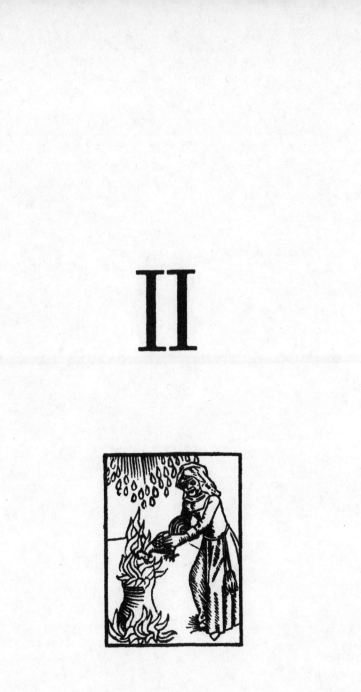

THE HEN FLOWER

1

Sprawled
on our faces in the spring
nights, teeth
biting down on hen feathers, bits of the hen
still stuck in the crevices — if only
we could let go
like her, throw ourselves
on the mercy of darkness, like the hen,

tuck our head
under a wing, hold ourselves still
a few moments, as she
falls out into her little trance in the witchgrass,
or turn over
and be stroked with a finger
down the throat feathers,
down the throat knuckles,
down over the hum
of the wishbone tuning its high D in thin blood,
down over
the breastbone risen up
out of breast flesh, until the fatted thing
woozes off, head
thrown back
on the chopping block, longing only
to die.

2

When the ax-
scented breeze flourishes
about her, her cheeks crush in,
her comb
grays, the gizzard
that turns the thousand acidic millstones of her fate
convulses: ready or not
the next egg, bobbling
its globe of golden earth,
skids forth, ridding her even
of the life to come.

3

Almost high
on subsided gravity, I remain afoot,
a hen flower
dangling from a hand,
wing
of my wing,
of my bones and veins,
of my flesh
hairs lifting all over me in the first ghostly breeze
after death,

wing
made only to fly — unable
to write out the sorrows of being unable
to hold another in one's arms — and unable
to fly,
and waiting, therefore,
for the sweet, eventual blaze in the genes,
that one day, according to gospel, shall carry it back
into pink skies, where geese

cross at twilight, honking
in tongues.

4

I have glimpsed
by corpse-light, in the opened cadaver
of hen, the mass of tiny,
unborn eggs, each getting
tinier and yellower as it reaches back toward
the icy pulp
of what is, I have felt the zero
freeze itself around the finger dipped slowly in.

5

When the Northern Lights
were opening across the black sky and vanishing,
lighting themselves up
so completely they were vanishing,
I put to my eye the lucent
section of the spealbone of a ram —

I thought suddenly
I could read the cosmos spelling itself,
the huge broken letters
shuddering across the black sky and vanishing,

and in a moment,
in the twinkling of an eye, it came to me
the mockingbird would sing all her nights the cry of the rifle,
the tree would hold the bones of the sniper who chose not to
    climb down,
the rose would bloom no one would see it,
the chameleon longing to be changed would remain the color
    of blood.

And I went up
to the henhouse, and took up
the hen killed by weasels, and lugged
the sucked
carcass into first light. And when I hoisted
her up among the young pines, a last
rubbery egg slipping out as I flung her high, didn't it happen
the dead
wings creaked open as she soared
across the arms of the Bear?

6

Sprawled face down, waiting
for the rooster to groan out
it is the empty morning, as he groaned out thrice
for the disciple
of stone,
he who crushed with his heel the brain out of the snake,

I remember long ago I sowed
my own first milk
tooth under hen feathers, I planted under hen feathers
the hook
of the wishbone,
which had broken itself so lovingly toward me.

For the future.

It has come to this.

7

Listen, Kinnell,
dumped alive
and dying into the old sway bed,
a layer of crushed feathers all that there is

between you
and the long shaft of darkness shaped as you,
let go.

Even this haunted room
all its materials photographed with tragedy,
even the tiny crucifix drifting face down at the center of the earth,
even these feathers freed from their wings forever
are afraid.

THE SHOES OF WANDERING

1

Squatting at the rack
in the Store of the Salvation
Army, putting on, one after one,
these shoes strangers have died from, I discover
the eldershoes of my feet,
that take my feet
as their first feet, clinging
down to the least knuckle and corn.

And I walk out now,
in dead shoes, in the new light,
on the steppingstones
of someone else's wandering,
a twinge
in this foot or that saying
turn or *stay* or *take*
forty-three giant steps
backwards, frightened
I may already have lost
the way: *the first step*, the Crone
who scried the crystal said, *shall be*
to lose the way.

2

Back at the Xvarna Hotel, I leave
unlocked the door jimmied over and over,

I draw the one,
lightning-tracked blind
in the narrow room under the freeway, I put off
the shoes, set them
side by side
by the bedside, curl
up on bedclothes gone stiff
from love-acid, night-sweat, gnash-dust
of tooth, and lapse back
into darkness.

3

A faint,
creaking noise
starts up in the room,
low-passing wing-
beats, or great, labored breath-takings
of somebody lungsore or old.

And the old
footsmells in the shoes, touched
back to life by my footsweats, as by
a child's kisses, rise,
drift up where I lie
self-hugged on the bedclothes, slide
down the flues
of dozed, beating hairs, and I can groan

or wheeze, it will be
the groan or wheeze of another — the elderfoot
of these shoes, the drunk
who died in this room, whose dream-child
might have got a laugh
out of those clenched, corned feet, putting
huge, comical kisses on them
through the socks, or a brother

shipped back burned
from the burning of Asians, sweating
his nightmare out to the end
in some whitewashed warehouse
for dying — the groan
or wheeze of one
who lays bare his errors by a harsher light,
his self-mutterings worse
than the farts, grunts, and belches
of an Oklahoma men's room,
as I shudder down to his nightmare.

4

The witness trees
blaze themselves a last time: the road
trembles as it starts across
swampland streaked with shined water, a lethe-
wind of chill air touches
me all over my body,
certain brain cells crackle like softwood in a great fire
or die,
each step a shock,
a shattering underfoot of mirrors sick of the itch
of our face-bones under their skins,
as memory reaches out
and lays bloody hands on the future, the haunted
shoes rising and falling
through the dust, wings of dust
lifting around them, as they flap
down the brainwaves of the temporal road.

5

Is it the foot,
which rubs the cobblestones
and snakestones all its days, this lowliest

of tongues, whose lick-tracks tell
our history of errors to the dust behind,
which is the last trace in us
of wings?

And is it
the hen's nightmare, or her secret dream,
to scratch the ground forever
eating the minutes out of the grains of sand?

6

On this road
on which I do not know how to ask for bread,
on which I do not know how to ask for water,
this path
inventing itself
through jungles of burnt flesh, ground of ground
bones, crossing itself
at the odor of blood, and stumbling on,

I long for the mantle
of the great wanderers, who lighted
their steps by the lamp
of pure hunger and pure thirst,

and whichever way they lurched was the way.

7

But when the Crone
held up my crystal skull to the moon,
when she passed my shoulder bones
across the Aquarian stars, she said:

You live
under the Sign

of the Bear, who flounders through chaos
in his starry blubber:
poor fool,
poor forked branch
of applewood, you will feel all your bones
break
over the holy waters you will never drink.

IV

VI

DEAR STRANGER
EXTANT IN MEMORY BY THE BLUE JUNIATA

1

Having given up
on the deskman passed out
under his clock, who was to have banged
it is morning
on the police-locked, sheetmetal door,

I can hear the chime
of the Old Tower, tinny sacring-bell drifting out
over the city — chyme
of our loves
the peristalsis of the will to love forever
drives down, grain
after grain, into the last,
coldest room, which is memory —

and listen for the maggots
inhabiting beds old men have died in
to crawl out,
to break into the brain and cut
the nerves which keep the book of solitude.

2

Dear Galway,

It began late one April night when I couldn't sleep. It was the
dark of the moon. My hand felt numb, the pencil went over the page
drawn on its way by I don't know what. It drew circles and figure-

27

eights and mandalas. I cried. I had to drop the pencil. I was shaking. I went to bed and tried to pray. At last I relaxed. Then I felt my mouth open. My tongue moved, my breath wasn't my own. The whisper which forced itself through my teeth said, *Virginia, your eyes shine back to me from my own world.* O God, I thought. My breath came short, my heart opened. O God I thought, now I have a demon lover.

Yours, faithless to this life,
Virginia

3

At dusk, by the blue Juniata —
"a rural America," the magazine said,
"now vanished, but extant in memory,
a primal garden lost forever . . ."
("You see," I told Mama, "we just *think* we're here . . .") —
the root-hunters
go out into the woods, pull up
love-roots from the virginal glades, bend
the stalks over shovel-handles
and lever them up, the huge,
bass, final
thrump
as each root unclutches from its spot.

4

Take kettle
of blue water.
Boil over twigfire
of ash wood. Grind root.
Throw in. Let macerate. Reheat
over ash ashes. Bottle.
Stopper with thumb
of dead man. Ripen
forty days in horse dung

in the wilderness. Drink.
Sleep.

And when you rise—
if you do rise — it will be in the sothic year
made of the raised salvages
of the fragments all unaccomplished
of years past, scraps
and jettisons of time mortality
could not grind down into his meal of blood and laughter.

And if there is one more love
to be known, one more poem
to be opened into life,
you will find it here
or nowhere. Your hand will move
on its own
down the curving path, drawn
down by the terror and terrible lure
of vacuum:

a face materializes into your hands,
on the absolute whiteness of pages
a poem writes itself out: its title—the dream
of all poems and the text
of all loves—"Tenderness toward Existence."

5

On this bank—our bank—
of the blue, vanished water, you lie,
crying in your bed, hearing those
small,
fearsome thrumps
of leave-taking trespassing the virginal woods at dusk.

I, too, have eaten
the meals of the dark shore. In time's

own mattress, where a sag shaped as a body
lies next to a sag—graves
tossed into it
by those who came before,
lovers,
or loving friends,
or strangers,
who loved here,
or ground their nightmared teeth here,
or talked away their one-night stands,
the sanctus-bell
going out each hour to die against the sheetglass city—

I lie without sleeping, remembering
the ripped body
of hen, the warmth of hen flesh
frightening my hand,
all her desires,
all her deathsmells,
blooming again in the starlight. And then the wait—

not long, I grant, but all my life—
for the small, soft
thud of her return among the stones.

Can it ever be true—
all bodies, one body, one light
made of everyone's darkness together?

6

Dear Galway,

I have no one to turn to because God is my enemy. He gave me
lust and joy and cut off my hands. My brain is smothered with his
blood. I asked why should I love this body I fear. He said, *It is so
lordly, it can never be shaped again — dear, shining casket. Have
you never been so proud of a thing you wanted it for your prey?*

His voice chokes my throat. Soul of asps, master and taker: he
wants to kill me. Forgive my blindness.
                                    Yours, in the darkness,
                                                Virginia

7

Dear stranger
extant in memory by the blue Juniata,
these letters
across space I guess
will be all we will know of one another.

So little of what one is threads itself through the eye
of empty space.

Never mind.
The self is the least of it.
Let our scars fall in love.

V

V

IN THE HOTEL OF LOST LIGHT

1

In the left-
hand sag the drunk smelling of autopsies
died in, my body slumped out
into the shape of his, I watch, as he
must have watched, a fly
tangled in mouth-glue, whining his wings,
concentrated wholly on
time, time, losing his way worse
down the downward-winding stairs, his wings
whining for life as he shrivels
in the gaze
from the spider's clasped forebrains, the abstracted stare
in which even the nightmare spatters out its horrors
and dies.

Now the fly
ceases to struggle, his wings
flutter out the music blooming with failure
of one who gets ready to die, as Roland's horn, winding down
from the Pyrenees, saved its dark, full flourishes
for last.

2

In the light
left behind by the little
spiders of blood who garbled

their memoirs across his shoulders
and chest, the room
echoes with the tiny thrumps
of crotch hairs plucking themselves
from their spots; on the stripped skin
the love-sick crab lice
struggle to unstick themselves and sprint from the doomed
    position —

and stop,
heads buried
for one last taste of the love-flesh.

3

Flesh
of his excavated flesh,
fill of his emptiness,
after-amanuensis of his after-life,
I write out
for him in this languished alphabet
of worms, these last words
of himself, post for him
his final postcards to posterity.

4

"I sat out by twigfires flaring in grease strewn from the pimpled limbs
    of hen,
I blacked out into oblivion by that crack in the curb where the forget-
    me blooms,
I saw the ferris wheel writing its huge, desolate zeroes in neon on the
    evening skies,
I painted my footsoles purple for the day when the beautiful color
    would show,
I staggered death-sentences down empty streets, the cobblestones as-
    sured me, *it shall be so,*

I heard my own cries already howled inside bottles the waves washed
    up on beaches,
I ghostwrote my prayers myself in the body-Arabic of these night-
    mares.

"If the deskman knocks, griping again
about the sweet, excremental
odor of opened cadaver creeping out
from under the door, tell him, 'Friend, *To Live*
has a poor cousin,
who calls tonight, who pronounces the family name
To Leave, she
changes each visit the flesh-rags on her bones.' "

5

Violet bruises come out
all over his flesh, as invisible
fists start beating him a last time; the whine
of omphalos blood starts up again, the puffed
bellybutton explodes, the carnal
nightmare soars back to the beginning.

6

As for the bones to be tossed
into the aceldama back of the potting shop, among
shards and lumps
which caught vertigo and sagged away
into mud, or crawled out of fire
crazed or exploded, they shall re-arise
in the pear tree, in spring, to shine down
on two clasping what they dream is one another.

As for these words scattered into the future—
posterity
is one invented too deep in its past
to hear them.

7

The foregoing scribed down
in March, of the year Seventy,
on my sixteen-thousandth night of war and madness,
in the Hotel of Lost Light, under the freeway
which roams out into the dark
of the moon, in the absolute spell
of departure, and by the light
from the joined hemispheres of the spider's eyes.

VI

IV

THE DEAD SHALL
BE RAISED INCORRUPTIBLE

1

A piece of flesh gives off
smoke in the field —

carrion,
caput mortuum,
orts,
pelf,
fenks,
sordes,
gurry dumped from hospital trashcans.

Lieutenant!
This corpse will not stop burning!

2

"That you Captain? Sure,
sure I remember — I still hear you
lecturing at me on the intercom, *Keep your guns up, Burnsie!*
and then screaming, *Stop shooting, for crissake, Burnsie,*
those are friendlies! But crissake, Captain,
I'd already started, burst
after burst, little black pajamas jumping
and falling . . . and remember that pilot
who'd bailed out over the North,
how I shredded him down to catgut on his strings?
one of his slant eyes, a piece

41

of his smile, sail past me
every night right after the sleeping pill . . .

"It was only
that I loved the *sound*
of them, I guess I just loved
the *feel* of them sparkin' off my hands . . ."

3

On the television screen:

Do you have a body that sweats?
Sweat that has odor?
False teeth clanging into your breakfast?
Case of the dread?
Headache so perpetual it may outlive you?
Armpits sprouting hair?
Piles so huge you don't need a chair to sit at a table?

We shall not all sleep, but we shall be changed . . .

4

In the Twentieth Century of my trespass on earth,
having exterminated one billion heathens,
heretics, Jews, Moslems, witches, mystical seekers,
black men, Asians, and Christian brothers,
every one of them for his own good,

a whole continent of red men for living in unnatural community
and at the same time having relations with the land,
one billion species of animals for being sub-human,
and ready to take on the bloodthirsty creatures from the other
        planets,
I, Christian man, groan out this testament of my last will.

I give my blood fifty parts polystyrene,
twenty-five parts benzene, twenty-five parts good old gasoline,
to the last bomber pilot aloft, that there shall be one acre
in the dull world where the kissing flower may bloom,
which kisses you so long your bones explode under its lips.

My tongue goes to the Secretary of the Dead
to tell the corpses, "I'm sorry, fellows,
the killing was just one of those things
difficult to pre-visualize — like a cow,
say, getting hit by lightning."

My stomach, which has digested
four hundred treaties giving the Indians
eternal right to their land, I give to the Indians,
I throw in my lungs which have spent four hundred years
sucking in good faith on peace pipes.

My soul I leave to the bee
that he may sting it and die, my brain
to the fly, his back the hysterical green color of slime,
that he may suck on it and die, my flesh to the advertising man,
the anti-prostitute, who loathes human flesh for money.

I assign my crooked backbone
to the dice maker, to chop up into dice,
for casting lots as to who shall see his own blood
on his shirt front and who his brother's,
for the race isn't to the swift but to the crooked.

To the last man surviving on earth
I give my eyelids worn out by fear, to wear
in his long nights of radiation and silence,
so that his eyes can't close, for regret
is like tears seeping through closed eyelids.

I give the emptiness my hand: the pinkie picks no more noses,
slag clings to the black stick of the ring finger,

a bit of flame jets from the tip of the fuck-you finger,
the first finger accuses the heart, which has vanished,
on the thumb stump wisps of smoke ask a ride into the emptiness.

In the Twentieth Century of my nightmare
on earth, I swear on my chromium testicles
to this testament
and last will
of my iron will, my fear of love, my itch for money, and my
     madness.

5

In the ditch
snakes crawl cool paths
over the rotted thigh, the toe bones
twitch in the smell of burnt rubber,
the belly
opens like a poison nightflower,
the tongue has evaporated,
the nostril
hairs sprinkle themselves with yellowish-white dust,
the five flames at the end
of each hand have gone out, a mosquito
sips a last meal from this plate of serenity.

And the fly,
the last nightmare, hatches himself.

6

I ran
my neck broken I ran
holding my head up with both hands I ran
thinking the flames
the flames may burn the oboe
but listen buddy boy they can't touch the notes!

7

A few bones
lie about in the smoke of bones.

Membranes,
effigies pressed into grass,
mummy windings,
desquamations,
sags incinerated mattresses gave back to the world,
memories left in mirrors on whorehouse ceilings,
angel's wings
flagged down into the snows of yesteryear,

kneel
on the scorched earth
in the shapes of men and animals:

do not let this last hour pass,
do not remove this last, poison cup from our lips.

And a wind holding
the cries of love-making from all our nights and days
moves among the stones, hunting
for two twined skeletons to blow its last cry across.

Lieutenant!
This corpse will not stop burning!

VII

LITTLE SLEEP'S-HEAD
SPROUTING HAIR IN THE MOONLIGHT

1

You scream, waking from a nightmare.

When I sleepwalk
into your room, and pick you up,
and hold you up in the moonlight, you cling to me
hard,
as if clinging could save us. I think
you think
I will never die, I think I exude
to you the permanence of smoke or stars,
even as
my broken arms heal themselves around you.

2

I have heard you tell
the sun, *don't go down*, I have stood by
as you told the flower, *don't grow old*,
don't die. Little Maud,

I would blow the flame out of your silver cup,
I would suck the rot from your fingernail,
I would brush your sprouting hair of the dying light,
I would scrape the rust off your ivory bones,
I would help death escape through the little ribs of your body,
I would alchemize the ashes of your cradle back into wood,
I would let nothing of you go, ever,

until washerwomen
feel the clothes fall asleep in their hands,
and hens scratch their spell across hatchet blades,
and rats walk away from the cultures of the plague,
and iron twists weapons toward the true north,
and grease refuses to slide in the machinery of progress,
and men feel as free on earth as fleas on the bodies of men,
and lovers no longer whisper to the presence beside them in the
    dark, O *corpse-to-be* . . .

And yet perhaps this is the reason you cry,
this the nightmare you wake screaming from:
being forever
in the pre-trembling of a house that falls.

3

In a restaurant once, everyone
quietly eating, you clambered up
on my lap: to all
the mouthfuls rising toward
all the mouths, at the top of your voice
you cried
your one word, *caca! caca! caca!*
and each spoonful
stopped, a moment, in midair, in its withering
steam.

Yes,
you cling because
I, like you, only sooner
than you, will go down
the path of vanished alphabets,
the roadlessness
to the other side of the darkness,

your arms
like the shoes left behind,
like the adjectives in the halting speech
of old men,
which once could call up the lost nouns.

4

And you yourself,
some impossible Tuesday
in the year Two Thousand and Nine, will walk out
among the black stones
of the field, in the rain,

and the stones saying
over their one word, *ci-gît, ci-gît, ci-gît,*

and the raindrops
hitting you on the fontanel
over and over, and you standing there
unable to let them in.

5

If one day it happens
you find yourself with someone you love
in a café at one end
of the Pont Mirabeau, at the zinc bar
where white wine stands in upward opening glasses,

and if you commit then, as we did, the error
of thinking,
one day all this will only be memory,

learn,
as you stand
at this end of the bridge which arcs,

from love, you think, into enduring love,
learn to reach deeper
into the sorrows
to come — to touch
the almost imaginary bones
under the face, to hear under the laughter
the wind crying across the black stones. Kiss
the mouth
which tells you, *here,*
here is the world. This mouth. This laughter. These temple bones.

The still undanced cadence of vanishing.

6

In the light the moon
sends back, I can see in your eyes

the hand that waved once
in my father's eyes, a tiny kite
wobbling far up in the twilight of his last look:

and the angel
of all mortal things lets go the string.

7

Back you go, into your crib.

The last blackbird lights up his gold wings: *farewell.*
Your eyes close inside your head,
in sleep. Already
in your dreams the hours begin to sing.

Little sleep's-head sprouting hair in the moonlight,
when I come back
we will go out together,

we will walk out together among
the ten thousand things,
each scratched too late with such knowledge, *the wages
of dying is love.*

VIII

VIII

THE CALL ACROSS
THE VALLEY OF NOT-KNOWING

1

In the red house sinking down
into ground rot, a lamp
at one window, the smarled ashes letting
a single flame go free,
a shoe of dreaming iron nailed to the wall,
two mismatched halfnesses lying side by side in the darkness,
I can feel with my hand
the foetus rouse himself
with a huge, fishy thrash, and re-settle in his darkness.

Her hair glowing in the firelight,
her breasts full,
her belly swollen,
a sunset of firelight
wavering all down one side, my wife sleeps on,
happy,
far away, in some other,
newly opened room of the world.

2

Sweat breaking from his temples,
Aristophanes ran off
at the mouth—made it all up, nightmared it all up
on the spur
of that moment which has stabbed us ever since:
that each of us

is a torn half
whose lost other we keep seeking across time
until we die, or give up—
or actually find her:

as I myself, in an Ozark
Airlines DC–6 droning over
towns made of crossroads, headed down
into Waterloo, Iowa, actually found her,
held her face a few hours
in my hands; and for reasons—cowardice,
loyalties, all which goes by the name "necessity"—
left her . . .

3

And yet I think
it must be the wound, the wound itself,
which lets us know and love,
which forces us to reach out to our misfit
and by a kind
of poetry of the soul, accomplish,
for a moment, the wholeness the drunk Greek
extrapolated from his high
or flagellated out of an empty heart,

that purest,
most tragic concumbence, strangers
clasped into one, a moment, of their moment on earth.

4

She who lies halved
beside me—she and I once
watched the bees, dreamers not yet
dipped into the acids
of the craving for anything, not yet burned down into flies, sucking
the blossom-dust
from the pear-tree in spring,

we two
lay out together
under the tree, on earth, beside our empty clothes,
our bodies opened to the sky,
and the blossoms glittering in the sky
floated down
and the bees glittered in the blossoms
and the bodies of our hearts
opened
under the knowledge
of tree, on the grass of the knowledge
of graves, and among the flowers of the flowers.

And the brain kept blossoming
all through the body, until the bones themselves could think,
and the genitals sent out wave after wave of holy desire
until even the dead brain cells
surged and fell in god-like, androgynous fantasies —
and I understood
the unicorn's phallus could have risen, after all,
directly out of thought itself.

5

Of that time in a Southern jail,
when the sheriff, as he cursed me
and spat, took my hand in his hand, rocked
from the pulps the whorls
and tented archways into the tabooed realm, that underlife
where the canaries of the blood are singing, pressed
the flesh-flowers
into the dirty book of the
police-blotter, afterwards what I remembered most
was the care, the almost loving,
animal gentleness of his hand on my hand.

Better than the rest of us, he knows
the harshness of that cubicle

in hell where they put you
with all your desires undiminished, and with no body to appease
    them.

And when he himself floats out
on a sea he almost begins to remember,
floats out into a darkness he has known already;
when the moan of wind
and the gasp of lungs call to each other among the waves
and the wish to float
comes to matter not at all as he sinks under,

is it so impossible to think
he will dream back to all the hands black and white
he took in his hands
as the creation
touches him a last time all over his body?

6

Suppose I had stayed
with that woman of Waterloo, suppose
we had met on a hill called Safa, in our own country,
that we had lain out on the grass
and looked into each other's blindness, under leaf-shadows
wavering across our bodies in the drifts of sun,
our faces
inclined toward each other, as hens
incline their faces
when the heat flows from the warmed egg
back into the whole being, and the silver moon
had stood still for us in the middle of heaven —

I think I might have closed my eyes, and moved
from then on like the born blind,
their faces
gone into heaven already.

7

We who live out our plain lives, who put
our hand into the hand of whatever we love
as it vanishes,
as we vanish,
and stumble toward what will be, simply by arriving,
a kind of fate,

some field, maybe, of flaked stone
scattered in starlight
where the flesh
swaddles its skeleton a last time
before the bones go their way without us,

might we not hear, even then,
the bear call
from his hillside — a call, like ours, needing
to be answered — and the dam-bear
call back across the darkness
of the valley of not-knowing
the only word tongues shape without intercession,

yes . . . yes . . . ?

IX

THE PATH AMONG THE STONES

1

On the path winding
upward, toward the high valley
of waterfalls and flooded, hoof-shattered
meadows of spring,
where fish-roots boil
in the last grails of light on the water,
and vipers pimpled with urges to fly
drape the black stones hissing *pheet! pheet!* — land
of quills
and inkwells of skulls filled with black water —

I come to a field
glittering with the thousand sloughed skins
of arrowheads, stones
which shuddered and leapt forth
to give themselves into the broken hearts
of the living,
who gave themselves back, broken, to the stone.

2

I close my eyes:
on the heat-rippled beaches
where the hills came down to the sea,
the luminous
beach dust pounded out of funeral shells,
I can see

them living without me, dying
without me, the wing
and egg
shaped stones, broken
war-shells of slain fighting conches,
dog-eared immortality shells
in which huge constellations of slime, by the full moon,
writhed one more
coat of invisibility on a speck of sand,

and the agates knocked
from circles scratched into the dust
with the click
of a wishbone breaking, inward-swirling
globes biopsied out of sunsets never to open again,

and that wafer-stone
which skipped ten times across
the water, suddenly starting to run as it went under,
and the zeroes it left,
that met
and passed into each other, they themselves
smoothing themselves from the water . . .

3

I walk out from myself,
among the stones of the field,
each sending up its ghost-bloom
into the starlight, to float out
over the trees, seeking to be one
with the unearthly fires kindling and dying

in space — and falling back, knowing
the sadness of the wish
to alight
back among the glitter of bruised ground,

the stones holding between pasture and field,
the great, granite nuclei,
glimmering, even they, with ancient inklings of madness and war.

4

A way opens
at my feet. I go down
the night-lighted mule-steps into the earth,
the footprints behind me
filling already with pre-sacrificial trills
of canaries, go down
into the unbreathable goaf
of everything I ever craved and lost.

An old man, a stone
lamp at his forehead, squats
by his hell-flames, stirs into
his pot
chopped head
of crow, strings of white light,
opened tail of peacock, dressed
body of canary, robin breast
dragged through the mud of battlefields, wrung-out
blossom of caput mortuum flower — salts
it all down with sand
stolen from the upper bells of hourglasses . . .

Nothing.
Always nothing. Ordinary blood
boiling away in the glare of the brow lamp.

5

And yet, no,
perhaps not nothing. Perhaps
not ever nothing. In clothes

woven out of the blue spittle
of snakes, I crawl up: I find myself alive
in the whorled
archway of the fingerprint of all things,
skeleton groaning,
blood-strings wailing the wail of all things.

6

The witness trees heal
their scars at the flesh fire,
the flame
rises off the bones,
the hunger
to be new lifts off
my soul, an eerie blue light blooms
on all the ridges of the world. Somewhere
in the legends of blood sacrifice
the fatted calf
takes the bonfire into his arms, and *he*
burns *it*.

7

As above: the last scattered stars
kneel down in the star-form of the Aquarian age:
a splash
on the top of the head,
on the grass of this earth even the stars love, splashes of the
    sacred waters . . .

So below: in the graveyard
the lamps start lighting up, one for each of us,
in all the windows
of stone.

X

X

LASTNESS

1

The skinny waterfalls, footpaths
wandering out of heaven, strike
the cliffside, leap, and shudder off.

Somewhere behind me
a small fire goes on flaring in the rain, in the desolate ashes.
No matter, now, whom it was built for,
it keeps its flames,
it warms
everyone who might wander into its radiance,
a tree, a lost animal, the stones,

because in the dying world it was set burning.

2

A black bear sits alone
in the twilight, nodding from side
to side, turning slowly around and around
on himself, scuffing the four-footed
circle into the earth. He sniffs the sweat
in the breeze, he understands
a creature, a death-creature
watches from the fringe of the trees,
finally he understands
I am no longer here, he himself
from the fringe of the trees watches

a black bear
get up, eat a few flowers, trudge away,
all his fur glistening
in the rain.

And what glistening! Sancho Fergus,
my boychild, had such great shoulders,
when he was born his head
came out, the rest of him stuck. And he opened
his eyes: his head out there all alone
in the room, he squinted with pained,
barely unglued eyes at the ninth-month's
blood splashing beneath him
on the floor. And almost
smiled, I thought, almost forgave it all in advance.

When he came wholly forth
I took him up in my hands and bent
over and smelled
the black, glistening fur
of his head, as empty space
must have bent
over the newborn planet
and smelled the grasslands and the ferns.

3

Walking toward the cliff overhanging
the river, I call out to the stone,
and the stone
calls back, its voice hunting among the rubble
for my ears.

Stop.
As you approach an echoing
cliffside, you sense the line
where the voice calling from stone

no longer answers,
turns into stone, and nothing comes back.

Here, between answer
and nothing, I stand, in the old shoes
flowed over by rainbows of hen-oil,
each shoe holding the bones
which ripple together in the communion
of the step,
and which open out
in front into toes, the whole foot trying
to dissolve into the future.

A clatter of elk hooves.
Has the top sphere
emptied itself? Is it true
the earth is all there is, and the earth does not last?

On the river the world floats by holding one corpse.

Stop.
Stop here.
Living brings you to death, there is no other road.

4

This is the tenth poem
and it is the last. It is right
at the last, that one
and zero
walk off together,
walk off the end of these pages together,
one creature
walking away side by side with the emptiness.

Lastness
is brightness. It is the brightness

73

gathered up of all that went before. It lasts.
And when it does end
there is nothing, nothing
left,

in the rust of old cars,
in the hole torn open in the body of the Archer,
in river-mist smelling of the weariness of stones,
the dead lie,
empty, filled, at the beginning,

and the first
voice comes craving again out of their mouths.

5

That Bach concert I went to so long ago —
the chandeliered room
of ladies and gentlemen who would never die . . .
the voices go out,
the room becomes hushed,
the violinist
puts the irreversible sorrow of his face
into the opened palm
of the wood, the music begins:

a shower of rosin,
the bow-hairs listening down all their length
to the wail,
the sexual wail
of the back-alleys and blood strings we have lived
still crying,
still singing, from the sliced intestine
of cat.

6

This poem
if we shall call it that,
or concert of one
divided among himself,
this earthward gesture
of the sky-diver, the worms
on his back still spinning forth
and already gnawing away
the silks of his loves, who could have saved him,
this free floating of one
opening his arms into the attitude
of flight, as he obeys the necessity and falls . . .

7

Sancho Fergus! Don't cry!

Or else, cry.

On the body,
on the blued flesh, when it is
laid out, see if you can find
the one flea which is laughing.